D0045399

FIC TOD
Todd, Charles
Pale horse

0801182

A
PALE
HORSE

A
PALE
HORSE

Charles Todd

wm WILLIAM MORROW
An Imprint of HarperCollins*Publishers*

HarperCollins books may be purchased for educational, business, or sales promotional use. For information please write: Special Markets Department, HarperCollins Publishers, 10 East 53rd Street, New York, NY 10022.

FIRST EDITION

Designed by Laura Kaeppel

Library of Congress Cataloging-in-Publication Data
Todd, Charles.
   A pale horse / Charles Todd.— 1st ed.
      p. cm.
      ISBN 978-0-06-123356-2
1. Rutledge, Ian (Fictitious character)—Fiction. 2. Police—England—Fiction. 3. Great Britain—History—George V, 1910–1936—Fiction. I. Title.
   PS3570.O37P35 2008
   813'.54—dc22

                                                  2007018088

---

08   09   10   11   12   OV/RRD   10   9   8   7   6   5   4   3   2   1

To Martha Lynn,

Whose voice is her gift,

As words are mine . . .

With much love for so many reasons

T.

I

Early April 1920

It was nearing the full moon, and the night seemed to shimmer with light.

He walked down the lane and turned to look up at the hillside.

The graceful white horse cut into the chalk by ancient Britons galloped across the green slope without stirring from its place.

He couldn't see it without remembering. That was the only reason he had chosen to live in this Godforsaken place. To torment himself until he couldn't bear it any more.

The horses had died too, in that first gas attack. It wasn't just the men. The poor beasts couldn't know what the low-lying mist wafting toward them brought in its wake.

An eyewitness had likened the cloud to a great horse moving across a barren meadow, ambling toward the barn for its dinner. Not hurrying, not drifting, just moving steadily, without apparent purpose, without apparent design, following the wind as the horse followed the scent of its stall and the fresh hay heaped in the manger. But like the pale horse of the Apocalypse, on his back rode Death. And Hell had truly followed them.

He smiled grimly at the imagery.

He hadn't been there when the Germans unleashed the chlorine attack against the Allies at Ypres. Yet it had changed his life in ways no one could have foreseen.

He wished he'd never heard the name of that medieval Belgian town. He wished the Germans had never reached it. Or that the British had left well enough alone and let them have the wretched place.

There was a silver flask of brandy in his pocket, and he felt for it, uncapped it, lifted it to his lips, then paused.

What if he drank it to the dregs and crawled into the ruins of Wayland's Smithy to die, like a wounded animal hiding itself away until it either healed or breathed its last?

Would anyone care?

A shadow was coming up the road toward him. It was Andrew Slater, the smith. It was impossible not to recognize him, even at this distance. Andrew was built like a church tower, tall and broad and solid. But the man didn't turn at the lane. He passed by without speaking, as if sleepwalking, moving on toward the Smithy. Like to like.

It would be crowded inside with the two of them there, he told himself with black humor. Not counting whatever ghosts lingered in that narrow Stone Age tomb.

I envy Andrew Slater, he thought, there in the darkness. *He* lives only in the present, while I have only the past.

He drank a little of the brandy, for courage, saluting the pale horse with his flask. Then he turned and trudged back to his cottage and turned up all the lamps for comfort.

2

Ian Rutledge walked into his flat and sat down in the darkness. He was too tired to deal with the lamps. It had been a long and trying day. The hours he'd spent searching for a murderer had ended in the man's attempt to leap through the tenement window on the wild chance he could still elude capture. It had taken Rutledge and two constables to prevent it, and all three of them bore bruises to show for their efforts. Rutledge's shoulder ached, and the top of his left thigh felt as if it had been kicked by a horse. But then desperation had lent strength to the man.

In the darkness the voice of Hamish MacLeod answered him. A dead man's voice, but for nearly four years now it had seemed to Rutledge as real as his own. He had never grown used to hearing it, and yet with time he had come to terms of a sort with it. It was either that or madness. And he feared madness more.

"Ye nearly went out yon window with him."

It was true, he'd been faster than the stunned constables, and got there first. He'd read the flare of intent in the man's eyes, and reacted to that just as the man's muscles had tightened to turn his back on them and race for the casement.

"A better death than hanging," Rutledge said, "if he'd succeeded. But he'd have gone scot-free if he'd been lucky enough to land on that shop roof just below and to the left. I couldn't chance it. He'd have killed again. It was in his nature."

Rutledge let the silence wrap him, closing his eyes and resting his head on the back of his chair, waiting for jangled nerves to find solace if not peace.

He had nearly let himself drift into a shallow sleep when there was a knock at his door.

Shaking off the torpor of exhaustion, he got up reluctantly and crossed the room. When he opened the door, he found his sister Frances standing there.

"Ian? Are you all right?" Her gaze went beyond him to the dark flat, and that sixth sense of hers seemed to catch the atmosphere like a sleek cat scenting danger.

"Tired, that's all. Come in. I've yet to turn up the lamps. I haven't been home long."

"Well, I'm here to dig you out of your cave. I'm meeting friends for dinner, and I need an escort."

"Frances. There must be half a hundred men who would gladly take you anywhere, including Paris. What's happened to them? They can't all have decided to throw themselves off Westminster Bridge in despair."

Laughing, she followed him into the flat and waited as he lit the lamps and made the shadows retreat. Those in the room, she found herself thinking, as well as those of the spirit. Her instincts to come here had been right.

"Yes, well, they're none of them as handsome as you, Ian, and I might as well take the veil. It's hopeless."

Beneath the humor, her voice betrayed her. Either she was lying, or there was something wrong that she wasn't ready to talk about.

"Is there truly a dinner party?" he asked quietly.

"As a matter of fact, there is. You remember the Farnums. They're taking Maryanne Browning out to dinner, invited me, and included a friend of yours. At least I think you count her among your acquaintances if not your friends."

Maryanne was a widow, her husband Peter a victim not of the war but of the Spanish flu. Rutledge had spent New Year's Eve at her house, at a party that he didn't care to remember.

"You aren't matchmaking, are you?"

"Good God, no! I'm truly fond of Maryanne, but I'm harboring no hopes in that direction. We've been trying to keep her busy, Ian, rather than leaving her to mope. And so all of us in her circle take it in turns seeing to it that she's not forgotten. Or left out of things."

He believed her. It was a kindness Frances would think of— and do.

"I'm tired, I told you. Do you really need me to make up your numbers?"

He caught something in her expression as she said offhandedly, "Simon can't come tonight. He's in Scotland."

And that was the nub, of course. She was growing quite fond of Simon Barrington. She hadn't shown a preference for any of her suitors, not for years. Not since Richard, who never was her suitor, but possibly the only man she'd loved. She was clearly disappointed that Barrington was out of the city.

More than usually disappointed.

He made a mental note of it, then answered, "All right, I'll come, if you give me a quarter of an hour to change. Help yourself to a drink, if you like."

She gave him a swift embrace. "I knew I could count on you."

As he walked into his bedroom he called, "Who is the other person? You mentioned that I knew him?"

"It isn't a him—it's a her. Meredith Channing. She and Maryanne have become friends."

He stopped on the point of taking off his coat.

Meredith Channing . . .

An attractive woman who knew far too much for comfort. About him, about the war, about—

He'd almost said Hamish, but he was nearly certain she hadn't read that nightmare in his mind. He'd blocked it for so many years now that it was habit to keep the Somme and Hamish and the firing squad shut firmly away where no one could find it.

Hamish said, "Don't go."

And Rutledge caught himself just in time, before he answered aloud. "I've already promised," he said silently. "I can't go back on it without explaining why. And that I shan't do."

3

Hugh Tredworth, the ringleader, possessed a goodly amount of charm. It was his stock-in-trade. Whispers claimed that his real father had been a Scottish tinker, but Hugh's grandfather had had the same red hair and wicked smile—and his auntie as well, come to that. As his mother was fond of pointing out. Hugh had also been cursed with older brothers, the butt of their jokes and malicious tricks for as long as he could remember. These had sharpened his wits and taught him cunning, which he was careful to conceal.

At eleven, he was the eldest of his four cohorts. Johnnie and Bill, cousins, were ten, as was Tad. Robbie, only nine, tagged along because he had always been his brother Tad's shadow. They had fallen under Hugh's spell when he'd missed a year of schooling after complications of scarlet fever. Their scrapes and escapades had never drawn blood, and for the most part their parents looked the other way.

This night—it was well on toward morning in point of fact—the five boys had tramped nearly five miles cross-country to reach their destination.

Robbie, tiring, lagged a little now, and Tad threatened to leave him by the wayside. Hugh hissed them to silence. "Hurry! Or we'll be too late."

Ahead lay the grounds of the estate and, beyond, the ruins of the great abbey. One of Hugh's neighbors had worked as undergardener there for a summer, regaling everyone with descriptions of all he'd seen. Only, everything appeared larger and harder to find in the dark. Or else Mr. Pritchert had been a liar and made up half his tales. Hugh moved his precious book from one hand to the other, unfamiliar nerves getting the better of him.

He'd purloined the book from the schoolmaster's shelf. The subject was alchemy, about which he knew nothing. But there were spells in these pages, and he intended to try them out.

Bill, the tallest, carried a sack with apples, a corner of cheese, and a heel of bread in it. Like Napoleon's army, he traveled on his stomach. They'd wanted to bring cider, but hadn't discovered a way to steal a stone jar for the night.

They skirted the grounds of the estate—Mr. Pritchert swore it had dogs that bit first and barked later—then threaded their way through a wood so dark the moon vanished. But soon enough they arrived at a point where they could see what lay ahead.

It was awe inspiring. An enormous complex of mellow stone stood before them. Ranges of monastic buildings jutting across the lawns, a square soaring tower, great arches running high into the moonlit sky, tall, haunted windows with no glass, doorways that opened into blackness unlike any they'd ever looked into.

"Gor!" Johnnie whispered, stopping short.

Robbie felt his bowels stir.

"It's naught but a ruin," Hugh scoffed. "At least, naught until we work the spells. Come on."

He started forward toward the nave, but when they didn't follow, he said in disgust, "I should have brought my sisters."

They crept at his heels then, hoping that whatever struck him down would spare them if they could only appear small enough. Bill, trying for bravado, said, "It's stood empty long enough for bones to rot."

Robbie squeaked.

An owl flew out of the empty west window above their heads, gliding on silent wings across the moonlit sward.

"I told you there were owls," Hugh whispered. "Has to be, if there's spirits here. And a black cat."

"We could have brought Cinders," Tad offered.

"And have Ma down on you like a thunderclap?" Robbie demanded. "He's her cat, not yours."

"Not to harm him, silly. Just to borrow."

"I thought people sacrificed to the Devil," Johnnie asked.

"Only if you want something. Do you?" Hugh retorted.

"No," Johnnie admitted, minding his footing as they went through the gaping door.

Now they were in the shadows cast by the massive columns, in the long roofless nave with moonlight visible above. The moon was past the full, but it helped, a little, with the gloom. The high walls seemed to stretch forever, pinning them in the eye of God.

"We aren't desecrating the altar, are we?" Tad was an altar boy. "Vicar won't care for that."

Even Hugh was having second thoughts. "We'll begin in the cloister. There should be a way to it along there. Nobody can say we didn't show respect."

With more relief than they cared to admit to, the other boys hurried after him in the direction of the doorway leading into the cloister.

There was brighter moonlight here, but the gallery was ominously dark. It seemed to be peopled with the unseen dead. Whispers of sound came to their ears, like monks walking to compline and condemning the souls of interlopers on sacred ground.

"The wind," Hugh told them when his followers stopped to listen. "See? Over there. We can use that stone in the center. It'll work a treat." He glanced up at the moon, then went sprawling. Scrambling to his feet, he looked down. But nothing he could see had tripped him up.

He'd have sworn a hand had caught at his ankle. The fingers had felt cold on his flesh.

Shaking off his own fears, he blamed them on his companions.

"Didn't anybody think to bring a candle? We'll break our necks, without."

Tad held out three, with a fistful of matches. Hugh lit them with a flourish, dripping wax onto the round stone and then setting the candles into each puddle. They formed a rough triangle.

He opened the schoolmaster's book at random and found a page where there was a drawing of a great iron kettle on the boil and an oven red hot to one side.

He scanned the words, found them very unlike a spell, and turned the page. Ah, much better. This was what he'd seen a week ago and determined to try out. He'd only a nodding acquaintance with Latin, but if God understood it, so would the Devil.

He stood up straight, his hands above his head, palms out in supplication, and began to intone the words on the page, turning them into gibberish as he struggled with them. An echo, soft and unintelligible, sent a shiver down Robbie's spine, and he clutched his brother's hand.

The words rolled on, and Hugh thought his voice had deepened toward the end as his confidence grew.

But nothing much happened, and he was disappointed.

He tried twice more with other spells, and still the Devil was afraid to come to him.

Tad said, tentatively, "He's busy elsewhere?"

But Hugh wasn't to be deterred.

"It's not sacred enough ground here in the middle. We need to stand closer to the church wall," he told them, as if he knew what he was doing. "See, just over there."

They turned to look, then got up from their haunches and followed him into the shadows, carefully shielding their candles. But the night wind blew out one of them, just as Robbie tripped, plunged headlong into the cold grass. He began to scream, high-pitched and terrifying.

They turned to clamp a hand over his mouth, then saw what he had seen first.

The Devil was already there, sitting against the wall, his grotesque face staring up at them with wide, blank eyes and the long nose of a donkey disappearing into the hood of the cloak he was wearing.

They ran until their lungs were ready to burst and their legs were trembling with the effort.

Away from the ruins, through the dark wood, as far as the road, and on toward the path they'd taken across the fields to reach the abbey.

When Robbie fell behind, Tad stopped for him, and then Bill, his hands on his knees and his breath still coming in frightened gasps, stopped too. His cousin pulled up, and Hugh, a little ahead, turned back to them.

"What was it?" Tad asked, his voice quivering.

"The Devil," Hugh retorted. "It must have been." He had never been so shaken.

"No, it was a man," Bill said. "He was wearing *shoes*."

"Do you think the Devil goes about with that cloven hoof in plain sight?" Hugh demanded, regaining a little of his confidence.

"What are we going to do about it?" Tad asked. "If we tell, we'll be blamed. Pa will take a strap to me!"

"What if Vicar won't let us come to service?" Robbie added. "Mama won't like that."

"We'll swear a blood oath never to tell," Hugh suggested dramatically. "I've my pocketknife. We'll cut our thumbs and swear."

"I don't want my thumb cut," Robbie said, and to his great shame, began to cry.

"Ma will see the cuts," Tad agreed. "She won't give us any peace over them until she knows everything."

"Why can't we just swear?" Johnnie asked. "And we'd better hurry about it, or someone will be up milking before we're back in our beds."

They swore, as fierce an oath as Hugh could devise on the spot.

"May our tongues blacken, and our faces run down our chins like hot pudding, if we speak one word about tonight to any soul, living or dead, good or evil. So help us God!"

They turned then to hurry home. But Johnnie spoke for all of them when he said, halfway there, "What if he follows us? *What if he wants us to be dead, because we've seen him?*"

I t wasn't until the next morning that a caretaker stumbled across a dead man in the ruins of Fountains Abbey.

The owner of Studley Royal was in London with his family, and so the caretaker took it upon himself to summon the police.

The local man, standing over the body, took note of three things. That there was no immediate indication of cause of death. That the man was wearing a cloak like a monk's, complete with a hood that had fallen away from his face. And that over his face there was a respirator, one from the war. He reached down and pulled the mask away.

He didn't recognize the face staring back at him.

"No one from around here," Inspector Madsen said aloud to the two constables standing at his back.

"No," the older of the two said. "But what's he doing here?"

"If I knew that," Madsen answered repressively, "I might know how he died and who has killed him. If anyone did." He had been called out before he'd had time to eat his breakfast and his wife had had a thing or two to say about that. She was a great one for cooking, and expected those she cooked for to enjoy and appreciate her efforts.

"Yes, sir." The younger constable trailed him as he turned to survey the cloisters and began a slow circle. "There're three puddles of wax, sir, on that stone in the center. A stub of candle over here, and that book you've noticed, just by his foot." He had been first on the scene.

Madsen examined the wax puddles, noted they were in the shape of a triangle, and grunted. He went next to the stub of candle. The kind, he told himself, his unthrifty wife would throw out. She was particular about her candles.

"Was this one longer to start with?" he mused. "Was this the third night of a vigil? It would explain the three puddles."

"The caretaker swears no one had been here before last night. He says he'd have noticed."

"Any sign that someone else was with the dead man?"

"It's hard to say, not knowing how active he himself was."

"All right, then, let's have a look at yon book."

Madsen picked it up and closed it to examine the title on the spine. "Alchemy, for God's sake." He flipped it open and saw the name of one Albert Harris Crowell on the name plate, and under it, Nether Bromley School.

"Is this Crowell, then?" he asked, lifting his gaze to Constable Hood, his voice flat.

"No, sir. I've seen Mr. Crowell, sir. He comes sometimes to The Dog and Cart—that's the pub near Dilby. A quiet man. Before the war he was schoolmaster in Nether Bromley, and now he's at Dilby School. Well respected, from what I'm told."

The younger constable stirred. "He was a conscientious objector in the war, sir. I've heard my father speak of it."

Madsen turned his gaze to Constable Pickerel. Pickerel's father had been a policeman as well, retiring from the Elthorpe force as sergeant just at the end of the war. Six months before Madsen himself arrived. "How does your father know what Crowell did in the war?"

"My father also drops in to The Dog and Cart from time to time.

It's the talk there, some evenings." Madsen was still staring at him, and Pickerel found himself adding, "The pub was never on his patch, you might say, and he likes that. Nobody to bring up what's past."

The next village over might as well be in a foreign land, in the eyes of most. Though the war had changed that notion to some extent, people clung to their prejudices.

"Does he never come to Elthorpe? Crowell?" Madsen asked him.

Pickerel glanced at Hood for confirmation. He shook his head.

Madsen held up the book. "Then he's made an exception last night. Maybe he can tell us who it is we have on our hands."

L ater that morning he found the schoolmaster in a classroom, seven or eight boys busy with a project involving, as far as Madsen could tell, catapults and castle walls of small mud bricks.

Crowell came out to speak to the inspector. Madsen tried not to stare at him like a specimen under glass, but this was the first time he'd set eyes on the man. Youngish, with that fair slimness that came from long lines of pedigree. His manner was composed, and his voice well bred. Glasses perched on the end of his nose, and he removed them as if suddenly aware that they were there.

If he felt any anxiety about confronting an inspector of police, he hid it well.

"Inspector Madsen, isn't it?" Crowell extended his hand. "What brings you to Dilby? Not one of my students, I hope." He smiled and nodded his head toward the half-closed door behind him. "They're a handful, but there's no meanness, I can tell you that."

"Yes, sir." Madsen took the proffered hand, then held out his own to Constable Hood just behind him. Hood passed him the book. "Can you tell us, sir, if this is by any chance your property?"

Crowell took it, frowning. "Yes, here's my name in it, but if you'd asked me, I'd have told you my copy is in the bookshelf in my office."

"Shall we have a look?"

Crowell cast a glance into his classroom. Three of the lads were staring back at him, their eyes large with alarm, as if the police had come for them. He made a mental note to discover what mischief they'd been up to, and said repressively, "Young Tredworth, mind you finish your section of the wall. Don't be standing about just because I'm not there. That applies to your workmen as well. I want to see progress when I return."

Hugh Tredworth ducked his head and turned back to his task. His cronies followed his example with suitable haste. "Very well, then," Crowell said to the policemen, and led the way.

As Madsen followed him down the passage, he asked Crowell, "Interested in alchemy, are you, sir?"

"Not particularly. When I teach science, I often make more progress with something that's exciting than I do with dull experiments. I say, how did you come by this? It's an old book, I doubt it's still in print."

"We'll attend to that in a moment, sir. This your office, is it?"

Crowell went in and crossed directly to the low bookshelf behind his desk. But when he put his finger out to tap his copy, the finger stopped in midair. "It isn't here." He turned back to Madsen, frowning. "I'm at a loss to explain how it got away, but I thank you for taking the trouble to return it, Inspector." He slid it into its proper slot, then straightened and waited, as if expecting Madsen either to take his leave or explain why it was an inspector and a constable had come to deliver a lost book.

"The problem is," Madsen began slowly, "that this book—your book—was discovered lying by the foot of a dead man."

"Good God!" Crowell was speechless for a moment, then recovering, said, "I don't understand, Inspector, but I expect we should discuss this. I'm available at three o'clock."

"Indeed, sir. Is there anyone who can take over your class, sir? I'd like you to come with me."

"What? *Now*? In heaven's name, can't it wait until the end of the school day? We're in the middle of a very important lesson. I have no idea why this man or anyone else would be interested in my book on alchemy, but surely it isn't a pressing matter? This is a harmless enough study, it can't do anyone any harm."

"I'm afraid not, sir. It could be a case of murder we're looking at."

Crowell stood there, uncertain quite what was expected of him. Then he said, "I shall have to ask my wife to step in. At this age, boys are inclined to rowdiness if left unsupervised."

As he went to find his wife, accompanied by Constable Hood, Madsen walked back to the classroom.

There was a ripple of wariness as the students turned one by one to look at him. He saw boys at the edge of the group hang their heads as if wishing the floor would swallow them up, and he smiled to himself. He could remember when he was that age and small sins loomed large.

"I'm having to borrow Mr. Crowell for a bit. I don't want to hear you've been rude or rowdy with his missus," he said, his voice stern. "You'll answer to me if there's any complaint of your behavior. Is that clear?"

There was a chorus of *Yes, sirs!* that made the rafters echo.

He nodded to the class collectively as he heard footsteps approaching. A young woman with a scar across her face walked past him into the room, taking the chair at her husband's table. She ignored Madsen, but he saw that her hands were trembling as she folded them together, and he shoved his own into his pockets as if to still them as well.

The students went quickly back to work, and Crowell smiled reassuringly at his wife before following Madsen out into the passage.

It was a long drive back to Elthorpe, not so much in miles but in the silence that neither Madsen nor Crowell felt free to break. But as they stopped in front of the police station, Crowell said, "All right, I'm here. As you asked. It's time you told me what this is all about."

"Where were you last evening, sir?" Madsen asked as he led the way into the station and back to the office where he kept his files and his pipe. "If you don't mind telling us?"

"I was at the school. Reading. My wife can verify that, you needn't have dragged me here. And what's this about a dead man and possible murder?"

"I was just coming to that, sir." Madsen sat down, leaving Crowell standing. "We found a body early this morning in the abbey ruins. A man none of us recognizes. But he'd spent some time there, from the looks of things, and it's likely he wasn't alone. My question is this. If he died of natural causes—and we'll know the answer to that when the doctor has examined him—why didn't the person or persons with him come for help?"

"As I wasn't there, I can't answer you."

"But you were there, in a manner of speaking. There was candle wax on a stone in the center of the cloisters, a stub of candle nearby, and at the dead man's foot, your book, with your name in it. A book you admit is kept in your private office."

"And I've explained to you that I have no idea how it came to be there. I'd have sworn it was on my shelf along with the rest of my books. I can't even tell you when it went missing, or how."

"Indeed, sir. You've told me the book was old, out of print. There can't be that many other copies floating about, and none of them, I expect, with your book plate inside. What we're hoping is that you can put a name to our dead man. If he had your copy in his possession, he very likely knew *you*. If it wasn't in his possession, why did you bring it to this meeting? No, don't interrupt, let me finish. Did the shock of seeing him die put the book out of your mind? Was that how it got left behind? There has to be a simple explanation, sir, and we would be greatly obliged if you could tell us why he was hanging about in a medieval abbey ruin in the middle of the night. It must have been important, whatever it was you met to discuss, and a private matter at that."

"Look, I've told you—I wasn't in the abbey ruins last night or any night this past year. I don't know who the dead man is or why my book should be there. I didn't meet him, and when you find out who stole my book, you'll have your other person." Crowell was angry now, and feeling more than a little defensive as the evidence against him was being presented.

"Then you'll have no objection to coming with us to look at the dead man."

"I—don't like the dead. That is, I've seen more than my share, and I'll live very happily if I never see another one."

"That's as may be," Madsen said. "All the same, I shall have to ask you to tell us if you can identify him." He rose. "We can walk to the doctor's surgery from here. I'm sure I can accept your word that you won't make any trouble for us?"

"Make any—of course not, damn you."

Madsen smiled as he led the way. He had his man now, he was sure of it.

But in the back room of the doctor's surgery, where the body had been taken, Crowell stared down at the face on the bed and slowly shook his head. "I've never seen him before in my life."

"Can you swear to that?"

"Of course I can. I have never laid eyes on him as far as I know."

But there was a subtle shift in what he'd said before and what he was willing to swear to. Madsen made a note of it.

The doctor came in just then and nodded to Madsen. "As far as I can tell on first examination I'd say he was overcome by gas. Which means he couldn't have been wearing that respirator when he died. Nor could he have died in the ruins."

Madsen frowned. "Are you saying he died elsewhere, was brought to the abbey, and left where he was found?"

"I can tell you he didn't walk there himself," the doctor retorted dryly. "Someone else was involved. Make of it what you will."

Crowell, standing there between the doctor and the inspector, flinched. "I don't have gas lamps. Not where I live." He'd blurted it out, nerves getting the better of him. His brother had died from chlorine gas at the second battle of Ypres. He had spent years trying to wipe that memory away. It had been a horrid death. He had carried the dying too many times not to know what his brother had suffered.

Madsen and the doctor turned to stare at him.

"I've never seen him before," Crowell repeated. "Can we go now? I've no taste for this."

"Conscientious objector in the war, were you, sir?" Madsen asked, making no move to leave.

"How did you know—" But it was obvious that the police had already looked into his background. "If you've seen my record, you've also read that I served in France driving an ambulance. I didn't want to kill, that's all. But I could do something about the suffering." He gestured toward the dead man. "And I've seen far worse than this poor devil, so making me stand here isn't going to help you." His voice had risen just a little, and he tried to get himself under control again. But it was hard. His temper these days was uncertain at best, and his wife had urged him to speak to someone about it. He wondered what Madsen would make of that if he'd learned of it.

But the inspector had already decided there was nothing to be gained here by trying to push the schoolmaster into betraying himself in the face of his victim. He nodded to the doctor and led the way out to the street.

Crowell felt himself sweating. A cold sweat that seemed to bathe him. "Am I free to return to my classroom, Inspector? I don't care to leave my wife alone with the older boys any longer than need be. They tend to rowdiness after a while."

"We shall have to speak to Mrs. Crowell. I'll take you back myself."

And so it was that Inspector Madsen found himself alone and face-to-face with Alice Crowell in the school's small office.

"How did you come by that scar?" he asked before he could stop the words. "You didn't have it when I knew you."

"It's not your concern." Her voice was husky, but he couldn't be sure whether it was fear or nerves.

There was a silence, fraught with what was not said.

"Did he do that to you?" Madsen pressed. "You may as well tell me, I'll find out in the end."

"What did you wish to see me about?" she asked. "Are you going to take my husband into custody?"

"Should I?" Madsen countered.

She made an impatient gesture. "Don't play with me, Harry. I saw your face when you took Albert away. Whatever has happened, it isn't just a matter of a truant student."

"Is there one? A truant student?"

"You know there isn't. I meant—never mind. What did you wish to see me about?" she repeated.

She had a very mobile face, her feelings clearly expressed. The scar seemed to alter with her emotions, emphasizing them in some fashion he couldn't understand. He wanted to run his finger along it, and tell her she was still beautiful. But he knew she could lie too. She had lied to him about her parents and how they had felt about a policeman in the family. That, he tried to tell himself in the face of his bitterness, was a *kind* lie. And she had told him another, that she hadn't loved him. He believed it then, but later convinced himself that it was to cover the first lie.

Madsen took a deep breath. This wasn't the place to open up the past. "Where was your husband last evening?"

Her expression changed. "Here. At the school. He was finishing going over papers that he's submitting for an award. Mrs. Scott's prize for the best essay on *Richard III.*"

Mrs. Scott was the widow of the former rector of St. Stephen's, in Elthorpe. She was something of a local historian, having written a small pamphlet on the architecture of the village church and another on the abbey. Both were available for sale on the table in the church porch. Madsen had seen them. It was typical of her that she'd asked Crowell to read the essays. Like to like. The schoolmaster in Elthorpe was an upstart from Liverpool. Well enough at what he did, but not the sort one invites to present prizes in a social setting.

"And you were here with him? Sitting in his office?" It brought such a cozy domestic scene to his mind that Madsen clenched his fists.

"No, I was at home, sewing the fringe on a shawl I was making for my mother's birthday."

"Then no one can actually prove he *was* here?"

"Of course he was here. Why would he lie to me about where he was? Where else would he go?"

To meet a man he planned to kill and whose body he intended to leave in the ruins of Fountains Abbey, to throw off the police. Madsen hadn't explained the presence of that book yet, but in time he would.

He found he was staring at her. "I'm married now, myself," he said. "Did you ever love me? Truly love me?"

She stood up. "I take it you have no more professional questions to ask me, Inspector. And I shan't answer personal ones."

But he stayed where he was, between her and the door. "There's a man dead. Didn't your husband tell you that this morning when he asked you to carry on in the schoolroom for him? A man dead, with one of your husband's books lying at his feet."

She drew in a breath. "Who was it?" she asked. "Who is dead?"

As if that were more important than the book. "We don't know. Your husband can't identify him, there is nothing in the man's pockets to tell us who he is, and all we can be certain of is that he didn't live in this part of Yorkshire. Else one of my men would have known him. And more to the point, no one has been reported missing."

"Well, then, if you don't know who the dead man is," she said tartly, "there's no reason to keep me penned up in here or to take my husband away. Meanwhile, there's the school to be seen to."

Her words stung him. "I haven't kept you penned up, Alice—Mrs. Crowell. I was doing my duty." He stepped aside and she swept out of the door as if he were invisible.

He watched her walk down the corridor, and he felt an urge to clap her husband up and throw away the key.

At the door of a classroom a boy stood watching him, wary and uncertain.

"What are you staring at, then?" Madsen snapped, and the child disappeared as if by magic, shutting the door softly behind him.

Hugh Tredworth was waiting for his friends at the end of the school day. One glance at his face made Bill distinctly uneasy as he came up to join Hugh, and Johnnie, trailing him, stopped to study his boots at a little distance, as if uncomfortable in Hugh's presence. Then Tad came through the door, starting at the sight of them standing together in silence.

"What's happened?" he asked anxiously.

"Where's Robbie?" Hugh demanded accusingly. "He wasn't at school today."

"Sick," Tad answered shortly. "Couldn't keep his breakfast down this morning."

"He's not telling, is he?" Bill wanted to know. "We swore an *oath!*"

"Of course he's not telling," Tad replied with more force than he'd intended. But he couldn't hold their eyes.

"Remind him," Hugh urged. "Remind him his tongue will turn black if he's not in school tomorrow."

"Leave him alone," Johnnie spoke up, and they all wheeled to stare at him. "You'll only make it worse," he said, "trying to frighten him. Why were the police here? What did they want?"

"I couldn't hear." But Hugh had seen the book in the constable's hands, if no one else had, and he had had to swallow hard to keep his own breakfast down, the shock was so great. "It was Mr. Crowell they wanted, wasn't it? Nothing to do with us."

"Why did they come for him?" Bill persisted. "All the way from Elthorpe. And then take him away."

"They brought him back, didn't they?" Hugh pointed out.

"Someone found the candle we dropped," Tad said. "It's a matter of trespass. None of us missed school, so there's nothing to point at us.

Not counting Robbie, but they're not to know that, are they?"

The four of them had been walking down the road as they argued, earnestly trying to assure themselves that there was nothing to show they'd summoned the Devil and succeeded in raising him.

Then Bill shattered their illusions. "Did *he* leave scorched grass, where he lay? The Devil? Is that why they're questioning schoolmasters, they've found the grass and want to know if anyone's *different*?"

"How different?" Tad asked anxiously. "Nobody else has been sick, just Robbie."

"He's possessed," Bill said. "That's why he's sick. He's *possessed*."

Tad shouted at him, "There's nothing wrong with him. There's nothing wrong with my brother!" And he marched off down the road, leaving them to look after him, their faces tight with sudden worry.

The doctor's report was brought in to Madsen. The man hadn't died where he was found, it was impossible that he could have, considering the cause of death. In fact, he'd been dead at least four-and-twenty hours before he was discovered.

Furthermore, there were no scars or other marks to make it a simple matter to identify him. He could be anyone. From anywhere.

And Madsen, though he didn't care for unfinished business on his watch, reviewed the evidence and decided that his next step would have to be identifying the corpse before he could make any connection with Albert Crowell stick. If he could prove that Crowell knew the man, it would go a long way toward building his case. If there was anything between them, he could take the schoolmaster into custody.

But that was easier said than done. Where, for instance, should he begin?

He considered bringing Alice Crowell in to Elthorpe to look at the dead man. He even toyed with going back to the school to ask Crowell where he had been every minute of the past three days. But he already knew what Alice Crowell would say. Her husband had been with her—busy at the school—listening to her read. Standing by him even with a possible charge of murder hanging over the man's head.

Madsen kept the file open on his desk where it could nag him every time he looked at it, and it became an obsession even when he was not there.

Why had Crowell's book been found by the corpse's feet? An old book, on alchemy of all things. He pondered that as he dealt with a quarrel between two farmers over the death of a prize ram. What did the book have to do with the dead man, except to betray the name of his murderer? Why had Crowell been carrying this book with him? Was it concealing something? Had it been the excuse that allowed Crowell to approach the victim?

Over his tea, Madsen was beginning to believe the two men must have met at the ruins, gone somewhere else, and the body had been carried back there to throw the police off. The caretaker could have been wrong, he might have simply glanced into the cloisters the day before and missed the corpse up against the wall. In a hurry as he made his rounds, and not wanting his employers to know he'd been slack.

Madsen went back to the doctor's surgery and stood looking down at the corpse. Why the respirator that hadn't saved the victim's life, and why the cloak that at first glance looked like a monk's habit? To lay a false trail for the police?

He tried to put it all together, but there was no making sense of it.

Walking back to his office he considered the fact that neither Crowell's house nor the village school was served by gas. So where had he taken the dead man to kill him? Why did the man have to die?

He shut himself in his office to think.

Debts owed? Some scandalous connection between the two men that didn't bear looking at? Then why leave the body here, if the man hadn't died here? It only made the killing more blatant. What was it in aid of, that respirator and the cloak? A warning to someone else?

What was the schoolmaster involved in and how would it affect Alice Crowell when the truth came out?

It all came down to that bloody book, he told himself for the hundredth time as he walked home for his dinner. If the book hadn't been there, the police would have been mystified. An oversight, a mistake, the kind that got murderers hanged.

What was there in Albert Crowell's life that he was desperate to hide?

By morning, Madsen was unable to stay away from the Crowells. Three more visits to the school, three more frustrating interviews with the schoolmaster, three more missed encounters with Alice, who seemed to have an uncanny ability to be other than where he wanted her to be. And yet he couldn't bring himself to ask for her outright. Not while he badgered her husband.

In the dark hours of the night he'd even considered the possibility that she had killed her lover and left the book to muddle the case. But he knew it wasn't true. The man, according to the doctor, was pushing fifty and not the sort who could sweep any woman off her feet.

Twice on his excursions to the Dilby School, he found himself faced with staring boys, nosy little bastards, more eyes than face. He never remembered being so fond of his own schoolmasters that he wouldn't have cheered to see them taken away for a week.

He had spoken to one of them, the Tredworth boy. "What are you hanging about for? Know anything about this business, do you?"

Hugh had shaken his head vigorously. "No, sir. I—it's just—" He took a deep breath and blurted, "Thought I might be a policeman when I grow up, that's all. And nobody will tell me what's happened. They change the subject when I come into the room."

"It's not a matter for children's ears," Madsen had said, annoyance creeping in. "Stay clear of it, or I'll have you in for questioning myself."

After that he saw no more of Hugh or his friends.

4

The dinner had, in many ways, been trying.

Rutledge had sat opposite Meredith Channing, and he had spent the evening trying to keep his mind closed to her. It was difficult, with Hamish restless and more intrusive as the hour stretched into two and then into three. The soft Scottish voice railed at him, warning him no' to lower his guard, as if they stood in the darkness of France, waiting for an attack they couldn't see but knew would surely come. For a moment he could smell the war again, and it shook him, it was so real.

Frances, beside him, had been brittle, her laughter forced, her smile too bright. Rutledge began to wonder if there had been more to Simon Barrington's departure for Scotland than met the eye—or that Frances had been prepared to confide.

The Farnums, thank God, had been their usual cheerful selves, and Maryanne Browning seemed to revive in the warmth of convivial-

ity. Widowhood had been a blow. Like most women of her upbringing, she'd relied on Peter for everything, and suddenly faced with
taking charge of her own life and fortunes when Peter dropped dead
in the second influenza epidemic, she had been at a loss to know how
to begin. There had been no time to prepare, to learn how certain
things were done, how to cope with lawyers and bankers and men of
business. *Peter* had done all that. He should by rights still be here to
lift the burden from her. The struggle had taken its toll, though to her
credit Maryanne had never shirked her duty. That too had been part
of her upbringing—to accept duty and responsibility, however difficult or distasteful they might be.

Frances had been right about this evening, a much-needed pallia-
tive for her.

He recalled his question to Frances—was this a matchmaking attempt, including him in the gathering? But it seemed to be the farthest
thing from Maryanne's mind. She treated Rutledge like the friend he
was, *Peter*'s friend, and therefore someone to trust and turn to but not
to consider romantically. A brother that Peter had never had. Conse-
quently, he returned the compliment and treated her in much the same
way he treated Frances, although without the worry that she would
see through him as his sister did. Maryanne was not in Frances's
league when it came to reading people.

Without a conscious shift in thought, he found himself recalling
that Meredith Channing never spoke of her late husband. He had
no idea how she had mourned him, or what gaps he had left in her
life. That innate composure seldom cracked far enough to show the
woman inside.

Images of Meredith Channing as he'd first met her on the eve of
the new year, when she'd conducted an amusing séance for Maryanne
Browning and her guests, had stayed with him. She had known more
about him than he'd felt comfortable with, and her voice was mesmer-
izing, soft and melodious and warm. Her eyes held secrets that he with
all his experience couldn't fathom. But she had stood by him when

they met again in Northamptonshire, and he had been forced to trust her then.

She made no reference to that during the dinner, greeting him as a friend of friends and giving no indication she had seen him deal with murderers.

At one point under cover of the laughter surrounding them, she had said quietly, "I hope you are well." It was a statement, not a question, as if she already knew the answer.

"Well enough. It was a long day." He couldn't for the life of him understand why he had added that, and swore silently.

She nodded, as if she could see he was speaking the truth, then joined in the general conversation. He began to relax a little, unaware until the meal was nearly over that somewhere in the course of the evening his fatigue had dropped away, the shocks of the day no longer weighing heavily on his mind. Mrs. Channing had not singled him out for attention, indeed he could hardly recall a word spoken directly to him save for her brief "I hope you are well." And yet the warmth of her voice, something in her manner that was inexplicably soothing, and the stillness that was her nature seemed to touch him in some fashion.

He told himself that that was nonsense, it was the wine and the good conversation and the laughter that had done the trick. But Hamish was there, warning him to mind he didn't betray himself, to keep a tight grip on his self-control.

To Rutledge fell the task of holding Mrs. Channing's coat for her when they were leaving, and a faint fragrance like jasmine on a warm summer night's breeze wafted toward him as she settled her scarf around her throat. He was used to the perfumes of England—lily of the valley, attar of roses, forget-me-nots—floral scents that most women wore, sometimes with the spicy touch of carnations or the richness of heliotrope. He found himself remembering the scent that Olivia Marlowe had used, even after her death still surrounding the desk where she had worked.

A line of Olivia's poetry from the volume *Wings of Fire*—O. A. Manning's poetry—filled his mind, unbidden.

I have not forgotten you,
The pleasure of your touch,
The depth of your voice.
It's as if you never left me,
And my heart is full.

He nearly dropped the coat, but Meredith Channing appeared not to notice. Hamish had.

Rutledge had envied Nicholas Cheney, Olivia's half brother. He still did. And Hamish knew that all too well.

There were general farewells, giving Rutledge time to collect his wits and shake hands, say the right thing, and turn away as the next cab drew to the curb. Frances was adding, "Mrs. Channing is going my way, Ian. You needn't worry about seeing me home. Did you enjoy the evening? I hope you did."

"Very much so," he answered, kissing her cheek.

And then he was alone, traveling toward his flat. *Damn Barrington, if he broke Frances's heart!*

Three nights later Rutledge met friends for dinner, this one masculine and taken in a club off St. James's Street. Their conversation avoided the war, but even so, the toast, "To absent friends . . ." had brought it back like a specter at the feast. One man had just returned from a tour of duty in South Africa, his face burnt brick red by the sun, and they spoke of his journey home, then moved on to where the government was heading with its policies, the state of the economy, and most depressing of all, a rise in the crime rate as ordinary people struggled to make ends meet. As the dinner broke up, Freddy Masters informed them that he was thinking of immigrating to Canada.

"My uncle has business interests there, and he lost his son—my cousin Jack—in the war. I'm what's left of the family, and while I'm not particularly enthralled with providing electricity to millions, there you are. I don't have much choice."

There was general agreement, and Mark Hadley said, "My neighbor has much the same idea. He'd considered Argentina and even Australia, but Canada seems less of a change."

Talk of Canada reminded Rutledge of Jean, married and living there now with her diplomat. If it hadn't been for the war he'd have married her himself. When he came home from France shell-shocked, a broken man, she had been horrified, unable even to look at him. He'd released her from the engagement there and then, but it had taken him a very long time to come to terms with the anguish of her desertion. It had seemed to underline the bleakness of his future.

He was wondering if she missed England, just as Freddy continued. "My wife's not best pleased, leaving schools and friends behind. I'll let you know what we decide."

"I can tell you my wife wasn't best pleased with Cape Town," Edward Throckmorton commented. "But we managed. You find a way."

Mark smiled at Rutledge. "Lucky man, you have no wife to make your decisions for you." And then he too remembered Jean and looked away.

Rutledge said only, "I don't know if it's luck or a curse. My sister keeps me in line."

Freddy said, thoughtfully, "I saw Frances some ten days back, walking along Bond Street with Simon Barrington. Good man, Simon." As if to say he'd seen which way the wind blew there. And as if to reassure Rutledge that she might make a worse choice.

"He's in Scotland at the moment," Rutledge answered.

"Scotland?" Mark was surprised. "He dined with the Douglases last night. I'm sure of it."

Rutledge heard him, but managed to say, "I must be wrong, then. I may not have a wife, but I know how to listen with half an ear."

That brought a round of laughter, and they said their good nights.

Driving to his flat, Rutledge tried to recall some of the evening's conversation, but it was a blur, already fading. All he could hear was Hadley's voice: *He dined with the Douglases last night. I'm sure of it.*

Tomorrow he would make it his business to find out what had happened between Frances and Simon Barrington. It had been a long day, and a good night's sleep would show him how best to go about it.

A night's sleep he was not to have. There was a constable on his doorstep, standing there with the stoic air of a man prepared to remain at his post until Doomsday, if that was required of him.

When he saw Rutledge step out of his motorcar, he waited until his quarry turned toward him to say, "Evening, sir. Chief Superintendent Bowles's compliments, sir, and will you come to the Yard at once."

Rutledge doubted that the chief superintendent had said anything about compliments. But he nodded and replied, "Come in, while I change."

"I'm to bring you as soon as I find you, begging your pardon, sir."

"Constable Burns, isn't it? Well, Constable, I am not appearing at the Yard in evening dress, and there's an end of it. Another five minutes won't matter." He unlocked the door to his flat and added with more humor than he felt, "I won't tell him if you don't."

"No, sir. Yes, sir," Burns replied woodenly, and followed him into the flat as if expecting him to escape through a back window.

It was, in fact, seven minutes before Rutledge was ready to leave. He felt as if he were moving in treacle, every task seeming to require more effort than he could muster.

Rutledge drove, and Burns sat silently beside him like a waxwork figure. Rutledge found himself thinking that he would be asleep before he reached the Yard. In an effort to keep himself alert, he said, "How long have you been waiting, Constable?"

"Two hours, sir. A little over."

"At least it was a pleasant night."

"Yes, sir."

Was I ever that green? Rutledge found himself wondering. It seemed a long time ago that he'd been a constable. Centuries. Eons. But it hadn't been ten years.

They arrived at the Yard, and Burns waited while Rutledge saw to the motorcar, then accompanied him inside and to the door of the Chief Superintendent's office, as if half afraid his quarry would bolt if left alone.

Rutledge knocked, and then entered at Bowles's curt command.

Burns disappeared down the shadowy passage, duty done.

Rutledge shut the door and faced his superior.

Bowles was in a subdued mood. Instead of what Rutledge expected to hear from him—"It took you long enough to get here!"—the Chief Superintendent said, "I want you to leave tonight for Berkshire, if you will. Your destination is half a dozen houses not far from Uffington. They're called the Tomlin Cottages. Hardly enough of them to dignify the name hamlet, but there you are. You've a watching brief, nothing more."

"Why not use a local man?" Rutledge asked.

"It's not something for the local people to worry themselves about. The War Office has misplaced one of its own, and they don't want him to get the wind up, thinking they're watching him. But the fact is, they are. Rather an odd sort, I'm told, tends to do things his way, disappears sometimes, and for all I know gets roaring drunk and alarms the neighbors. A routine look-in was unsatisfactory, and in the event he's got himself into trouble, they want it dealt with quickly and efficiently, to avoid gossip."

"But the Yard—"

"Isn't in the business of minding fools. My view as well. But when you've been asked nicely, you do as you're told." He turned to look out the window. "They were impressed, they said, with the way you handled matters in Warwickshire last June. See that you don't disappoint them now." It was grudging, as if the words were forced out of him. Or required of him?

"What excuse do I have for being there?"

"There's that damned great white horse on the hillside." Bowles turned back to the room. "Done in chalk. People come to stare at it, and strangers are taken for granted. Not liked, mind you, but for the most part ignored."

The damned great white horse was a chalk figure from the prehistoric past, and of all the chalk figures, possibly Rutledge's favorite. He'd been taken to see it as a child and allowed to walk the bounds.

"Who is the man I'm to watch? How will I know him?"

"It's Partridge, of all the bloody names. Gaylord Partridge. The cottage with the white gate. He matters to the War Office, and that's what you're to keep in mind at all times." He passed a sheet of paper to Rutledge.

Not even on official stationery, he thought, scanning it. A name, a direction. Nothing more. Spoken rather than written instructions. Sydney Riley, the infamous spy, could have done no better in the cloak-and-dagger world.

Rutledge left soon afterward, not happy about the long drive that lay ahead, but in other ways glad to be out of London. The daffodils would be rioting among the hedgerows, and the air was sweet in the countryside.

Hamish reminded him, "There's yon Simon Barrington," as Rutledge put the kettle on and then went to pack his valise.

"He'll still be in London when I return. It can wait." But Frances's face when she'd come to ask him to take her to dinner with Maryanne Browning was before him, even as he answered Hamish aloud.

He could hardly pound Barrington into admitting he'd lied to Frances, or arrest him for cruelty to his sister. And there was always the possibility that perhaps it was Frances who lied about Scotland, to keep herself from blurting out the truth—that something had gone wrong between the two of them.

"It can wait," he said again to Hamish as much as to himself. "It might work out better without my meddling."

Hamish said derisively, "Aye, that's a comfort."

Rutledge filled his Thermos with tea, then turned out the lamps. He paused there in the darkness, wondering again if he should leave a message for his sister, then thought better of it. A letter was no way to deliver bad news, if she truly didn't know where Simon was. And it was always possible that he had dined with the Douglases and then traveled north with them.

Cutting across London, Rutledge set out in the direction of Uffington, and drove through the darkness, stopping only to stretch his legs when he felt himself drowsing at the wheel and to drink from the Thermos.

It was a remarkably soft night, one of those April evenings when the world seemed pleased with itself. When he'd left the busy towns ringing London behind, he could sometimes smell plowed earth and, once or twice, the wafting fragrance of fruit trees in bloom. The road emptied as the night moved on toward the early hours of morning, a handful of lorries making their way to the east and the occasional motorcar passing him. At one point he smelled wood smoke, and wondered if gypsies were camping in a copse of trees in the middle of nowhere. The policeman's instinct was to stop and investigate, but he drove on, ignoring it.

Around two in the morning, he pulled into a small clearing and slept, awaking to the dampness of an early dew. For several seconds he was disoriented, not sure where he was, in France or in England, but then his mind cleared and he got out to walk again and to finish his tea.

It was just getting light when he drove past his destination, a cluster of nine cottages that seemed to stand in the middle of nowhere, much of a sameness in design as if they were built to match. Stone and thatch, they seemed out of place here. He saw that one a little to itself boasted a white gate in a low stone wall.

On the hillside above him was the White Horse, pale in the morning light, an early mist hiding its feet, giving it the appearance of floating across the ground, silent and mysterious.

He stopped the motorcar in the middle of the road, swept by such an intense emotion that he could feel his heart thudding heavily in his chest.

The mist, moving gently, blotted out everything else until it was all he could see.

Gas. Floating across the battlefield, and the shout going up, *Masks!*

He was back in France, the tension and fear spreading around him as he and his men watched the slow-moving cloud, fumbling to put on their gas masks, hastily making sure not an inch of skin showed. He thrust his hands in his pockets, unable to find his gloves, digging them deep until he could feel his knuckles hard against the fabric. And Hamish saying in his ear—

"Are you lost, then?"

He came back to the present with a jolt, staring at what appeared to be a giant of a man standing at his elbow.

For the life of him, he couldn't have told how long the man had been there or what he'd been saying.

"I— Admiring the horse," he managed, trying to bring it into focus against the backdrop of his slip into the past.

The young man turned to look at it. "Impressive, right enough. I like it best at moonrise. But you're blocking the road."

Rutledge glanced in his mirror and saw a large wagon behind him and a patient horse between the shafts. On the wagon was a harrow.

"Sorry."

He let in the clutch and drove on, still lost in that nightmare world that all too often shared his real one.

The cottages were behind him, and ahead lay Wayland's Smithy in a copse of beech trees. He could make it out clearly, an arrangement of great stones that encompassed a small space with a narrow opening. It had probably been a Stone Age tomb, not a blacksmith's shop. Still, legend maintained that if a man left his horse there overnight to be shod, and a coin to pay for the work, the animal would be waiting for him in the morning. More likely, local smiths had discovered a way to expand their trade. For centuries fire and those who used it to work metal were held in high regard, and sometimes feared as well.

A few miles along, he found a small inn by the road, lorries in the yard and a motorcar or two as well.

He stopped to ask if they were serving at this hour, and inside saw a pot of tea standing on a small table near the door, a stack of mugs beside it, sugar and a pitcher of lukewarm milk just behind it.

He poured himself a cup, wandered into the tiny reception area, and sat down by the window overlooking the road.

It was two hours later that he opened his eyes again.

A woman was clearing away the tea things, and she smiled as he stirred and then straightened up in his chair.

"You're not the first to nod off in that chair," she said, her eyes merry, "nor the last. That your motorcar by the lilacs?"

"I'm afraid so. When do you begin serving breakfast?"

"Lord love you, we closed the kitchen more than an hour ago. Most of the lorry drivers have moved on. I'd have thought their racket would've wakened the dead."

"Not this dead," he said, standing and stretching his shoulders. "Do you by any chance have rooms here?"

"We keep a half-dozen beds for travelers. Clean sheets and good food, as well as good cheer. That's what we offer. And all we offer." She considered him. "It's not very posh—"

Rutledge smiled. "Still, I'd like a room for tonight, if you have one. I'm here to see the horse."

"Oh, yes? It's early for the day-trippers, but I expect you aren't the usual visitor. What are you, then?"

Her face was red with the morning's rush, her hair pinned back out of her way, and her clothing sober, as if she worked hard and had no time to worry about how she looked.

He hadn't been prepared to deal with questions of this sort.

"I was tired of London, and I drove all night." Following her into the dining room, he added, "I needed to see something besides walls and pavement and people."

"Disappointed in love, are you?"

He was on the point of vigorously denying it when he realized that she was teasing him. And he must have looked the picture of the rejected lover, unshaven, his clothes unpressed, his face marked with fatigue.

"No. Foolish in the extreme."

She laughed. "Sit down over there in the corner—that cloth's clean—and I'll bring you whatever's left from breakfast. There's usually cold bacon, bread, and hard-boiled eggs in the cupboard. There's coffee as well as tea. Some of the lorry drivers prefer it to keep them awake."

"I'll stay with tea."

When she brought his plate it was large as a charger, and as promised there were rashers of bacon, eggs, toasted bread, and pots of butter and jam. Rutledge thanked her and added, "I've just come past those cottages not far from the spot where you can look up and see the White Horse. Odd place to put them, I should think, unless they're intended for viewers to stop in." He couldn't remember seeing them there when he'd come to Uffington as a boy, but then the horse had been all that mattered, firing his imagination.

"Well, I hope you're not thinking of wanting one. They're taken, the lot of them. They were put up near the beginning of the late Queen's reign, leper houses they were. But no lepers came, and then they were let to anyone who was willing to live there. The local people don't much care for them, but there's no dearth of people who do."

"Why leper houses? Was leprosy a problem here?"

She paused on her way back to the kitchen. "It was a Miss Tomlin, they say, who was set on them, having been a missionary and seen her share of suffering. And there's a leper in the Bible, you know. I expect that was what put her in mind of doing something for them. She sold off another parcel of land her grandfather had left her and sent for a builder to make cottages where the poor things could live without being tormented. But she never found any 'children of God' as she called them, and she died not long after."

"At least she cared enough to try."

"Well, there's that, I expect. Or a guilty conscience. The fact is, she could have done more good with her money in other directions, in my opinion. A touch of the sun, it's what my granddad always said. Too much sun and too long in heathen lands. She'd lost sight of what truly needed doing in *England*. And I've dishes to see to. My husband's gone to market, and the girl who dries for me has a bad thumb, so I'm on my own. Give me half an hour, and there'll be a room for you."

She was gone, leaving him to the hearty breakfast.

Afterward she showed him to a small room that seemed Lilliputian, and he remembered the young man on the road. *He'd have played the very devil getting himself into this box,* he thought.

And the cramped space sent his claustrophobia reeling. The first order of business was to open the only window, which looked out on the road. He stood there breathing in the morning air and fighting an urge to run back down the stairs after Mrs. Smith, begging for something larger. But there weren't any larger rooms, given the size of the building.

Fatigue overtook him after a few minutes, and he lay down on the narrow bed, asleep almost as soon as his head touched the pillow. The fragrance of sun-dried sheets folded with lavender was the last thing he remembered.

I t was late morning when he drove back to the White Horse and climbed the hill. His legs were longer than they had been at age nine, and he made short work of it now. As a child he'd huffed and puffed in his father's wake, trying to keep pace but stumbling as he tried to see everything at once.

Hamish, unhappy with this heathen horse, kept him company with a vigorous objection to having any part of it.

When one stood on the crest of the hill looking down at the figure, it was difficult to pick out what the expanse of white chalk represented. Aware of what the design was, it was possible to identify the flowing tail, the legs stretched in a gallop, the reared head. But the ancient people who had cut the turf here to create the figure must have had someone standing on the ground below, guiding them.

As, he realized, someone was standing now, looking up at him.

He began to walk back the way he'd come, and the man stayed where he was. It wasn't the young giant from early this morning, but an older man with gray in his hair and a lined face. His eyes, when Rutledge was near enough to see them, were brown but the whites were yellow.

Malaria.

Rutledge had seen troops from the Commonwealth, especially India, with just such yellowing.

"Good morning," he said to the man, for all the world a traveler taken with the local sight. "It's quite a piece of work, isn't it? I expect it was dug with wooden mattocks or antler horn. I wonder how long it took to create the full figure."

"Don't ask me, I don't know a damned thing about it. And care less. Is that what brought you here, the horse?"

Warily, Rutledge said, "Should there be another reason?"

"Well, Partridge has gone missing again. There's generally someone from London looking in on him or waiting for him to come back when he's on one of his walkabouts."

It was an Australian term, and the man seemed to use it as if from habit.

"How do you know he's—er—gone missing?"

"I feed his cat, don't I? When he's not to home, she comes to my door. That's the arrangement we have. And I don't mind, she's a good mouser."

Rutledge held out his hand and introduced himself.

"Quincy," the other man said, briefly. "Well, since you're down, you'll want to come for a spot of tea."

"Thank you, Mr. Quincy."

"No, just Quincy," he retorted, turning on his heel to lead the way to the cottage across from the one with the white gate.

Rutledge bent his head to follow his host inside. The rooms were small but of a size for one man to manage well enough. Or one woman. He'd glimpsed a woman's face peering out at him from her windows as he had turned from the road into the lane that linked the cottages.

"That chair's got better springs," Quincy said, pointing it out.

Rutledge sat down and looked around. From the sitting room/parlor, he could see a kitchen in the back where Quincy was busy, a second room across the entry from this one, its door shut, and in the middle of the house, stairs up to a loft.

"Quite comfortable here, are you?" Rutledge asked.

"If you like small places," Quincy answered, putting on the kettle. "I've had to store some of my belongings under the bed upstairs. Where did you drive from?"

"London," Rutledge answered and they talked until the kettle whistled about the city, which Quincy seemed to know, although his information was often more than a little out of date as if he hadn't been there for some time.

The closed door creaked, a paw came out and around it, followed by a long gray cat with orange eyes. Behind her, Rutledge could see a burst of color in the room, as if tins of paint had been splattered everywhere.

"Dublin!" Quincy, catching sight of the cat, swore and came to scoop her up to put her outside. But first he'd shut the inner door quickly as if not wishing Rutledge to know what was in the room beyond.

But Rutledge had already guessed. Birds, in every hue, every size, all naturally posed. And all quite dead.

He said nothing, accepting the cup of tea he was offered. "These cottages are interesting. What's their history?"

"Not much," Quincy told him bluntly. "Built at a guess some fifty years ago by a woman who had more money than sense. Comfortable enough, but I need a bicycle to go anywhere. It's out back."

"And how did Partridge get around?"

"He had a motorcar. It's in the shed behind his house. I expect he wasn't going far and left it in favor of his own bicycle."

"Does he usually wander off like this?"

"He's mad as a hatter," Quincy responded sourly. "Goes where the wind blows."

"And who comes here looking for him?"

"Business associates. So they tell me. It seems he worked for a firm in London before he was put to pasture, and apparently someone there still cares what becomes of him."

"That's thoughtful," Rutledge answered.

"Not thoughtful, careful. I expect he was someone important enough that they didn't want the world and its brother knowing he's gone balmy."

"When was the last time he left?"

"February, it was. The man here when Partridge came back told me he'd been spotted on a street corner in Birmingham, preaching peace and harmony to the world."

"That's cold work in February."

"Yes, well, I don't think he cares. I don't think he cares for anything except Dublin, the cat. A young woman came here once and he wouldn't let her in. I expect it was his daughter. There was a resemblance, at least."

"His wandering off must worry her."

"Most of the time it's only a day, a day and a half that he's away. Occasionally it's a longer period of time. Someone told me, I forget who it was, that he must have another house elsewhere. That that's where he goes. But he's never spoken of it, so my guess is that it isn't true. Gossip is not always reliable. And in his case, not always helpful."

"And his daughter never came back?"

"Not that I'm aware of."

"A pity. It sounds as if Partridge needs her."

"He doesn't need anyone when he's right in his head. Which is most of the time. You're very interested in him, for a passerby."

"Yes, well, I've time on my hands. And people intrigue me. Partridge's walkabouts as you call them. Your birds." As a diversion, it worked beautifully.

"Seen them, did you? Well, there's no law broken in having them."

"None that I know of."

Rutledge had finished his tea, and stood up. "Thank you for your hospitality."

"If you're needful of seeing in the cottage, Partridge never locked it."

Surprised, Rutledge said, "I have no right to trespass on his privacy."

"The other watchers weren't so particular about that."

"Yes, well, as it happens, I'm not one of the other watchers. Thank you again, Quincy."

"I'll see you about. Watcher or not."

Rutledge left. The woman who had been peering out her window at him was in her back garden, hanging a morning's wash on the line. He wondered if it was to see who he was and what he did next. A better vantage point than the window.

He walked back to his motorcar to find the young man he'd met earlier with his head deep in the bonnet.

He jerked it out as he heard Rutledge approaching, and said, "I like mechanical things. Engines. Whatever. Do you mind?"

"Not at all. The name's Rutledge."

The other man held out his hand, saw that it was filthy and drew it back again. "Andrew, Andrew Slater."

"I've been admiring the White Horse," Rutledge said as Slater dove back into the inner workings of the engine.

"I saw you this morning. Asleep on the road."

"Yes—" He let it go at that.

"We don't get many visitors this time of year," Slater went on, voice muffled. "The horse is most popular in the summer. People bring baskets and spread out a cloth and have their lunch or their tea there. I don't think the horse much cares for that."

"I needed to get away from London," Rutledge said. "This was as good a place as any. Why should the horse care?"

"Someone put him there, a long time ago. He was a god, then. But we've forgotten why today. And so to most he's only a chalk figure."

Slater withdrew his head and folded the bonnet back in its place. "She runs sweetly, your motorcar."

"Thank you." Rutledge looked at the filthy hands, the black ground into the creases and whorls of the skin. "A smith, are you?"

Slater grinned widely. "Yes. Or to say it another way, I was. Until the war came and took away the horses. I work with motors now, and mend things. My dad didn't have the knack of that, but I do. Do you want to see?"

Without waiting for an answer, he led Rutledge to one of the cottages, the outer one in the half circle they formed.

Slater dwarfed it just walking through the door, and Rutledge felt a spasm of claustrophobia when he went in and was asked to shut the door behind him.

The house was surprisingly tidy. On a table under the back window, an array of work was set out.

"I don't keep such things at the forge," Slater was saying as he gestured shyly to the table. "Don't want anyone walking off with them. They do, thinking I won't notice."

Rutledge saw a set of hinges in wrought iron, with matching knobs in the shape of a beaver, and the cabinet for them on the floor next to a table leg. They were beautifully done, as was the butterfly hook for hanging a plant by a door and a set of fire irons, shaped like deer, with the basket made to look like entwined antlers.

It was remarkable workmanship.

To one side stood a lovely Georgian teapot, where Slater was in the process of setting the handle back in place.

He saw Rutledge's glance and said proudly, "That's from St. Margaret's, part of the tea service, and the handle had worn right off. They'll never know it's been repaired when I finish with it."

"You're very good with your hands," Rutledge told him. "It's fine work."

Slater seemed to expand with the praise. "It's a gift. I was given it. Do you know those great stones in the beech grove farther along this road? The ones they call Wayland's Smithy?"

It was the prehistoric tomb. "Yes, I do."

"I slept there one night. As a boy. And I was given the gift. Even my father had to admit to it. He could shoe horses and mend wagon tongues and put a latch on a barn, whatever needed doing. But this work—" Slater swept his hand above the table. "He couldn't do it. Even he said as much."

"He must have been very proud of you."

A rueful smile dimmed the brightness in his face. "He told me I was dreaming, thinking the smithy had anything to do with gifts. Foolishness, he called it."

"What do your neighbors think of your work?"

"I don't show most people. I don't know why I showed you." He seemed to consider that for a moment. "You have a way of listening. Most people don't hear what I say to them. It's always been like that."

"How well do you know your neighbors?" Rutledge persisted.

Slater shrugged. "I see them from time to time. Mr. Partridge stands in the dark and looks up at the White Horse. I've lost count of the evenings I walk by him and he never speaks. I'm one to like walking in the dark, I go to the Smithy if there's moonlight. But he just stands there.

And the lady—she's quite strange, you know. I think she's afraid of the dark. House is shut up tight long before sunset, and stays that way until full light in the morning." He frowned. "We're outcasts, if you ask me. That's why we live here. Nobody else would have us. I was always the biggest in my school, bigger than many of the older boys. And the parents, they was always protecting their little ones from me, thinking I'd do them a harm." He looked down at his hands, huge and strong. "I've never hurt a thing, not so much as a butterfly. But I wasn't allowed to play with the other children, and they laughed at me sometimes. Gullible, they called me, after a giant in a book. I learned soon enough to stay away from them."

Rutledge could see the hurt in the big man's face. "I expect they didn't understand that giants could be—gentle."

"They never tried to know." Slater took a deep breath. "I didn't mean to trouble you with my life."

"People are people," Rutledge said. "Each one interesting in his or her own way. Good or bad, mean or generous, helpful or not, they make up the human race. You must take them as you find them, because few of them ever really change."

"I've been happy here, going in to the forge when I have heavy work to do, staying clear of them all when I can. But it's lonely, all the same." He studied Rutledge's face. "Did you fight in France?"

"Yes, I did." He answered the question simply, wondering where it was going.

"Aye, I thought as much. You brought it home with you. And you aren't the first I've met with such a look. No offense meant, it's there for anyone to see. The army wouldn't take me. I told them I was strong, but they told me I wasn't up to the work. I told them I could shoe the horses and keep the wagons and caissons moving, but they didn't believe me." He shook his head, the disappointment still raw. "I don't read very well. But what's that got to say to what I can do with my hands?"

"Very little," Rutledge answered and turned toward the door. "All the same, you were lucky. It was not a war you'd have liked."

"What does liking have to do with it?"

He followed Rutledge out into the sunshine again, and noticed when Rutledge took a deep breath, almost unwittingly. "You don't like small spaces. I'd not sleep in the Smithy, if I were you." He stood there on his threshold, looking up at the sky.

"Ever think about the old gods?" Slater asked. "The ones before we was all Christians?"

Rutledge remembered a woman named Maggie in Westmorland, who knew the Viking gods in her own fashion. "Sometimes," he answered.

"They're still out there, aren't they? Displaced, but still there, waiting to come back. And they will, one day, and catch us all off our guard. That will be a day of reckoning, when it comes."

He nodded to Rutledge and went back inside, shutting the door quietly.

5

Walking back to his motorcar, Rutledge tried to see if Partridge's own motor was still in the shed by the house, but it was impossible, given the direction of the sun, to judge if the light struck metal.

Hamish said, "If ye're here to see yon horse, ye've done precious little to show an interest."

"I thought you didn't like the horse."

"Oh, aye, it's a wicked beast, but it wasna' me who told the world and his brother it's the thing that brought ye here."

"I could hardly explain that I was looking for Partridge."

"They ken you arena' a day-tripper wi' a taste for what's cut into the chalk. If ye stay anither day, they'll no' need to be told the truth."

"Then let's hope Partridge comes home before that."

Hamish said, "I dona' think he will."

"Why?"

"Ye ken, this time they sent a policeman."

Rutledge climbed the hill again and walked to the head of the great horse. There he stood and looked across the valley. There was another hill here where Saint George slew the dragon—Dragon Hill, as he remembered it was called. One of many places where the militant saint was said to have encountered dragons. Rutledge recalled a page in one of his mother's books where Saint George on his white horse—this one?—quelled the dozen-headed, fire-breathing beast with a single spear. Gilt edged and delicately painted, the scene was taken from a plate in an ancient manuscript, and the artist had captured the quality of the original work. Saint George was handsomely robed in crimson and sapphire velvet, no workaday dented armor for him.

He turned to study the cottages. Nine of them. It would have been more efficient if the War Office had given him the names of the other residents here. He had met two of them, seen a third, and Partridge made a fourth. Where had the other five inhabitants been as he wandered about, walking into Quincy's house like a welcomed guest, and then into Slater's?

He drew himself a mental map of the cottages. They were set out like a horseshoe, appropriate enough here. Four to a side and one at the top of the bend. A lane ran between them, cutting the horseshoe in half, and from the lane paths led to each door.

Slater lived in Number 1 on the left, then Partridge at Number 2, his white gate distinctive, as if shutting out his neighbors. Quincy was the first cottage on the right-hand side, Number 9 on the map, and the woman with the wash hanging on the line lived in Number 8.

Someone opened the door of Number 4 and stepped out into the sunshine, shading his hand to see better as he scanned the cottages and then turned slightly to stare up at the horse. Even at that distance, his eyes seemed to meet Rutledge's, and he stood there, not moving, for a dozen seconds more. Then he turned his back and stepped inside, shutting his door firmly behind him.

That accounted for five of the residents. And this hadn't been a casual interest shown by a curious resident. There was more to it. Not a challenge precisely, but an acknowledgment.

"Anither watcher?" Hamish said.

Rutledge wouldn't have been surprised. Someone who knew that Rutledge would be coming and while having no intention of working with him, at least wanted it to be known that he was present as well.

The government kept an eye on certain people. Quietly and unobtrusively as a rule.

What had Partridge done to excite interest? Knowing that might make a difference in deciding where to look for him.

His only choice now was to wait for dark and then search Partridge's cottage. He could come to it by a roundabout way, passing unseen. He'd been told this was merely a watching brief. But if Hamish was right and Partridge wasn't coming back, there could be an advantage in knowing what the man was up to.

Rutledge left the hill of the White Horse half an hour later and went back to The Smith's Arms, where he had taken a room. He found he was in time for luncheon served both in the dining room and at a handful of tables that had been set up outside with benches round them for the lorry drivers.

It was a rough crowd. Men who drove long distances for a living were often footloose by nature and had more in common with one another than with families left behind. They'd cast glances in Rutledge's direction when he drove up and walked into the inn, curious and suspicious. Then conversation had picked up again when he disappeared from view.

The innkeeper's wife—Mrs. Smith—greeted him with a harried nod and went on serving tables with quick efficiency and a laugh that kept the men jolly and at arm's length. Rutledge glimpsed Mr. Smith; the swinging doors into the nether regions showed him briefly. He was the cook here, not his wife.

Rutledge wondered if their name was Smith or if they enjoyed the play on words as well as their anonymity. It would explain why they kept their inn for transient custom and showed no ambition to cater to a different clientele.

Mrs. Smith reappeared from the kitchen with a tray for Rutledge. "If you won't mind eating it upstairs," she said apologetically. "There's not a table to spare for a single."

He took the tray and thanked her. In his room he looked under the serviette that covered it and found generous sandwiches of beef and pork, a pickle, a small dish of tinned fruit, and a glass of beer.

Sitting by the window he ate with an appetite, listening to the voices rising from the tables below. Someone had started a political argument and found himself shouted down by his comrades good-naturedly calling him a fool. But he stuck to his guns, clearly possessed of a grievance against a proposed tax on goods shipped to France or the Low Countries.

"It'ul put me out of business, I tell you, and you as well," he said gruffly. "Wait and see."

"Rumor," another voice replied. "It'ul never happen, see if I'm not right."

They moved away, still talking, and then it was quiet for a moment before lorry engines roared into life and began to roll out of the yard.

A bird was singing now, a chat, the song filling the air with brightness.

Then a male voice called, "Betty?"

And Mrs. Smith answered from the doorway almost at Rutledge's feet, her voice was so clear. "If you're hungry, you're out of luck. That lot ate everything but the rats in the barn and the straw in the mangers."

"That man—the one who owns the motorcar in the yard. Is he staying here? What do you know about him?"

"Only that he's from London and unlucky in love." Her voice was light, deflecting his questions.

Rutledge set his plate aside and stood up, hoping to see who had come to the inn. But the man was just out of sight.

"I need to know, Betty," he went on urgently. "Are you sure he's from London?"

"I don't think he said," she answered him. "I just assumed . . ."

"I don't like it. Is he staying?"

"He's taken a room for tonight." It was a reluctant admission. "You're building castles in quicksand," she added. "What would *he* want with the likes of *you*?"

The man's answer was lost in the clatter of feet on the stairs and someone calling, "Good-bye, love, I'm off to make my fortune—oh, there you are! Thought you were in the kitchen. Well, then," the voice went on, "I've left what I owe on the table. And you can count on me again in a fortnight. Anything you'd like from Wales?"

"Wales, is it? I'll take one of those wool shawls, in a paisley pattern. Like the red one you brought Ma."

"Right you are!" And a young man who looked enough like Mrs. Smith to be her brother dashed into sight heading for the last lorry, standing by a plane tree.

When he'd gone, there was no further conversation. Rutledge could hear Mrs. Smith moving about below, humming to herself. The man who had questioned her had gone.

Hamish said, startling Rutledge, "Ye canna' ask her who it was."

"No. But it wasn't Quincy or Slater. Someone else. I didn't recognize the voice. And there's no certainty he came from the cottages."

He sat down again, finished his meal, and then carried the tray back to the dining room.

It was interesting, Rutledge thought, walking out the inn door, that Mrs. Smith asked no questions of him. Her pleasant nod as he passed indicated no curiosity about where he might be going or why. And she had answered the man at her door with circumspection, as if she were accustomed to keeping secrets.

He drove back toward the Tomlin Cottages, but passed no one walking in that direction.

The remainder of the afternoon he spent prowling about the chalk horse, while keeping a surreptitious eye on the cottages below him.

Rutledge had the strongest feeling, supported by the uneasiness of Hamish, that he was being watched in his turn.

But if Partridge had come home, learned of Rutledge's presence, and then questioned Mrs. Smith at the inn, there was no sign of him here at the cottages.

Rutledge drove some twenty miles for his dinner, lingering over the meal far longer than its quality justified, and it was nearly dark by the time he drove back to the inn. He left the motorcar in the yard, went up to his room, and stretched himself on the bed.

When he heard the clock in the downstairs dining room strike one, he got up, dressed in dark clothing, and quietly left the inn. In his pocket he carried his torch. From the companionable snores coming from the room where the Smiths slept as he went down the stairs, Rutledge was certain they hadn't heard him go. As far as he could tell, he was the only guest this night.

Rutledge walked back to the cottages, standing under a tree for some time to let his eyes adjust to the ambient light and listening to the sounds around him.

There were steps coming his way, and he faded into the shadows where he was fairly certain he couldn't be seen.

Andrew Slater appeared farther up the road, heading for his own cottage. He carried something in his hands, Rutledge couldn't see what, and disappeared through his door without any indication that he knew someone was about.

But as Hamish was busy pointing out, a man like Slater often knew more than ordinary people, as if to make up for his simplicity. Not so much a sixth sense, but a knowledge that often came to such people. Not animal, either, that wariness of a fox or even a deer, but something generated by the need to protect himself from those who would trick him, take advantage of him, or cheat him.

Rutledge gave the smith another hour to fall asleep and then walked softly across the dew-wet grass to the house with the white gate.

He didn't pass through it, but went over the wall on the side that couldn't be seen from the other cottages.

The door was unlocked, as Quincy had told him it would be.

He opened it cautiously, listening for sounds inside that indicated someone was there. Silence came back to him.

He went inside and began his search. But there was nothing of interest in the cottage. Shielding his torch, he looked around at the furnishings—mainly castoffs, he thought, though there was a chest under a window that appeared to have come from a different life. It was locked. He glanced at the books on the low shelf by the hearth, and found that most of them were scientific, although there was an odd mixture of historical materials as well. Renaissance Italian history, African exploration, South American botany, and a Chinese herbal. Heavy reading for one's spare time. Sections marked were often macabre, descriptions of the way everyone from Socrates to victims of curses died.

The bedroom was tidy, the kitchen cleared, and dishes set as if by habit to drain by the sink. Nothing out of place, an empty valise under the bed, clothes still hanging in the armoire.

Wherever Partridge had taken himself, he clearly intended to come back.

Rutledge returned to the sitting room and looked at the desk there. He found nothing of interest, as if it were seldom used.

There was a single framed photograph on the desktop, grainy and yellowed, showing a man and a small boy standing together in what appeared to be the marketplace of a Georgian town. There was nothing in the shop windows to indicate which town or where in England it might be. Rutledge lifted the frame, slid open the back, and looked to see if there was any inscription on the other side of the photograph. And indeed there was. A schoolboy hand had scribbled, "the day we climbed the white horse."

Had Partridge come here as a boy? Was that what brought him back as a man?

Rutledge reassembled the glass and the frame, and set it where he'd found it.

In the basket to one side of the desk, however, was a crumpled sheet of paper. He reached for it, spread it out, and in the shaded light of his torch found that there was only one line on it.

My dear

The start of a letter? To a friend, a lover, a relative? There was no way of knowing.

He crumpled it again and dropped it back into the basket.

Nothing here to tell him who Partridge was, where he might have gone, or when he intended to return.

Certainly nothing mysterious enough to make London worry about where he was.

When Rutledge stepped out of the cottage, he nearly leapt out of his skin as something warm and sinuous wrapped itself around his legs.

"'Ware!" Hamish warned in the same instant.

It was all he could do to stifle a yelp even as his brain absorbed the sound of a soft purr.

Dublin the cat.

He bent down to pet her, and she accepted the salute but was more intent on finding her way into the house. He managed to get the door shut first, and as if displeased, the cat stopped purring and trotted off.

Rutledge stood there for a moment as his heart rate steadied and then made his way to the shed where Partridge kept his motorcar. It was still there, and a bicycle stood in the deeper shadows beyond the bonnet.

The only unusual thing was a small length of carpet that lay crumpled by the boot, a trap for unwary feet. The oil stains down its length, dark as blood in the little light there was, explained its use.

Wherever Gaylord Partridge had gone, he had left on shank's mare, not his bicycle or his motorcar.

But then he needn't have gone far to find someone to take him away. For a price, the lorry drivers at The Smith's Arms would have been willing to let him ride with them as far as he liked. From there he might have gone anywhere by train or bus.

And come back just as inconspicuously.

Gaylord Partridge's walkabouts, as Quincy had called them.

Rutledge slipped out of the shed and made his way through the darkness in the deepest shadow he could find, until he was well past Wayland's Smithy.

Where did Partridge go, and why? he asked himself as he walked without haste, listening to the night around him.

Hamish said, "If he was in the war, it's possible he doesna' remember where he goes, or why."

At the clinic where Frances had taken Rutledge to learn how to deal with his own shell shock, there was an officer who went away for days at a time. Physically present, but his mind lost in some other world where his body couldn't follow, Lieutenant Albany would sit by his window staring inward, and simply not hear or see or feel anything. As if the empty shell of himself waited for him there knowing that in the end he would come back to it. And then, quietly, he did just that, moving and speaking and acting as if nothing had happened, incurious about the hours or days that had passed meanwhile.

Rutledge had no way of knowing if Partridge was a victim of the war. Nothing in his cottage indicated military service, not the way he'd made his bed or the clothing in his armoire. But then that might have been deliberate.

The letter beginning "My dear" could mean there was someone he regularly went to see. And if the Government had no knowledge of that someone, it could well be a woman he preferred to keep secret.

A rendezvous far from the War Office's prying eyes, a brief escape from whatever it was he'd done to have people watching his every move?

It was distasteful to spy on a man, entering his house without his knowledge, looking at his personal correspondence. The fact that the

search hadn't yielded any useful information made matters worse. No
body in the bedroom to explain away Partridge's absence, no souvenirs of Brighton to point to his whereabouts, no letters giving Rutledge the direction of the man's family. Was the young woman who'd
knocked on Partridge's door a daughter—or a lover?

Which brought him back to the unseen man who had been questioning Betty Smith at the inn door. If that was Partridge himself, back
again and worried about the stranger hanging about in his absence,
he'd taken off.

Rutledge reached the inn, and removing his shoes, went up the
stairs as silently as he could. The snores from the Smith bedroom
rumbled in counterpoint.

R utledge woke to the early arrival of three more lorries, and as he
shaved, he considered his instructions from London.

A watching brief. Waiting for Partridge to come home, and then
reporting to the man's masters, whoever they were, through Chief Superintendent Bowles.

How long had the man been gone? Three days? A week?

It was time to find that out.

At breakfast he asked Mrs. Smith who it was she'd been talking
with just after lunch the day before.

"Just as your brother was leaving. I happened to hear the man mention my motorcar." Rutledge added when she frowned, "He seemed to
know you well. He called you by your first name."

"Lord have mercy, half the people in and out this door know me
by my Christian name. It was a busy day from the time I opened my
eyes until I shut them again, and with Larry underfoot as well, I was
behind most of it."

"It wasn't a man named Partridge, by any chance? I'd been hoping
to see him."

"Partridge? No, that's not likely. And if it was your motorcar whoever it was had an interest in, he's not the first nor will he be the last. Most of my regulars want to know if the King is staying here." She laughed and bustled back into the kitchen, leaving Rutledge to his meal.

He drove back to the White Horse, and when Quincy appeared to feed Dublin the cat, Rutledge walked down to speak to him.

Quincy saw him coming. He straightened and waited, while the cat ate its food without haste, unconcerned by the man from London coming to stand close by its dish.

"You do your duty by your neighbor," Rutledge began, looking down at the scraps minced for the cat.

"It's a dumb animal, it doesn't know when to expect its owner. When there's no one about to feed it, at least it knows it won't starve."

"Which is far from being a dumb animal," Rutledge observed. "How long has Dublin's owner been away this time?"

"How should I know? I'm not his keeper."

"Would any of his other neighbors be able to tell me?"

"I feed the cat, not them."

"What happens if you aren't here by the time your neighbor returns from his walkabout? Surely the woman up the way would take pity on Dublin."

"Why?" Quincy shrugged. "I'm not likely to be going anywhere. I leave the walkabouts to Partridge."

"Partridge? An odd name. What part of the country did he say he came from?"

"He didn't. And it's no odder than Quincy," he retorted. "Why is it you're really here? Not the horse yonder."

"Does it matter?"

"It does. Because every one of us in these cottages is afraid of something. And Partridge was always afraid of strangers."

"What frightens you?" Rutledge asked, curious.

"My dreams," Quincy retorted, and went back inside his cottage.

Later in the day, Rutledge drove to London. His mood was mixed, frustration warring with duty.

Hamish said, "Have ye no' thought? Ye're a red herring."

Rutledge was beginning to believe that might be true.

He found Chief Superintendent Bowles in his office, finishing a report.

Bowles looked up as he entered, frowned, and said, "What brings you back so soon?"

"There's nothing to be gained by staying where I was. I was beginning to arouse suspicion. And if I'm not mistaken, there's a watcher there already. Partridge's motor is in the shed, his bicycle as well. He's not in the house ill or dead. And with lorries passing through at all hours of the day and night, he has ample opportunity to disappear wherever he pleases. Unless I'm given more resources, there's nothing more to be done."

"They won't like it at the War Office." Bowles's voice was thoughtful. "But I'll tell them, all the same."

That same morning, as Rutledge was questioning Mrs. Smith about the man he'd heard from his window, Alice Crowell sat down to write a letter to her father.

He hadn't approved of her husband's declining to fight in the war, but felt that Albert Crowell's duty driving an ambulance had in some measure made up for it. It took considerable courage to pull men out of shell holes under fire and dress the wounds of men lying helpless in No Man's Land. The Germans had no compunction about shooting ambulance men, and Crowell had distinguished himself several times, even shooting at a diving plane with a borrowed rifle and hitting it before it could fire on his vehicle.

And so she began her letter with "Dearest Papa . . ."

She went on to tell him that her husband was being persecuted by the police inspector in Elthorpe, and unfairly so since he had had nothing to do with the dead man in the Fountains Abbey ruins.

But she wisely omitted any reference to the book found at the man's feet.

Ending the letter with a plea for her father's help, she added, "What disturbs me is that the intense scrutiny he's given Albert may have its roots in Inspector Madsen's previous relationship with me, and I daren't remind him of that for fear it will only make matters worse."

She sealed the letter, posted it, and told no one.

Her father, colonel of an East Anglian regiment, went directly to London and presented the letter to a friend at the War Office. He didn't know the Chief Constable of Yorkshire well enough to approach him, but he rather thought that Martin Deloran might.

The matter might have languished in limbo but for the fact that Colonel Ingle and the man he met with had both been at Sandhurst. He had come prepared to argue. It wasn't necessary.

For one sentence in the letter seemed to leap off the page, startling Deloran.

> . . . *the poor man was wearing a respirator, which causes the police to think his death might have something to do with the war, but if Albert couldn't shoot the Hun, how could he kill a man he swears he has never seen before?*

The man behind the desk fingered the sheet of paper for a moment, and then, choosing his words with care, said, "Interesting story. Yes, well. Consider it done. But I'd rather you didn't tell your daughter that you've brought the letter to me. Better to let her believe help arrived before you could act in the matter. Sensibilities of the local police, and all that. This needs to be sorted quietly—if she's to continue living in Yorkshire, that is. And I know just the man to look into matters."

Colonel Ingle was no fool.

"Thanks very much, Martin." He waited to see if more information might be forthcoming. "I'll be on my way then."

"Anything for an old friend," Deloran assured him.

But Colonel Ingle knew that friendship had nothing to do with Martin Deloran taking on this matter with such speed. He was jumping in for reasons of his own.

Deloran got to his feet. "What do you say to a spot of lunch, while you're in London?"

Sometime later, Rutledge was summoned to Bowles's office, and he found his superintendent in a dark mood.

"Bloody army, they think we have nothing better to do than run their errands for them. You're wanted in Yorkshire now. I asked if it was the same business, and they declined to tell me. Bloody Cook's Tour, if you want my view of the matter. Give me what's on your desk, and I'll see that it's dealt with."

"What is it in Yorkshire that I'm supposed to be investigating?"

"There's a dead man found in Fountains Abbey, of all places. The police are harassing a local schoolmaster over it. You're to deal with it. The Chief Constable has requested you by name. But he let it be known the request came from higher-ups."

"Little enough to go on—a dead man in an abbey."

Bowles considered him. "Getting a reputation for yourself, are you?"

Rutledge laughed without humor. "My sergeant used to tell me that once the army gets you in its clutches, you're never free again."

"That's as may be," Bowles answered. "But see that you do better with this matter than you did in Berkshire. It was tricky, telling the War Office you'd failed to find their precious lost sheep."

Walking out of the building, Rutledge found himself already tying the two cases together. He wasn't sure why, except that each request had come from the army, and if Gaylord Partridge was still missing, someone was scouring the countryside for bodies.

6

It was a long drive to Yorkshire, and Rutledge broke the journey in Lincoln, staying in the shadow of the great cathedral there. After a late dinner at the hotel, he walked through the gate into the precincts to view the magnificent west front. It was quiet, shadows giving the carvings depth and reality, and he stayed for some time, letting the peace wash over him.

It was rare that he had time to dwell on something other than murder. Just as in the war, death pursued him as a policeman as well. It was his chosen profession, but he found himself thinking that the men who had built such splendor had left a greater legacy than most. Names long since forgotten, they lived on in what their hands had wrought. Not guns or tanks or deadly gas, but in stone, defining the human spirit's capacity to create rather than destroy.

Hamish, good Covenanter that he was, preferred unadorned simplicity.

Rutledge said to him, his voice echoing against the towering west front, "Ah, but is man better off without something to stir him and lift him and carry him through the darkness?"

Hamish responded, the deep Scots voice trapped in the narrow space between Rutledge and the massive gate, "It didna' serve you well in the trenches, no more than plainness served me. Where was your God or mine then?"

It was unanswerable. Rutledge turned and walked back to his hotel, the moment broken.

The next morning, he drove on to Elthorpe, his mind already busy with what he could expect to find.

No one had given him either a description or a photograph of Gaylord Partridge, and he wasn't certain what it was he was supposed to achieve when he arrived. But accustomed to the mysterious workings of the army, he wasn't surprised.

He came into Elthorpe after lunch when the streets were relatively quiet and the April sun had vanished behind clouds.

Yorkshire's landscape was varied—the rolling dales of the North Riding, a long shoreline to the east, and very fertile land along the rivers that flowed through the West Riding. It was small wonder that medieval monks established so many houses here, building abbeys by the handful. Their ruins, dramatic and quite beautiful, were reminders of a distant past. For someone who loved architecture, it was a feast for the mind and the eye.

Fountains stood on the plateau west of the city of York, and it was still sheep country, though on a smaller scale, feeding the looms and the mills nearer the coal deposits.

Elthorpe, small and tidy, stood upright in the sun, as if absorbing as much of its warmth into stone walls as the waning afternoon permitted. A wind had come up, promising a cool night, but the few people on the streets still wore only sweaters or coats against the chill.

Rutledge found a hotel close by the church, though its name, The Castle Arms, was far too elegant for what was on offer—a comfortable lobby, a lounge beyond an arch, and a desk manned by a very attractive woman about his own age.

She smiled at him in a way that offered no familiarity, merely an acknowledgment that he was custom newly arrived.

"I'm looking for a room for several nights," he said, and she nodded, her eyes flicking to the book in front of her.

"There's number ten, which should suit you. Would you care to see it, Mr. . . ."

She paused, waiting for him to give her his name.

"Rutledge," he replied pleasantly. "From London. Thank you, number ten will be fine."

She nodded, and wrote his name in the hotel register, then handed him an ornate key on a knob that wouldn't fit comfortably into a pocket. Embossed on the end of the knob was a brass inlay of the Great Tower at Richmond Castle. Behind her on a board were similar keys, and a quick glance showed him that there were three other guests at present.

"Shall I help you carry your luggage up the stairs?" she asked, but it was perfunctory, and she made no move to come round the desk.

"I should manage very well, thank you."

He went back to his motorcar, smiling to himself. The people of Yorkshire were not unfriendly but their reserve was legendary. A man, he thought, might live here forty years before he was accepted in the inner circle. And perhaps not then, if there was any suspicion that he might not be deserving of it.

Two men some twenty yards from him were talking together, and Rutledge found himself listening to the local dialect. The English had such a variety of voices, and his, in this place, stood out as foreign. A stranger.

He wondered how he would be received by Inspector Madsen.

Oddly enough, it was with relief.

Madsen rose from behind his desk to shake hands, his face tired and his eyes troubled.

He launched into a brief report on the murder as if he had re-hearsed it a dozen times that morning.

"We've got nowhere in this business. The schoolmaster is involved but we don't know how—or why. It's his book there at the dead man's feet," he said. "The book was dew damp, but hadn't been there any longer than the body, judging by its condition." He reached behind him for a book lying on a shelf and passed it to Rutledge.

"Alchemy," Madsen went on. "Nonsense if there ever was one. But we've looked through the book with care, and there's nothing to say it isn't what it appears to be—a book wildly out of place. But if the schoolmaster, Crowell, brought it to the meeting, why? And why leave it where it was found? Does it say something about the dead man that we don't understand? What's *in* the blasted book that took it to a scene of violence?"

Rutledge opened the book and thumbed through it. A history of alchemy, the philosopher's stone, the centuries-old search for a way to turn lead or other base metals into gold.

A good many famous men had dabbled in alchemy. A good many more had used it to cheat unsuspecting people out of their money. He'd heard a professor say that it was merely a forerunner, early at-tempts to explain chemistry. But there had been an overtone of other interests in the study of this quasi-science—a search for the elixir of life and for spells that forced the spirits of evil to obey commands and serve the alchemist. It had sometimes been called heresy and com-merce with the Devil, and even witchcraft.

He scanned several of the purported incantations that had come down through the years, and they were laughable. The garish illustra-tions next to several of them showed someone very like Roger Bacon standing in a cavelike room, smoke circling his head, the fire at his back roaring up the chimney, and an array of vessels spread out on the table before him.

Hamish, who had been silent for some time, startled him by speaking so normally that he was sure the man across the desk heard the words.

"Yon man in the drawing is wearing a robe."

Roger Bacon had been a monk. And his robe was very much like the description Madsen had just given Rutledge of the cloak the dead man had been wrapped in.

So perhaps there was a connection, though not the most obvious one. Not meddling with spirits but with something else.

"And still no word on the identity of the dead man?"

"None. If he'd dropped out of the sky, we'd have been no wiser."

Rutledge said, "I'd like to see the victim for myself."

Madsen considered him for a moment and then said, "He's at the doctor's surgery."

"And the cloak, the respirator?"

"There as well."

They walked down the street to the doctor's surgery, and were admitted by a nurse who looked to be close to forty, trim and dark haired. Madsen asked to see the murder victim and was shown into the room where the body was being kept until the police were finished with it. Madsen nodded to the woman, and she left them.

Rutledge raised the sheet over the body. The man looked to be of good height, his shoulders broad and well muscled. Rutledge took a moment to look at his hands. Not those of a laborer—no calluses in the palms, the nails clean and well shaped. The face was not one that would stand out. The man could walk down any London street or one in Manchester and never attract attention. His hair was a light brown, showing gray strands throughout. Forty-five? Fifty? It was hard to tell. There were lines in his face that death hadn't smoothed away, as if he had been ill or aged before his time.

"What about his clothing?"

"Good quality. They're in the box, there."

That matched the condition of the man's hands. "London labels?"

"See for yourself."

Rutledge squatted to examine the contents of the box. Madsen was right, the clothes were of good quality but had seen a great deal of use.

As if the dead man had fallen on hard times or lost interest in what he wore. Even the shoes had seen hard use.

"Anything in the pockets?"

"Nothing. Not so much as a handkerchief."

Rutledge stood up. "I'd like to see the cloak and the respirator."

The cloak was of fine wool, well made, with a hood. Rutledge fingered it, felt the weight of it, and the thickness. Unlike the clothes, it appeared to be almost new. Because it wasn't something that might be worn every day?

Hamish said, "An actor, then?"

But no smudges of grease paint or powder marked the neckline or the edges of the hood.

The gas mask was a 1917 small box respirator, standard equipment during the war. No one had felt safe, once the Germans had used poison gas in the field.

But the tab underneath the chin was missing, leaving a small tear and making the mask useless. It wasn't uncommon for the tab to come off, and there was no way to tell how long ago or how recently it had happened. The question was, why had anyone gone to the trouble of putting the respirator over the face? A mockery of the manner of death or to make the death seem more macabre?

"There were no scars, no indication of a surgery, no identifying marks on the body? No irregularities in the teeth?"

"The doctor says not."

Once this man was buried, there would be nothing to show he had lived. Nothing to identify him in a report, nothing to hand in evidence to witnesses or suspects, nothing to set him apart, if someday someone came looking for him.

Anonymous . . . which explained why the man wasn't known in this part of Yorkshire. He wasn't meant to be identified. A mystery, an unclaimed body, a nine days' wonder, buried and soon forgotten.

Rutledge said, "Is there someone here—in Elthorpe—who could make a drawing of his face?"

"A drawing?" Madsen was caught off guard, busy with his own thoughts as Rutledge went through the box.

"If we're to locate someone who knows the victim, we need something to be going on with."

"Why not a photograph?"

"Because it will show that he's dead. People might be more willing to talk to us about a missing person."

No one wanted to be drawn into a murder inquiry. It was a stigma, something that happened to other, less savory classes. And Rutledge had a feeling that this man had had secrets. Otherwise, why should he wind up dead, like a buffoon, wearing a respirator and a monk's cloak, a long way from home? Why not simply leave the body in a ditch or throw it into a lake or shove it off a cliff?

Madsen was saying, "Benson. He's one of the employees at The Castle Arms. He did a pen-and-ink sketch of my house for my wife's birthday. Mrs. Madsen was quite taken with it."

"That's where I'm staying. We'll speak to him now."

Madsen went with Rutledge back to the hotel, where Miss Norton, at Reception, told them they would find Mr. Benson in the kitchen, discussing menus with the cook.

Rutledge waited in the small sitting room while Inspector Madsen went in search of the artist. He was a short, thin man with the carriage of a soldier.

"Sketch the face of a dead man?" He stared from one policeman to the other. "I've—I'm not really good with faces. Why not take a photograph?"

"Yes, I'd considered that," Rutledge told him, "but I think a sketch might serve us better. It doesn't make an issue of the fact that we're trying to identify a corpse."

Benson wiped a hand across his mouth. "I'm not sure I can do this. I've seen enough dead men to last a lifetime."

"Yes, I can sympathize," Rutledge responded. "All we ask is that you give it a try."

Madsen added, "He's not unpleasant to view. Dead, yes, but not—er—marked in any way."

In the end, Benson collected a pad and his box of charcoal sticks and went with them across to the doctor's surgery.

Rutledge was already regretting his request. Benson's face was pale and strained as they waited for the doctor. He said, "I'm sorry—"

But the doctor was coming out of his consultation room, nodding to Madsen and shaking hands with Rutledge.

Five minutes later, Benson was sitting on a high stool looking down at the body of the man no one knew.

He sketched quickly, using the charcoal with deft strokes, creating the shape of the head, the placement of the ears, the dark hair springing from a high forehead. And then he began to put in the features, the eyes first, getting them right before tackling the straight nose and a surprisingly mobile mouth.

At one point he looked up at Rutledge, his face set as if his mind had withdrawn to somewhere safe. "I—I can't see the color of his eyes . . . ?"

"Blue," the doctor told him from where he stood by the wall, watching. "They're a pale blue."

Benson nodded and kept working.

He took his time, and when he'd finished, the likeness was so fine that he forgot where he was for a moment and studied the dead face on the pillow.

"It's first-rate, isn't it?" he asked. "I've got it right." There was surprise and satisfaction in the words.

Rutledge thought, He's captured something I hadn't seen—a subtle sense of the person whose face it was. A man with such talent oughtn't be running a hotel dining room.

And an instant later Benson came back to the present, where he was and what he'd been doing. He looked as if he might be sick on the spot. He hastily passed the sheet of drawing paper to Rutledge before hurrying out of the room, his footsteps beating a rapid tattoo as he ran down the passage.

Rutledge caught up with Benson just outside the surgery door, where he was standing in the cool air, his face lifted to the watery sun.

Rutledge said briskly, "Thanks sounds insufficient. I'll make your excuses to Miss Norton while you take your time getting back to work."

Madsen was behind him, holding out the pencil box and pad of artist's paper.

But Benson said, his voice rough, "I'm all right. Don't fuss." He took his things and walked away, toward the hotel.

Halfway there, he turned to ask, "He's the man from the abbey?"

"Yes."

"Pity."

And he walked on.

Madsen said quietly, "He went through a rough patch on the Somme."

Hamish said, "He wasna' one of your men."

And Rutledge answered silently, "He could have been."

He nodded to Madsen and followed Benson back to the hotel. He was nowhere in sight when Rutledge stepped through the door.

Miss Norton stopped him. "Would you care for some tea, Mr. Rutledge? You look tired—I don't know, worried, perhaps."

He said, not knowing how to answer, "It was a long drive from London."

"That's not the kind of tired I meant. Were you in the war?"

"Yes."

"Yes," she repeated. "I thought perhaps that was it. If Julian had come home, I think he would have looked the same. Haunted by what he'd done and seen. He sometimes wrote about his life in the trenches. Not the whole truth, I'm certain of that. But enough, I think, to warn me not to expect him to be quite the same. When I look at Mark Benson, I wonder."

"Your brother?" he hazarded, in an effort to redirect the conversation.

"My fiancé. He died at Ypres. Lingered in hospital for a week, and died. Gassed. He was Albert Crowell's brother. They were so close."

"The schoolmaster?"

"Yes. Poor man. Inspector Madsen is certain he's done murder. That's what Alice wrote to me yesterday. The gossips haven't picked up the news yet, but they will."

"And you? What do you think?"

She sighed. "I don't think he could. Kill, I mean. Julian once said that Albert is not made up like most men. He should be a Quaker. They're an odd lot, Quakers. There's an iron strength to them. A coldness. I think sometimes they must be hard people, to stand aside and watch."

"Is that how you see Albert Crowell?" Rutledge asked with interest.

She shook her head, confused. "I don't know. He forgave the man who scarred his wife's face. It was a terrible ordeal for her. I don't think I could have done that. My own suffering, yes, but not someone else's."

"I hadn't heard the story. How did it happen?"

"They were at Whitby. On holiday. She went out alone a little while after tea, to shop for Albert's birthday gift. There was a man near the corner. He'd been drinking, and was flinging his arms about, shouting. He was angry or upset, I don't know. And he shoved her out of his path. She fell against a wrought-iron railing, cutting her face badly. Passersby rushed to help her, and two men held on to her assailant. The police came and took him up for public drunkenness. He was quite sober by that time, crying and apologizing. But it was too late, wasn't it? The damage had been done. She was taken to hospital, bleeding profusely, and the doctors feared for her eye. They took her directly to surgery and sent someone to find her husband. Albert called it an accident. Of course it was, but if the man hadn't been drinking—if he'd been in his right senses rather than looking for trouble—nothing would have happened to Alice."

"And Albert forgave him, you say? In public or private?"

"Both. He was—" She stopped, horrified. "You aren't thinking—? This man they found dead—it couldn't have been the one in Whitby, could it? Is that why Inspector Madsen has gone back to Dilby so many times?"

Rutledge answered, "Early days yet, but I'll take the sketch to Mrs. Crowell and ask her. She won't have forgotten what he looked like."

"But that will just bring it all back again."

"Did you see the man, could you identify him instead?"

"I wasn't engaged to Julian then. I knew about the incident, of course. It happened just before the war. Early July, I think. Julian and I weren't engaged until August. It wasn't—I wasn't involved. Ask Albert. He'll be able to tell you."

"He's already told the police that he can't identify the dead man. I have no choice, you see, but to speak to Mrs. Crowell."

She came out from behind the desk, her face set. "I'm going with you, Inspector. Let me find someone to mind the desk while I'm gone."

"No, I think it best—"

"It isn't a question of what you think, Inspector. I won't have Alice upset about this business. I'm coming to be certain she isn't. A woman ought to be there with her."

7

Ten minutes later Miss Norton climbed into Rutledge's motor-car and settled herself. "The quickest way is as the crow flies, of course. But as we aren't crows—" She began to direct him, out of Elthorpe, then around the skirts of the estate on whose grounds the great abbey ruins took pride of place, and down an unmade road that wandered for several miles before dividing. The right branch contin-ued to the west, while the left turned more to the south.

"To your right," Miss Norton said. "It's only another mile or two."

They soon came into a small village clinging to the road. "There's the school," she said. "Alice should be upstairs. Alone, I hope."

He passed the row of shops, a tiny lending library, a church more the size of a chapel, and came to a house a little larger than the others he'd passed, the front façade softened by stonework around the win-dows and above the door.

"It was a prosperous merchant's home," Miss Norton was saying, her nervousness showing in the tenseness of her voice. "And left to the village some sixty years ago to be used as a school. I wish I'd never mentioned Alice," she went on. "How did you trick me into saying anything about her?"

"It wasn't a trick," he replied, drawing up in front of the school. "You were telling me about your fiancé. Julian."

"Yes, and somehow—"

He got down and went around to her door as she added, "You won't tell Inspector Madsen about this foolishness, will you? He's already brought Albert in for questioning four times now. It will only make him more anxious to prove something."

"If Mrs. Crowell identifies this man from the sketch, then I've no choice."

"Oh, blast the sketch," she said furiously, slamming her door behind her. "I wish I'd never seen you."

She marched ahead of him, back ramrod straight, her face closed. She went directly into the school, leaving him to follow or not, as he pleased.

There was a central hall with stairs leading up to the first floor. The building was quiet, the students gone home at the end of the day. The sign over the nearest door read SCHOOL OFFICE.

Miss Norton passed it by and was already halfway up the stairs.

An echo of voices, a child's and a woman's, reached them, disappearing down the passage ahead of them.

"Alice?" Miss Norton called.

"Yes? Mary? Is that you?" Mrs. Crowell turned to stare. "What on earth brings you here at this time of day? Who's minding the hotel?"

"I asked Velma to step in for me." As they came closer, Mary Norton indicated the man behind her. "Alice—this is Inspector Rutledge from London. Scotland Yard." Her words seemed to fill the passage, floating ahead of her, echoing behind her.

To his surprise as he caught up with the two women, Mrs. Crowell turned warmly to him, extending her hand.

He took it as she said, "How nice of you to come!" as if she'd been expecting him.

A classroom door opened farther down the passage, and a head popped out, vanishing again just as quickly. Rutledge glimpsed a pale, startled boy's face. Then it was gone.

He followed the two women into a tidy office, and Mrs. Crowell shut her door.

"I'm so glad you came to see me first," she went on, speaking directly to Rutledge, "because it's important to know the facts behind my concerns. There *is* a history of sorts between my husband and Inspector Madsen." She was intense, earnest, as if she had rehearsed the manner of her presentation many times over. "This may well explain why he's so anxious to prove that my husband is guilty of murder. But he isn't—truly he isn't. I can think of no reason in this world why he should kill a stranger. I can't explain how my husband's book got to the ruins either, but if you think about it, is it likely that he'd take such a silly thing with him if he were intent on murder?"

Rutledge could see the scar clearly now, running across her face from the corner of her left eye to the line of her jaw on the right, near her ear. It had healed smoothly without pulling at the flesh around it, but it was still ugly, marring the rather classical features of straight nose, square jaw, and well-set gray eyes. She had not been strictly beautiful, but was certainly a very attractive woman, before the wound. He couldn't tell if she was still self-conscious about it or had grown used to it.

Hamish said, "She doesna' look in the mirror verra' often."

Before Rutledge could answer Mrs. Crowell, Mary Norton said quickly, "He's brought a sketch to show you, my dear. Will you look at it and tell me if you recognize this man?"

"The dead man?" Alice Crowell paused as she was about to take her chair behind the desk. "But—" she faltered. "Why—I mean why should I wish to see it?"

"Because—well, to assure the police that Albert is telling the truth when he says he never saw this person before." Mary's words were hurried, as if to break the worst news quickly and avoid any mention of the man who had scarred Mrs. Crowell's face.

"Oh. Very well." Alice reluctantly held out her hand for the folder that Rutledge was carrying. "He isn't—I shan't have nightmares, shall I?" she asked as he passed the folder to her.

"It's merely a man's face. Nothing more frightening than that."

As the two bent over the sketch he'd brought, Mary's dark head close to Alice's fair one, Rutledge wondered how he would have felt about someone who did such injury to Jean. Or to Frances, for that matter. If he could have forgiven the drunken man with such apparent grace. Or perhaps Crowell had seen the change in his wife's appearance as a way of keeping her here in this small, dingy school when it was clear that she wasn't from this part of the country. Her accent, like Rutledge's own, spoke of good schooling and a wider circle. Righteous men, he thought, often feel the need to serve in the most forbidding places.

He watched Mrs. Crowell's expression as she examined the sketch, but all he could read there was puzzlement.

"I don't think he's anyone I know," she said doubtfully, still bending over the drawing. "Should I recognize him?"

"It was important to ask, on the off chance you did," Rutledge told her.

Mary Norton bit her lip. He could almost read the thought in her eyes. *Better with you here than with Inspector Madsen . . . finish it now.*

Before he could stop her, she said, "Think back, Alice. To Whitby. Could this be the man who knocked you down and hurt you? You told me once you'd never forget his face." Mary spoke urgently, trying to protect and going the wrong way about it. "Could it be he?"

"Oh, my God," Alice Crowell said softly, her shock apparent even to Rutledge. "Do you think—? But no, it couldn't have been this man. I know his name. Henry Shoreham, that was the man's name."

Mary Norton said triumphantly to Rutledge, "It's *not* the man." And then to Alice she went on. "Be quite sure! And we needn't speak of it again. To Inspector Madsen or Albert or anyone else. Ever."

It was almost as if Mary Norton's anxiety sent the wrong message to Mrs. Crowell, twisting her promise into a warning.

Rutledge leaned forward and took Miss Norton by the arm. "Let Mrs. Crowell take her time and look at the drawing in her own fashion," he said gently, drawing her out from behind the desk to one of the chairs in front of it. "Don't put words into her mouth."

"But I'm not—" Mary Norton protested.

He cut off her indignation. "Please. Give her time to *think*."

Mary Norton sat down, body stiff and still resisting.

Alice Crowell looked from one of them to the other. "Are you saying you believe this was Henry Shoreham? I can't believe it is. It just doesn't *look*—"

There was a tap at the door, and one of the schoolboys stuck his head in.

"Mrs. Crowell?"

She straightened up. "Yes, Hugh, what do you want? I have visitors."

"Oh, sorry, Mrs. Crowell. It's Johnnie, he's been sick, Mrs. Crowell. All over the floor." His face was tight with worry. "Can I take him home, then? We've almost finished cleaning the desks—please can I go?"

"I'll be there shortly, Hugh—"

"He'll not make it, it's all I could do to keep him from being sick in the passage. He's at the door now, waiting for me."

"Yes, very well," Alice Crowell said impatiently. "But I'll speak with you both tomorrow. Is that understood?"

"Yes, Mrs. Crowell, thank you, Mrs. Crowell." And he was gone, shutting the door quickly behind him.

Mary Norton had risen again to look out the window. "Should you see to them, Alice? There's a boy out there, doubled up. He doesn't look as if he'll make it home."

But Alice Crowell was saying, "There's been a rash of suspicious sickness among that lot. One of the younger boys is at home and hasn't come to school this week. His mother thinks he's malingering, but he's in bed crying and begging her to look at his tongue. His brother was sick two days ago, and now Johnnie." She turned back to the sketch but the uncertainty of a moment ago was gone. "This isn't the man. He was larger, for one thing, and I remember his chin, it had a cleft in it. I remember that very well." She shivered, and turned away from the desk. "He bent over me, and that was all I could see, and his breath—"

"There's no cleft here," Mary Norton began, looking across at Rutledge. "Are you satisfied now?"

Rutledge ignored her. "Please take your time, Mrs. Crowell. We need to be certain."

She shook her head. "No. I will swear to it."

"Thank God," Mary Norton said, her breath catching. "You don't know how worried—"

Mrs. Crowell was considering Rutledge. "You've only come because of the sketch? To see if I'd remember the face, because of Henry Shoreham? But I thought—I thought Mary said you'd come from London?"

She seemed to be waiting for him to say something, to confirm that something else had brought him here.

"I was sent from London to look into the matter here," Rutledge replied, choosing his words. "It was only after I'd spoken to Miss Norton that I felt it was important to ask you if you knew this man."

"I see." Her gaze went back to Mary Norton. "Why on earth were you telling him about that, Mary? How could it have come up?"

"I don't remember," she said, her face flushing. "Mr. Rutledge spoke to me after Mark Benson sketched the man, and I was saying something about the war, somehow, and then Julian, and somehow the conversation came round to you."

Rutledge stepped in. "I'm sorry, Mrs. Crowell, but it's essential to look at all the possibilities, even the far-fetched ones. Do you know, by chance, what this man Shoreham did for a living?"

"He was a clerk in a bank, as I remember. He'd been passed over for a promotion. He claimed."

The door opened and a young man stepped in, his eyes going straight to his wife.

"Am I missing something?"

She quickly got herself in hand and said, "This is Mr. Rutledge—from Scotland Yard. He's come to look into what happened in the abbey. He asked me to look at a sketch of the dead man that a Mr. Benson made for him. But I don't know him—the victim."

"That wasn't very pleasant for you, my dear," Crowell said, then turned to Rutledge, offering his hand. "You should have spoken to me first, before disturbing my wife."

"Would you have preferred that I take her into Elthorpe to see this man for herself?"

"Doubting *my* word?" It was a challenge.

"No. Verifying it, so that the police can get on with this case. We've lost enough time, chasing wild geese in the wrong direction."

"I see." He moved around the desk to look at the sketch Mrs. Crowell was still holding. "This is well done, a good likeness. But no more familiar than the man himself was, when I first saw him."

"Then I needn't trouble you further," Rutledge replied, taking the measure of Crowell. Irritated and sensitive from his previous encounters with Madsen, if he was any judge. And this wasn't the time to press. "Thank you, Mrs. Crowell. I am grateful for your help."

He turned to go. Mary looked at him, something in her expression that warned him what to do next.

"Miss Norton, I've kept you long enough. I'll be happy to take you back to the hotel."

She appeared reluctant, saying at first, "I really should stay—"

But Alice Crowell broke in. "Nonsense. Mr. Dunn won't care to have you away too long. Go with Mr. Rutledge, Mary. I'll see you at the weekend."

Mary went to the door with Rutledge. "Albert—"

He said, "Don't worry, I'll sit with her for a bit."

And then she was in the corridor with Rutledge, casting him a grateful glance.

Outside, Rutledge looked up and down the street, but there was no sign of Hugh and his classmate.

When they were back in the motorcar, Rutledge asked, "What were you afraid of? Does Crowell have a temper?"

"No. Not a temper. He—sometimes I just feel as if it would be better if he did explode into anger. He's so—so controlled. I don't know why Alice fell in love with *him*. And not Julian."

"It's not a matter for the head but for the heart," he replied, turning the motorcar to go back the way he'd come.

Out of the corner of his eye he saw something among the trees in the churchyard. The boys who had asked permission to leave while he was interviewing Mrs. Crowell.

He pulled the motorcar to the verge and said to Miss Norton, "I'll just be a moment."

He walked briskly across the churchyard, and the two boys, who had ducked behind the apse of the chapel, turned wide-eyed as he came round the corner. There was no time to run. And nowhere to run to. They stood their ground of necessity.

The other boy, the one Hugh claimed was sick, looked it, his face pale and his eyes red. Even Hugh was drawn and wretched, his gaze dropping to his shoes after that one wild glance at Rutledge.

"We couldn't make it home," Hugh said finally. "You can see, he's been sick all down his front."

"I was worried," Rutledge said. "Can I offer you a lift?"

"Oh, no," the other boy—Johnnie, was it?—began.

Hugh said quickly, "If he's quiet a bit, he'll be all right."

Rutledge considered them. "If you're sure?"

"Yes, sir." It was a fervent chorus.

He turned to leave, then stopped. "What do you know of this business the police have been speaking to your schoolmaster about?"

Children heard their elders talk and were sometimes better at putting two and two together than adults.

But Hugh's reaction was unexpected. Like a cornered animal, he backed against the stone wall of the chapel and seemed to have lost his tongue.

Johnnie was sick again, dry heaves jerking his body.

Rutledge waited until the worst had passed, then handed him a handkerchief.

Hamish said, "Ye can see he's in no case to answer ye."

Johnnie, looking as if he wanted nothing more than his bed at home, leaned against the nearest tombstone.

Rutledge persisted, speaking mainly to Hugh but keeping his eye on Johnnie. "Did you see something the night when someone was killed near Elthorpe? Did you see Mr. Crowell leave the school where he was working that evening, and go to meet someone?"

Hugh took a deep breath. "We were home in bed, weren't we, Johnnie? There was nothing for us to see."

It was the truth. Even Hamish could read that in the boy's fervent manner.

And yet it wasn't the whole truth.

"Who did you see leave the village?" Rutledge persisted.

"Nobody!" they exclaimed loudly, in unison.

"You needn't be afraid. If there's something you want to tell me, I'll see that no harm comes to you."

The boys stood there, hangdog but refusing to budge.

Hamish said, "Ye havena' found the key."

Rutledge changed direction. "Do you like Mr. Crowell? Is he a good master?"

They nodded vigorously. Reassuring him, proving that they had no reason to step forward, no reason to be afraid.

"Is there anyone else at the school, other than the Crowells?" He'd seen no one, but that might be the rub. If not Mr. Crowell . . .

"There's Old Fred. He cleans," Hugh said, as if offering up a sacrifice to hungry gods. "We had two other masters, but they were killed in the war. Mr. Crowell has had to manage on his own since he came back."

"And Mrs. Crowell. Does she walk at night? Without her husband?"

"I never saw her," Hugh maintained. And the ring of truth this time was clear, unequivocal. "What would she be going about at night, alone, for?"

"Johnnie?"

"No, sir. Never. You can ask anybody."

Rutledge gave it up. "You're sure I can't see you home? Johnnie? Do you have far to walk?"

"Not far." He gripped his stomach with both arms wrapped around his body. "Please, can we go now?"

"Yes, be on your way."

Rutledge watched them scurry away, like mice frantic to escape the claws of a cat.

Mary Norton was looking after them also as he reached the motorcar and stopped to turn the crank.

"I think you've put the fear of God into those two. Was it really necessary?"

"I think they've put the fear of God into themselves, and I'd like to know why."

"Then you're still harassing Albert Crowell," she said, making it a statement and not a question.

"I'm trying to get at the truth," he answered her as he closed the door on his side of the motorcar and let in the gear. "I'm not here to badger anyone."

"That's what people always say, but the police have made a good job of upsetting Albert and his wife."

He wanted to tell her that she herself had caused Alice Crowell anxiety in her earnest and misguided effort to prove that the dead man wasn't Shoreham. "The problem is that the only piece of evidence we have points to Crowell. And once I find out why it does, it may serve instead to clear his name."

"The sooner the better, then, before he's lost his job and his reputation. Have you policemen thought of that? No, I expect not. He's the fox and you're the hounds, and there won't be any peace for him until you lot have caught him."

She sighed, and said nothing more for the rest of the journey.

After dropping Mary Norton at the hotel, Rutledge went back to the police station, intending to report to Madsen.

But the inspector had left, he was told by an elderly constable. "He'd missed his luncheon. Not knowing when you'd return."

Rutledge thanked the constable and walked back to the hotel.

Hamish said as Rutledge closed the door to his room, "Was it a lie, that the man in the sketch wasna' the one who scarred the schoolmaster's wife?"

"I don't think she lied. But I think she's tried to forget his face and has partly succeeded. I'll ask Gibson at the Yard to track down Shoreham. But if that's who the dead man is, why meet him at the ruins, take him away and kill him, then bring him back? And what does a book of alchemy have to do with revenge?"

"A lure?"

Rutledge put the sketch in his valise and then, on second thought, pulled it out again to keep with him. After a brief half hour given over to his lunch, he left almost at once, intending to visit the abbey.

He approached the abbey through a quiet parkland that led him to a stream crossed by stepping stones. And soon he was there, in front of the great arched ruin soaring into the gray sky.

Hamish said, "There are abbey ruins in Scotland. Burned by the Borderers who came for revenge."

"I'm not sure these weren't destroyed for revenge," Rutledge said, looking up at the elegance of simplicity in design. The abbeys were wealthy, and wealth Henry VIII envied.

The monks had built well here. Something of what they'd done had survived Henry VIII by three centuries and more. The King had destroyed the abbey and what it stood for, but not the memory of its beauty. Or its greatness.

A strange place, Rutledge thought, to leave a dead man. Why here?

He went through into the nave, his footsteps alternately echoing on stone and whispering on the grass. The cloister was open to the sky, constructed for contemplation and peace, where monks could walk or sit in the noonday sun or pray in private.

He found the wax drippings from a candle, then the crushed grass where the victim had lain, but too many other feet had come and gone here, there was nothing to tell him about the dead man or who had been here with him.

He turned to look at the stone surrounding him, at the curve of an arch and the delicacy of a wall. *Why here? Why meet here?*

This was private property, the chance of being discovered at any moment was a risk that had had to be considered. Or did it appear safe, because it *was* private and therefore there was nothing to fear?

He heard a dog bark outside the church, and a voice call, "Is anyone there?"

Rutledge turned to walk back the way he'd come, stepping out of the nave to be greeted by a sleek Irish setter sniffing suspiciously at his heels.

The man standing some fifty feet away stared at him.

"Inspector Rutledge, Scotland Yard," he said easily, ignoring the dog. "Were you the man who found the body?"

"I was."

"And you are?"

"The undergardener. Hadley."

"Did you notice anything the police might have missed, Mr. Hadley?"

"No."

"Did you look at the man's face, under the respirator?"

"I could see he was dead. There were flies about. I went directly for the police."

"You didn't look at the book lying beside the body?"

"It wasn't beside it. It lay at his feet."

"Open or closed?"

"Open, like a tent."

"Not where the man might have been holding it?"

"No."

"Could you or your dog tell how the man had come this far? Or how the killer might have left?"

"By the time I'd thought of that, the police had come and gone. There was a muddle of scents."

"If you think of anything that might be useful, however insignificant it might seem to you, will you contact Inspector Madsen at once?"

"I'm not likely to remember anything more. The dog stood here barking, as he did at you, and when no one came out of the ruin, I went to see what he was on about. I wondered, just now, if there might be another dead man in there."

It was a grudging admission.

"There's a sketch of the dead man in my motorcar. Will you come and look at it?"

"I needn't see it. I was here when they first took off the mask."

"Did you recognize him? Or had you seen him before?"

"He was a stranger."

"But the family might have known him."

"It's not likely they'd know a murdered man."

Murder didn't happen in nice circles . . .

Hamish said, "He's no' concerned with the dead, now. It's no' a part of his duties."

It was true.

Rutledge thanked the man, waited until he'd called off the still sniffing dog, and then walked back the way he'd come.

Rutledge realized, driving back to Elthorpe, that what he'd been sent north to do was to put a name to the victim.

And that didn't appear to be a simple matter.

But he could see, he thought, what the army was about—searching out unidentified bodies in the expectation that one of them might be Gaylord Partridge. Because the man still hadn't returned to the cottages in Berkshire, or London would have recalled the Yard's emissary by now.

Why did they think Partridge might be dead?

Did he have other enemies? Or was it that the army didn't want to step forward and publicly claim the man's body? If Rutledge identified him in the course of a murder investigation, there would be no connection with officialdom.

It was possible that Partridge's earlier forays had been made to prepare an escape route, so to speak, away from his watchers. And this time, unlike before, he had no intention of coming back.

And instead of going missing and causing an uproar, he'd died and inconvenienced everyone.

Rutledge was tempted to take the sketch to show at the Tomlin Cottages, to see what Quincy and Slater and the others might say about it.

But early days for that, now.

He found he'd driven back to Dilby, where the schoolmaster lived.

Hamish said, "It willna' be useful."

And yet Rutledge left his car by the church and walked through the village, getting a sense of it.

He'd seen much of England over the years, both as a policeman and as an ordinary visitor. Wherever he had traveled, he'd found a sense of place—a shared history, a shared background. But this little spot on the map seemed to have none of that. No sense of the past in the square buildings with their slate roofs, gray in the cloudy light. No sense of history, no armies marching through the churchyard, no Roman ruin under the baker's shop, no medieval tithe barn on the fringe of the village. The abbey must have wielded some influence here—if not Fountains, then one of the others. Ripon, perhaps. What had the monks run here? Sheep, or even cattle? Or was this tilled land? Beyond the village, where he could see green and heavily grassed pastures, there must have been good grazing from the earliest days. Surely the inhabitants of Dilby had been tenants of the abbeys, not monks. Laymen or even lay brothers, earning their keep and owning nothing until the Dissolution of the Monasteries by Henry VIII had left them masterless and destitute, scraping out a living where they could or falling under the sway of whatever lordling had coveted these acres.

He had come to the end of the village now, and turned to walk back.

Hamish said, "It's no' a place of comfort."

Rutledge was about to answer him when he saw a face in an upper-story window staring down at him.

A young boy's face, so terrified that he seemed to be on the verge of crying. Glimpsed for only a moment, then gone, as if Rutledge had imagined it.

It wasn't Hugh or his friend Johnnie. He was certain of that.

What did these children know? What were they so frightened of?

Rutledge walked on, an unhurried pace that took him back to his motorcar, nodding to men he passed on the street, touching his hat to the women. No one stopped him to ask his business.

They already knew. The blankness in their eyes as they acknowledged his greeting covered something else, an unwillingness to be a part of what was happening.

How long could the schoolmaster go on living here, if the cloud of suspicion wasn't lifted, and soon? He would be sent packing, no longer the proper person to form young minds. Miss Norton was right about that.

Rutledge drove back to Elthorpe in a bleak mood, as if the village had left its mark on him.

On the outskirts lines from the poetry of O. A. Manning seemed to express what he felt about Dilby. It had been written about a shell-gutted village in France, empty of people, empty of beauty, empty of hope.

> *There is something cold and lost*
> *Here, as if the people died long ago,*
> *No one left to mourn them or tell me why.*
> *My footsteps echo on what was the street,*
> *A rose blooms in a corner where no one sees*
> *The beauty that it offers to the dead.*
> *I thought to pluck it and take it away,*
> *But it belongs here, a memorial to them.*
> *No birds sing in the ruined trees,*
> *No fowl scratch in unweeded kitchen gardens,*
> *No child's laughter answers a mother's voice.*
> *There's only the wind searching for something to touch*
> *And passing through unhindered.*

A fleeting memory came to him—Alice Crowell's welcome, as if she had been expecting him. And yet as far as he knew there was no reason why she should.

8

The next morning found Rutledge back at the Dilby school, encountering a surprised Albert Crowell in the passage just as he came out of a classroom. Rutledge had brought the sketch of the dead man back with him.

"Inspector. What can I do for you?" Crowell asked.

"I'd like a word with your wife, if she's here."

There was a wary expression in his eyes now.

"In regard to what?" Crowell asked bluntly.

"I'm afraid that's police business at the moment."

Crowell gave some thought to the request and then said, "She's in the small room we call the library. Four doors down and to your left."

"Thanks." Rutledge walked on, feeling the man's gaze following him as he counted doors and stopped to knock lightly on the fourth.

A woman's voice called, "Come in."

But whoever it was Alice Crowell was expecting, it wasn't Rutledge this time. Surprise crossed her face, and she bit her lip before saying, "You haven't come to arrest my husband, have you? Please tell me you haven't."

"Not at all. I didn't intend to alarm you," he said easily, coming into the room and shutting the door.

As if Hamish knew now what he was about to do, the voice in his head seemed to swell into angry remonstrance.

"No' here, it isna' wise, what if yon schoolmaster is guilty?"

He ignored it as best he could.

There were handmade bookshelves around the walls, most of them half full. The titles ranged from simple children's works to more serious books on history and geography and biography. He recognized a tattered copy of Wordsworth, and another of Browning, among the poetry selections. A meager library, but for this small place, it must seem handsome.

Mrs. Crowell gestured to a chair across from the one where she was sitting. It was an intimate arrangement in the center of the room, two chairs and a scattering of benches for the children. A woven carpet covered the floor, and there was a fireplace in one wall.

"It's here we read to the children at the end of the day," she said. "They may never have access to such books after they've left us. Sadly, most of them are destined to work on the farms for their fathers or their uncles. But on the other hand they've known that since they were old enough to understand anything, and they take it as a natural course of events."

"It must seem to you a waste, at times. With a particularly bright student."

"Education is never wasted. But yes, we've taught a few who might have gone on to university. We encourage them, of course we do. But who will work the farm while they're away? And what will happen to that farm if the son of the house comes to prefer London or Ipswich or Canterbury to Dilby? Do you have children, Inspector? Do you expect them to be policemen?"

He could see that she was avoiding asking him what had brought him to her.

"Sadly, I'm not married," he told her, "but if I had a son, I'd hope he chose the career most suited to him." He found himself remembering a small boy in Scotland, named for him but not his son. "Did the war reach as far as Dilby?" he went on quickly, before the memory took hold.

"Oh, yes," she replied with sadness in her voice. "We paid a high price here, considering our numbers. Most of our men wanted to serve together, and so they were killed together as well. A good many of our children were orphaned. It's been very hard for them. And Albert lost his brother, Julian. But Mary has told you about him, hasn't she? I'm sure she has."

"Your husband was in the war, I understand."

The wariness crept back into her eyes. "Yes."

"We didn't disparage the men who drove ambulances," he said. "They were very brave to go where they were needed most. And they were caring. In the worst of the fighting, they were often the last touch of England that many dying men knew."

A smile brightened her face. "Thank you," she said softly. As if she too had wondered about her husband's bravery under fire and had had no one to ask.

He went on, "I've come to make a request. I'd like to speak to several of your students, alone if possible."

"Why? And which of them do you have in mind? I didn't think you knew any of them."

"The one called Hugh. And his friend. Johnnie. The one who went home because he'd been sick."

"Why on earth should you be interested in those two? They're troublesome, but nothing beyond the usual mischief one expects of boys who are not good students and find school boring."

"Something appears to have frightened them."

She frowned. "How do you mean? Are you saying that *someone* has frightened them?"

"Not necessarily someone. Perhaps something."

"But what has this to do with my husband?"

"Nothing at all, for all I know. But until I speak with them, I can't tell you how they fit into this business. And it might be best to do that here, rather than in their homes. Less intimidating, perhaps."

All the while, Hamish was reminding him that Crowell was the chief suspect. "Ye could verra' well be putting yon lads in harm's way."

Mrs. Crowell was intelligent, her mind working quickly as she sorted through several thoughts pressing for her attention.

"And if I say no?"

"Mrs. Crowell, I would prefer your cooperation. But if you refuse to give it, I shall have to approach the families directly."

"You don't seem to understand. John Standing isn't here today, he's not well enough to return. And for several days, another boy, Robbie Medway, has been ill. His mother was saying to me only last evening that she was at a loss to know what was wrong. His brother Tad and John's cousin Bill have been very distracted in class. And that's not like them. It isn't boredom. I expect they're worried about their friends. The four of them are also friends with Hugh Tredworth. He's not been himself either. Very subdued. It would be best not to add the distress of speaking to a policeman to the problems in their home situation just now. You see, one of our brightest boys died a few months ago of complications from measles, and any illness is disturbing to the children now. One of the younger students asked me only this morning if Robbie was going to die too. There's your frightening something."

Hamish chided Rutledge, "You wouldna' heed me. They're afraid of yon schoolmaster."

"I appreciate your concern for them, Mrs. Crowell. It's admirable.

All the more reason to interview the boys here. If you would bring them to me now . . ." He left the words hanging in the air between them, leaving her no way out.

"I believe as a teacher I'm in a better position to judge." She tried another tactic. "Inspector, these are *children*. It's cruel to drag them into something as horrid as a suspicious death. I don't understand how schoolboys here in Dilby could possibly know anything about your dead man at the abbey. I expect they've never set foot in the ruins."

He cut her short. "It will be done, Mrs. Crowell. Here. At their homes. Or in the police station at Elthorpe. The decision must be yours."

Mrs. Crowell capitulated with what grace she could muster. "Hugh is here. I'll find him and bring him to you."

He could almost read what was running through her mind. Better to know what was happening than be in the dark.

"Before you go. I'd rather you didn't tell Hugh or your husband why he's being taken out of class."

She couldn't contain her fear any longer. "I know what it is you're intent on asking. If they've seen my husband out walking late at night. After all, their house windows overlook the street. But he does walk sometimes. Albert suffers from headaches, he has since the war, and the cool air helps at the end of the day. Inspector Madsen will use that against him, and it isn't *fair*." A slow flush rose to her cheeks. "I thought," she added accusingly, "that you had been sent here to put an end to this harassment of my husband."

"I shan't know that until I've spoken to Hugh. If you please."

Ten minutes later she returned with a very flushed Hugh Tredworth. He edged into the room, staring at Rutledge as if the Devil himself were awaiting him.

Rutledge smiled at Mrs. Crowell. "Thank you. I'll let you know when we're finished."

That alarmed Hugh, who was clearly not happy with being left alone with the tall man standing there by the window.

"I think I should stay. In lieu of his parents—"

But Rutledge cut her off again. "This is not a police interview, Mrs. Crowell. Merely a conversation."

She left reluctantly, casting a last glance at Hugh as she closed the door behind her. It could have been interpreted as a warning or as encouragement. Rutledge rather thought that Hugh took it as the former. He seemed to shrink, as if his last protector had betrayed him.

He stood there, waiting for martyrdom, staring at his executioner with a complex mixture of bravura, fright, and a deep-seated worry.

And it was the worry that intrigued Rutledge.

"Hugh, my name is Rutledge. I've come from London to help the local police in a matter that perplexes them. You had nothing directly to do with this problem, but I have a feeling that you might know some small piece of the puzzle that will help us sort out what really happened at Fountains Abbey."

"I don't know anything. I told you that yesterday, didn't I?"

"Is that true? Your friend Johnnie was very upset yesterday. Is he the one I ought to be speaking with this morning?"

"No!" It was explosive. As if Hugh were afraid that Johnnie could be persuaded to tell more than he should.

Rutledge gestured to the chairs in the center of the room. "Sit down, Hugh, I'm not here to persecute you or your friend. No, not on the bench. On the other chair. This is man to man."

Hugh sat gingerly on the chair, as if suspecting a trick. His face was set now, his mind racing. But his stomach was about to betray him, his nerve close to breaking.

"Who are your friends, Hugh?" Rutledge asked, trying to put him at ease.

But it was the wrong question.

"Don't have any," he said gruffly. "Nobody likes me."

"That's not true. You were very concerned about Johnnie yesterday."

"He's not my mate," Hugh said stubbornly. "He doesn't like me."

"Are you protecting someone? Is that why you're so afraid?"

"I'm not afraid of anything!" It was almost a shout, but one that rang of pain rather than anger.

"Who left the village on Monday night, the evening that someone was killed in the Fountains Abbey church?"

"No one, I didn't see anyone."

It was a plea now, and Rutledge heard more than Hugh intended.

Hugh and at least one of his friends had been out that night, bent on some adventure of their own. One that their parents knew nothing about. And that was keeping them tongue-tied. The knowledge that any confession would get them into serious difficulty with their fathers, never mind the law. Rutledge wondered if Hugh had made a habit of late-night forays.

I didn't see anyone . . .

No, I was in my bed that night . . .

He said, while Hamish thundered in his head, "Hugh. You'll be safer if you tell me what's been happening. You know, don't you? You and John Standing, his cousin William, Tad and his brother Robert."

Rutledge had no way of guessing that in Hugh's mind, not even a London policeman was a match for the Devil. Probing, listening, he was trying to build a picture of what had so disturbed this distraught, tense child. But he was going about it from an adult's perspective, knowing the truth and trying to work backward from it. That these boys had actually been in the abbey ruins was the last thing to cross his mind.

Hugh was living in a different reality, one in his mind that was so unforgivable he could find no way back to the safety of his old life. What had begun as a daring escapade had turned into a nightmare. His knowledge of history, scant as it was, included burning witches at the stake for summoning the Devil. It hadn't even occurred to him on his way to Fountains Abbey that he was going down that path, but it had struck him forcibly later. His concept of the Devil had been a simple one, more like the spirit in a magic lamp than the fiend they'd met. Something to brag about, not something that could destroy him.

Hugh's brows flicked together, and Rutledge could almost hear the thoughts rushing through his head. *Who told? Who spoke out of turn?*

"If you won't tell me, I must ask the other boys. Robert is younger, he might not be as stubborn as you are, or as determined to protect his friends."

"Robbie has nothing to do with us." The words were angry, and full of fear as well. "Leave Robbie out of this."

"I'm afraid I can't. There are suspicious circumstances surrounding a man's death, you see, and I've come north to find out why he died. If he was killed."

It was all Hugh could do to stop himself from blurting out, *None of us killed him—it was the Devil!*

Rutledge tried another direction. "Do you know the book on alchemy that belongs to Mr. Crowell?"

"I've seen it," Hugh said warily. He had nearly forgotten the book by the time the Elthorpe inspector brought it back to the school. That had shaken him. But with a child's sense of what was important, he could now safely deny all knowledge of it. It was where it ought to be, wasn't it, and no one knew he'd borrowed it. Now he dredged up his first acquaintance with it. "He shows it when he's trying to explain how people get things wrong, but in the end, each bit of knowledge helps the next person looking for the truth."

Even to his own ears that sounded very much like a memorized lesson he was parroting.

"Police work is much the same," Rutledge told him, seizing his opportunity. "We try this bit of knowledge and that bit, and in the end, we learn the truth. We—the police—found that book in Fountains Abbey the night a man died. And so we came to speak to Mr. Crowell. His name was in it, you see. And the police believe he might have been in the ruins of the cloister talking with the man who was later killed."

"Mr. Crowell wouldn't kill anybody. Not even in the war, he couldn't."

"Then how did his book come to be in the ruins beside a dead man? Who else could possibly have left it there? That's our dilemma. That's why we must know who might have met the man that night. Someone did. We found candle wax in the cloister as well. They must have stood there and talked at some point."

Hugh was silent, confused, his face working with his thoughts, his body tense as a cornered animal's.

"We have a body, we have a book with another man's name in it, Mr. Crowell's name, and no answers to the puzzle," Rutledge persisted. "You can see, surely, that we must get to the truth if we're to show whether Mr. Crowell is to blame for what happened. Otherwise, he'll be held responsible."

Hugh said, as if he thought it was all a trick, "There's no one dead I heard of. Who is it, then? And what was he doing in the abbey late at night?"

Rutledge answered him with honesty. "We don't know his name. He's a stranger." He reached for the file on Mrs. Crowell's desk and opened it to show the sketched face to Hugh. The boy hesitated, then curiosity got the better of him.

"That's him, then?" Hugh stared at the face. "He doesn't look dead."

"I assure you he is. We don't know where to find his family."

After a moment Hugh looked away. "What killed him?"

"He was—er—overcome by gas." Rutledge had debated what to say, knowing that the question would surely come up. It was important to be honest with the boy, now.

That took Hugh aback. "Like in the war?"

"No. Not like in the war."

"I never saw him before." There was a wealth of relief behind the words. "Never."

"He hasn't come to call on someone in Dilby? Perhaps met him by the church or at the edge of the village? On the road, or even out in a field?"

Hugh shook his head vigorously.

"Perhaps you didn't see his face, only his back or a silhouette. The problem is, who did he come here to see?"

"He never came to Dilby that I know of. It's God's truth."

"And so we're back to the book of alchemy. And why it was left at this man's feet. In an ancient abbey cloister, of all places."

Another thought had struck Hugh. He frowned fiercely, as if concentrating on something. What was running through his head was the fear that the Devil they'd raised had found another victim after they had fled the ruins. If this were true, he was as good as a murderer. He felt sick again, his stomach clenching and twisting.

Rutledge was saying, "He was lying on his back, this man. He wore a respirator on his face and was wrapped in a dark cloak."

Drawn out of himself, Hugh was staring, his face so pale Rutledge realized he'd touched on something that was shocking to the boy.

"Say again?" It was a croak, coming out of a tight, dry throat.

"I didn't mean to frighten you, Hugh."

"No, sir, tell me that bit again." There was urgency in the boy's posture and his voice.

"The dead man was wearing a respirator. You've seen them, during the war. We don't know why this was on his face, and it was broken, but there you are. And the cloak was heavy, black. *What is it, Hugh, what's wrong?*"

Rutledge was on his feet as the boy slumped in his chair, starting to shake as if he were running a fever.

His eyes stared at Rutledge accusingly, begging.

"For God's sake, young man, what's *wrong*?"

"You're lying to me." It was a whisper.

"I don't lie, Hugh. I can take you to Elthorpe and show you these things."

Hugh nodded. "I want to see them."

But he sat there, as if he couldn't manage to stand on his own two feet.

Rutledge was watching him. "What is it, Hugh? Tell me what you're afraid of."

Hugh struggled with himself, then got up and said, "Can I go now?"

Rutledge thought he meant, was he free to leave. Then realized he was actually asking to be taken to Elthorpe.

"Yes, now."

Hugh nodded, followed Rutledge from the room, and in the passage outside he ran into another boy Rutledge hadn't seen before. The boy was staring at Hugh, and he said shortly, "There's nothing wrong, Tad. There's nothing *wrong*!"

Rutledge said, "Do you want Tad to come with you?"

Hugh shook his head forcefully, and Tad seemed to melt back into the wall, making room for the policeman and Hugh to pass.

It was a silent ride to Elthorpe, though Hamish was still vocal just behind Rutledge's right ear. At one point, Rutledge retorted sharply, "It was the right thing to do."

Hugh looked across at him, startled. Rutledge tempered his voice and repeated, "It was the right thing to do, Hugh. You're a brave lad."

When they reached the doctor's surgery, Rutledge explained that he'd come to show Hugh Tredworth the clothing that the dead man had been wearing. The doctor's nurse took them back to a door at the end of the passage, and Hugh began to drag his heels.

"I don't have to see him, do I? You didn't say I had to see *him*. Just his things."

"That's right. I'll bring them out to you."

The nurse opened the door into a room lined with shelving, storage for blankets, medical instruments, an array of bottles, and other paraphernalia. On a lower one, tidily boxed, was the folded cloak and on top of it was the respirator.

On a bench outside the closet, Rutledge spread the cloak out for Hugh to see, and set the mask in at the head, the way it had covered the dead man's face.

Hugh stood there, absorbing the image Rutledge had created. His eyes squinted, as if he were comparing a memory with what lay before him. Then he looked up at the man from London. There was a mixture of emotions in his expression. Understanding, alarm, confusion, distress. Rutledge could have sworn that among them was disappointment.

"It wasn't the Devil, then." The boy's voice was flat, without feeling.

"The Devil?"

Hugh turned and marched out of the surgery, Rutledge hastily thanking the nurse and following him out to the motorcar.

Hugh was leaning against the wing, his face hidden.

Rutledge gave him time to recover and then said quietly, so that passersby couldn't hear, "Will you tell me what you know, Hugh?"

"I want to go home now." Hugh turned and scrambled into the passenger's side, waited for Rutledge to crank the motorcar, then join him.

They were nearly out of Elthorpe before Hugh spoke.

"We thought it was the Devil lying there," he said, beginning at the end of the tale, tears suddenly welling in his eyes. He looked away. "That's when I dropped the book, we were all so afraid."

"You were there?" Rutledge tried to absorb that. "What took you there, Hugh? Why should you think it was the Devil?"

"Because we'd been trying to raise him, weren't we? With that book of Mr. Crowell's."

"That's a book of alchemy."

"There's spells in it. That's why I took—borrowed—it."

The story came tumbling out, relief so great that there was no stopping the pent-up words. Backward, leaping ahead, sometimes garbled, but clear enough. The boy ended, "It wasn't Mr. Crowell who carried the book there. It was me. I went to his office when I was running an errand for Mrs. Crowell, and I took it. Must you tell him? Must you tell my father? There'll be the strap for the lot of us—even Robbie."

Rutledge said, "Have you told the whole truth, Hugh? Nothing left out, nothing made up?" But he was sure nothing had been held back. The boy had needed the release of telling the whole story to someone. Even a policeman.

"It's the truth," Hugh said fervently, "I swear it!"

"Is this why you and your friends were so afraid? Because you believed you'd raised the Devil?"

"We swore an oath not to tell. But Robbie wanted to tell, he was so afraid. I warned him his tongue would turn black." He brushed his lips with his own tongue. "And look who it was broke first." There was disgust in his voice.

"You swore not to tell about raising the Devil. But you didn't raise him. What you saw was a human being, lying there in the shadows."

"It doesn't matter, does it? An oath is an oath."

"It matters a great deal. What you've done today is help with a police inquiry. You can rightly be proud of that. Should I speak to your friends, tell them you've done your proper duty? They may remember details that you haven't."

"I'd rather you didn't. I've told you the lot. What about Mr. Crowell, then?"

"Leave this to me. Once the book has been explained away, there's nothing to link him to this other man, is there?"

Hugh still seemed uncertain.

Rutledge asked, "Was there anyone else in the ruins that night? Did you see anyone on the road? Or hear anything, men arguing, someone walking fast to make sure he wasn't seen?"

"There was no one on the road or in the woods but us. And no one in the ruins. I'd swear to it."

"If you remember anything, however small the detail might be, will you ask Mrs. Crowell to find me? This is true of your friends as well. Any small detail, Hugh."

He said again, "No, there was no one. We'd have run for home if there'd been any such thing."

Which Rutledge thought was more true than any spoken denials.

He returned the boy to the school, spoke briefly to Mrs. Crowell, and then went looking for her husband.

"You're in the clear, Crowell. As far as I can see. I'll tell Inspector Madsen that you weren't in the abbey ruins that night."

"Why are you so certain? And why did you take Hugh Tredworth away from the school without my permission?"

"He was out that night, and you'd best leave it at that."

"What do you mean, out that night?"

"It's police business, Crowell, and if I were you, I'd let sleeping dogs lie. It's in your best interest, after all."

Crowell's face had taken on a stubborn tightness.

"He's one of my pupils—"

"But not your son, is he? And he wasn't in school at the time. If he requires discipline, leave it to his father."

"I don't understand how that boy could clear me of a charge of murder. My book was there, beside the dead man. How does a child explain that away?"

"If you wish, I'll take you to speak to Mr. Madsen. He'd like very much to see you charged. We can try to persuade him otherwise, but I'm not sure you'll be successful. He has a grudge against you, as far as I can tell, and if he pursues this matter, it's very likely to cost you your position here at Dilby."

Crowell considered that. "It's true. He's not counted amongst my friends."

"Then leave me to deal with him. I haven't much time. Make your decision."

"Very well. But I can tell you, it's against my better judgment."

"And leave Hugh Tredworth alone. Don't question him yourself. If you do, it's likely that he won't be able to testify on your behalf at any trial, should it come to that."

"Did Hugh take my book without my knowledge? But he couldn't have carried it to the abbey, not that far, in the middle of the night. Who did?"

Rutledge could follow his line of thought—that somehow the pointing finger of accusation was swinging toward his wife.

"It has nothing to do with Mrs. Crowell. Stop second-guessing me, you'll do more harm than good."

He could see that Crowell had a tenacious mind and it would worry at the problem until it came up with a satisfactory conclusion.

It was also the kind of mind that might harbor a wrong until it grew into a monstrous weight that had to be addressed. Or avenged . . .

Hugh Tredworth had explained away the alchemy book. Albert Crowell might still bring down on himself a charge of murder because he couldn't let well enough alone.

Driving alone back to Elthorpe, Rutledge listened to Hamish in his mind.

"Ye've cleared the schoolmaster, aye, but there's still a dead man with no name and no suspects to take the schoolmaster's place."

There was also one Henry Shoreham, who had to be found and discounted. For the record.

"Are you saying you don't believe Hugh Tredworth?"

"He told the youngest lad his tongue would turn black and drop oot if he spoke."

"He told all four of them that."

"But it was the youngest lad who believed it."

"I think because Robbie needed so badly to confide in someone."

"Yon inspector willna' be happy you've spoiled his chances."

9

Inspector Madsen, in fact, was livid.

He paced the small office and asked Rutledge what he was about, to make an arbitrary decision about a case that was his only by courtesy.

Rutledge said, "You can't hang a man for murder because you dislike him, Madsen. And there's no other proof Crowell was involved in any fashion, now that the book is explained away."

"Too conveniently explained away if you ask me. I should have been present when you interviewed Hugh Tredworth. Why wasn't I sent for? You don't know this part of the country the way I do. How can I be sure he was telling the truth? Damn it, *you don't know these people.*"

Rutledge said only, "I know when I'm being lied to. Your case is wide open, man, it's time to get on with it. If London can place the victim from the sketch, then you'll be the first to know. Meanwhile, you're letting what evidence there is grow cold. I'd speak to the undergardener on the estate, for one. And talk to the nearest stationmaster. He may remember a stranger arriving by train. Hold the inquest, and ask the coroner to bring in the verdict of murder by person or persons unknown, to give you more time."

"Don't teach me how to run an inquiry," Madsen went on, fuming. "And why are you here in the first place? Because Alice Crowell's father has friends in high places, looking after his daughter. I tell you, the schoolmaster thought he was killing the man who'd scarred his wife, and you'll not convince me otherwise. Oh, yes, I got that story out of Mary Norton."

"It's a dead end, Madsen. I'll have to return to London tomorrow. I need to look into several other possibilities."

Or to put it another way, reporting to the Colonel, Madsen told himself in disgust. "Good luck to you then."

It was bitter, far from wishing him well.

As Rutledge walked out of the station, Madsen watched him go. The man from London hadn't come to discover who the dead man was, whatever he said, Madsen told himself. He'd been sent by Alice's bloody family to keep her precious husband safe. Once that was done, it was good-bye to Yorkshire, leaving the local man with an unidentified corpse and no murder suspect.

He let the legs of his chair slam back to the floor, relishing the sound. He'd have liked to throw the chair after the departing Londoner, but that would be the end of his own career. And he was having none of that.

There was one thing to be done to spike the Londoner's guns.

Find Henry Shoreham, or failing that, someone who knew him well enough to say if the dead man was Shoreham or not.

And if it was, then Crowell could damned well take his chances in a courtroom, Colonel Ingle be damned.

———

During the long drive back to London, Hamish was insistent, railing at Rutledge for his handling of Madsen and Crowell alike.

"Ye didna' gie yon inspector the whole truth."

"It's not mine to give, is it?"

"It would ha' gone a long way toward placating him."

"The War Office can look at this sketch and tell me if we've found our man. If we have, then I'll be back in Yorkshire before the week is out, to discover what happened to him and why."

"And if it isna' Partridge?"

"Then very likely I'll be sent back by the Yard. The Chief Constable will be involved by that time. Madsen will complain to him before we've reached Cambridge."

"Ye should ha' told him as much. That you'd be back."

"I'm not at liberty to explain why I think there's more to this case than he realizes. If those boys hadn't confessed, Crowell could well be facing the hangman. And if the victim turns out to be Shoreham after all, he's still the chief suspect."

"Then why the robe, why the mask?"

"To throw us off. As it did. Although if it was Crowell, he should have been clever enough to rid himself of the body altogether."

"He couldna' leave his wife long enough to take the body verra' far."

"I'm still not convinced that dying so easily would provide a satisfying retribution. A shotgun in the face perhaps, or throttling with one's bare hands would be a more convincing vengeance."

"Aye, but there's nae weapon, in a gassing."

Which was an excellent point.

Rutledge arrived in London too late to return to the Yard, but the next morning, he was there before Chief Superintendent Bowles had arrived.

Sergeant Gibson, passing Rutledge in the corridor, said, "Walk softly."

Which meant that the Chief Superintendent was not in a good humor.

Rutledge stopped him and said, "Can you find me information on one Henry Shoreham, of Whitby, Yorkshire? Taken up for public drunkenness after accidentally knocking a young woman into an iron fence and scarring her badly."

"I'll speak to a constable I know in Whitby police station, if you like. What's he done?"

"Nothing that I'm aware of. But he could well be a murder victim. In Yorkshire. I'm particularly interested in his appearance—whether he has a cleft in his chin."

Gibson nodded. "I'll do my best."

Gossip had it right. Superintendent Bowles had just had a dressing-down by his superiors, and he was nursing his wounds. No one was safe.

There had been a very careful watch set up for a killer cornered in the East End, and somehow the man had slipped quietly through the net and escaped. Bowles had borne the brunt of official displeasure.

As Rutledge came through the door, Bowles looked at him with narrowed eyes. "And what are *you* doing here? I thought I'd sent you north to Yorkshire."

"You had. I brought back a sketch of the dead man. I think some-one in the War Office ought to have a look at it."

"Very clever of you," Bowles declared in a growl. "What makes you think they want to meet with you, pray? Sketch or no sketch?"

"Because I don't think they're very keen on traveling to Yorkshire themselves to see the body. There are no distinguishing marks, and any description would fit half the men walking past our door. If they want Partridge badly enough, they'll agree."

Bowles grunted, but picked up the telephone and put in a call. It took nearly a quarter of an hour for someone to get back to him.

He sent for Rutledge and told him shortly, "Martin Deloran. Some-one at the War Office will take you to meet him. They're waiting. Bloody army."

Rutledge retrieved the sketch from his office and left.

When he was finally admitted into Deloran's presence, Rutledge had had enough of secrecy and chains of command. He sat down in the chair pointed out to him and said without preamble, "It's possible I've found Partridge. It's for you to decide."

Deloran took the folder that Rutledge passed across the desk and said, "I'm told by Chief Superintendent Bowles that this body was found in the ruins of Fountains Abbey, wrapped in some sort of cloak, with a respirator on his face. Hardly sounds like the man we've somehow mislaid."

"The respirator was torn. The cloak I think is theatrical."

He had a sudden image of his parents leaving for a party, his mother in an Elizabethan costume, the ruff around her face framing it becomingly, the scent of her perfume mixing with the heavier one of cedar shavings. And his father, looking like Charles II in a wig that reached below his shoulders.

Deloran said, "Well, that's not Partridge, I can tell you. I doubt he ever went to the theatre in his life."

"A masquerade," Rutledge said. "Not theatrical." It fit—the fineness of the weave and the quality of the robe . . .

Nothing changed in Deloran's face. But the fingers holding a pen tightened. He said, "I doubt Partridge would have been caught dead in a masquerade." Then he realized what he'd just said, and smiled. "Sorry. But you take the point, I'm sure."

He picked up the folder, almost as if to satisfy Rutledge rather than from any curiosity on his part. Looking at the sketch, he said thoughtfully, "It's hard to say, given the inferior quality of the drawing. But I can tell you that this looks nothing like our man."

He closed the folder and passed it back to Rutledge. "It appears we were wrong about Yorkshire. I expect Partridge will show up in his own good time, whether we look for him or not."

"This man was very likely murdered," Rutledge told him bluntly. "He didn't die there in the ruins. He was carried there, after he was dead."

"Yes, very sad." Deloran prepared to stand, ready to dismiss Rutledge. "Thank you so much for your help in this matter. We are more grateful than you know."

He was standing now, and he gestured to the sketch. "I hope there's a successful conclusion to this case. Are you returning to Yorkshire?"

"At the moment, no." Rutledge stood also.

"Just as well. Let them sort out this inquiry. I'm sure they'll manage very well. Local people know best, oftentimes, deep roots in their patch, and all that. Sorry to have muddied the waters."

"Are you quite certain this couldn't be your man Partridge?"

"Absolutely." Deloran offered his hand, and Rutledge took it. "Innis will see you out."

As they walked out of the room, Hamish said, referring to Deloran, "I wouldna' care to play cards wi' him."

Innis was waiting to escort him out of the building. Rutledge, considering the gray-haired man, would have placed him as a retired sergeant-major, ramrod back, calm face, an air of unquestioned authority that had nothing to do with a uniform.

On the street once more, Rutledge answered Hamish. "I'll give you any odds you like that our dead man *is* Partridge. The question is, why wouldn't Deloran admit to it?"

"He's deid," Hamish said. "And that pleases someone."

"Yes," Rutledge answered slowly.

His dismissal rankled. The bland lies, the willingness to abandon a man who was inconvenient, even though someone had murdered him, the arrogance of the assumption that Rutledge would walk away as well, case closed, not even warning him off so much as believing that a policeman could be so easily gulled, left a bad taste.

And in the meantime, Inspector Madsen, with a corpse on his hands and his main suspect cleared, was to be left in the dark.

Back at the Yard, Gibson was waiting for him outside his office.

"I've been on the horn to Whitby. They remember your man Shoreham. He was never tried for the injury to Mrs. Crowell. The family refused to take the matter further. Shoreham left town shortly after that, and Whitby has quite lost track of him."

"Shame, I should imagine."

"Very likely," Gibson responded. "After losing his position, he found there was no use staying on where he wasn't wanted. Another town, another life."

"Quite," Rutledge answered.

"No one remembers his chin."

"I'm not surprised."

"And so far as Whitby knows, he never came to the attention of the police again. No inquiries in regard to a troubled past."

"A lesson learned. Yes. Thank you, Sergeant. Well done."

He was about to walk on, when Gibson added, "No inquiries, that is, until this morning. From an inspector in Elthorpe, or so I was told."

Rutledge stopped in his tracks. "Indeed."

"Seems they have a dead man they can't identify. And they're coming round to thinking it could be Shoreham."

Rutledge swore.

"Keep searching for Shoreham, then. I need to be sure he's alive. More important, I need to know where he's currently living."

"That's a tall order," Gibson said doubtfully.

"Yes, well. If we don't find him, someone is going to hang for his murder."

Rutledge walked on down the passage to Chief Superintendent Bowles's office. As he went, he made up his mind about what he was going to say.

Bowles looked up as he entered the cluttered room.

"Well?"

"The case is closed. At least as far as Mr. Deloran is concerned. I'm not so sure."

"You don't want to run afoul of that lot."

"No. On the other hand, I have a feeling that they'd rather sweep a murder under their carpet than tell us the truth. There's a man dead in Yorkshire, and they would just as soon ignore him. I'd like to clear up a few loose ends before I accept their verdict. Frankly, I wouldn't put it past them to have got rid of this man Partridge themselves."

"We can't go meddling into matters that are none of our business." There was alarm on Bowles's face now. He'd already run afoul of his superiors this week.

"The dead man could be anyone. From anywhere in England. But if Inspector Madsen has his way, he'll call him Henry Shoreham and take one Albert Crowell, the schoolmaster, into custody on a charge of murder. We can't seem to lay hands on Shoreham. Before we can say with any certainty that he's the victim, we must make certain to eliminate the choice that sent me to Yorkshire in the first place. I'd like to ask someone who knows—knew—Partridge well to tell me the man in the sketch I had made is not Partridge. It will clear the field to pursue the issue of Shoreham's whereabouts. If it is Partridge, we can save a good many man hours searching for Shoreham."

Bowles considered his options. In the end, it would be his duty to report to his own superiors how and why Rutledge came to be meddling in affairs that were none of his business. On the other hand, the Chief Constable of Yorkshire was not to be trifled with. He was vocal and did not suffer fools lightly. If there was any chance that one of Bowles's men was intent on pursuing a wrong course that could lead to a public embarrassment—

He wiped a hand across his face.

"Damned if we do, and equally damned if we don't," he said. "All right. Look into the business. But hear me, Rutledge! I won't have toes stepped on for naught. You'll go about this quietly, whatever you do. Tying up loose ends is all very well, but we needn't bruit it about. Ask your question without prejudice and come back to London with your answer. Understood?"

"Understood, sir. I'll leave in the morning."

He went back to his flat that evening, packed his valise with fresh clothing, ready to set out for Berkshire.

He got a late start through no fault of his own.

His sister was at his door just after breakfast, and he could tell from her face that all was not well.

She toyed with a slice of toast in the rack, buttering it and then putting it down untouched.

The purpose of her visit was—ostensibly—to ask his opinion of a new hat she'd bought the day before.

It was quite fetching, as her hats generally were. On the other hand, Rutledge thought, on her, most anything would look fetching.

"You aren't here at this ungodly hour because you have doubts about your milliner," he said lightly. "What's happened?"

"It's Simon," she said, keeping her voice steady with an effort. "He's been avoiding me. I know that for a fact, I have it on good authority, so don't tell me I'm imagining things. I don't know why he's doing this. I thought—well, I thought we were good friends."

"Why should he avoid you?" He threw up a hand, adding, "No, I'm not saying you're imagining anything. I want to know what reason you think he might have. Something you commented on, for instance, that you regretted as soon as it was out of your mouth. A remark you shouldn't have made about one of his friends. Something you said that might have led him to believe your feelings for him were stronger than his for you."

"Ian. I'm not likely to make stupid remarks, and I'm not likely to criticize him or wear my heart on my sleeve. You aren't helping."

He laughed. "I'm a policeman, not a seer."

"And a very good policeman at that," she retorted. "But you've given me an idea. I think I'll invite Meredith Channing to have lunch with me."

He was immediately on alert. "Frances. I think that's a very poor idea. Mrs. Channing isn't going to look into a crystal ball and tell you what's in Simon's mind. Or heart."

"I don't expect her to look into a crystal ball. She's a very astute woman, Ian, she can give me her opinion. And it could be what I need, to understand how to go on. I mean, people are *asking*. We've been seen together more than a little these last two months. I don't know how to answer them. 'Where's Simon, my dear? I saw him last night at the Collinses' and you weren't with him.' Or, 'What's happening between you and Simon? Has there been a falling-out, a quarrel? Have you lost interest in him?'" Her eyes filled with tears but she refused to let them fall.

"And how do you answer these questions?"

"I say that I've been terribly busy and so has Simon. Or that I couldn't make the Collinses' party, I had other plans. But it's growing *old*."

She stood up. "You'll be late, Bowles will be clamoring for you. I'll go and speak to Meredith Channing. If nothing else, she'll cheer me up. I'm in need of cheering right now."

And she was gone, despite his protests, smiling at him over her shoulder as she went out his door.

He spent the better part of the morning scouring London for news of Simon Barrington. There was no one he could ask outright, and so he had to make time to listen to various friends they held in common.

Hamish was not pleased with his decision.

"It willna' help, even if ye find him. Ye ken that as well as I do. Ye canna' speak to him."

"I don't intend to speak to him. Or try to fix whatever happened between Barrington and my sister. But if there's something wrong, something I ought to know, then the sooner the better."

"Aye, but are ye the brother now? Or the policeman?"

He couldn't answer that. And at the end of the day, there was still nothing he could point to as a reason why Barrington should avoid his sister without explanation. The closest he came to an answer was an offhand remark by Tommy Aspell. That Simon had something on his mind and had been damned poor company for a fortnight or more.

With that he had to be satisfied.

It was close to nine in the evening when he arrived in Berkshire. But The Smith's Arms was well lit, the bar noisy with shouts of laughter and the stamping of feet. Not a drunken crowd, from the sound of it, but one where men were relaxed and enjoying themselves.

Rutledge went to the tiny desk in Reception and signed the register. Then he walked into the bar.

There was a sudden silence as patrons looked up at the newcomer and judged him from his clothes.

Half a dozen lorry drivers were busy with a game of darts. One man, in the process of taking his turn, scowled at the interruption. Two farmers were watching the proceedings from the bar, keeping to themselves.

Rutledge nodded to them as the game resumed and found himself a table in a corner by the front windows. He smiled as Mrs. Smith came over to him and asked what he'd have.

"A room, if you please. I've signed the register. And dinner, if there's any left."

"This lot isn't staying over. There's the room you had before, and a bit of roasted ham and some bread left. Mustard sauce as well."

"That will do very well." He'd missed his lunch, and could hear the growling of an empty stomach.

"What will you have to drink, luv?"

"A Guinness, if you please."

"Smith u'll bring it shortly." She skirted the players and disappeared into the kitchen as another burst of laughter met a wild throw.

Rutledge watched this leg end in a victory for the bald man with a birthmark on his face. The man went to the bar to claim his wager, another glass of his choice. A shorter man, broad in the shoulders, called out to Rutledge, as he pulled the darts out of the board. "This is a worthless lot. Will you have a turn?"

It was a dare, not an invitation.

Rutledge got to his feet, shrugging off the long drive, and answered, "I'll give it a try."

They eyed him with interest as he took the three darts and lightly hefted them in his hand. Judging his skill. Or lack thereof.

Hamish was saying, "I won best of three in the canteen."

Suddenly, without warning, Rutledge could feel himself slipping back, reliving a night in France.

He had been invited to the canteen by his men. It had been his birthday, and he never knew how they'd found that out. Darts was a working-class pastime, but he'd held his own with a good elbow and a better eye. He'd been grateful not to disgrace his men in front of the other onlookers.

Hamish had stood them all down, the quiet young Scot already respected by his men, his corporal's stripes still new on his uniform.

It had been a brief respite from the Front, tired men pulled back for a few days of rest after a hard week of fighting, and nowhere to go in the rain and the mud and the dark save the popular canteen set up in a small stone barn—all that was left of a French farmhouse—that had been too rat infested to serve as a field hospital. Rumor was, officers turned a blind eye to the use it was put to by a trio of enterprising Welshmen, miners at home outside Cardiff but sappers now.

Someone had found a great gray and black tomcat, and it soon made short work of the earlier residents. A broom and some odds and ends of scavenged paint, and a rough bar built from whatever wood could be found or stolen, and the canteen was in business. A large oil painting of a French officer of the Napoleonic wars had materialized from somewhere, hung at one end of the barn by a length of scorched rope. It had become a habit to salute the officer on entering.

Evenings were usually rowdy, some of the strain and fatigue draining away as young soldiers old before their time had tried to forget the war.

He and his men had walked through the door and lifted the blanket behind it. Lamps had been hung from the rafters, the room was smoky from cigarettes, and the scent of moldy hay still lingered. Rusted kettles were whistling on a wood stove that gave off sufficient heat to keep the building just barely comfortable.

When Rutledge took the mug of steaming tea handed to him by one of his men, he nearly choked on the first swallow. In lieu of sugar, someone had added a liberal spoonful of brandy to it. But he said nothing, aware of anxious eyes on his face.

They had played darts after that, though the numbers on the board were badly worn and the colors had faded to a uniform brown. But the sisal still held each throw firmly where it landed.

At the end of the evening, Rutledge had returned to his quarters feeling not relaxed but burdened by guilt. How many of the men who had shared this wartime birthday tonight would be alive by month's end?

Ten had died the first day back in the line. And he'd heard a year later that the Welshmen had died outside Ypres when a tunnel they'd been digging had collapsed prematurely, burying them alive. By the time help reached them, it was too late.

Rutledge brought himself back to the present as a lorry driver, a man his mates called Jimmy, said, "Loser buys drinks all round."

There was general agreement to the terms, since the general opinion was that the man from London would pay the accounting.

Rutledge found the rough line drawn on the floor, put the outside of his right foot against it and considered the target. This one was worn too, but from long use, not from rain and mud and countless journeys across northern France in haversacks.

He forced his mind to concentrate on what he must do.

Hamish warned, "They'll want to see your mettle."

His fingers closed around the first dart. Worn, like the board, and comfortable in his grip. He pumped his hand twice, gauging his shot, then threw firmly toward the board.

It landed precisely where he'd intended—in the wood above the board. From the bar, Smith called, "Here! That's my wall."

"Sorry," Rutledge apologized as the lorry drivers and even the farmers slapped their knees and bent over laughing at his expense.

He waited for the racket to die down and took his second throw. This time the dart landed in the number ring, between eleven and fourteen.

There was more laughter, and the bald-headed man said to Smith, "Set them up, man, this 'ull be a short leg."

"Nay, he hit the board, didn't he?" another driver answered. "We could go on all night."

The point of the game was to put his dart somewhere in the pie-wedge-shaped section numbered 20.

Rutledge took aim for his third and final throw—and this time his dart landed perfectly in the triple in section 20.

There was an intake of breath, and someone said, "You're a damned lucky man."

He'd made his three. He walked to the board, pulled out his darts, and scored his throw, amid much joshing.

It was still his turn.

This time the section was 19, to the bottom and left.

His first dart hit the black.

One man said, "Not bad, for a toff."

He missed his other two throws, and went to retrieve his darts.

His opponent, a slim, dark man called Will, came forward to take them from him, and showed off his own skill, earning a second turn and then a third. But he was off on his next throw and that jarred him just enough to make him miss again. He wound up losing his turn, and went to fetch the darts for Rutledge.

Rutledge threw well this time, keeping pace with his opponent. There was partisanship among the observers now, the farmers taking his part and the drivers banding together behind their man.

Rutledge could have hit the outer bull with ease, but he chose to put two throws into the inner bull, the third one missing its mark.

Still, he had finished the leg just behind his opponent. There was general celebration and someone slapped him on the back as Smith handed him his glass before setting up for the rest of the men.

They stopped after splitting two more legs, sitting down at the bar or the nearest tables instead to talk to Rutledge about London and eventually the war. Four of them had served in France, while the other two had been in the navy.

Rutledge let them talk and then led them into stories about their experiences on the road.

"Ever give a lift to someone who wanted to go to, say, Liverpool or York?"

They shook their heads.

"I'd be sacked," one of them said, "if it got out."

"Not for any amount of money," the bald man added. "Can't say I like company on the road."

"Why, do you want to go to Manchester tonight?" Will, the thin man asked, finishing his beer. "I'll give you a lift."

"I've been to Manchester," Rutledge answered him. "Once is enough."

They laughed, and someone said, "Nay, Manchester's not all that bad."

Soon talk shifted to the struggles these men faced making a living wage, the hardships of being away more often than they were at home, coping with the growing tangles of traffic and the winter's toll on the roads.

"Although it's a damned sight better than being shot at by the Hun's aircraft, I swear," one of the men said. "My mate was blown up by the Red Baron. I saw that Albatross coming in and blew the horn but there was no time. Never is. He was carrying shells, and my windscreen blew out with the force of the blast. They never did find anything of my mate to bury. I took his wife a bit of the lorry, that's all I could do. If anyone had been sitting beside me, he'd have had his head took off when something slammed into the seat and carried it through into the bed. I don't miss France, I don't."

Hamish said, "They'll no' tell you, if they had taken up yon dead man."

But Rutledge had been watching faces as he'd asked his questions. And if Partridge had got himself out of Berkshire with a lorry driver, he'd have wagered it wasn't one of these men.

Smith was calling time, and Mrs. Smith said to Rutledge as he looked around for it, "I'll bring up your dinner, if you like."

He hadn't touched it, hadn't had the time, hungry or not.

He bought a final round, then said good night, leaving the drivers to drink in peace. The farmers had already left half an hour before.

Mrs. Smith met him at the stairs as he came out of the bar, his plate on a tray.

"Were you thinking about Mr. Partridge?" she asked him. "When you wanted to know if someone might find a ride with a driver?"

He was caught off guard.

"Yes, I was, as a matter of fact," he answered, lowering his voice.

"He was here, once. Playing darts and later asking about traveling to Liverpool. But it was the roads he wanted to hear about. What sort of time he could count on making."

"When was this?"

"Six months ago, at a guess. Longer, for all I can remember."

The state of the roads.

"You're certain it wasn't the prelude for asking for a lift?"

"No, sir, he has his own motorcar, I can't think why he would need a lift with the likes of them."

"How well do you know Mr. Partridge?"

"He wasn't one to come around in the evening, as a rule." She smiled ruefully. "I think it's when he can't stand his own company any longer."

"Why do you say that?"

"Well, he's a widower, isn't he?" There was pity in her voice.

"Did he tell you he was?"

"Lord, no, sir, we never spoke about his private life. No, it was young Slater who said he'd lost his wife and hadn't much use for company. Mr. Partridge kept to himself at his cottage, and seldom went out. We were that glad to see him, when he did come."

And yet this wasn't the sort of pub a man like Partridge would frequent. Granted it was the nearest one to the cottages, but he wasn't working class, if the army was keeping an eye on him.

That reminded him of the dead man in Yorkshire, whose hands were soft and uncallused.

Hamish said, "Why did ye no' show her the drawing?"

Rutledge wasn't sure himself why he hadn't. But he wanted no rumors reaching the Tomlin Cottages before he himself could go there in the morning.

He slept poorly that night. As if the memory of the dart game on his birthday had stirred up the past too deeply, he could hear the guns in France, and men calling and screaming and swearing, bringing himself up out of the depths to lie awake until the sounds receded. And then he would drift into sleep again for another quarter of an hour, sometimes longer, before the guns started shelling his position. Muzzle flashes in the distance seemed to light up the sky, and the flares were sharp, brilliant, nearly burning his eyes.

Once when he awoke, he could hear Hamish talking to someone, and then he realized that the someone was himself, answering the familiar voice of a dead man, even in his sleep.

"I'm trained to it," he said aloud, and then lay still listening. But from the other rooms came the regular snores of occupants luckier than he was, comfortable in their beds. "Like a dog who knows his master's voice."

Hamish's laugh was harsh. "Oh, aye? More like a man wi' blood on his conscience, who canna' find peace."

"You left me no choice but to execute you. You wouldn't heed me when I warned you what would follow, if you didn't relent and obey the orders given you. *I warned you, and you didn't listen.*"

"I couldna' watch more of my men die while the colonel who gave the orders sat safe and ignorant miles behind the lines. You *knew,* you knew as well as any of us that it was hopeless."

"No more so than the whole bloody campaign. We did what we were *told,* because there was no other choice left to us but to obey. One man, two men, a dozen, couldn't have stopped the madness. We had to carry on to the end, and die if we had to."

"I wasna' afraid of dying. Ye ken that well. I couldna' bear to watch the ithers die. There had been too many, for too long."

"You refused an order under fire. You left me no choice, damn you!"

"Aye. And afterward, ye couldna' let me go."

"You didn't want to go. Then or now."

Hamish said, something in his voice now that was unbearable, "I didna' want to die. But I couldna' live, no' even for Fiona. I couldna' stand before my men and break as we went o'wer the top. It was a question of pride. I'd have shot mysel', else."

"But you let me do it instead. You let me call up the men and order them to shoot you. My men, your men. You put that on their souls and mine. If I could ever understand why, I'd find some peace. Why not let the Germans do it for you. You wouldn't have been the first. Nor the last."

"Aye, it's what ye did, but no' even the Hun could touch you. You were left wi' your shame. Ye ken, it's why I willna' go. No' now, no' yet."

"For God's sake, tell me why!"

There was a knock at his door, cutting through the darkness in his mind. Smith called out, "Mr. Rutledge? Are you all right?"

He realized that the snoring had stopped—had been stopped for some time, for all he knew. And his shouting could be heard all over the inn.

Rutledge cleared his throat.

"I'm sorry, Smith. It was a bad dream. I didn't mean to disturb the house."

There was a moment of silence on the other side of the door. "If you're sure then?"

"I'm sure."

He listened to the man's footsteps receding across the passage, and a door shutting.

Rutledge lay back against his pillows, his body still tense, his fists clenched, not certain when he'd sat up in bed or for how long the exchange with Hamish had been loud enough to be heard.

Hamish said, in the darkness, "But they canna' hear me. Only you can."

10

Rutledge was awake when at the back of the inn a rooster crowed, welcoming the early spring dawn. He got up, shaved and dressed, and went outside to walk off his mood.

For a mercy, Hamish was silent.

He found pansies blooming in the shadow of the small barn, and a clutch of hens picking busily at the sparse grass of the yard, then he walked on, down the road to Wayland's Smithy.

It was smaller than he remembered from childhood, but still an impressive grave. For whom? A chieftain? A warrior? Or perhaps a high priest, the Merlin of his age.

Whoever had lain here, the power of his name had given him a great stone tomb, monoliths that time had barely eroded. And whatever grave goods had been buried with him were long since taken away as the power of his name faded in human memory. And the bones, had they also been scattered?

Rutledge squatted down to look inside and shuddered. A narrow room in which to spend eternity. Claustrophobic and dark.

He thought about Gaylord Partridge, who was being left to rot in an unmarked, unmourned grave, because in some fashion he had offended people with a long memory for revenge.

An outcast. Like the others who lived in the Tomlin Cottages. Lepers, without the sores.

What had Partridge done to deserve his fate? A spy would have been tried and shot behind walls where no one could see him die. How had he offended? That was the crux of this business, to know why he was better off dead in a back corner of a Yorkshire graveyard—a fortuitous death, surely, for those who had hated him.

Or had it been somehow engineered?

That was something to be considered. The army looked after its own, but transgressors were beyond the pale. Abandoned.

T. E. Lawrence had offended and been snubbed. Would anyone weep if he died conveniently on a back road where no one knew him?

It was time to go back to the inn. Rutledge turned away from the tomb and retraced his steps, thinking.

When Rutledge had finished his breakfast in the quiet of the bar—empty and well scrubbed by Smith before the tea had steeped—he refreshed his memory about the nine people who lived near the foot of the great White Horse.

He had met only two of them, these neighbors of one Gaylord Partridge.

Slater, the smith, first to the left. Then Partridge, with the only gate in the low walls of the cottage gardens. The next five in the horseshoe he hadn't met, but Rutledge had seen Number 4 staring up at him as he paced along the mane of the horse. Although Martin Deloran in London had never indicated that there was another watcher, Rutledge's training told him it must be so. At the far right of the half circle was Quincy's cottage, with the birds hidden in a back room. Behind him, at Number 8, a woman lived. Rutledge had seen her hanging out her wash as well as peering at him through a window.

Finishing his second cup of tea, he left for the Tomlin Cottages.

There was one thing he disliked about what he called a cold road—coming back into a place where he had got the pulse of the people and the way they lived and then had to walk away for whatever reason. He had done that here in Berkshire, and he had done it as well in Yorkshire. Possibly all because of one mysterious man.

Much would depend on what Partridge's neighbor Quincy had to say.

He pulled his motorcar to the verge of the road, near the path up the hill of the White Horse. Near the muzzle of the great beast, he looked down on the cottages and waited for a door to open below him or a window curtain to twitch.

What were the connections between these nine residents? If connections there were. Englishmen were not by nature gregarious, even abroad. But surely human curiosity made them draw conclusions about each other from what they had observed from a window or a stroll down the lane.

The woman, he decided. From her windows she could see Partridge come and go. And women were sometimes less reserved than men, if approached in a sympathetic way.

Or was it wiser, after all, to speak to Quincy?

Quincy appeared to keep to himself. Would he admit to recognizing the sketch? He would most certainly want to know when it had been made and why. Driven by curiosity, yes, but beneath all that was his own reason for considering himself a leper of sorts and choosing to live here. He might well prefer to keep his distance from any trouble involving Partridge for fear of the impact on his own seclusion.

The smith, then. A simple man, he wasn't the sort to look below the surface of a question for hidden traps and meanings. And he was an honest man, as far as Rutledge could tell, with no secrets. His reason for living here was plain—he preferred to be left alone because his experience with people had taught him that they were unkind.

Rutledge sat there on the hillside in the April sun, and waited until he saw the smith walk into view from the direction of Uffington.

The man looked tired, his gait measured, as if there were something on his mind, holding him back.

Rutledge waited until he'd disappeared into his cottage and then went down the hill. By the time he knocked at the door, the smith had put the kettle on and Rutledge could hear it whistling cheerfully in the background as Slater opened to him.

"I saw you on the Horse," he said. "What brings you back?"

"Curiosity," Rutledge answered. He had brought the file with him from the motorcar and put it aside for the moment on a small table near the door.

"Curiosity?" Slater repeated. "It killed a cat, you know," he added, quoting the old saying.

"Yes, well, I'll be careful."

Slater said, "Would you like a cup of tea?" He gestured toward the tiny kitchen, where the kettle was still whistling.

"Thank you. I would."

While Slater was preparing the tea, Rutledge watched his deft, sure movements, big hands handling the tea things with the same ease as he handled his tools.

The cup Slater offered him was thin porcelain, with cabbage roses around it. The man could have crushed it like eggshell, and it was lost in the large, callused hand.

"How is work on the silver teapot handle faring?" Rutledge asked, to open the conversation.

"Fancy you remembering that," Slater answered, his face brightening. "It's very well. Polish it and I'm finished."

"I hope the church is pleased."

There was a bitter smile now. "I'm told I charge too much."

"Who tells you that?"

"The sexton. He says he could have done it at half the cost."

"Could he?"

"I doubt it. But he's one who opens his mouth and doesn't care much what harm he does with what comes out."

"Tell them I've offered to buy the teapot myself. For twice the cost of repairs." He couldn't stop himself from saying it. Or cursing the sexton for his callous cruelty.

Slater looked at him. "What do you want with a teapot? It's not yours to start with. It belongs to the church service."

"Yes, it does. And I'll make a gift of it back to them, so that it stays where it should."

"You're mocking me."

He had got off on the wrong foot unintentionally, and Hamish was already telling him as much. But Rutledge said, "I'm mocking no one. You showed me that teapot, and I think the sexton is wrong. Good work deserves good pay, and I for one recognize that."

"Well. It's not your problem. It's mine. What have you come for?"

"To show you a sketch, if you don't mind."

"Of work you wish me to do?"

"Sorry, no. I'd like to ask if you recognize the person in the sketch. I'm looking for this man."

There was instant hostility. "What's he done, then?"

"Nothing that I'm aware of. But friends are anxious about him. I'd like to put their minds at ease." If Deloran could be considered any man's friend . . .

"You're being fair with me?"

"Actually, I've told you the truth."

"Why do you think I might know him?"

"Look at the sketch first. And then I'll give you the answer to that."

He lifted the folder from the table and opened it.

Slater looked down at it, but his eye went first to the quality of the drawing. "It's well done, this sketch. Who made it?"

"A young man in Yorkshire. He takes as much pride in his work as you do in yours."

"And so it's a good likeness."

"We hope it is."

Slater didn't need to study the face on the paper. He said at once, "Yes, I know him. As you know very well I do."

"Who is he?"

"It's Mr. Partridge." Slater looked up. "He's dead, isn't he?"

The certainty of identification was what Rutledge had been expecting, but not the conclusion that Slater had drawn from the face in his hands.

Yet it was too easy. Deloran must surely have realized that, armed with the sketch, sooner or later Rutledge would learn who the dead man in Yorkshire was.

"He couldna' be sure you would come back here," Hamish answered the thought. "He's used to being obeyed."

"Why do you think Mr. Partridge is dead?" Rutledge asked the smith, but he already knew the answer. Slater worked with his hands, he had a feeling for skill and observation and how to translate that to whatever he was creating. And it was true, the likeness caught something that perhaps the living man had lost.

"Because it's a good likeness, that's why. How could it be this good from memory?"

"The artist might have used a photograph."

"No, I don't think he did. He saw the man. And Mr. Partridge isn't here, is he? Hasn't been for a bit. And you were here earlier, looking for him, weren't you? Somehow I have a feeling he's dead."

"But how? And where?"

Slater shrugged. "Ask a policeman to answer that for you."

"I *am* a policeman," Rutledge said slowly. "Inspector Rutledge, Scotland Yard."

There was a pause. Then Slater said, "You *have* lied to us." More than the words, his tone of voice and his face conveyed the sense of betrayal and dislike.

"I wasn't here as a policeman. I was here to see if there was an explanation for a man leaving his house and not coming back within a reasonable length of time. His motorcar and his bicycle are here. But he isn't. People don't disappear as a rule. When they do, there's always someone who wants to know why." Even as he said the words, in his mind's eye he could see the bland face of Martin Deloran as he figuratively washed his hands of Gaylord Partridge. "No, that's a lie as well," Rutledge went on. "I don't think, in the end, they really cared, these people, whether Partridge lived or died. What worried them was that he wasn't where he was supposed to be."

"He has a minder. Why should they send you here?"

"A minder?" He had suspected as much. But hadn't expected confirmation.

"I'm not a fool," Slater said, "even though people believe I am. He drinks, does Mr. Brady."

"The man in Number Four?"

"The first time Mr. Partridge went missing, he was beside himself. He'd got very drunk that night and passed out in his front garden. I put him to bed, and in the morning he must have thought he'd managed it alone. I never told him otherwise. He took his field glasses up the hill with the Horse, and searched everywhere. Even in the Smithy. But Mr. Partridge came home again, and all was well. Mr. Brady stayed sober for several weeks afterward, then went back to his drinking."

"Where do you think Partridge went?"

"It's his own business, isn't it? If he'd wanted me to know, he'd have told me."

"Still, if he's dead, it's no longer his business. It's a matter for the police."

"He didn't die here. How could any of us be responsible?"

"How do you know where he died?"

"I don't. But if the sketch was made in Yorkshire, then it must be that he died there."

Simple Slater might be, but stupid he was not.

"A good point. But the fact is, we don't know where he died. His body was found in Yorkshire. Hence the mystery. And the concern."

Slater shook his head as Rutledge finished his tea. "I've nothing to do with this. I'm sorry he's dead, he wasn't a difficult neighbor, though I didn't know him well, but I had nothing to do with his death."

Rutledge set his cup aside and stood up. "I didn't expect you had. But you're a man with clear eyes, and it was important to ask you. Thank you for the tea."

He took up his sketch and walked to the door.

As he was opening it, Slater, behind him, said, "I'd not ask the man in Number Seven about the sketch, if I were you."

Rutledge turned. "Why is that?"

Slater said, "Whenever I see him, I feel the darkness in him. I try to stay out of his way."

"I'll remember that. Thank you." And with that, he closed the door.

Slater had identified the sketch, just as Rutledge had expected. Moreover, he believed the smith. What he needed now was information of a different kind. And for that he chose to call on Quincy next.

Quincy wasn't at home—or at least failed to answer his door—when Rutledge knocked. And so Rutledge moved on to the next cottage, where he'd seen a woman's face at the window on his earlier visit.

She opened the door only, he thought, because after he knocked he stood there waiting.

Through the crack she said, "Yes?" As if he had come to sell brushes or produce from a barrow. He couldn't see her face clearly. But he could tell from her eyes that she was frightened.

"My name is Rutledge. I'd like to speak with you."

"You were here before. Who sent you?"

"Sent me?"

"Was it my husband? He only sends someone if there's bad news."

"I can't bring you bad news," Rutledge answered her quietly. "I don't even know your name."

"It's Cathcart," she answered him. "Maria Cathcart."

"I'm sorry if I frightened you, Miss Cathcart—"

"It's Mrs. Was and still is, whatever he may tell you."

"Mrs. Cathcart. I'm here to ask if you recognize the man in a sketch I'd like to show you. Would you mind if I came in? I'll only stay for a moment, I promise you."

Grudgingly she let him in. The cottage was obsessively neat, as if she had nothing better to do than keep it that way. House-proud? And yet she didn't seem to be the sort of woman who would do her own cleaning. As if she came from different circumstances than he found her in here. Tall and slim, tired and afraid. It was the only way to describe her. The circles under her troubled blue eyes indicated sleepless nights.

She didn't ask him to sit down. Instead she said with some anxiety, "Show me this man's face."

He opened the folder and held it out to her. She didn't take it, just glanced at the sheet of paper inside, seemed relieved that it was not the person she'd been expecting, and said, "Mr. Partridge, I think. I don't know him well. But I daresay that's him."

"He's been away for some time. Do you have any idea where he might have gone? Or why? Or with whom?"

"I'm not his keeper, nor is he mine," she answered him.

Rutledge said, "Did he have family? Friends who came to call? You can see his cottage well from your windows. You might have noticed who came and went."

"I might have," she agreed. "But I didn't. He was of no concern to me. I doubt we said good morning more than a dozen times all told."

"You never saw anyone at his door?"

"Once when I was in my garden I saw a young woman come to

his door. But if he was in the house, he didn't answer her knock. And shortly afterward she left."

"What did she look like?"

"A well-dressed, fair-haired young woman. I couldn't see her face. I made no effort to try. It had nothing to do with me."

Was this the same woman Quincy had seen and assumed was Partridge's daughter?

"How long have you lived here, Mrs. Cathcart?"

"For fifteen years, this June."

"Which means you were living here when Mr. Partridge first came. Do you remember when that was?"

"Of course I remember. It was during the war. The spring of 1918."

"And he made no effort to be friendly with his neighbors?"

"He was polite. We all are. But we have no desire to befriend one another."

He wondered why she lived here, alone and with no interest in her neighbors.

"And so there's nothing more you can tell me about Mr. Partridge that might help us find him or learn what's become of him?"

"I have no idea what he did with his time or where he went when he wasn't here. I've told you."

"We have reason to fear he may be dead."

She heard him but seemed untouched by the news. "I'm sorry to hear it," she said, but it was perfunctory, good manners coming to the fore. "I've answered your questions. Good day, Mr. Rutledge."

Rutledge accepted his dismissal, but said on the threshold, "Did you know—or hear—what Mr. Partridge did for a living?"

"He appeared to be unemployed. That's all I can tell you."

Rutledge thanked her and left.

He went back to Quincy's cottage and knocked again.

This time the man came to the door and stepped aside to let him in. "Making the rounds of the neighborhood, are you?"

"In a way," Rutledge answered him. Dublin got up from a pillow by the fire and stretched before eyeing Rutledge with suspicion. "I see you're still feeding Partridge's cat."

"She doesn't bother me, nor I her."

Rutledge opened the folder. "Is this Partridge?"

Quincy looked at the sketch. "Yes. Yes, it is. You've found him then. If that's what you came for before."

"We think we might have, yes. He's dead. His body was lying in an old ruin, left for the caretaker to stumble over. There's a possibility that he was murdered."

"Good God!" He seemed genuinely shocked.

"Did he have enemies, that you knew of? I gather you knew him better than most."

"First of all, I'd like to know why you're here asking so many questions," Quincy said, drawing back and letting Rutledge close the folder.

"I'm with the police, you see. Inspector Rutledge, Scotland Yard."

"So your interest in the White Horse was all a ruse."

"No, I am interested in it. I always have been. But in other things as well."

"I see. This is now an *official* inquiry. My neighbors won't care for that, I can tell you!"

"Why not?"

"You know very well why not. We all have something to hide. Perhaps not murder, but something that to us is just as powerful."

Lepers all, indeed. "Perhaps you'd like to tell me what it is you must hide."

Quincy laughed. "I didn't kill Partridge. That's what I can tell you. The rest is none of your business."

"Besides the care of the cat, what did you talk to Partridge about?"

"My birds, if you must know. Oh, you've seen them in the other

room. I'm no fool. But he was curious about them, and wanted to
know where they had come from."

"I'd like to see them."

"Oh, yes?" He crossed to the inner door and flung it open.

Rutledge stood there, stunned.

Hamish, in the back of his mind, was speechless.

Rutledge had never seen such an array of birds—all of them dead,
yet perched on twigs or railings or stones, like so many toys that with a
turn of the key would dance and twitter and sing, to please a child.

Every shape and size, blazing with color and their eyes sparkling
like shoe buttons in the light from the windows, they seemed to watch
Rutledge.

"I have every right to them, you know. I brought them back to England under a license."

"Were they alive then?"

"No, of course not. I spent years collecting them. I think I was
slightly mad at the time, certainly I wasn't fully in my right mind. It
had become an obsession, you see. To find them and capture them
and mount them. It gave me something to do, a reason for living.
That's a keel-billed toucan over there. Next to him is a fiery-billed
trogon. You should see them flying about the trees. And that's a rufous
motmot. The chestnut one just there, with yellow in his tail, is a Mont-
ezuma oropendola. The little green one is a red-headed barbet. That's
a resplendent quetzal, with the long tail, and the bigger blue one is a
white-throated magpie-jay. The Jabiru stork is just behind it. And the
very small ones are hummingbirds. Marvelous little creatures. My
favorite is the little snowcap, the purple one with the white head. We
don't have them in this hemisphere. A shame. You see them dart about
flowers like tiny fairies, wings beating so quickly you glimpse only a
blur, and when the sun catches them, they're like tiny jewels. I'm told
that the Inca kings wore cloaks made from their feathers."

"Where do they come from? South America, I should think."

"Most of these are from Central America. The one with what

looks like a worm in his beak is a three-wattled bellbird. Over there is
the crimson-collared tanager. He was one of my first successes. The
odd one with the large eyes isn't an owl, it's the common potoo." He
seemed to enjoy naming his prizes. Dublin had slipped in behind the
two men and was staring at the array of color. Indeed, it reminded
Rutledge himself of a feathered rainbow.

Hamish said, "My granny would say he's bewitched."

"What took you there? An interest in these birds?"

"Good God, no. I hardly knew one species from another. I went
there to hire myself out as an engineer on the construction of the Panama Canal. The first try, the one that didn't succeed. In the end most
of us came down with malaria or yellow fever, and we hardly knew
what we were about."

"But you stayed."

"I stayed because there was nowhere else to go. I trekked through
jungle looking for ruins and gold. I climbed volcanoes and dragged
myself through caves. I reasoned that the Spanish couldn't have found
it all. But they must have done. All the gold I saw was on the high
altars of churches, great mountains of it, ceiling to floor. Nothing like
it in England. I just stood and stared at the first one I came across. I
worked for a time translating invoices and bills of lading for a coffee
plantation outside a place called Antigua, then moved on to manage a
banana company's plantation on the Caribbean coast. It wasn't a life
I'd recommend."

Rutledge said as Quincy reached out to smooth the wing of one
of his specimens, "With that background, you must have been in de-
mand."

"Oh, it wasn't as exciting as it may sound," he went on dryly.
"Sometimes I guided people coming out to look at land. I learned to
use a foot loom in a village on the side of a volcanic lake. Atitlán, it
was. Whatever came to hand. By that time I was drunk most of the day
and all of the night, and finally I went to see a shaman, to find a way
to sober up. Saint Maximón, they called him. Only it wasn't a man, it

was a lump of wood draped in shawls and wearing a black hat. They'd told me he was wise. I brought cigars and wine and a watch I'd stolen, as gifts. The room was dark, filled with incense and smoke, and I thought I'd suffocate before my turn came. The man who interpreted for him—it—told me that my salvation was in the colors of the rainbow. I thought him as mad as I was."

Satisfied that all was well with the bird, he added, "Then I remembered the birds, and the more I thought about them, the more the obsession grew. I went back into the jungle for them, and up and down the coast, and climbed into rain forests and sailed down rivers, looking for them."

"What did you intend to do with them? Bring them back to a museum?"

Quincy laughed. "Hardly that. No, I tell you it was an obsession. I just wanted them. And then one day I realized that they were all dead. Not flying about, not mating, not bringing up their young or foraging for food. They were *dead*. And I never touched another drop of whisky. I was stone-cold sober, and I had this enormous collection of dead things in my house, and I realized I wanted to go home. I sold most of them, kept these to remind me, and came back to England against all the odds."

"And so the wise man's prediction that your salvation lay in a rainbow was right. After a fashion."

"I don't know if it was his prediction or my liver. But I kept these to remember where I'd come from. And I've never killed anything since."

It was a remarkable story. How much of it had actually happened?

"Did you know Partridge before you came here to live?"

"Never clapped eyes on him."

It rang true, but Rutledge wasn't sure whether he believed Quincy or not. He thought, he's very likely a remittance man. Someone the family pays well to stay out of the country, where his behavior won't embarrass them. It would behoove him to lie if it meant trouble for the family.

And therefore the question might be, what had Quincy done before he left England that had to be hushed up?

But Rutledge said nothing of this, listening as Quincy rattled off the names of his precious birds, interspersing that with the story of his years in Central America.

It was as if the man had dammed up the past for so long that the pressure had been building behind it, the need to talk that sometimes made lonely people garrulous.

And Quincy seemed to realize this in almost the same instant, ushering Rutledge out of the room, picking up Dublin and taking her with him as he shut the door on his collection.

"Pay no heed to me," he said, trying to cover his lapse. "They were my salvation, those birds, and I'm fond of them."

"Back to Partridge," Rutledge said, and thought how appropriate the name was, in this house. "I think it's time I spoke to someone in his family. There was a young woman, and you suggested she might be his daughter."

"She favored him, although she was fair instead of dark. I have no idea where she lives. He didn't open the door to her when she came. From that you might reach the conclusion that there is no warmth between them."

"Does she live in Uffington, do you think?" It was the nearest town.

"I've never seen her there, but of course that's not proof of anything."

"I've also been told that he'd lost his wife."

Quincy's brows rose. "Indeed? Well, that could well explain why he's reclusive. And for all we know, when he disappears he's visiting her grave."

"I appreciate the help you've given me."

Quincy walked with him to the door. "What had friend Partridge done, to get himself murdered? He'd gone missing before."

"If I knew the answer to that, I wouldn't be here questioning his neighbors. He's an enigma. We know very little about the man."

"You might speak to Mr. Brady, then. He's shown an inordinate interest in Partridge and his whereabouts on previous absences. Most of us here try to keep our private life private, but when Brady came, he asked questions. It wasn't well received, I can tell you. And he's a nosy sod, sitting by his window day and night as if there's nothing better to do."

Not so much a helpful suggestion as a touch of revenge on Quincy's part?

"I'll bear that in mind." Rutledge was on the threshold when another thought struck him. "When is the post delivered here at the cottages?" He had seen no letters in Partridge's house, but that was not proof that none had come.

"In theory, around nine. But we seldom receive any mail, you see. Lepers don't. Nor do we write to anyone. Or if we do, it's posted in Uffington." His voice was suddenly bitter, as if this were a reminder of how completely he'd been cut off from his family.

He shut his door almost on Rutledge's heels.

Rutledge looked at the neat half circle of cottages, and thought to himself that murder could be done here, and no one would know except the other residents, and they would refrain from summoning the police until the smell of decay overwhelmed them.

He considered calling on Brady, but decided that this was not the time. As Quincy had pointed out, he'd already spoken to Slater and Mrs. Cathcart. Everyone was prepared for a visitor now. Better to let the matter appear to drop.

But there was a man standing in his front garden, watching Rutledge leave Quincy's cottage. If Rutledge had kept to his original itinerary, Number 3, between Partridge and Brady, would be the next cottage to be visited. And it seemed that the owner was outside, prepared to confront the interloper in their midst. His expression was hostile.

Rutledge was of two minds about the best approach, but the matter was taken out of his hands.

"What is it you want?" the man called to him. His voice was tense, as if his concern outweighed his caution. "Who are you? You were hanging about before, I've seen you."

Rutledge walked toward him, covering the distance in unhurried strides.

An elderly man, tall and slightly stooped. Rutledge guessed his age to be seventy. Still vigorous, but already beginning to feel the tug of Time.

"My name is Rutledge," he said, the folder ready as he chose his opening. "I'm looking for Mr. Partridge. Perhaps you can tell me where I might find him?"

"Partridge, is it? I don't believe you. You never stopped at his door. First Slater, then Mrs. Cathcart, after that Mr. Quincy. But not Partridge. Not at all."

"Yes, I'm afraid he's not there. That's why I didn't go to his door. Do you know him well, Mr. . . . ." He paused, waiting for a name.

"Willingham." Grudgingly.

"Mr. Willingham. Do you know how I can find Mr. Partridge's solicitor? Or failing that, any of his family?"

"What are you selling?" Willingham eyed the folder.

"I'm not selling anything. This is a drawing—"

"Then why don't you go away and leave the rest of us alone? We don't trouble Mr. Partridge and we don't expect Mr. Partridge's visitors to trouble us."

"Does he have visitors?"

"If he does, I don't stare out my window looking to see who they are. Now be off with you, Rutledge, or whatever your name is. We don't care for the likes of you here."

"I'm afraid you'll have to put up with my presence, unpleasant as it may be, until you've answered my questions."

"Then I'll summon the police and have you removed."

"I *am* the police, Mr. Willingham. From Scotland Yard."

Willingham stared at him. Then without another word, he turned on his heel and went inside his cottage, slamming the door in Rutledge's face.

For a man eager to summon the police, Hamish was pointing out, "he was no' very happy to find one on his doorstep."

"Interesting."

Rutledge turned and walked back the way he'd come, climbing the hill of the White Horse and looking down on the cottages from the heights.

He wondered what Miss Tomlin would think of what had become of her charitable gift. She had considered it a sanctuary. And perhaps in a way it had turned out to be one after all.

But the question now was how to go about tracking down Partridge's daughter. Without going back to Martin Deloran and asking him for the information.

"He willna' tell you that," Hamish warned him. "It wouldna' be wise to ask in that quarter."

Where had Partridge lived before coming here in the spring of 1918? What sort of work had he done, and where was his family?

There was the off chance his daughter might pay another call, but Rutledge thought it was unlikely after being turned away.

And so where to start?

If Sergeant Gibson at the Yard began making inquiries, it would attract attention in the wrong quarters.

Had Partridge been *in* the army? Was that Deloran's interest? He could have been drummed out for reasons even the army preferred to keep quiet. And that might explain the watcher, Brady. Whatever toes Partridge had trod upon, they were still very sensitive about what had happened. Better to let him die and be buried in Yorkshire as an unidentified victim of murder than bring the whole matter up again.

Did Partridge know about the watcher? Had he cared?

Was Gaylord Partridge, for that matter, his real name?

It was the first time Rutledge had considered that, although looking at Quincy's birds, he had been amused by the coincidence of "Partridge" and an aviary. Perhaps this man had thought so as well, and
on the spur of the moment, rechristened himself? It wouldn't be long
before Brady reported the new name to London.

It would also explain why Deloran had felt so certain that it was
safe to send Rutledge to Berkshire—it wasn't likely he'd learn more
than he should know, while he was searching for "Partridge." And
now, even if the other residents identified the face in the sketch as Partridge, that was as far as Rutledge could take the matter. Meanwhile
Yorkshire would soon see the missing man into a pauper's grave. And
there would be the end of it.

Gaylord Partridge would no longer be a problem for the War
Office.

But he was still very much a problem for the police.

If Deloran had his way, the daughter would never be told what had
become of her father. That might not matter to her now, but if there
was a will to be sorted, in time her father's fate would become important legally.

Martin Deloran be damned—Partridge hadn't walked back to that
cloister on his own, there was someone else involved. And whether the
man died by accident or was killed, Rutledge was determined to get to
the bottom of what had happened. If there was a murderer somewhere,
who could say if he'd killed before this, or if he would kill again?

II

Where to begin a search? The only information Rutledge had at his disposal was the small photograph on the dead man's desk.

He had no way of judging who the man and boy were, or even if one of them was Partridge. The photograph was not clear enough to tell. For all he knew the two people in it were close friends or even cousins. The possibilities were endless.

And yet—out of everything he might have owned before coming to this place—Partridge had chosen to bring only one personal possession with him: a framed photograph. It had mattered to him in some fashion to have it there.

Where then was the square in which the photograph was taken? Not in Uffington, Rutledge thought, ruling it out immediately. None of the houses there resembled that background.

"Anywhere in England," Hamish pointed out gloomily. "No' sae verra easy to find fra' what could be seen in yon photograph."

True. There were Georgian houses in Kent, to start with.

"the day we climbed the white horse..."

But not every market square in England possessed Georgian houses *and* a white horse cut into chalk that could be climbed on the same day as the photograph was taken in the town.

All right then, the second bit of evidence in hand. If the inscription was to be trusted.

What else was unique about this white horse, where he was standing? For one thing, it was the only one galloping with such elegant strides across its hill.

Most of the others he knew about looked more like cart horses.

What else, then?

Legend claimed that in the ninth century King Alfred had ordered this horse carved out of the hillside. It was, in fact, Iron Age workmanship, but the legend persisted.

There were any number of white horses in Wiltshire—it was famous for them.

Rutledge went down to his motorcar and dug maps out of the pouch on the door. He'd bought the set to serve him on walking holidays. Later he'd found it helpful driving.

He spread out the sheets for south England, found Salisbury Plain, and began running a finger up and down the adjacent squares in an orderly search, starting from the right.

When he came to the eastern boundaries of Salisbury Plain, he found a place to begin.

Westbury. The Bratton White Horse.

Which—legend said—King Alfred ordered to mark a victory over the Danes.

He had never been to Westbury. Did it have Georgian houses in its market square? It had been a wool town in its day, and made gloves as well, which meant there was money enough for handsome buildings to mark its success.

He shoved the maps back in the pouch, got out to crank the motorcar, and set off to the west, bearing south, stopping only for petrol. Along the way he scanned other town squares, but he saw nothing that would fit what he was searching for.

But when he drove into the center of Westbury, he had no doubt that he'd made the right guess. He not only found the marketplace but the exact building facing him in the late afternoon sun.

He had had no lunch and missed his tea as well, but he pressed on.

The main problem to solve now was how to go about proving he was right.

If he went to the police station, there would be questions. He wasn't ready for them. For that matter, what *could* he say? That he was giving his imagination free rein in a case that didn't exist? At least, not officially.

If he began asking about a man called Partridge in the shops, gossip would spread like wildfire. Perhaps to the wrong ears.

And the post office had rules.

That was still the best place to begin.

He arrived just in time to see the elderly man behind the grill putting up a sign.

CLOSED.

Rutledge called to him, and he reluctantly set the sign aside, mouth turned down, eager to be off to his late tea and comfortable chair.

Behind him on the floor lay a large, nondescript dog. Clearly both companion and bodyguard, because he lifted his head to stare up at Rutledge, sniffing the stranger's scent. Satisfied that all was well, he lowered his head to his paws once more and sighed, for all the world commenting on the delay in departure.

"The name's Rutledge. I've come down from London to find a Mr. Partridge. We haven't been able to reach him, and I wonder if you can tell me whether or not he's moved."

The postmaster regarded him sourly. "Moved, you say?"

"Yes. It's the only explanation we can come up with."

"I don't know of a Mr. Partridge hereabouts."

He reached for his sign again, but Rutledge said quickly, "I think we have the name right. I have a sketch here, perhaps you'd be willing to look at it?"

"What do you have that for?" The man's tone was suspicious.

Rutledge brought up the file without answering the postmaster and opened it.

"That's not Mr. Partridge."

"I thought you said Mr. Partridge didn't live in Westbury."

"I never said that. I told you I didn't know of a Partridge hereabouts."

"Then how can you be so certain this isn't Partridge's likeness?"

"Because it isn't. I just told you."

Rutledge was losing patience.

"Quite," he said. "Then perhaps you know the name of the man in this sketch."

"I do."

"Will you kindly direct me to his house?"

"You never told me why you have a drawing of him."

Rutledge had never been so tempted to take out his identification and tell the postmaster that this was police business and none of his. "I expect that's a family matter. No one could find a recent photograph."

"Then you should have said so."

"I should like to find Mr. Partridge this afternoon, if that's possible."

"I told you he wasn't Mr. Partridge." The postmaster's expression was smug. He was quite enjoying being bloody-minded.

"Who, pray, is he?"

"That's Mr. Gerald Parkinson, and he doesn't live in Westbury."

"Parkinson? Where does he live?"

"Between here and Dilton."

"Get to the point, if you will. Where shall I find him?" Rutledge's mounting anger must have shown in his face or his voice. The dog lifted his head again and stared.

The postmaster said, "Here, now, there's no call to be rude. Follow the main road south, and halfway to Dilton, there's a turning to the left. Take that for three miles, and you'll see the gates of the house."

"Thank you."

Rutledge turned on his heel and left. He took ten minutes to find himself a sandwich and a cup of tea, and then, blessing April's longer evenings, drove south out of town.

He found the turning, no more than a lane and not clearly marked, as if it led nowhere in particular. But it was reasonably well made, indicating traffic, and he passed first one and then another house—neither with gates—whose windows were golden in the early evening sunlight. The next house was surrounded by a low wall with a pair of white posts and a graceful white gate where the drive came down to the road. The gate was firmly shut.

There was a placard set into the right post, bronze, he thought. It said PARTRIDGE FIELDS in elegant script.

Rutledge stopped the motorcar, and Hamish startled him as he spoke.

"You will no' trespass." It was the British outrage at a stranger's encroachment. "The gate is closed."

"But apparently not locked. I'll walk up to the house and knock at the door, as any guest would. All very civilized."

Hamish was silent. Rutledge opened the gate and started up the drive. As in the other houses on this lane, tall shrubs lined the way, cutting off a view of the house. But when he reached the end of the plantings, he found himself in a circular drive before a Georgian brick house. There was a semicircular portico held up by slender fluted columns and a black paneled door reached by three shallow steps. He went up them, lifted the brass knocker, and let it fall.

It seemed, as he stood there, that it echoed through an empty house beyond, and no one answered the summons, though he stood there for a good five minutes, waiting.

He went down the steps and looked up at the shining windows, wondering if someone was there, looking down at him. Then he turned to his right and started around the house. There was a terrace on this side, French doors leading down to a French-style garden of roses and perennials. Beyond the garden was a square shrubbery of boxwoods, and he could see wrought-iron benches and a stone fountain inside the small sheltered garden they created. Inside the bowl of the fountain was a horse, head to one side, tail and mane flying. It was a lovely thing, but no water splashed over it. The fountain was dry.

He went on to the back of the house, and saw that the kitchen door was shut. No signs of servants going about their duties, the kitchen garden more than a little overgrown compared to the formal plantings, and the outbuilding doors were barred.

The house, for all intents and purposes, was closed up.

Rutledge came back to the French doors and stood with his hand shielding his forehead, trying to look inside. Dust sheets covered the furnishings, and even the small chandelier was swathed in what looked to be a pillowcase.

Why had Partridge—Parkinson—left behind this jewel of a house to live in a tiny cottage in the middle of nowhere?

Hamish had had enough of trespassing. Rutledge turned to go, with one last look over the gardens. Someone kept them up, though not the kitchen garden, and came here often enough to see that no weeds marred the symmetry of the beds or weather damaged the plants. There wasn't so much as a twig underfoot on the small well-mown lawns at the far side of the house, ringed by flowering trees. A croquet lawn? It was smooth enough for that. And a long pair of windows from what appeared to be a study looked out over the green carpet. There the draperies had been drawn and he could see nothing.

He took one last look at the house. It seemed to be standing there waiting for its owner, and if he was right, that the dead man in Yorkshire was Parkinson, then its owner could never come again.

Hamish said, "He lost his wife."

And that might have explained the man's exile—too many memories here to let him heal.

But it didn't explain his death.

Rutledge drove back to The Smith's Arms, too late again for his dinner. Mrs. Smith was waiting up for him, as if half afraid that he wasn't coming back, his account unsettled.

She said, "There, you're in. I was just tidying up a little. I'll be off to bed, then."

Saying good night, she mounted the stairs, and he looked into the bar before following her. It was already shut and dark.

He went up to his bed and stretched out fully clothed, too weary for more than that.

Why had Partridge—Parkinson—changed his name? To fit into his surroundings without attracting attention? But then that was the name that Deloran had given him too. Either Deloran was content to go along with Partridge's need for anonymity or it suited the War Office very well.

Who was he? What sort of man had he been before the spring of 1918? And what was it that had triggered this abrupt change in his life? Losing his wife, yes, that would account for much.

How had he made his living, to be able to afford a house of that size with well-kept gardens? Even if he was independently wealthy, he must have held some position during the war years. In industry, perhaps, or in some capacity with the military. Men with certain skills worked at code-breaking, others at perfecting aircraft and weaponry or translating documents. There was always a need for clever minds. Stage designers had turned their talents to creating camouflage patterns for ships and gun emplacements and even trenches as spotter planes flew longer sorties over enemy lines. The list was endless.

Was that why the army was concerned about his whereabouts? Had he worked in something that was still under wraps, and therefore his erratic behavior had drawn attention to the need to keep an eye on him? It seemed far-fetched.

This was April 1920. The war had ended in November of 1918. According to Mrs. Cathcart, Parkinson/Partridge had moved into his cottage in the spring of 1918. What might have seemed important in the waning months of the war when the outcome was still in doubt wouldn't explain Deloran's secretiveness now.

Rutledge gave it up and lay there staring at the ceiling, listening to the night sounds, an occasional vehicle passing on the road, a dog barking in the distance, and then the sudden patter of rain on the roof.

The fine weather had broken.

It was still raining when Rutledge woke up in the morning. Sometime in the night he'd changed out of his clothes and gone to bed, only half awake as he fumbled with the sheets.

Mrs. Smith was serving breakfast when he came down, and he discovered just how hungry he was. The warm charger she set in front of him was demolished in short order, and he sat there drinking his tea and eating the last of the toast.

The door opened and the thin man—Will, wasn't it?—with whom he'd played darts earlier in the week stepped into the inn and shook the last of the rain off his hat.

He nodded a greeting to Rutledge and went to find Mrs. Smith. Rutledge could hear their conversation over the banging of pots and pans.

When he came back, he had a Thermos of tea in one hand and a cup in the other. He sat down at Rutledge's table with a polite, "D'you mind?"

"Not at all," he answered. "Driving all night, are you?"

"More or less. The rain wasn't so bad at first, but by dawn it was heavier. I've stared at the road for longer than I like. It was coming to look the same, every curve and straightaway. Played darts since that night?"

"No opportunity."

"If my mother hadn't taught me my manners, I'd wonder aloud what a man of your stripe is doing here at The Smith's Arms."

"It's convenient."

"To what?"

"To nowhere."

The man smiled. "I know when to stop. She taught me that as well."

"I came here to solve a riddle," Rutledge said. "And it's not likely to be solved as easily as I'd hoped."

"About the White Horse? There's a legend, you know. That on certain nights it comes down to the Smithy to be shod."

"Indeed."

"There's more than a few say they've seen it. But I reckon they were not as sober as they claimed to be. Are you here to keep an eye on us? The lorry drivers?"

Rutledge laughed. "Hardly that. Should I be?"

"A man gets an itch between his shoulder blades sometimes and looks around to see who might be watching."

"Watching for what? Surely you can't be smuggling this far inland?"

"Smuggling? No. The war put an end to that, as a matter of fact. Ships couldn't put in to a small cove and off-load goods there. Likely to find a submarine staring back at them as they up-anchored. Or a coastal warden coming to see what they were up to."

He finished his tea and prepared to go. "I'm off."

"Ever see anything strange here at the White Horse? On nights you or your mates were driving through?"

Will grinned. "Like seeing it come down to be shod?"

"No, more human agency than spectral."

He shook his head. "It's quiet through here, which is why some of us choose this way. Better time, with the roads so empty." He walked to the door, then paused. "I was told not long ago that a fair woman in a motorcar was stopped at the side of the road, and she was crying. Close by Wayland's Smithy. The driver drew up alongside her motorcar and asked if there was aught wrong. And she said no, she was fine. He drove on, but he told me later he'd seen that motorcar before, and it wasn't a woman driving then."

"Where had he seen it?"

"Here. Outside the inn."

"How long ago did this happen?"

The driver shrugged. "A fortnight? More or less."

"Interesting story."

"I think it must be true. He's not the sort given to lying. He said she didn't look like a whore. Who knows? Since the war, they're bolder, aren't they? Not enough men to go around, like."

And he was gone, his lorry roaring into life and rolling down the road, spray from the tires throwing up mud and muck like a brown bow wave.

Rutledge watched him out of sight.

Now he had a second report of a fair-haired woman in the vicinity of the Tomlin Cottages. Difficult to connect this one with the woman who had knocked at Parkinson's door. Still—it could mean that she'd come back to try again and encountered him along the road, where no one else saw the meeting. And the interview hadn't gone well.

Any query through Sergeant Gibson at the Yard about Parkinson's family would surely jangle tins on the wires that directly or indirectly reached Deloran. And then Deloran would have Rutledge back in London and on the carpet.

It was one thing to pursue a man who didn't exist. Quite another to look into the past of one who not only existed but was also safely dead.

What, then, were his choices?

Hamish said, "Return to London."

That made sense. He hadn't been able to contact Sergeant Gibson to see what had turned up about Henry Shoreham. And there was still the nameless victim on Inspector Madsen's hands to be officially identified. Not to mention the mystery of why Partridge or Parkinson had died in Yorkshire. The best place to draw these threads together was in London.

Hamish said, "A man could bribe a lorry driver to take away a body. It wouldna' be the first time sich a thing was done."

"If Partridge had been found by the road, I'd agree. But what lorry driver would risk carrying a dead man deep into Fountains Abbey's ruins, and setting him down by a cloister wall?"

"Ye ken, it would depend on how much the man was offered to take sich a risk."

And if that was the case, the driver had long since vanished into a new life.

"There has to be some trace. Somewhere."

He hadn't been aware he'd spoken aloud. Mrs. Smith stuck her head around the door and said, "More toast, sir?"

"Thanks, no. I'll be leaving in two hours. But first there's something I must do."

"I'll have the accounting ready for you when you come back."

"Thank you." He folded his serviette and set it beside his plate. *Where to begin?* That was always the policeman's dilemma. It could spoil chances as well as open doors.

He went up to his room, packed his valise, and then left it on the bed.

The rain was heavier now, and he could feel it across his shoulders, through the wool of his coat. He thought of the old cliché about April showers. Last April he had hardly known who he was or where he was. Had he come this far in only a year? If it had rained at all last April, he couldn't remember it. At the clinic the days ran into one another, and the nights were torments.

The cries of other disturbed patients in the darkness, nothing to distract his churning mind, no routine to force him to shut down his memories, nothing between him and a fear so great he couldn't close his eyes. That was before he learned that Hamish couldn't follow him into sleep. And so he had fought sleep, he had paced the floor of his room until his feet were numb and his legs ached, and still he walked. Anything to stave off sleep. He'd even pinched his arms until they bled, to keep himself awake. And then, at dawn, he would fall into a stupor and sit in his chair staring at the wall, a sleep of sorts, but never deep enough to dream.

Night after night. And in the rooms around his, other men suffered as well, banging on their walls, crying out for something to stop the anguish—a true madhouse of fear that was worse than anything found in an asylum.

The doctors had had to keep him drugged to let him sleep, and if he could have found the powders the sisters brought him, he would have swallowed them all, to end it. Not a bad way to die, a way where dreams couldn't follow him.

He cranked the motorcar and got in, sitting there shaking. It had nothing to do with the rain.

Hamish said roughly, "Aye, that was the heart of it. You wanted to die. I wanted to live. And we neither of us got our wish."

"And so we're damned, both of us, because God got it wrong. I wish you had lived and I had died. I would have come to haunt you, and when you married your Fiona, I would have been the skeleton at the feast."

"No," Hamish said, his voice cold. "I would ha' forgotten you, and left you rotting in France."

12

Rutledge wasn't sure how he had driven to the Tomlin Cottages. When his mind cleared, he was there, the motor still ticking over quietly and the White Horse washed clean in the rain.

He got out and walked to one cottage he hadn't called on yet. He knocked on the door and waited.

It was opened finally by a broad-shouldered man whose prematurely white hair was brushed back from a young face. It was hard to judge his age, but when he spoke, it was clear that he was of a class that possessed Victorian manners.

"Good morning. Are you lost?"

Rutledge introduced himself. "I'd like to ask you a few questions," he went on. "Mainly about one of your neighbors, Mr. Partridge."

"Silly name," the man said. "I should think he dreamed it up. We're not a friendly community, you see. I've often wondered how many of us use the name we were born with. Come in out of the rain, man."

He stepped aside and allowed Rutledge to enter the main room of the cottage. It was a parlor, with a Georgian desk in one corner and a tall shelf of books along the inner wall.

"Singleton is the name," he continued. "Tell me why you've been looking for Partridge."

"You know he was away, then?" Rutledge asked, taking the chair offered him. "His friends have been anxious about him."

"Were they indeed? I shouldn't have thought he had many friends. No one ever comes to call." He smiled, the austerity of his face relaxing. "I can see the horse from my desk, and his cottage as well. We have very little to occupy us, you see, and while none of us is anxious to have his own business bruited about, we are curious about our neighbors to the point of nosiness."

"There was, I understand, a young woman who came to his door."

"Yes, I remember. But she wasn't admitted, and I found myself thinking that she had stopped to ask directions. She never came again, you see."

It was a possibility that Rutledge hadn't considered.

In the pause, Singleton asked, "In the war, were you?"

"France," Rutledge answered.

"Then you were lucky to survive. I salute you. It was quite different in my war. Skirmishes in the Empire mostly, though some of them turned nasty of course. For the most part we played polo, set a good example, and dined rather well."

"India?"

"For the last ten years. I spent some time at the Khyber Pass, for my sins. The tribesmen were a wretched lot, troublesome in the extreme, and knew the country far better than we did. Keeping them bottled up was a bloody business, any way you looked at it."

Rutledge gestured to the cottage. "This is not the England you fought for."

It was a statement.

Singleton shook his head. "Sadly, no. It's far from that. We learn to cope, you know, it's what we're trained to do. I'm writing about my experiences. Not for publication, you understand, but for my own satisfaction. We're too busy living to fully understand our lives, you see. Where we came from, where we were going. What went wrong. It's a way of making sense of the past." As if he'd said enough about himself, he changed the subject. "Is there anything else I can tell you about Partridge? We spoke, the usual platitudes—'good morning, lovely weather we're having, I see your hollyhocks were knocked about by the wind last night, yes, a pity isn't it, cold enough to be thinking about a fire again, heavy mist this morning, wasn't it.' Nothing of consequence."

"Was he interested in the chalk horse on the hill?"

"Strange that you should ask that. I sometimes saw him standing in front of his door, staring up at it at odd times of the day. Or by those trees just down the lane, where he could see the beast at night. It has an ambient glow, you know. Starlight, I suppose. I'm sure most of us have noticed that. Slater, the young smith, is fascinated by it as well. I expect we are all aware of the horse in one way or another, living here. But some more than others."

"I'm told Partridge left a time or two, for several days. Did you see him leave? Or return?"

"I don't think he wanted us to know when he went away. The chap in Number Nine takes care of the cat when it comes to him for food, but there's no formal announcement about leaving. He's there and he's not there."

"Any idea where he might have gone on these occasions?"

"Good Lord, no. We don't pry. Not in that way. If it can't be seen at a distance, then we leave it alone."

"That makes for good neighbors," Rutledge said dryly.

"Actually it doesn't. One of us could die here and no one would wonder, until the smell reached him. Have you spoken to the man in Number Four? He seems to spend an inordinate amount of time studying Partridge's cottage. I've seen him at his window, using field glasses."

Number 4 was Brady's cottage. Deloran's man.

"No, I haven't. I've just stopped at the cottages closest to Partridge's."

"Yes, we've all seen you coming round. I had wondered when it would be my turn."

Rutledge smiled. "I've called on a few of the residents, yes. Quincy, Slater, Mrs. Cathcart, Willingham—"

"He gave you short shrift, didn't he? I think I've spoken to him fewer times than I spoke to Partridge."

"—and there's Brady. Who are the other two?"

"There's Miller in Number Seven, just up from Mrs. Cathcart. He's a curmudgeon by nature and we leave him alone. I'd go to anyone else before him if I needed help. And the last of our happy little family is Allen. My neighbor in Number Six. He would have made our dear patroness proud. I'm told he's dying of tuberculosis. Sometimes of a summer's evening, one can hear him cough. Not precisely leprosy, but a wasting disease, nonetheless."

"I appreciate your time, Mr. Singleton," Rutledge said, rising. "And I'll be on my way. I have business to attend to in London. But I expect to be back before long. If you see anyone at Mr. Partridge's door, make a note of it."

"I shall, if the occasion arises." Singleton saw Rutledge to the door and added, "I hope you conclude your business with us shortly. We've all secrets here, and none of us enjoys the attention of strangers."

"I'll bear that in mind," Rutledge replied, and before he was five paces down the path, the door behind him was quietly closed.

Hamish said, "We're no' what you'd call sociable in the Highlands, but we're no' sae unfriendly as this lot."

"As he said, they have secrets. Not necessarily murder, but to them just as important."

"Aye. Important enough to kill for?"

It was a thought that had already occurred to Rutledge, sitting in Singleton's tidy parlor.

But how would any of these eight householders manage to take a body to Yorkshire?

"Partridge has a motorcar."

"And it's still here."

"Aye, so it is. But that doesna' mean it never left."

Rutledge settled his account with Mrs. Smith and turned the bonnet of his motorcar toward London.

He hadn't been in his flat five minutes when he saw the note propped up on the small table by his bed.

It was in Frances's handwriting and said only, "If you are home to read this, call Gibson at the Yard."

She had been to his flat in his absence and found a messenger on his doorstep. What had brought her here? Simon Barrington? A need to talk to someone? Another invitation to a dinner she didn't want to attend alone?

Rutledge put the thought aside and looked at the time. He could just catch Sergeant Gibson, if he hurried.

Turning on his heel, he went back to his motorcar and drove to the Yard.

Gibson was just coming down the walk as Rutledge was looking for a space in which to leave his vehicle.

The sergeant recognized him at once and came to the nearside of the car. He was a big man, and he bent down to see Rutledge's shadowed face.

"There's trouble," he said.

"Bowles?"

"Not this time. For one thing, I couldn't find Henry Shoreham. No one has seen him since he left Whitby. Vanished from the face of the earth."

Damn.

"You're quite sure?"

Gibson drew back, offended. "I'm sure."

"Sorry. I meant to say, given the case in Yorkshire, that this is the worst possible news."

"That it is. For one thing, if he's nowhere to be found, he can't speak for himself. And Inspector Madsen has taken it in his head to send his men for the schoolmaster, to help in his inquiries."

Rutledge swore again. "I told Madsen the book on alchemy had nothing to do with the dead man."

"He said as much. But since no one can produce Mr. Shoreham, Inspector Madsen is convinced he's the victim."

"And what does the Chief Constable say? Or Bowles, for that matter?"

"They're reserving judgment."

There was no point in going to Deloran. He'd washed his hands of this business. He would say now that since Partridge hadn't died in Yorkshire, there must be some truth to Madsen's suspicions. And leave Crowell to deal with the consequences.

But where was there any connection between a man named Parkinson, from Wiltshire, and Albert Crowell? Partridge—Parkinson—hadn't attacked Mrs. Crowell in Whitby. The man Shoreham had been taken into custody; he was a clerk, known in his community. He'd admitted his responsibility.

But turn the coin the other way—

Rutledge said, "Do we have a photograph of Shoreham? Was there one taken when the newspapers carried the story about Mrs. Crowell's injuries?"

"I've not been told there were any."

All right then, look at it from a different perspective, Rutledge told himself.

In the dark, how much did Henry Shoreham resemble Gaylord Partridge or rather Gerald Parkinson? Could a man with a grudge mistake one for the other?

But then where had he taken his victim to kill him? Not to the school. And Parkinson hadn't died along the road. Why, when the evidence might in the end point in his direction, had Crowell left the body in the ruins of a medieval abbey, where it was bound to be found, and only miles from where he lived?

Was he so arrogant that he didn't believe a connection would be made? Or when he realized he'd killed the wrong man, had he felt sure he was safe?

Hamish said, "There's Mrs. Crowell. He would ha' done his best to keep her out of it, even if she'd killed her tormenter."

Rutledge didn't relish the long drive back to Yorkshire. But there was no other choice now. *Damn Deloran!*

"Is Bowles sending anyone north?" he asked Gibson.

"He sent a constable to see if you'd returned home."

"Then I'll report to him first thing in the morning." He said good-bye to Gibson and went back to his flat.

There he found Frances sitting in his parlor drinking his whisky.

She lifted her glass to him. "I saw your valise by the door. So this time I stayed."

"I'm leaving tomorrow for Yorkshire."

She pretended to pout, pursing her lips and looking at him out of the corner of her eyes. "I might have known. Here my life is in total crisis, and you're nowhere to be found."

"How's Simon?"

The pretense vanished. "Would that I knew."

"Frances."

She put down the glass. "No, I didn't come for a lecture. I just needed to hear a friendly voice."

"Frances," he said again, but in an entirely different tone.

"I don't want to talk about it. Take me to dinner and make me laugh."

He rephrased her response. "Would that I could."

"I sometimes do wish that Mother had had a large family."

Rutledge laughed. "All right, dinner it is. Let me change." But at the door to his bedroom, he stopped. "Do you know a Gerald Parkinson?"

"Parkinson? No, I don't think I do." Her interest sharpened. "Should I?"

"I doubt it. I ran across the name in Wiltshire, and I didn't want to ask the Yard who he is. At least not yet."

"Forget him for one night. I'm sure he's not going anywhere at the moment."

As he went through his door, he said to himself, "No, he's not going anywhere. He's dead. And I don't know for certain what name will be on his stone."

Dinner was quiet, Frances in a mood of reminiscence and Rutledge distracted by his thoughts and Hamish's crushing presence. Hiding his demons from his sister proved to be trying.

But the next morning he presented himself at the Yard, found a glowering Bowles waiting for him as he walked down the passage toward the Chief Superintendent's door, and with a sinking heart, followed him into his office.

"Well? I'll not be made a fool of, Rutledge. Who's this dead man stirring up trouble in Yorkshire?"

"I've reason to believe he's one Gaylord Partridge, who also answers to the name of Gerald Parkinson. His neighbors and a postmaster confirm that."

"And Inspector Madsen has reason to believe he's one Henry Shoreham. He can't be both, damn it!"

"I'll go to Yorkshire and get to the bottom of it."

"See that you do. Who's Gerald Parkinson, when he's at home? Never heard of him."

"He's from Wiltshire. He's known there, he has an estate there.

For some reason he left it and moved to Berkshire, not far from Uff-ington, content to live in a small cottage under a different name. His neighbors found him aloof, and none of them seems to know he had a past different from the one he's given out to them. Which is precious little."

"Are you certain this sketch of yours is a good likeness? You'll look a fool and so would I if it's off the mark."

"No one in Yorkshire admitted to recognizing the body—or the sketch."

"Humph." Bowles rubbed his eyes. "Well, it's time to get to the truth. Find out why Inspector Madsen is hell-bent on causing trouble. Or what he knows that we don't. Either way, settle it. Don't come back until you do."

"I'll do my best."

"No, man, you'll do more than your best. If we're to have a hornet's nest burst about our ears, we want to make certain we can survive it." He leaned forward in his chair. "I have no more use for this Deloran than you do. I don't like outsiders meddling in an inquiry, and above all I don't relish being made to look a fool. Do you understand me?"

Bowles had been an unexpected and unwilling ally when they faced a common enemy in the War Office. Now he was back to his irascible self.

Rutledge took a deep breath. "I'm fairly certain Deloran is hiding information that might make our work easier. But I can't find a way to get at it without bringing Partridge to his attention again."

"If you're asking me to beard the lion in his den, you've another think coming. You're expendable, Rutledge. And don't you forget it."

During the long drive north, Rutledge had much on his mind, and there was only Hamish to break the silence that pursued him mile after mile. When, the next morning, he pulled into Elthorpe, he had the odd feeling that nothing had changed since his first arrival only days ago. As he switched off the motor, he could have sworn the same faces were on the street, the same wares displayed in the shop windows, and the same rain clouds hovered in the distance. He sat for a moment looking at nothing, considering how best to say what must be said to Inspector Madsen.

A cold wind blew across the dales and into the narrow streets, reminding him that here April had not brought the same spring softness that was awakening the south of England.

Finally he got out of the motorcar and crossed the road to the police station.

There was a distinct pause in conversation when he entered and asked for the inspector.

Madsen was not pleased to see him. He met Rutledge's gaze with righteous hostility as he came through the door, waiting for him to speak first.

"I've been told that Albert Crowell has been taken into custody."

"Oh, yes, you explained away that book on alchemy very well. It's harder to explain away Henry Shoreham's disappearance less than a week before we found our corpse in the abbey."

Rutledge said, "I've had a positive identification of your victim. He lived in Berkshire, and as far as I know, never met Alice Crowell."

"From a sketch."

"You yourself saw both the sketch and the victim. Are you telling me that the sketch is faulty?"

"Then what was your Berkshire man doing, hanging about in Yorkshire?"

"I don't have the answer to that. Yet. My sergeant told me," Rutledge went on, "that Shoreham had left Whitby shortly after the Crowells refused to press charges against him, and no one has seen him since. Where has he been, these last few years?"

Madsen sat down in his chair and leaned back, suddenly smug. "London isn't as thorough as a good Yorkshire man can be when he puts his mind to it. We ran Shoreham to earth in the village of Addleford, living quietly with a cousin. Only, he went to stay with another cousin, and vanished. *This* cousin, one Lewellyn Williams, swore he never arrived. And he left Addleford because a family from Whitby moved there and he feared he'd be recognized."

"Why didn't one or the other of these cousins raise the alarm when Shoreham failed to arrive in Wales? Surely they were concerned about him?"

"The one in Wales thought Shoreham had changed his mind about coming just then. The one in Addleford thought he was snug in Wales. Constable Pickerel got the distinct impression that the cousin in Addleford hadn't been in any great hurry to contact Williams."

"How did Crowell find Shoreham, if it was impossible for the Yard to locate him?"

"It's our view that Crowell ran into him quite by chance. Lucky for him, not so fortunate for Shoreham. The Crowells weren't living in Dilby when the accident happened. Shoreham had no way of knowing his danger."

"For the sake of argument, let's say you're right—"

Madsen smiled. "Very well."

"Where did Shoreham die? And why did Crowell take the risk of leaving him in the abbey ruins? It was not the cleverest thing to do."

The legs of Madsen's chair smacked the floor with a sharp thump. "Early days yet, Rutledge, but we'll have that soon enough."

"I'd like the name of the cousin in Addleford. And the direction of the Welsh cousin as well."

"Where's the need? We've been over that ground already."

"So you have," Rutledge responded with more patience than he felt. "But the Yard will require assurances that all the evidence has been thoroughly examined. More to the point, we appear to have some confusion about identity. I'll remind you that Mrs. Crowell didn't recognize the drawing, and Crowell himself said he couldn't identify the body, when he was taken to the doctor's surgery."

"Well, they *would* say as much, wouldn't they? Crowell because he had no intention of drawing attention to himself, and Al—Mrs. Crowell, that is—because she's not about to betray her husband."

Rutledge saw something in Madsen's face as he said the last few words that was very different from his manner to this point. "Nothing in *my* conversations with her made me feel she would lie for her husband's sake. And what about Crowell's feelings about killing? They're on record."

"This is the man who ruined his wife's face, for God's sake. It's all very well to make a public display of forgiving the bastard, but deep down inside? Crowell was probably biding his time for a bit of quiet revenge." Madsen shook his head. "I don't hold with conscientious objectors. I never have. They were perfectly willing to let someone else die in their place, weren't they? I'll stay home, cozy by my hearth, thank you very much, and leave you to do the fighting!"

"I remind you he drove an ambulance."

"Yes, that's all very well. A bit of conscience overcoming him, for a guess." It was a sneer. "And Alice thought him quite the hero, didn't she, bringing back the wounded and saving lives. And those of us who had to carry on back in England, doing the job we were meant to do, were not good enough—"

Madsen stopped short, but not before Rutledge had seen more than he was meant to see.

Alice . . .

And those of us who had to carry on here in England were not good enough . . .

As Madsen struggled to rein in his temper, Hamish said, "Ye ken, he's jealous, and he canna' live with it."

The inspector looked away from Rutledge, his gaze going to a half-dozen folders lying on top of the table at his elbow. "It could be she's afraid to tell us what she really thinks. There's no getting around the fact that every time she looks in her mirror, the scar is there, staring back at her."

He picked up one of the folders and opened it. "Peter Littleton. That's the cousin in Addleford. And this man Williams lives outside Aberystwyth in a place called Hill Farm."

Rutledge took the sheet of paper that Madsen held out to him. "I'll let you know what I discover."

"Precious little, I'll be bound," Madsen said under his breath as Rutledge left.

Rutledge made a detour to Dilby, to find Alice Crowell. She was trying to keep the school open in her husband's absence. There were shadows under her eyes and a tightness in her face that spoke of her distress. The white scar seemed to shine in the morning light as if newly burnished by the reminders of how it had begun.

There was a flare of hope in her face as she saw Rutledge in the passage outside the bookroom, and she glanced beyond him to see if her husband was following in his wake. And then it vanished as she realized he was alone.

"Have you seen Albert?" she asked anxiously. "They won't allow me to speak to him."

"I haven't seen him. I'm sorry," he told her gently. "But he'll be safe enough where he is, until Inspector Madsen gets to the bottom of this business."

She shook her head. "But he won't do that, will he? Where's the point?"

Mrs. Crowell opened the door behind her and ushered him into the empty room. She indicated a chair for him, but he stood, as she did. There wasn't a great deal to be said by either of them.

"What's behind Madsen's dislike of your husband?" Rutledge asked, coming directly to the point.

"We were about to be engaged once. My parents didn't care for my choice and I was young, I listened to them instead of my heart. I realized later, when I'd met Albert, that they'd been wiser than I. But at the time I was heartbroken."

"I understand that Inspector Madsen has since married."

"Yes, that's true. But his pride was hurt when I had to tell him my father wasn't happy with the match. Father promised he'd speak directly to Harry. But you see, my father was in the army, and there was no opportunity. Harry—Mr. Madsen—wrote to him finally, but there was no reply. My mother, who was alive at the time, always thought that the war had prevented Papa from answering. I knew that wasn't true. He didn't want to encourage either of us. He felt I was making a poor choice. A working-class man."

"Is your father still living?"

"Yes. He's offered to come and fetch me now, but I won't leave Albert." She sighed. "I thought, when you first came here, that my father had sent you. I wrote to him when I saw how Albert was being persecuted. I asked him to intervene."

"And did he?"

"I don't know," she answered him frankly. "He's the colonel of an East Anglian regiment. I thought he might know someone, bring a little pressure to bear in the right quarters. But look how it's all turned out. I expect there was nothing he *could* do."

Her voice trailed off forlornly, and she looked at the windows. There was a bright sunshine outside, but it failed to light the room, as if sensing the despair that filled it.

Rutledge was tempted to ask her outright if she knew one Martin Deloran but thought better of it. Instead he approached the subject indirectly. "Do you know a man called Gaylord Partridge?"

"What an odd name. I should remember that, if we've ever been introduced. Should I know him?" Hope seemed to spring awake again. "Is there any way he can help me?"

"Later perhaps. And Gerald Parkinson. Did you or your father know him?"

She frowned, digging for the memory. "I went to school with girls by the name of Parkinson. They were much younger; we didn't have a lot in common. But they used to tell everyone the most absurd stories about their father. He was eccentric, if half of it was to be believed. Always tinkering with things. I can't think that he's the same person you're asking me about."

"I agree, it doesn't sound like it. Martin Deloran. Do you know him?"

"Deloran? No, that's not a name I recognize either."

"I'll do what I can for your husband, Mrs. Crowell, but don't count on miracles."

"But I told you—" she began indignantly.

"Yes, so you did. The fact is, you aren't a reliable witness. If the victim of murder is Henry Shoreham, then you have a reason to conceal your knowledge of him. Or anyone associated with him."

Her mouth was open to protest vehemently. He held up a hand to stop her.

"I understand. But you must examine this matter in the same way that the police must do. First a book is found by a dead man's feet, one that has your husband's name in it. That can be explained away very well. Then there's some reason to believe that Henry Shoreham disappeared shortly before the corpse was discovered. If the man in the sketch is Henry Shoreham, then you lied to me and to Madsen. If it isn't, then where *is* Shoreham? Let's look at it another way. Until we can identify the victim with absolute certainty, we must investigate all the possibilities. *Someone* is dead, and he deserves to have justice. The police are bound to see to it that he will."

Alice Crowell, no fool, looked at Rutledge with weary resignation.

"I don't know that this poor man will receive justice of any kind. He's too convenient a whipping boy, to make my husband suffer."

"Could Albert Crowell have killed him? Either because he was certain he was Shoreham or thought he looked like the man?"

Her gaze moved toward the books on the shelves. "He believes in forgiveness. He forgave Henry Shoreham, and when he has done that, he wouldn't take it back and kill the man." Her mouth took on a grim expression. "For some time after *this* happened," she touched her face, "I could have killed Henry Shoreham myself. I was asked to forgive him, and I said the words. But in the depths of my soul, I knew it to be a lie. And I hid it from everyone."

Her eyes came back to his face, as she added, "I wouldn't ask my husband to do murder for my sake. If Inspector Madsen wasn't so blinded by his own anger over my turning down his proposal of marriage, he'd realize that he has the wrong Crowell in custody. I'm the one who had the best reason to kill Henry Shoreham."

13

Addleford was a small dale village that had begun to shrink in the nineteenth century as men found work in the mills or mines. It had continued to shrink into the twentieth. On the outskirts of town were barns without roofs and houses with boarded-up windows. But the heart of the town, with its plain church and churchyard, its one pub and its tiny shops, seemed to be hanging on for dear life.

The houses on either side of the winding street were well kept and the white lace curtains in their windows were cheerful against the gray stone of the walls.

There was no police station here, but Rutledge went to that other source of gossip and information, the local pub. He ate tough beef with a mustard sauce and fresh baked bread, enjoying the peace and quiet of the small dining area next to the bar. The man who served him limped, one leg shorter than the other, giving him a swaying walk that spoke of years of pain. He set down the charger with Rutledge's food and went about his business, taciturn and without curiosity about the stranger who had walked in and asked if luncheon was still being served.

Hamish was telling him that this was a wild-goose chase. Better to leave the troublesome Henry Shoreham to Inspector Madsen.

But Rutledge wanted every loose end tied up before he went south again. And so as he finished his flan, he asked the man who brought it where he might find one Peter Littleton.

"He's the shoemaker, two doors down from the greengrocer. You have business with him then?"

"Indeed."

The barkeep looked at him. "He'll be finished his dinner in a quarter of an hour. He always goes home for it."

"Then I'll walk in the churchyard while I'm waiting." He paid his reckoning and went out in the chilly air. The churchyard's wall cupped a small purple flower growing in a crevice, and when he stopped to look at it, he recognized heartsease. It seemed forlorn there, as if it had lost its way from someone's garden.

Hamish said, "It's Fiona's favorite among the flowers."

Rutledge went through the gate and walked among the stones until he saw the shoemaker striding back to his shop.

Crossing the road after him, Rutledge waited until he'd opened the shop before going inside. The musical ring of a small bell above the door announced his presence, and the shoemaker raised his head from the leather he was trimming. He bore a faint resemblance to the dead man—around the same height, the same unremarkable shape of face, brown hair, and blue eyes. Nothing to set him apart from hundreds of other Englishmen.

I'm looking for Henry Shoreham," Rutledge said. "I'm told you can help me find him."

Littleton's face changed from the smile he used to welcome custom to a wariness that went deep.

"Who's asking?" He smoothed the leather with his fingertips, as if judging its quality without looking at it.

"Rutledge, Inspector, Scotland Yard."

The shop was redolent with the scents of leather, wood, and polish. A cobbler's bench sat by the window and there were lasts on the shelves against the back wall. Patterns lay on a table below. And two chairs, high enough to allow the shoemaker to work on the footwear of a client without squatting, were set into the near wall, facing the counter.

"He never went to trial for what he did." It was defensive, as if Rutledge had come to take Shoreham back to Whitby. "So it never ended, you might say. No one let him forget what had happened. There was the young woman of course, she suffered and was scarred, mind you, but Henry also paid dearly for his drunkenness. And he never set out to hurt anybody. He wasn't that sort."

"I'm not here to charge him. The problem is we can't seem to locate him at present. Is he still living with you?"

"If you've come this far, you know he's not here. Inspector Madsen will have told you."

"Quite. Why did Shoreham choose to come to Addleford? Because you were here?"

"Because he didn't have two pennies to rub together. They didn't want him back at the bank. Bad for business, they said. Everyone recognized him. There was nothing else he knew how to do but clerking. When no one would take him on and his savings ran out, he left Whitby and came to me to get back on his feet. But he couldn't get the hang of shoemaking, and then a neighbor of his from Whitby moved here as well, and the story was spread about again. He decided to go to another cousin in Wales. Sheep aren't easy to manage, but they don't have to fit someone's foot just right."

Hamish said, "Ye canna' judge how he felt about his cousin."

It was true, there was a distance in what Littleton was saying, as if he were discussing a stranger.

Rutledge asked, "When did he leave?"

"I could tell he'd made up his mind, and I let him go. And the house was crowded with seven people under our roof, I'll admit it. My wife was just as glad to see him move on. But then he's not her kin, he's mine."

"When did he leave?" Rutledge repeated his question.

"It must be getting on to a week, now." Littleton shrugged. "A fortnight even. One of the little ones has been ill. I've had more to worry about than keeping in mind when Henry set out. I had no way of knowing, see, that it would matter to have the exact day."

"Did Constable Pickerel or Inspector Madsen tell you there was a dead man at Elthorpe who might be your cousin? Surely that should have worried you."

"Constable Pickerel said nothing of that when *he* first came here. He was all for leaving for Wales straightaway. My cousin Llewellyn knew Henry was coming, but there wasn't a fixed date. You could have blown me over with a feather when the constable reported Henry never got there. Then Inspector Madsen came, going on about a dead man. I was afraid that it might be Henry. That he'd finally done himself some harm, out of remorse. That he never intended going to Wales."

"Yet you felt no need to travel to Elthorpe, to be sure?"

Littleton looked him in the eye. "It was the inspector telling me Henry was dead. Add to that, he'd never arrived in Wales, had he? So I believed what I was told. My going to Elthorpe wouldn't bring Henry back, would it? I have a wife and family to feed. A child that's ill, and the doctor is costing us more than we can pay. I have a shop that brings no money in when I'm not here to open it. Besides, we never had a suicide in our family. I'd not want that getting about."

"Who told you it might have been suicide?" Rutledge asked sharply.

"What else could it be? I know, the inspector was hinting that it was murder. As I explained to the constable, Henry was persecuted. It might have ended differently if he'd gone to prison instead, but the woman and her husband forgave him. That turned everyone in Whitby against Henry. When the law wouldn't punish him, everyone else did. There was a great outcry."

"You never considered the fact that Albert Crowell might have killed your cousin, that they ran into each other by accident, and Crowell took the chance offered to avenge his wife?"

"Then why did this man Crowell forgive him in the first place, if that's what he wanted to do?"

"To keep Henry Shoreham out of prison? To make sure he could be found and killed? Only he came here to Addleford and Crowell couldn't find him."

In spite of himself, Rutledge found that it made a certain sense—perhaps explained why Crowell had chosen to teach at Dilby. Looking for Shoreham. Madsen could easily make that case.

"That was before the *war*—a long time to wait to get even."

"Then you'll leave your cousin to a pauper's grave, and let the police sort out how he died?"

"I'll pay what I can for a decent burial. Inspector Madsen knows that. But I won't do more. Truth is, the scandal affected all our lives. Harboring Henry was what I had to do, because he was my blood. I'll not bring him back here and put him in the churchyard for everyone to stare at and remember."

Rutledge could hear Martin Deloran's callous dismissal of the dead man. Did no one care what became of him?

"An interesting point of view, Mr. Littleton. Still, I'll have to speak to your wife and your neighbors. I need to know precisely when Henry Shoreham left Addleford. How he was traveling, and in what direction."

"You're not understanding me. Henry kept to himself. Most particularly after the Jordan family moved to Addleford. I doubt my neighbors have clapped eyes on him since. He never came to town, went to church services, called in at the pub. He just sat in his room and stared out the window."

There was evasion here, almost a washing of the hands. Why?

Rutledge had brought the folder in with him and opened it now to pull out the sketch. "Perhaps you know this man?" he asked.

Littleton looked intently at the face. "He's the dead man?"

"Yes."

Littleton shook his head, then glanced up at Rutledge. "The description Inspector Madsen gave of the body was too close for comfort. The hairs on the back of my neck stood up. But this is like seeing Henry younger and happier."

"There's no cleft in this man's chin."

Littleton was rattled. "Should there be? I don't see it here, and Inspector Madsen never said anything about one."

"Shoreham didn't have one?"

"No."

Then either Mrs. Crowell had been mistaken, or she'd lied. It had been six years. And she had been in shock and pain at the time.

"Who else besides Crowell might have wished your cousin ill?"

"If you found Henry, he's dead by his own hand," Littleton answered stubbornly.

Rutledge considered the possibility that Littleton himself had killed his cousin. But judging the character of the shoemaker, he thought not. If the man went to prison or was hanged, who would support his family?

"Did Inspector Madsen tell you that this man, the one you see in this drawing, died somewhere else, not in the place where he was found?"

It was clear that Littleton didn't know what to make of this information. Inspector Madsen, for reasons of his own, had kept some facts of the case to himself.

"Here! I can't tell you what happened to him. He left my house, he told me he was going to Cousin Llewellyn in Aberysthwyth. Then along comes Inspector Madsen, saying he never got to Wales, that he was dead and lying in a doctor's surgery in Elthorpe. I've told the police all I can. You must ask him—Inspector Madsen—what this is all about."

Rutledge was again reminded of Martin Deloran, willing to give any name to a dead man for his own ends. But what end could Peter Littleton have, unless he'd killed Shoreham long ago and hidden the body?

Hamish said, "Ask yon cousin in Wales."

Blood was thicker than water . . . How far would Henry Shoreham's relatives go to protect him? Or be rid of him?

Rutledge said, "If this man in Elthorpe isn't your cousin—if you're obstructing the police in the course of their duties, it will go hard for you."

The threat registered in Littleton's eyes. But he answered only, "I haven't gone to Elthorpe asking about this dead man. It was Inspector Madsen who came to *me*."

The door opened and a woman walked in, her eyes red with crying. She stopped short as she saw Rutledge. "Peter. If you could hurry—?"

But before Peter Littleton could answer, Rutledge said, "Mrs. Littleton, is it? We've nearly finished our business, your husband and I. I was just asking him about his cousin."

Her gaze sharpened, whatever had brought her here quickly set aside. "Peter?" She didn't glance at her husband. She stood there trying to collect her wits.

"It's all right, love. This is Inspector Rutledge. He's come about Henry."

"But I thought they'd found a body and were satisfied." Her voice was accusing.

"So we were told. Here, see for yourself. This is a drawing of the dead man. Does it look like Henry to you?"

She took it and stared at it. "They're the same age," she replied after a moment, looking not at Rutledge but at her husband. "And the same coloring. I don't understand. I thought it had been settled?"

"He's come to tell me this man was murdered."

Mrs. Littleton gasped. "But—there must be some mistake. You didn't tell me—what did Henry have worth stealing? And he hadn't touched a drop of gin since that day in Whitby. How do they know he was murdered? You told me it was suicide. I don't understand."

She was begging for help, for reassurance. Her husband said, warningly, "We're trying to sort it out, Beth."

"Let it wait. I'm sick of Henry Shoreham. I've come to fetch you. The baby's worse, we must find the doctor."

Peter Littleton's face lost its color. He said, "Oh, God," and pushed past Rutledge to his wife. "Go home, love, I'll bring the doctor to you." And over his shoulder to Rutledge he said, "She's had whooping cough—"

And he was gone, leaving Rutledge to close the shop door behind them.

Rutledge spent half an hour asking round the village for Henry Shoreham, and met with a shake of the head. Most people had no idea that he'd gone.

"One to stay close to home," the greengrocer said. "Early on, I saw him a time or two in the evening, but not to speak to. You'd never guess he was in the house. When I went to make a delivery, he never came out to say good morning."

"He never came to services. Not even to his niece's christening," the rector told Rutledge. "Not a religious man, Peter Littleton said. But he ought to have been. If ever there was a man in need of prayer, it was that one. Looked like a ghost of himself, the way I remember him when Peter and Elizabeth were married."

A woman pushing a baby in a pram told Rutledge, "He was in the shop once when I stepped in to see about the heel on my best pair of shoes. But he didn't know what he was about, and so I told Peter. After that, he never came to work at Littleton's."

And a man sweeping the doorstep of the ironmonger's said, "I didn't know him well. He used to walk about at night, to stretch his legs. We talked once or twice, as I was taking Harriet out—she's my dog—and she would sniff at his shoes and growl, as if she didn't much care for him. Strange man. My wife was glad when he went away."

"When was that? Do you know?"

"I didn't even know he'd left until I'd asked Peter how he was getting on. And Peter said he'd decided to live with a cousin in Wales. Made sense. I doubt they had room in the house, and it was one more mouth to feed. Peter did his best, mind you. But it was a strain on the family."

"Were you ever told why he'd come here to live?"

"Fell on hard times, Peter said. I didn't press for more. It wasn't my business, or anyone else's. But my wife always thought he must have been in gaol somewhere, and afterward had nowhere to go. She said Peter was a good man to take on responsibility like that. She said that if Henry had nothing to hide, he'd be helping more in the shop or walking the children to school or coming to services of a Sunday. The Jordans said he'd been in trouble in Whitby. Attacked a woman."

He shook his broom against the wall of the shop to clean it, and went back inside. "Gossip, for all I know," he ended as he prepared to shut the door in Rutledge's face. "He mayn't have had anything to hide. But he'd have fared better, wouldn't he, if he'd been open about it."

Hamish said as Rutledge turned toward the motorcar, "He willna' be missed. Even by his cousin."

Which would go far to explaining Littleton's assumption of suicide, the decision to move to Wales notwithstanding. Good riddance, a body to bury, a family skeleton disposed of, and on Christmas or Easter, a prayer to be said in passing for Shoreham's soul. . . .

Reaching the motorcar, Rutledge decided to drive on to Wales without going back to Elthorpe today.

He spent the night in Shrewsbury, then crossed the border in a fine rain that seemed to wrap the river valleys in playful mist, rising now, then thinning, the great sweep of hillsides and heavy clouds barely visible before they were veiled again. He saw sheep sometimes, not yet shorn of their winter coat, huddling in the lee of whatever shelter they could find, but the land was empty save for the few towns he had to pass through. There were scattered farms at the end of long and winding lanes, and even they appeared to be deserted, as if all the people of Wales had gone away somewhere else. And yet it was a beautiful drive.

Aberystwyth sat on Cardigan Bay, the water curving into the town and a ruin of a castle standing out on the headland to the right. Rutledge stopped in the town only long enough for a meal in a small, dimly lit café where he was regarded with interest. Asking at shops that catered to farmers, he finally discovered where Llewellyn Williams lived. There were seven men of that name within a twenty-mile radius. He backtracked along the way he'd come until he found the lane leading into a village with an unpronounceable name. Beyond it he soon spotted the track that continued into the Williams farm.

It was a small house with a sagging slate roof, surrounded by outbuildings. As he stopped, a dog came out to sniff at his motorcar before baying toward the house. As a welcome it lacked a great deal, and although Rutledge, good with animals as a rule, did his best to befriend the dog, he thought it best to leave well enough alone after a tentative move to leave the motorcar won him a low growl.

After some minutes, a man came to the door. He was of medium height, thin, dark, nondescript. But he didn't resemble the sketch at all.

"Llewellyn Williams?" Rutledge called.

"What do you want with him?" It was wary, as if strangers weren't welcomed here.

"Call off your dog. I need to speak to you, and it's too wet to stand here shouting at each other."

The man hesitated. After a moment, he whistled to the dog and it came to sit grinning up at him. His hand went to its massive head, a gentle touch.

Rutledge walked across to him. "I'm Inspector Ian Rutledge, Scotland Yard. I've come in search of Henry Shoreham."

"What's he wanted for?" the man asked.

"He's done nothing more than disappear. His family is worried for him."

"I doubt it. He has no family to speak of. But I haven't seen him. I told another English policeman as much. If you'd spoken to him, it would have saved you a journey."

"You aren't Welsh." It was a statement.

Williams shrugged. "My family is—was. I moved to England when I was a child. My mother's cousin lives in Yorkshire. Littleton is his name. Henry was staying with him."

"But left to come and live with you."

"You can look about if you like. He's not here."

"So I'm told. There's a possibility that he was murdered."

Williams's eyebrows rose. "That other policeman simply told me he thought Henry was dead. He didn't say anything about murder."

"Yes, well, murder it was." He pulled out the folder with the sketch, trying to shield it from the rain. "Here's the dead man's likeness. Inspector Madsen has arrested someone for his murder."

Williams looked at the sketch for a long moment and then said with resignation, "You'd better come inside."

The house was plainly furnished, many of the pieces early Victorian. But it appeared to be comfortable enough, weather tight and warm with the coal fire on the hearth.

"How long have you lived here?" Rutledge asked with interest as the dog slumped down on the hearthrug and sighed.

"I inherited the property from my father's cousin. He had no children. Neither do I, but there it is, the house is mine. He ran sheep here, but I couldn't manage it. A neighbor offered me a good price for them, and I'm living on what I was paid for them."

"How well do you know your cousin Peter Littleton?"

"He's on my mother's side of the family. I haven't seen him in many years."

"And Henry, from Whitby? Did you see him often?"

Williams shook his head. "It's a long way to travel. We were never close."

"Yet you offered him houseroom here."

"Which he never took me up on. Just as well, I don't know how the two of us would manage. The house is large enough, but the money I have isn't. I don't know that I could afford to keep him."

"He left Addleford, to come here to you."

"And changed his mind, as far as I know. I expect he was walking or looking for a lift, and found another place he liked better. You drove here, you know how long a journey that would be. I'm not saying he's dead, mind you. He just never came to this part of Wales."

There was no anxiety over Shoreham's fate, no concern about the long walk across Wales, no interest in what the man might have encountered, poor and alone and with no friend to turn to.

"You never made any attempt to learn what had become of him? If he were ill, dependent on the charity of strangers, dead and buried somewhere as a pauper?"

Williams had the decency to look ashamed. "It's not that we don't care," he said hotly, "it's that life is hard enough without taking on another man's troubles. Henry isn't here. You can search the house, if you like. You won't find him. If I knew where he was, I'd want to help him, but I can't go searching half of England in the hope of finding him. There's not the money for it."

"And what about the man dead in Elthorpe? I could make a case that you and Peter Littleton between you tired of your cousin and killed him, leaving him to be found by strangers."

Williams's face paled, his dark eyes wide and alarmed. "But you can't do that. We've not touched Henry. We've not left him anywhere but where he wants to be—away from Yorkshire."

"Inspector Madsen has one Albert Crowell in custody, to be charged for Henry Shoreham's murder. There's evidence enough to see him hanged."

Williams sat down heavily. "You're lying to me."

"I'll bring Inspector Madsen to you, to confirm what I've said."

"But why would this—this Albert Crowell wish to harm my cousin?"

"Because Shoreham scarred his wife for life. You know this, it's the reason Shoreham is unemployed and living on the charity of his family."

Williams shook his head, shock still washing over him. "I know about the accident. That's what it was, an accident. Henry swore it. What do you want me to do, help you prove that this is Henry? I haven't seen him in years. Did you show this sketch to Peter? What did he say?"

"He avoided answering me. He cared as little for your cousin as you appear to do."

"No, that's not fair, it isn't a matter of caring. God knows—" He broke off, swallowing hard.

"If you pass off a dead man as your cousin, and Albert Crowell is hanged for it, what then? Henry Shoreham has done enough harm to the man and his wife, and this will compound it."

Williams began to cry, his face worn with grief. "Go away and leave me alone. I won't hear any more of this. It's all a trick, and I won't be taken in by it."

"Then I shall have you summoned for the trial. You can sit there and watch what happens, and then if your conscience pricks you, you can tell the court what became of your cousin." It was harshly said, and intended to be.

"I can't afford to come to Yorkshire. I have no money, it will break me."

"Better to break you than to hang an innocent man."

Rutledge had drawn his conclusions by this time. He knew what was coming and he braced for it.

"You can't do this to me, I've been punished enough. Leave me alone."

"Then you're a coward, Shoreham, and I'll have you in that court-room if it's the last thing I do."

He turned and walked through the door, the dog, hackles rising, coming to nip at his heels. The man did nothing to call him off. But Rutledge had just turned the motorcar to go back the way he'd come when Shoreham was in the doorway, calling to him.

"Stop—"

Rutledge paid no heed.

"For the love of God, wait!"

Rutledge braked but didn't turn. He could hear Williams splash-ing through the puddles to the side of the motorcar, his face ravaged.

"All right. I'm Henry Shoreham. Peter wrote me about the dead man, nobody knew who he was, even Inspector Madsen didn't. We thought—we thought if he was nameless, it wouldn't matter to anyone if we let the police think it was Henry. Me."

"How long have you lived here?" Rutledge asked again.

"For two years. Since my cousin Llewellyn died and left the house to me. I thought—I thought I could take his place, use his name, find work again, and live like a man and not someone else's dependent. Peter had done his best, but they couldn't keep me." He wiped the rain from his face. "Then two years ago a man from Whitby and his wife came to live in Addleford with her mother. They'd done their banking where I worked. They *knew* me. I couldn't stay on. I came here and looked after Llewellyn until he died, and I took his place. Peter pretended I was still there, in Yorkshire, and everyone believed him. They never saw me, I was known to be a recluse. How would they know if I'd gone away or not?"

"Your cousin couldn't go on lying forever. You hadn't expected him to do that."

"We played a little game. He'd tell the rector I'd seen him pass by the house. Or the butcher that I'd appreciated the bit of beef for Sunday dinner. But Peter's children were getting to an age where someone might ask them how I fared. We were casting about for a way to explain I'd gone to London to search for work when the constable came looking for Henry Shoreham. They told Peter no one knew the dead man, and he was quick to see how it might help me to be dead and buried. We didn't know the Crowells were back in Yorkshire."

"You were interfering with a murder inquiry. It was a stupid thing to do."

"I never meant harm to anyone, I swear it. You don't know what it has been like. The Crowells are everywhere I turn, and I can't escape them. He forgave me, did you know that? In public. I fell on my knees and cried afterward, but he never knew that. Others blamed me, though, and word that I wasn't to be tried ran round like wildfire. I couldn't go on. If Peter hadn't asked me to come and stay, I'd have killed myself somehow. I didn't mean to harm Alice Crowell, but she's repaid me in kind. I've suffered as much for my sins as she has for my carelessness. What am I to do to find any peace?"

"Come to Yorkshire with me. The case will be closed and you can come back here and get on with your life. I don't think Inspector Madsen is going to make a great noise about any of this. It can be done quietly."

Shoreham looked up at him. "I have no money. If I go to Yorkshire, I'll have no way to get back to Wales. I can't ask Peter, he's strapped as well."

"I'll see you safely back," Rutledge said.

"Inspector Madsen will be furious. He'll know we lied to him."

"It might do him some good," Rutledge said. "He needs a lesson as much as you do."

"I'll pack my things and find someone to see to the dog. If you'll come back later, I'll be ready."

"And find a dead man here in your place?"

"I won't end it, I swear it."

"The temptation may be stronger than you think." He began to turn the motorcar again, and Shoreham walked beside it to the house.

Rutledge waited until the battered valise was closed, then took up the dog in the motorcar with them, to leave with a neighbor while Shoreham was away.

Then they turned toward England.

It was a silent drive. Only once did Shoreham break the silence. And that was to say, "Who's the dead man, then?"

Rutledge answered, "A man who also lost his way, I expect."

R utledge drove straight through to Elthorpe, fighting drowsiness and an ache across his shoulders as he took the most direct route back—Shrewsbury to Manchester, Leeds, and then Harrogate. Rutted roads, slow-moving drays, overladen lorries, and the occasional wandering livestock made the journey feel longer than it was. Outside Shrewsbury he waited impatiently for cows to make their way along the road for morning milking, and in Cheshire, the Royal Mail had come to grief in a ditch, where heavy rains had made a bend tricky. A farm cart and a half-dozen burly men were doing their best to pull it out again.

Hamish said, "They willna' manage without help."

Rutledge caught himself just before he answered aloud, then called to the driver to offer his services. He gratefully accepted, and in short order the Royal Mail was on the road again.

They stopped for food and petrol and sometimes to stretch their legs.

Shoreham was quiet, resigned now, though Rutledge kept an eye on him throughout to gauge his mood.

One act of drunken unruliness, unintended yet preventable, had altered the direction of Henry Shoreham's life. And Crowell's forgiveness, well meant, had only driven the guilt deeper, without hope of expiation. It had become, in a way, retribution.

It was possible he'd change his mind at some stage of the journey to Yorkshire, preferring to take his chances alone and nearly penniless rather than revisit his nightmare.

And in truth, if he did change his mind, there was no legal way to stop him. The need to identify a stranger had brought him back to his own personal hell, and indeed, the closer they got to Elthorpe, the more noticeably anxious Shoreham got.

Still, he said nothing, and the silence was a strain on both men. Hamish filled it instead, his voice alternately hostile and questioning.

At one point Rutledge asked, just to silence it, "Shoreham. Do you know a Gerald Parkinson? Or Gaylord Partridge?"

"No. Should I? Is this another test?"

"Not at all."

And the silence reigned once more.

When the motorcar pulled at last into Elthorpe in the late afternoon, a cold rain was falling and the streets were empty. In the teashop they passed, the tables were filled and steam clouded the windows. The pub was dark, but there was a motorcar in front of the hotel, two men descending and walking briskly through the door.

Shoreham said, "Peter Littleton lied as well. But for my sake. Don't punish him for my sins."

Rutledge didn't answer.

Inspector Madsen had gone home for his tea. Elthorpe was tranquil once more and no murderers wandered in the ruins of an abbey, or anywhere else. He could afford to take his time.

Rutledge sent the constable on duty for the inspector, and it was with studied reluctance that the man did as he was asked.

In short order, Inspector Madsen came striding in, confident and in good spirits. His gaze swept over the stranger and moved on to Rutledge.

"Well, then, what brings you north again? Track down Littleton, did you? Fool's errand, I could have told you as much, but there you are."

"Not quite," Rutledge replied. "Don't you recognize this man?"

Madsen turned his attention to Shoreham's face, and he frowned. "The Welshman, is it? What possessed you to bring him back with you?" Some of the confidence in his face faltered.

"His real name is Henry Shoreham, not Llewellyn Williams."

Madsen laughed. "I daresay you could find a dozen Henry Shorehams across the breadth of England, if you set your mind to it." But the laugh rang hollow.

"You found Littleton, I grant you, and Shoreham had stayed with him for some time. But it was two *years* ago, not two weeks, when Shoreham left to take up a cousin's farm in Wales. Littleton was clever, he saw a chance to bury his cousin, and the two of them were convincing."

"You're mad!"

"Hardly that. Bring out Crowell, if you will, and see what he has to say."

"Of course he'll identify your man as Shoreham. He's no fool."

Shoreham said, his voice not quite steady, "They will know me in Whitby. You've only to take me there, to the police. I don't want to see Crowell. Or his wife."

Madsen was staring at him with a hard expression on his face now, convinced against his will, and yet unwilling to admit to it, he was wishing Shoreham at the very devil.

Rutledge said into the silence, "He's right."

"Then who is the dead man from the abbey? Answer me that, if you're so damned *clever*."

"It is my belief he's one Gerald Parkinson, of Wiltshire."

"Wiltshire, is it? And what was he doing in Yorkshire?"

"I'm not sure. But there was this business of Shoreham to settle once and for all. You'll have to let Crowell go, you know."

"Maybe he mistook this Parkinson for Shoreham," Madsen snapped.

"Do they look that much alike to you?" Rutledge countered. "Generally, of course, in coloring and height. The same could be said of your constable, there by the door. But there's no question about the features. They aren't the same."

Madsen said, "Bring me Parkinson's murderer and I'll let Crowell go. Not before."

But it was bravado. They had only to look at Shoreham, standing there with his eyes downcast and his face pale, the strain evident, to know that Rutledge had found his man.

"All the same, I'll take him to Whitby," Madsen went on.

"At your expense. And after that, he's free to return to Wales. Agreed? I'll leave you the money to pay for his journey."

"Agreed." It was reluctantly promised, but Madsen knew he had lost his gambit. He'd been wrong about Crowell. If in fact he had ever truly believed that the schoolmaster was a killer. And now it was time to save face and back out with as much grace as he could muster.

Rutledge took Shoreham to the hotel across from the police station and found rooms for them. He said to Shoreham as they turned toward the stairs, "You couldn't have hidden forever. You couldn't have lived with the lie."

Shoreham stared at him for a moment, then said, "Yes, I *could* have done that, if you hadn't come to my door. I could have ignored the truth and told myself the man was dead, and there was no harm in giving him a name—my name. He didn't have one of his own, did he? But when you stopped in my yard, it was different, somehow. I couldn't pretend after that. I'd lost the chance." He held out his hand for his key and added, "You told me you'd pay for my way back to Wales."

"The money will be waiting at Inspector Madsen's office, when he's finished with you."

Shoreham grimaced. "I wasn't going to run." And then he was gone, the door shut behind him.

————

After four hours' sleep, Rutledge left Elthorpe and turned south. He took with him the words that Madsen had said to him when he brought the money for Shoreham's journey home.

"It must be nice to sleep at night, knowing you're always right."

"I wasn't blinded by wishful thinking, Madsen. There's the difference."

"Still and all," the inspector told him bluntly, "I wish you'd never come here. We'd have managed very well without you."

"Let go, man, before you destroy your career."

"It'ud been worth it. I'll say that to you and no one else. I don't know which of them I wanted to hurt more. Him or her. It wouldn't have changed anything, but it might have taken away a little of the pain on my side."

It was something Rutledge was to remember in the days ahead.

14

Rutledge put in a call to Bowles when he stopped for the night in Lincoln.

Chief Superintendent Bowles wasn't there, he was told. But Sergeant Gibson had a message for Inspector Rutledge.

There was a delay while the sergeant was located and brought to the telephone.

He was gruff. "You're to come directly to London, sir."

"What's happened?"

"I'm not to say, sir. It's a family matter. Your sister will be waiting for you at your flat."

If she was waiting there, she must be all right. But she wouldn't have had the Yard pass on a message if it were only another snag in her relationship with Simon Barrington. He could feel his mind searching for a solution, and finding none.

"Very well. Thank you, Gibson. I'll be at the Yard in the afternoon."

"Yes, sir." He sounded doubtful, but then Gibson was not known for his cheerfulness.

Rutledge put up the receiver and turned around, on his way out of the small room where the hotel telephone had been installed. As he opened the door, he was surprised to see Simon Barrington walking into the hotel dining room, a woman on his arm. Rutledge could see only the back of her head, dark hair and a slim figure.

He decided on the spot to find somewhere else to dine. He had no wish to come face-to-face with the pair.

But what was Barrington doing here in Lincoln?

Hamish said, "Ye're too weary to go on to London. It would be foolish."

He had read Rutledge's mind.

The policeman, however, walked briskly to Reception and turned the book toward him to see who had registered with Barrington.

There were two names. Separate rooms. S. Barrington and J. Fellowes. Barrington had given his address as London, but Fellowes had listed Boston.

The clerk saw what Rutledge was doing and came out of the office. "Here—"

"Police business," Rutledge said curtly, and went out to find his dinner.

He reached London in the late afternoon, stopping twice on the road for a brief respite.

Hamish had rumbled through the night, as he'd often done in the trenches, and the soft Scots voice had brought tension with it.

Rutledge went straight to his flat, and he found Frances waiting as promised, her face filled with concern. He knew at once that someone was dead.

"Who is it?" he asked, bracing himself. "Not Melinda—"

Melinda Trent, the intriguing elderly woman who'd lived through the Great Indian Mutiny of 1857, had been a friend of his family for as long as he could remember, and cared for him as well. He returned that love in full measure, leavened by a strong suspicion that she saw through him more often than not. If she'd found Hamish in his shadows, she had spoken of that only obliquely. Her home was in Kent, and he promised himself he would find a way to go on there tonight, taking Frances with him.

"No." She crossed the room to greet him, hands on his shoulders, and said, "Oh, my dear, I don't know how to tell you."

"Quickly would be best," he replied tightly.

"It's Jean," she told him then. "She's dead."

"Jean—"

The woman he should—would—have married, if there had been no war.

He had got over her, he had told himself that often enough through a long dark year. Now it struck him that he had never said good-bye. That day in the clinic when he'd broken off their engagement so that she wouldn't have to ask him to set her free, letting her go because it was what she desperately wanted and didn't know how to tell him, she had walked out of his room promising to come again as soon as she could. But she never had. He had known she wouldn't be able to brace herself for another visit.

Dead—

He could feel Frances's hands on his shoulders, hear her voice, and knew that she was there.

"Who told you?" he asked hoarsely. "How did you find out?"

"Melinda telephoned to me. A friend of hers had sent her a cable from Canada. It was in the papers in Toronto."

That too was a blow. That Jean had died and he had felt nothing.

"How did it happen?"

"Complications of pregnancy. She lost her child—a miscarriage—and infection set in afterward. They did all that was possible to save her."

Women died in childbirth every day. Only he hadn't expected one of them to be Jean.

"Is she coming back to England?"

"The obituary says she'll be buried in Canada. Her husband is still serving there."

And so he would never say good-bye. Not now.

The last time he'd seen her, she was coming out of St. Margaret's Church, where she was soon to be married. A cluster of her friends surrounded her, their voices traveling to him where he stood. Her face was shining with happiness and excitement as she discussed flowers and candles and ribbons. It had broken his heart—and yet he had never hated her for leaving him. He had known what sort of husband he would have made. She was better off without him.

Still, he felt a surge of guilt for letting her go.

If she had stayed in England—

But that was pointless.

Rutledge set Frances aside and went to the window to look out on the street, not seeing it.

She went away, and came back presently with a cup of tea.

Rutledge drank it, the hot strong liquid cutting through the shock of Frances's news.

There was nothing he could do. No word of comfort for the bereaved husband—who probably had never known Rutledge existed— and no flowers for the raw earth of the grave.

He finished his tea and said, "I need to walk. Will you wait?"

"Of course."

He had never taken off his coat. He just went out the door.

An hour later, he saw that there was a church on the next corner, smoke-stained stone, with a spire that gleamed in the sun.

The door was unlocked and he went inside into the silent dimness. His footsteps echoed against the stone walls, and he got as far as the first row of chairs. There he sat down. It wasn't the comfort of God he sought so much as the need to be alone. And Hamish, mercifully, was quiet.

He hadn't expected it. That was the problem. The loss was emotional, sharp.

Their engagement had not been spent growing closer to each other, settling into a warm and responsive companionship that would carry them into old age, as it should have been. Four years of war had seen to that and changed them both. She was another man's wife, now. Not his, never his. And while he grieved for the girl he had asked to marry him in 1914, she had left a long time ago.

He rose after a while and walked back the way he'd come.

Hamish, at his shoulder, said only, "It was verra' different with my Fiona. I should ha' come home to her, and left you dead in France. Your Jean wouldna' have missed you . . ."

The voice was sad, as if half convincing himself that this was true.

Together the two men, one of whom didn't exist, went back to the flat.

15

Frances was waiting, as she'd promised.

She said as he came through the door, "The Yard sent someone. You are to come at once."

Rutledge swore silently. There was never any time . . .

"Yes, I'll go. Shall I give you a lift home?"

"As far as Trafalgar Square, if you don't mind. Ian—are you all
right? Do you want me to call the Yard and ask them to give you an
hour or two?"

"Work," he said bitterly, "is its own panacea. But thanks."

He stopped long enough to change clothes. And then he shut the flat
door behind them as he led the way to his motorcar. He couldn't help
but wonder how long it would be before he crossed his threshold again
without remembering the news that had been waiting here today.

Frances kept him busy with trivial gossip until he put her down in
the square, and she leaned across to kiss him before she got out.

He watched her walk briskly in the direction of St. Martin's in the Fields, and then turned toward the Yard. He hadn't mentioned seeing Simon Barrington. It hadn't seemed the right moment, and then too important to be a parting remark.

It was Simon's business and none of his, after all. As long as Frances wasn't hurt. But he thought she was going to be.

His eye was caught by a familiar figure walking toward him along the street. It was Meredith Channing, dressed in a becoming dark red coat and matching hat. She didn't look his way, but he could have sworn she had seen his motorcar and recognized it as quickly as he had recognized her.

Bowles was waiting for him at the Yard and almost as he walked in the door asked abruptly for his report.

"There's no time to write it out, but I want to know what's going on."

Rutledge gave it orally, as Bowles stood fuming by the window.

When he'd finished, Bowles grunted, and Rutledge couldn't tell whether he was satisfied or still irritated. It was often difficult to read the man's moods.

"Stepping on toes is never prudent. I want you back in Berkshire tonight. I want to see the end of this business with Partridge or Parkinson or whatever his name is. Finish it as fast as you can, and report to me. Yorkshire is complaining we're playing merry hell with their inquiry, and giving them damn all in return. They still have that godforsaken body, and don't know what to do with it."

Rutledge was as eager to leave London as Bowles was to send him away. But he said, "If I get too close to the truth, Deloran will be knocking at your door, complaining."

"And that's when I'll know you're doing your job. Get on with it."

Rutledge had been driving for three days, but he said only, "I'll be leaving within the hour."

Somehow the road west seemed longer this time. But in the end Rutledge saw the familiar shape of the White Horse galloping silently across its grassy hillside. He drove on, passing it, then stopped in the darkness to look up at it.

What had it seen, this chalk horse? Why had it brought Parkinson here, and why had he died in Yorkshire, and not in Berkshire?

He got out and walked a little way up the hill. Somehow it seemed peaceful and comforting. The horse had been there since time out of mind. Rutledge squatted in the dew-wet grass and studied the dark, silent cottages.

Hamish said, "No one wants this dead man."

"Except to use him," Rutledge answered aloud. "A convenience. Sad, isn't it? The cottages are the end of the road for most of the people down there. A place to grow old and die without fuss. Did death come looking for Parkinson, or did he go out to find it?"

"It's a long way to Yorkshire fra' here."

There was movement below. Rutledge could just make out the smith coming home. He slowed for an instant, as if he sensed being watched, then walked on toward his door.

A curtain twitched in Brady's cottage, a sliver of lamp light flashing briefly and then vanishing. The lane was quiet again.

Rutledge was content to sit here on the hill and listen to sounds of the night. His mind was tired, and even the puzzle of Parkinson's life and death failed to interest him. It could wait until tomorrow.

A cat—Dublin?—trotted across the open space between Quincy's cottage and Mrs. Cathcart's. A dog barked in a farmyard a long way off, the sound carrying without urgency.

For a moment Rutledge wondered why he had ever chosen to become a policeman and deal so closely with death. And he knew the answer even as he posed the question. It was still the same as it had been at eighteen, when he'd told his father that he intended to join the metropolitan force when he came down from Oxford. Tired he might be of death, yet he was still here to speak for the dead. Only it was proving more difficult to speak for Parkinson. It was possible, he thought, that Parkinson didn't want anyone to learn the truth about him. That he would be glad to lie in an unmarked grave and be forgotten.

Then, without warning, as if it had been busy this last quarter hour without his knowing it, his mind offered Rutledge a solution to the puzzle of Gerald Parkinson.

He had been working on the theory that the man had had something to hide, like the other residents of the Tomlin Cottages. And perhaps it was true. But the overriding factor behind what had brought Parkinson here was guilt. A strong sense of guilt.

And that was where to begin, if Rutledge expected to unravel the puzzle of this man's life and his death.

Rutledge stood up and walked back down the hill, cranked the motorcar, and drove on to The Smith's Arms. It took him several minutes to wake Mr. Smith and bring him down to unlock the door.

"Back again, are you? Your room's empty, if you want it. We'll settle on that tomorrow."

"Fair enough." Rutledge thanked him and followed him up the stairs in the wake of his flickering lamp. As he opened his door, the room smelled of lavender and fresh air, as if the sheets had dried in the sun.

He undressed in the dark and went to bed.

Tomorrow he'd find out why guilt had changed Partridge's life.

After breakfast, Rutledge drove on to Wiltshire, a good two hours one way, then found again the turning for Partridge Fields, the house where Parkinson had lived.

Once more there appeared to be no one about as he walked through the gate, leaving his motorcar in the lane.

The sun was slanting through the trees beyond the house and long shafts of golden light barred the lawns and gardens. It was a tranquil scene, and he wondered again why Parkinson had preferred the cottages to this place.

He went around the house, through the gardens and the shrubbery that shut off the kitchen yard, listening to a silence broken only by a bird calling from the miniature dovecote birdhouse in the kitchen garden. Was no one ever here?

Moving on, he was just on the point of taking the stone path through to the far side of the house, when a shrill voice stopped him in his tracks.

Hamish said, "'Ware!" in warning, and Rutledge turned slowly.

"Here! What are you about?"

A plump woman wearing an apron was standing in the door to the yard, arms akimbo and a frown on her face.

"I didn't think anyone was at home," he said in apology, "or I would have knocked. My name is Rutledge, and I've come down from London—"

"I couldn't care less where you're from. What are you doing here?"

"Looking, I think, for Mr. Parkinson."

"You're not one of them people from the newspaper, are you?" There was a challenge now in her tone. "I've told you before and I'll tell you again, he's not here, nor will he be here any time soon, and you might as well march yourself back the way you've come and leave the premises. Close the gate behind you or I'll see the police have a word with you for trespassing."

She was about to shut the door in his face, and he said quickly, "I'm from the police. Scotland Yard."

Her face altered, the hostility giving way to concern mixed with irritation. "The police, is it? What are you here for? Is there bad news you're bringing?"

Rutledge was walking back toward her now, and she stood her ground with the ferocity of an old and trusted servant.

"Here, you're not coming in this house, policeman or no!"

"I'm trying to locate Mr. Parkinson," he replied, his tone indicating a need for help rather than ulterior motive. "It's a police inquiry, you see, and I should like to ask his assistance." He'd left the sketch in his valise at the inn, and swore to himself. She would surely have recognized it.

"Well, you won't be finding it here—he's not in residence, and that's a fact." She looked Rutledge up and down. "You'd think a *London* policeman would know that."

He said, drawing on his experience dealing with watchdog servants, "My superiors don't always tell me everything they know. Much to my regret. How long has he been away? Surely he must have told you where to send along his mail."

"He doesn't receive any. None, that is, I'm aware of. And he left just a week after his wife died in the spring of 1918. Here, are you certain you aren't from the London papers?'"

Rutledge showed her his identity card, and she studied it with suspicion, as if certain it was counterfeit.

"I don't understand why the newspapers should be interested in Mr. Parkinson," he went on in a conversational tone. "Or disturb him. Perhaps the police ought to have been called sooner."

"They were, and they did nothing." Her sense of grievance went deeper than her circumspection. "It was on account of his poor wife, of course. Like vultures they came here, battering the door, upsetting the household. It was shameful, that's what it was. No respect for the dead."

"Was she well known in London circles? Was that their interest?"

"It was the way she died. She left the gas open by mistake, and they tried to say it was suicide, but of course it wasn't. She was a good and kind lady, she would never kill herself. But they told poor Mr. Parkinson it was on purpose, and he believed them."

It was the same way Parkinson himself had died. To follow her? But then how did he come to be in Yorkshire?

"I'm surprised the London papers saw anything newsworthy in the story."

She sighed. "It's because of what he did in the war, of course. And here at the bottom of the garden as well, with that workshop of his. Mrs. Parkinson told me herself she was heartsick over it."

Rutledge tried another tack. "I'm not sure I understand. London didn't inform me what Parkinson had done in the war."

"He worked at Porton Down, he was one of the scientists there. Gassed the Kaiser's men in return for *our* boys. Got our own back, didn't he? Mrs. Parkinson was squeamish, but not I."

He was startled by her vehemence, even as his mind registered *Porton Down.*

It was a military facility on the eastern border of Wiltshire, across the county from here. A place where absolute secrecy was the order of the day.

And for the first time Rutledge understood why Martin Deloran was interested in the whereabouts of one Gerald Parkinson. The army didn't care to lose track of someone like that, someone whose knowledge was more valuable than his person. Eccentricity was one thing, disliked but oftentimes tolerated. Even madness could be overlooked. Parkinson, however, had walked away from a comfortable family home, lived elsewhere under a different name, and disappeared with unsettling regularity. The War Office could do very little about it, but that didn't mean they didn't watch his every move.

Very likely Deloran had put the change in Parkinson down to excessive grief after his wife's death—give him time and he'd recover, be himself again. The war's nearly over, we can afford to be patient . . . But two years had passed, and Parkinson still went his own way. And Deloran was still watching him.

Small wonder Deloran jumped at the chance to bury Parkinson under a pauper's stone in rural Yorkshire! What sort of secrets had safely died with him?

"Guilt, ye said," Hamish reminded him, and Rutledge remembered.

That would explain Parkinson's choice to live in the Tomlin Cottages.

It still wouldn't explain where he'd died.

"He worked on the development of poison gases?" Rutledge asked to clarify what Parkinson had done for a living. It would explain too the choice of reading material he had taken with him to the cottage.

"Well, of course he did," she said with pride. "Where else, and him fascinated by chemistry ever since he was a young man at Cambridge? Mrs. Parkinson was at her wits' end with fear for the children."

"Children?"

"Indeed, the light of her life, they was. I daresay Mr. Parkinson found them a nuisance when he had his laboratory at the bottom of the garden. Always looking in the windows, trying to see what he was up to. It was when he killed the cows by accident that Mrs. Parkinson put her foot down." She rested her back against the doorframe, a tired woman with no one to talk with as she worked. "But that caught the army's attention, didn't it? So he took himself off to a new laboratory there. Posh, he said it was, everything to hand. 'Martha, they value me. They know I'm right about this new direction. Germany hasn't got there yet. But we shall, wait and see. You'll be reading about it in the newspapers, because it's likely to stop the war and the dying.' My nephew, the one gassed at Ypres, my sister's only boy, was going to be avenged, he said. Germany was the first to use the poisonous gases, but we'd be the last. We'll show 'em, he said, wait and see."

"You've worked for the family for some time, have you?"

"I was maid to Mr. Parkinson's mother, and came here as housekeeper to Partridge Fields when he bought the place, Mrs. Miggs having just died."

"And Mrs. Parkinson didn't care for the work he was doing."

"She worried that they were testing these gases on the animals. She couldn't bear to think about it. She saw my nephew when he was sent home, lungs burned right out. He didn't last long and died hard. I told her the Hun had brought it all on themselves, whatever Mr. Parkinson devised, but it didn't matter. She stopped sleeping well, wandering about the house at all hours. Like her own ghost. Small wonder she forgot and left the gas on. She couldn't even kill a spider that crept in at the window, she was that troubled about hurting anything. Which is why I refuse to believe she killed herself. But Mr. Parkinson thought she'd done it out of spite, using the gas. I'm told it's as peaceful a way as any to go, falling asleep and not waking up."

The housekeeper turned and looked over her shoulder as if a ghost could give her the answer to her question. But it was the kitchen floors that concerned her, and she said, "It's dry in there, must be by now. And I've a good bit more to do before I close up for the day."

"And you're sure you have no way of knowing where Mr. Parkinson went?"

"His daughter Becky might know. But I doubt it. He left me instructions not to say anything, and I never have. It's not my place to decide such things. "

"Where will I find Miss Parkinson?"

"No, I won't tell you. She'll know who did, and I'll hear about it soon enough. No one stays in the house of a night anymore. Myself, I'm away before dark, I can tell you that. But she comes from time to time to tend the gardens."

And sometimes to knock at her father's door?

"You spoke of children—" Rutledge began, but the housekeeper shook her head firmly and disappeared inside without answering him, shutting the kitchen door in Rutledge's face.

He had no choice but to move on, rounding the house and coming again to the drive. He could almost feel the housekeeper watching him from the windows, making certain he was not sneaking about, as she would call it, but leaving the premises.

As he closed the gate behind him, he thought, *This house has seen tragedy* . . .

Rutledge found a small pub for his noon meal, and sat there over his pudding, thinking about Parkinson and the cottage in Berkshire. So much made sense now. The fact that the cottage had no touches of personal warmth—it was not Parkinson's home, this house in Wilt-shire was. And his disappearances.

Hamish said, "To his wife's grave? You ken, ye thought of that before."

"Deloran probably had the churchyard watched for all we know. And going there would have bolstered Deloran's theory that Parkinson was still grieving. Wherever Parkinson went, Deloran couldn't find him, and that was the trouble."

Hamish said, "It's verra' likely that he went away to torment Deloran."

"It wouldn't surprise me that he was just being bloody-minded, rebelling against being watched, showing the War Office that he was clever enough to outfox them all. A cat-and-mouse game, to worry Deloran."

Rutledge considered another possibility—that when Parkinson couldn't stand his own company any longer, when the walls of the cottage were closing in, he might well have needed to be around people. A crowded train station, a Wednesday market, a theater. Somewhere safe to remind himself he wasn't going mad.

It was dark when he reached The Smith's Arms. Rutledge left the motorcar in the yard, then walked down to Wayland's Smithy. It was a far better place to leave an unwanted body than an abbey cloister in Yorkshire.

Who had decided that it was time Parkinson should die? That's what it all came down to. Not where the body was left, but who had chosen to end one man's life now. It was useless to speculate, but *who* had become the bedrock of the case.

The heavy stone slabs that had created this ancient tomb caught his attention, and he thought about the numbers of men it would have taken to build this place for a dead chieftain or priest.

We spend our energies in different ways, he thought, standing there. How many aeroplanes and tanks and artillery caissons had it taken to end the Great War? Not to count the rifles and helmets, respirators and machine guns, the number of boots, the tunics and great-coats and the tins in which we had brewed our tea or the casings of the shells fired. A nation's fortune surely, greater than any man possessed in the centuries since this tomb was new and raw and the dead shut into it was still honored by those who had carried him here.

It was depressing to think about.

There was always a new weapon, something to kill greater numbers of the enemy than the enemy could hope to kill on one's own side. Parkinson must have been more than a pair of hands in the work he was doing on poisonous gases. Men like Deloran wouldn't have wasted an hour's thought on the whereabouts of a minor chemist who carried out tests and wrote reports. The housekeeper had said that Parkinson was pleased with something new that would help end the war sooner. Had he left with that work unfinished or at a critical stage?

If that had been the case, someone would have moved heaven and earth to get Parkinson back into the laboratory as quickly as possible.

Had he discovered a conscience when his wife died and decided that he was finished with what had always been his life's work? Had he been frightened by the man he'd become, and walked away?

Rutledge brought to mind the face in the sketch, and tried to probe behind it.

All he could find was an ordinary man, despite what he had done in his laboratories, nothing in his features to mark him, nothing that could have caught one's eye on the streets of London or Canterbury, nothing that would reflect what this person had chosen to do with his life. Neither evil nor good, just a man with no calluses on his hands and no scars, no means of telling him from a half-dozen others his size and weight and coloring.

Then what had happened to him if he was so ordinary?

Rutledge turned back toward the inn and asked Mrs. Smith if he could have his dinner brought to his room. After eating it by the window, he went on sitting there in the darkness even after the yard was silent and the road in front was empty.

Trying to picture Jean's face, the sound of her voice, the touch of her hand, he found it was difficult. He had loved her, or believed he had, and grieved for what might have been when the engagement ended.

Now, with her death, a door had closed. She was the last link with the bright summer of 1914, and happiness, and a world that was going to be his to grasp.

After a while he got up and readied himself for bed without lighting the lamp.

He had expected to lie there awake, listening to Hamish in his head. In the morning, he would go to the cottages and find out who might have wanted the death of one Gerald Parkinson, or if they had wanted to kill Gaylord Partridge.

Instead he'd drifted into sleep without dreams.

Best-laid plans have a way of going astray.

Someone was knocking on his door before the first light of dawn had penetrated his room, summoning him urgently.

He fought his way back from a deep sleep and answered.

Smith said, his voice husky, "There's been trouble at the Tomlin Cottages. You'd best come."

16

Rutledge dressed swiftly, asking questions as he worked. But Smith knew nothing more.

In the lobby he found Slater standing there, pale and agitated.

"What kind of trouble?" he asked the smith.

"I don't know. I heard a cry. And after that, nothing."

"From the Partridge cottage?"

"There? No. Please hurry!"

Rutledge went at once into the yard and Slater followed, going to the bonnet and bending to turn the crank with his massive hand.

Smith was calling after them, "Shall I come as well?"

"Not yet. You may be needed later."

He got behind the wheel, and Slater slid into the other seat, a hulking shadow in the light of the innkeeper's lamp.

"Which cottage?" Rutledge asked.

"Mr. Willingham's. Number Three, just above Mr. Partridge."

The old man, then.

They drove the short distance to the cottages in silence, but Rutledge could feel the anxiety in the man at his side, and reaction setting in.

"I didn't investigate," Slater said as the cottages came into view. "I've never heard anything like that. I fear there's murder done, Mr. Rutledge. Sure as God's above."

"Can you be certain he wasn't calling for help? Taken ill suddenly in the night—a fall?"

But he knew it must be more than that, to frighten Slater so badly. Slater walked the night and was of a size that brooked no interference. It wasn't fear that had shaken him, it was something closer to a primordial response to horror.

Slater said nothing, hunched in his seat, willing the motorcar to move faster.

They arrived at the cottages soon enough, and Rutledge left his motorcar beside the smith's door, rather than destroy any tracks or other evidence nearer Willingham's.

He reached for his torch, closing his eyes from habit because it was in the rear where Hamish sat. Groping he found nothing, and then suddenly his hand touched the torch, as if Hamish had pushed it nearer. He flinched, then gripped the cold metal, turning toward the cottage.

The windows were dark, the door closed, nothing to mark forced entry, but the question was, did Willingham lock his doors of a night or leave them off the latch?

Rutledge started toward it, and Slater made to follow him. Rutledge held up a hand. "No. Wait until I call you."

Slater argued, "You may need help. I'm stronger than you."

Rutledge said, "Then better to be outside than in."

The door was indeed unlocked. Inside, Rutledge's torch seemed to pierce the darkness like a spear. He moved it without moving himself, until he had a feeling for the furnishings and the shape of the room. It was very similar to other cottages he'd been in, but the placement of chairs and tables was different.

The sitting room just beyond the door showed no signs of disturbance. A rug before the hearth, a chair to one side, a shelf of books on the other. A small table by the window, with two smaller chairs, and a footstool by the winged chair under the lamp. An empty glass rested on the stand next to it, with a book open beside it.

The kitchen, tiny even by cottage standards, was tidy, but a stack of plates and cups stood waiting to be washed, while pans soaked in the sink. Guests for dinner, or was Willingham in the habit of washing up once a day?

The bedroom lay above the kitchen, and on the threshold Rutledge found splotches of blood, black in his torch's beam.

He stopped, flicking his light around the room.

Beyond, between the tall chest and the bed, Willingham lay on his side on the bare wood of the floor. His eyes were wide and empty, reflecting the light. Rutledge didn't need to cross the room to know that he was dead.

The bedroom still held a presence, malice and fear, as if the strength of the emotions that had ended in death still lingered. But there was no one else there.

Rutledge, used to scenes of violent death, quickly surveyed the bedroom, digesting what there was to see.

There had been a struggle—bedclothes pulled free and left trailing across the floor, the lamp broken and the oil spilling into a chair, soaking darkly into the green brocade upholstery. The nightstand was overturned as well.

Angered to find an intruder beside his bed, Willingham had apparently been galvanized to put up an energetic defense.

Walking into the room, Rutledge could see a slash on the left wrist and a knife, of the kind used to joint chickens, deep in Willingham's chest.

Stubborn and cantankerous to the end, Willingham had not died easily, and the killer must have suffered a shock.

Rutledge went down on one knee by the body. The cut on the wrist wasn't right, somehow. Not the sort of defensive wound he'd have expected to find. On the hands, perhaps, or on the arms, fending off the final blow, but not straight and deep into the wrist.

With that wrist wound alone, Willingham would have bled to death. The killer could have held him down in bed until it was over. Perhaps that had been the plan, to make this attack look like an old man's final retreat from a lonely and despairing life. Instead, it had been necessary to end the struggle violently before there was another outcry.

Hamish was saying, "I canna' see what this has to do with Partridge."

"I—"

He broke off as a footstep grated on the threshold, and flashed his light in that direction, tensing for an attack. Slater was outside, but the killer might still be within.

Just at that moment, someone said, "Mr. Rutledge? Where are you? Are you all right?"

Slater had followed him, contrary to orders. The torch's beam struck him full in the face, making him blink and duck his head.

Damn the man!

"Go back outside," he commanded sternly, and Slater hastily withdrew, moving quickly for such a large man.

Flicking off his torch to avoid attracting attention from the neighboring cottages, Rutledge followed him.

"I saw him. Willingham's dead, isn't he?"

Rutledge said quietly, "Take my motorcar and drive into Uffington. Ask the sergeant on duty at the police station to send someone here. Preferably an inspector. Tell them only that there's been a murder and someone should come at once."

Slater repeated, "He's dead then?"

"Yes. There's nothing we can do for him now."

Slater nodded and turned to walk back to the motorcar. Then he paused and said, "You'll be safe here alone?"

"I expect I will be. Thanks."

The smith nodded and was gone.

Rutledge stood there watching the first fingers of rosy light—rosy-fingered dawn, Virgil had called it—spread from the eastern horizon toward the road.

As he had so many times in the trenches, when dawn had broken softly without the guns or the whistles or the shouts of men going into battle, Rutledge heard himself quoting O. A. Manning aloud. Hamish had been fond of the lines as well.

> *The first reaches of light out of darkness,*
> *Pink with new birth,*
> *And then gold,*
> *Like apricots on silk,*
> *And the morning was here.*

The earliest riser, the man in Number 5, had stepped out his door and was staring in Rutledge's direction.

"What's that? Is there anything wrong?" Singleton asked. "The old man hasn't taken ill, has he?"

"I've sent for the police. They'll be here shortly."

"I thought you were the police."

"The local people, then. It's their patch."

Singleton nodded. "Die in his sleep, did he? I always thought his heart would send him off. Choleric old fool that he was."

"How well did you know him?"

He shrugged. "How well do any of us here know one another? It's a morning greeting, a nod in passing, a good night before we shut our doors. And in the end, only what we can see from our windows."

And the windows of Willingham's cottage had a clear view of Parkinson's.

They also looked out on Mrs. Cathcart's, and on Number 7, the man Miller's door.

Mrs. Cathcart opened her door a little, as if by recalling her name, Rutledge had summoned her spirit.

"Good morning, Inspector. Is something wrong with Mr. Willingham?"

"Do either of you know if he had a guest for dinner last night?"

"I shouldn't think so," she answered. "He was alone last evening when I saw him working in his garden. He seemed well enough then."

Singleton said, "I don't think I've ever seen anyone enter or leave his cottage."

They stood there awkwardly, uncertain what to say, watching Rutledge to see if he would tell them what was wrong.

Quincy came out his door, and Dublin ran ahead of him, released for a day of hunting.

"What's up?"

"It's Mr. Willingham," Mrs. Cathcart replied. "Mr. Rutledge has sent for the police."

Quincy disappeared inside his door and shut it firmly.

Allen was next to stick his head out. His face was pale, drained, as if he'd slept ill.

"Anything wrong?" he asked, nodding to Mrs. Cathcart. "Can I help?" A coughing spell sent him almost to his knees, but when it had passed, he said again, "Can I help?"

"There's nothing anyone can do," Rutledge replied.

"Then I'm for my bed again. Not at my best in the mornings."

He shut his door and they could hear him coughing again.

"He shouldn't be out at this hour," Mrs. Cathcart was saying. "The dampness . . ."

After a moment she herself went back inside, as if staying there and making conversation was more than she could cope with.

Singleton remained, standing with folded arms. Rutledge could see Brady's face at his window, staring with bleary eyes at the two men. Soon afterward, the sun's rays turned the window to brilliant gold, and Rutledge couldn't be sure if Brady was still there or not.

He had seen most of the residents now. Curiosity had got the best of them in one fashion or another, this break in the dull routine of their lives making them more willing to interact than they might have done otherwise.

Miller had yet to appear, but he could be a late riser, unaware of what was happening.

After a long while, Slater was back with a slim, dark man beside him in the motorcar.

They left the car by the road and walked toward the Willingham cottage.

"What's this?" the man said. "I'm told someone is dead."

"And you are . . ."

"Hill, Inspector Hill. You must be Inspector Rutledge."

They shook hands, and Rutledge began to point out his observations, but Hill said, "No, let me." He held out a hand for Rutledge's torch and went inside the still dark cottage.

After a time he came out again. By then Singleton had walked back to his house. "You were right to send for me. Any witnesses?" He looked in Singleton's direction, then focused his attention on Rutledge.

"None that I've found so far," Rutledge answered.

"Yes, well, if he was killed at night, who would notice? Although Slater here tells me he was awakened by a cry."

They turned as one to look at the other cottages.

"I've not had much call to come here," Hill said. "Peaceful enough little community. No problems."

"Until now."

"Until now," Hill agreed. "Slater didn't enter the cottage?"

"He came as far as the bedroom door. I sent him back out again."

"Well, if it were he who did the deed, the struggle would have been shorter. Someone nearer Willingham's size, if not his age?"

"A startled man might fight with more strength than a frightened one."

"I agree."

Rutledge gave Hill a quick overview of the other inhabitants, ending with Partridge. "He's not been seen for some time. The general view is that he's been away."

"And what," Hill asked, his eyes sharp on Rutledge's face, "has brought the Yard to our doorstep?"

"I'd been asked to learn what had become of Partridge. By interested parties. He left without telling anyone where he was going or when he'd return."

"I see. Very well. I'll take over here, if you please. No thoughts on who might have had it in for Willingham?"

"None. And I doubt you'll get much out of his neighbors. They haven't been very forthcoming about Mr. Partridge."

"Yes, well, a man going about his own business is one thing. I'll have a chat and see if murder might sharpen their memories."

Rutledge left him to it. He told himself that what had happened to Willingham most certainly had nothing to do with Parkinson. And yet a niggling doubt crept in.

Why would the killer try to make the old man's death appear to be a suicide? To silence him without creating a stir on the heels of Parkinson's murder? Willingham's windows looked down on the Partridge cottage at Number 2. Had he seen something he shouldn't have? Then why wait this long to dispose of him?

Hamish said, "It would be as well to wait until yon inspector went on his way before asking too many questions."

Rutledge was about to answer when he heard Mrs. Cathcart quietly call to him. Inspector Hill was busy questioning Slater, his back to them. She said, "Will you come and tell me what's happened? I'm afraid."

He turned to reassure her, and instead seized the opportunity offered him.

She let him in her door and shut it quickly.

"Mr. Willingham is dead," he said, stepping into the sitting room. "Did you know him well?"

"Oh, poor man! I don't think any of us knew him at all. He kept to himself. Was it illness?" She shivered. "I shouldn't like to die alone. But it's likely I shall."

"I'm afraid he was murdered, Mrs. Cathcart."

That shook her badly. "Murder? By whom? Why? Oh my God."

"It was most likely a personal matter, Mrs. Cathcart. There's nothing for you to fear."

"But his cottage could easily be confused with mine. It's happened before. A letter to me was taken to him by mistake. He kept it for a fortnight before he handed it to me. And another time, someone looking for me knocked at his door. What if the murderer thought he was coming into *my* cottage?"

She was genuinely disturbed, he could see it in her face.

"I don't think—" he began again, and she put a hand on his arm to stop him.

"No, you don't know my husband! He'd do anything to be rid of me. He lied to the court, he told them I was a terrible woman, unfit to be a mother, and he divorced me. He paid people to prove what he said was true. He kept the children from seeing me again and turned them against me. My son was killed in France, and I never knew he had enlisted. He was just a boy, and I never said good-bye to him."

She began to cry, and he gave her his handkerchief. "I'm sorry—"

But she went on, wrapped in her own despair. "There's another woman now. I've seen their photographs in the newspaper in the last few months. What if she refuses to marry him, because she doesn't want the shame of a divorce in her family? It's quite a good family, they could object, and he'd not stop at having me *killed*."

Rutledge took her arm and gently steered her into the sitting room, settling her in a chair. She was distraught, but when he turned away to bring her tea from the tray by the hearth, she clutched at him.

"I'm afraid to drink it now. What if someone slipped in and put something in the leaves? I'd never know until it was too late. I'll have to throw everything in the rubbish bin. I daren't trust my chances, don't you see?"

"Mrs. Cathcart, no one is trying to kill you. You've had a shock, that's all, and it frightened you. Mr. Willingham saw his killer. Whoever it was fought with him. There was no doubt that it was Mr. Willingham who was meant to die. This has nothing to do with you."

She tried to stop shaking, her sobs choking in her throat. He went to the pot and felt it. Still quite warm. He poured a cup, drank from it, and said, "You see, there's nothing wrong with your tea. Let me find you a fresh cup."

He went into the kitchen, found a pretty white porcelain cup to match the one he'd used, and filled it. He added sugar and milk from the jug on the tray, then had to hold her hands around the cup to keep her from spilling it.

After a few sips, she sat back, a little steadier now.

"I've made a fool of myself," she said, looking up at him in some embarrassment. "I couldn't think of anything but dying alone and afraid in the night."

"Why did your husband wish to divorce you?"

"He was tired of me. I wasn't exciting, the children mattered more to me than anything, and he was ambitious. He needed to be seen at parties and attend weekends in the country. He told me it was important to meet these people, that they could do so much for his career. He's a solicitor, you see, and wanted his own chambers. So he took away the only thing that mattered, and punished me for fighting him."

She drank a little more of the tea. "He's tried to do away with me. I'm convinced of it. I was on my bicycle, coming home from Uffington, and someone ran into me and left me in the ditch. The driver never stopped, and it was Ronnie, I knew it was."

Rutledge didn't know whether to believe her or not. But he sat opposite her, listening and offering what comfort he could.

She had been tormented to the point of convincing herself that her husband wanted her dead. And her son weighed heavily on her mind. She returned again and again to his loss, and the fact that she knew nothing of his death for months.

"Then someone sent me a cutting from the newspaper. Weeks old, the announcement of Harry's death circled in black. That was the letter that went astray, to Mr. Willingham. I think it must have been shoved under his door. There was no stamp on it. I wanted to kill myself when I read the cutting. And then I knew that's what he'd hoped I'd do. I wanted to die, but I wouldn't give him that pleasure, damn him."

Rutledge said, "Is there anyone I could bring to you? You're too upset to stay alone just now."

She smiled, the hurt in her eyes very plain. "I have no friends, Mr. Rutledge. They believed his lies and deserted me as well. 'Fair-weather friends' I call them. They couldn't withstand the storm. But it's kind of you to ask. I'll be all right, but I shall lock my door tonight and drag that table across it for good measure."

After a time, he got up to leave and she saw him to the door. He stood there listening to the tumblers fall into place as she locked it, before walking away.

There were two more vehicles here now, men from one of them carrying a stretcher for the dead. Others were gathering around Hill, listening to instructions.

The remaining cottages were shut tight. Ranks closed against outsiders, even with murder done. It was a matter of self-preservation, Rutledge thought.

Hamish said, "Aye, but they know one of them could ha' done this."

And he was right. Two dead . . . out of nine.

He walked on toward his car. He'd seen enough, he knew as much as Hill did at this stage.

Quincy's door opened and he said, "What's going on?"

"Willingham's dead," Rutledge answered.

"Indeed." Quincy looked thoughtfully in the direction of Willingham's cottage. "There was a cry in the night. I heard it. I thought Dublin was having a romantic interlude, and so I didn't investigate. Anything to do with events?"

"You'll have to ask Inspector Hill. He's the man in charge."

"Your only interest is Partridge, then. I wonder why."

"Because he's dead too. An uneasy coincidence, don't you think, in such a small community?"

"You'd better come in." Quincy opened the door wider, and Dublin scooted between his legs and into the house.

Quincy had finished his breakfast, and the dishes were still on the table. Dublin jumped up to sniff at them, then lost interest, moving on to curl up in a chair.

"Why do you think Partridge died? He's gone away before." Quincy was standing by the window, watching the activity up the lane. "And nothing happened."

Rutledge was at his shoulder. "He always came home again, in a matter of several days. You said as much yourself," he responded. "Someone knew his pattern."

"Yes, it's true. He was a man of habit, in some ways."

"Where did he go? And why? I can't find anyone who will tell me."

Quincy shook his head. "We never exchanged that sort of information. I don't like the police prowling about. Will they be knocking on doors, do you think?"

"I expect they will. Mrs. Cathcart is frightened. I doubt they'll persuade her to open her door."

Quincy hesitated, then said, "I saw Singleton walking late. He'd been up the hill. I wondered if he was looking for you. I saw you there, two nights ago."

"I stopped for a while. The horse is interesting to me."

"And so are we, your specimens under glass. I doubt Inspector Hill knows as much about us as you do."

"Because of Partridge. I'm not interested in your past, just whether or not you had a reason to dislike your neighbor."

"I don't have a reason to like or dislike him. But I'll tell you, I don't much care for Brady, he can't hold his drink. And Miller's a slippery sod. I wouldn't put murder past him, if you want the truth. Singleton is secretive, and that means he has secrets."

"What's yours?"

"Mine? I was a remittance man, and told never to set foot in England again. But I got homesick, tired of foreigners, their language, their food, their ways. So I slipped back into England and the family thinks I'm still in Mexico. My keep is paid into my account each month, and I like it that way."

It was a challenge, but Rutledge didn't take it up.

After a moment Quincy went on. "What's your interest in Partridge, anyway? I don't know that I believe the tale you tell. For all I know, Partridge is a red herring, and it's someone else who is on your watch list."

"I'd like very much to know why he's dead."

"Or you know why, but not who killed him. And my money is on Brady, because he hates Partridge, you know. God knows why, but he does."

Which was an interesting consideration. The watcher should be above reproach. And until Partridge—Parkinson—was a closed book, there was no release for Brady either. Was he tired of loneliness and orders?

Rutledge left, and was halfway to his motorcar when he heard Hill calling to him. He was just coming out of Miller's cottage, and jogged down to meet Rutledge, his fair face flushed as he caught up.

"I thought you'd agreed this was my patch. And here you are hobnobbing with the neighbors."

"I had agreed," Rutledge answered him, keeping his tone mild. "But Mrs. Cathcart and Quincy called to me, wanting to know what had happened. I told them Willingham was dead. They suspected as much, with the police summoned."

"Well, I'd be grateful if you kept away." He paused. "What about Slater? He tells me he knew you were here and came for you instead of me. He could have wielded that knife, you know, and used you for an alibi."

"I doubt Slater killed Willingham. In the first place, why?"

"Miller tells me Slater has something of a temper and Willingham was the devil to get along with."

"He was an unpleasant neighbor. I don't believe he invited his murder by tormenting Slater."

"Yes, well, you never know. Slights sometimes galvanize people like Slater into retaliation."

"What do you mean, slights?" Rutledge asked.

"You can see, Slater isn't the brightest star in the sky, is he? And he's had a run-in or two in Uffington. He's been accused of doing bad work, for one thing, and overcharging for it."

"Ah, the sexton. Yes, bad news travels fast. The work on that teapot was well done. I saw it myself. The sexton cheated Slater. If the sexton were dead, you might have a case."

Hill considered Rutledge with interest. "You do know these people, don't you? Better than you're willing to admit."

"I've held a conversation with several of them." Hill was beginning to annoy him, and he could feel Hamish stirring in the back of his mind.

"See that you don't hold any more until I've got to the bottom of this business. And you've never been clear about the Yard's interest here in Berkshire. No one's said anything to me about an inspector sent down."

"It has nothing to do with Willingham, I can assure you. A watching brief for the moment."

"Yes, Miller informed me that you'd shown an inordinate amount of interest in Partridge. Where is he? Not dead, by any chance? A knife in *his* back?"

"Hardly."

"Well, keep clear of my men and let them do their work." Hill walked away.

"He doesna' care for you stepping on his toes."

"I don't blame him. I'd not like anyone meddling in my case." He turned the crank and got in, but sat there with the motor idling, thinking.

He now had the perfect excuse to ask Sergeant Gibson to learn what he could about the people here in this tiny enclave of lepers.

It might be interesting to see what he could discover.

But he was no nearer to finding what had happened to Parkinson. A death in Yorkshire, a death in Berkshire, and both without the usual span of motives that often tipped the balance of an inquiry. There was no village here, in the real sense. And no threads or connections to be picked up and sorted through. The inhabitants of the Tomlin Cottages hadn't known one another before coming here to live, as far as he could tell—and that could hold just as true of Brady as any of the others. Martin Deloran wouldn't have trusted such a task to anyone who had been a friend of Parkinson.

Where was he to find the daughter that the housekeeper had spoken of in passing? Or the other children? There was time to go back to Partridge Fields and ask. Although he was of two minds over involving this daughter until he was prepared to tell her that her father was dead . . .

T he house, when he got there, was shut tight, and no one answered the knocker. Hamish, moody, had much to say about his failure to ask the housekeeper about the children when he had the chance. Instead he had pursued the subject of Porton Down, and then it was too late.

Rutledge drove on to the post office, and braced himself to face the elderly postmaster again.

The man was as irascible and unhelpful as he'd been earlier.

"I'm not supposed to give out information of this sort," he informed Rutledge.

"I'm searching for her father. She may know where he can be reached."

"I can't help you there. She doesn't live here."

"Very well. The direction of the housekeeper at Partridge Fields. Where can she be found when no one is in residence? It's police business."

They went in circles for all of five minutes. Finally, in exasperation Rutledge said, "I'll speak to the local police, then, and bring someone back with me."

"It won't do you any good. The housekeeper doesn't live here either."

Rutledge turned away, holding on to his patience with an effort. But as he was walking out the door a young woman with dark red hair and freckles who had been in the post office putting stamps on a small stack of invitations followed him out into the April sunshine.

She called to him and said, "You are trying to locate Rebecca Parkinson? I overheard you tell Mr. Walsh you were a policeman."

"Yes. I need to find her father."

"Is anything wrong? Is someone ill?"

"We've been asked to try to locate him. I'd hoped his daughter might help."

She frowned. "I doubt you'll succeed. They haven't spoken for two years."

"I can try," he said, smiling down at her. "If I knew where to find her. Do you know her?"

"We went to school together. Look, she and her father are estranged, but if it's important—"

"Very important."

"All right then. She's taken a small house about five miles from Partridge Fields. No one's lived at the house since Mrs. Parkinson's death. But Rebecca keeps up the gardens. If you go to the crossroads, and turn left instead of right, you'll find her at a place signposted Pockets."

He thanked her and went back to the motorcar.

The house was where the young woman had said it would be, small and well kept, the thatch overhanging the door and a pot of heartsease in tall stands on either side of it. The gardens surrounding it were filled with spring blooms.

He went up the front walk and knocked lightly.

After a few minutes, a young woman of perhaps twenty-four, blond and attractive, opened the door to him.

"My name is Rutledge," he said. "I'm from Scotland Yard—"

Her face went white, as if the blood had drained away and left only the flesh.

"What do you want?" she asked, holding tightly to the door, her voice low and husky.

"I'm trying to find your father. It's police business."

"I don't know where he lives. I don't care."

"I'm told you came to visit him once not long ago. A young woman of your description was seen knocking on his door."

Where she had been pale, she flushed now. And he thought it might be anger.

"I haven't knocked on any door of his. I can tell you that. He killed my mother, and I hate him."

She tried to shut the door, but he prevented her with a well-placed shoe.

"Miss Parkinson. I have reason to think your father is dead."

She stared at him, as if trying to read something in his face. "Dead?"

"It's very likely."

"Well, then, he's in hell, where he deserves to be. Go look for him there." And she shut the door with some force.

He stood there, on the tiny porch, and waited, thinking that she might be curious enough to want to know more.

But apparently she had meant what she said, and after a moment, he went back to the motorcar.

He had just reached for the crank when he thought he heard raised voices from the house. Only for an instant, and even then he wasn't certain whether Miss Parkinson was arguing with someone or venting her own anger—or her grief.

17

Rutledge found a telephone in a small hotel along the road back to Uffington, and put in a call to the Yard. Gibson couldn't be found right away, and it was a good quarter of an hour before the telephone rang and Gibson was on the line.

Rutledge gave him a list of names and asked him to learn what he could about each.

Gibson said, "It will take a while."

"I've got all the time in the world," Rutledge said with irony and told the sergeant when he expected to call the Yard again.

He ate his lunch at the hotel, and then traveled back to The Smith's Arms. There he found Smith eager to hear what had transpired at the cottages.

Rutledge said only, "Inspector Hill is dealing with it. Willingham is dead, that's all I can tell you."

"Willingham?" Smith seemed surprised. "I thought perhaps you'd found Mr. Partridge."

Rutledge let it go. But Smith was starved for information and said, "But how did he die? His heart, was it?"

"You must ask Inspector Hill."

"Pshaw, his like never show up here, at the Arms. I'll ask Andrew, when he comes for a pint. Care for a late lunch, Mr. Rutledge?"

Rutledge refused, thanking him, and went up to his room. Taking out paper and pen, he sat down and wrote an account of what he'd seen and done that morning at the Willingham cottage, signed it, and set it aside.

After that he went to stand by the window, looking out across the yard and the road, watching the wind dancing through the high grass there.

There was a letter, only just begun, that he'd found in the basket beside Parkinson's desk.

"My dear" was as far as he'd got before crumpling it up.

Had that been written to his daughter? Apologizing for whatever he'd done to make her hate him with such venom? Trying in some small way to make amends for the loss of her mother? Or asking her forgiveness for whatever role she felt he'd played in his wife's death?

And yet Parkinson had died as his wife had died, using gas. That would seem a bitter irony to Rebecca Parkinson, when she learned what had become of her father.

"Unless," Hamish pointed out, "the lass herself murdered him."

That had to be taken into account as well.

Except that the body had been found in Yorkshire . . .

Hamish said, "'Ware!"

And Rutledge turned to see Andrew Slater walking up the road toward The Smith's Arms.

Minutes later, Slater was mounting the stairs.

Rutledge had the door open, ready for him.

"Why did you leave?" the smith asked, aggrieved. "You left us to the mercy of Inspector Hill. He's half convinced that I killed Willingham. I ask you, why would I come and tell you I'd heard a cry, if I'd done the deed myself? It doesn't make any sense to me."

"Hill is doing his duty. And he'll begin by taking a long hard look at the dead man's neighbors. If you've done nothing wrong, if your conscience is clear, you'll see that's true."

"Yes, well," the smith said, gingerly lowering himself down in Rutledge's chair. It groaned under his weight. "If I survive, I'll applaud myself for my clear conscience."

"Who do you think might have wanted Willingham dead?" Rutledge had promised Inspector Hill to stay out of the case, but Slater had come to him.

"God knows. We didn't much care for him, and if we didn't, who did? He'd never spoken of a family. Who's to mourn him, then?"

"A good question," Rutledge answered.

"I can tell you Mrs. Cathcart is taking it hard. And so is Mr. Allen. Death came too close last night for his comfort."

"And the others?"

"Miller doesn't give a damn about any of it. If we all dropped dead in our shoes, he'd probably be pleased. Mr. Brady is trying to make himself very inconspicuous. He was drunk as a lord before he went to bed last night, and I doubt he'd have heard the angels' chorus after that. But he doesn't want it known to the world."

"Did Mr. Partridge have better luck with Willingham? Did they talk, do you think?"

Slater shook his head. "Where's a beginning for friendship? I expect I spoke with more of my neighbors than anyone else. I'm too thick to notice when I'm being ignored. Besides, I'm lonely sometimes."

"No one ever came to call on Willingham?"

"If they did, I never saw them. Mrs. Cathcart is afraid someone might visit her. That's sad." He looked down at his large hands, lying idle on his knees. "I wish I hadn't grown so. But there's nothing I can do about it. Just as she can't help being afraid. And I don't know if Quincy is his first name or his last. I never feel right, calling him 'Quincy.' Mr. Allen is dying, and there's no one to comfort him. I expect he doesn't want to be comforted. There's something stoic in that. Mr. Partridge had demons, and didn't know how to rid himself of them. And Singleton wants to be a soldier still. You have only to look at his carriage and how tidy he is. Hair clipped short, clothes immaculate. Mr. Brady is tormented too, because this isn't where he most wants to be. And Mr. Miller is the strangest of the lot, because I think he wants to be here."

It was an intriguing summation of the inhabitants of the leper cottages. Sometimes, Rutledge thought, a simple man saw more directly into the heart than one who was burdened with the sophistication of social behavior.

Slater got to his feet. "You won't let them arrest me, will you? I don't want to be taken into Uffington and put in a cell, with everyone staring at me. I think I'd go mad, locked up, and tell the police anything just to be let go. Even lies."

He went back down the stairs heavily, like a man carrying an enormous burden. Outside he turned to the Smithy, not back the way he'd come. It was odd how he seemed to find comfort and even acceptance there.

Slater hadn't been gone five minutes when Hill came looking for Rutledge.

He said, seeing the door open into Rutledge's room, "I'd like to have your statement now, if you please."

Rutledge turned to the desk and picked it up. "It's ready. I wanted to put it on paper while my memory of events was still sharp."

Hill took it and scanned it. "Fair enough. Any thoughts on who might have done this murder?"

"I leave that to you. But I will say, if I were in your shoes I'd be no closer to an answer."

"You were right, they're a stubborn lot. Won't come to the door, won't say more than yes or no when they do, and no one has seen anything. Granted, it was in the middle of the night, but I have the feeling that not much happens in those cottages that the rest of them don't know. I could feel the window curtains twitching like a palsy, eyes watching every move I make. Fairly gave me the willies, I can tell you. But if I had to pick one of that lot, it would either be the smith or the ex-soldier. Did you know he'd been cashiered from his regiment for dereliction of duty? Some years ago. That's the story I was given, anyway."

"By whom?"

"One of my men had seen him about and heard something of the sort. I'll look into it, find out if there's any truth in it. As far as I can tell, there's nothing missing from the dead man's cottage. So I have to rule out housebreaking. Although that might have been the original plan, come to think of it."

"Willingham's wrist was slashed," Rutledge said neutrally.

"Yes, probably while fighting off his killer. You saw for yourself how the room was wrecked."

"You don't think someone was trying to make the death appear to be a suicide?"

"No, no. Too preposterous. I talked to the man who calls himself Quincy. Seems a levelheaded sort. He thinks this murder is connected with Partridge's disappearance. He predicted they'd all be killed in their beds if I'm not quick."

"Willingham by all accounts was an unpleasant man who had probably made himself a pariah long before he came to the Tomlin Cottages. His murderer could have come from his past."

"I'd considered that too, and will be looking into it." He'd been standing leaning against the doorframe, nonchalant as if Rutledge's opinion carried no weight with him. He straightened, preparing to go.

But Hamish believed his coming to the inn was a fishing expedition.

Rutledge tended to agree with that summation.

"You'll be returning to the Yard?" Hill asked from the head of the stairs. "I'm of the opinion your man Partridge is dead. That's Mr. Brady's view as well."

"I expect he may be right," Rutledge answered.

"Well, at least I have a body to be going on with. That's more than you can say—so far."

He turned and ran lightly down the stairs.

Rutledge watched Hill leave the inn and walk briskly back the way he'd come.

In the afternoon, he drove back to Pockets, to speak again to Rebecca Parkinson.

She was there, in the house. He could sense it. But she refused to answer his knock.

He tried to sense how she had responded to it—whether she was stock-still, waiting for him to go away, or hiding behind the stairs, where she couldn't be seen. Or lying on her bed, looking at the ceiling, telling herself that she didn't care.

And he found himself wondering if Meredith Channing, if she were standing next to him under the overhang of thatch, would have been able to tell him if he was right.

Unwilling to leave, Rutledge waited in his motorcar for over an hour outside the house. But it was a stalemate. He couldn't go in, and she couldn't come out.

Finally he gave up and drove away. The house at Partridge Fields drew him, and he went there to sit in the gardens for a time. This time the house felt empty, and he knew there was no one inside. He was about to leave when a motorcar turned in the gates and followed the drive round to the kitchen yard.

He realized it must be Rebecca Parkinson, and he walked swiftly toward the shrubbery, to catch her before she had gone inside.

But she must have seen him, or perhaps glimpsed his vehicle where he'd left it, behind a shed. She gunned the engine, swung the vehicle in a circle to turn it, tires spewing gravel and earth as they bit for a grip, and then sped away down the drive before he could stop her.

He stood there, winded from dashing after the motorcar, and swore.

It was useless, following her back to Pockets. By the time he retrieved his own motorcar and started after her, she would have a head start, enough to be safely inside again before he could get there.

But he was angry enough to try, and drove after her anyway, flying down the lane in her wake.

When he got to Pockets, there was no sign of the car or of Rebecca.

He realized that she must have expected him to follow her and instead of going directly home, as he'd anticipated, she had foxed him again and disappeared.

Rutledge drove back to Berkshire, his mood dark, and found the inn full of drivers stopping for dinner or the night.

Avoiding them, he went directly to his room. Tomorrow he would call Gibson again and see what, if any, information he'd come up with.

In the event, it was very little. Although Hill had been right about Singleton. He'd been cashiered from his regiment but not for dereliction of duty. He had lost his temper once too often, and been asked to resign after he'd struck a fellow officer.

The reason for the argument wasn't clear, but Gibson believed it was the excuse Singleton's commanding officer had been looking for.

Mrs. Cathcart's nasty divorce had been as bad or worse than she'd told Rutledge. Her husband, in Gibson's view, had set out to make her life wretched, and succeeded beyond his wildest expectations. After the divorce, he'd cut her off without a penny, and she had had to scrape a living as best she could. The rent at the cottages was cheap enough, and she had inherited just enough from an aunt to live there frugally.

Allen, who in fact was dying, had gone off like a wounded animal to spend his last days away from friends and family. The general belief was that he'd wanted nothing to do with surgery or cures, and expected to die within the first six months. He hadn't been that fortunate.

There was no information on the man who called himself Quincy, and none on Miller or Brady. Gibson suggested that Brady was using a name other than his own, and there were too many Millers to be sure which one was living in the shadow of the pale horse. And with only one name to go on, Quincy hadn't turned up in the files or memories of the policemen Gibson had spoken to. Rutledge found himself thinking that perhaps Quincy had spoken the truth, that he was a remittance man back in England and careful to conceal that fact.

Willingham had a rather sordid past, as it happened. He had been involved in dubious schemes designed to leave the investor poorer and himself richer. Skirting the law carefully, he had managed to avoid trouble, but in the end, bitter and running out of money, he'd come to a place where he felt safe from persecution as well as prosecution. Although a few of his former clients had threatened to sue him over the years, the general consensus had been that in doing so they would reveal their own avarice and their willingness to bend the rules to their own advantage. Still, more than one had voiced physical threats.

"He's been there for more than ten years, and the taste for revenge must have grown cold by now," Gibson concluded. "But then you never know."

"This didn't appear to be a case of revenge. As far as I can tell, the intent was to make his death appear to be a suicide. Not much satisfaction there."

"None," Gibson agreed. "On the other hand, it would confuse the police."

Rutledge thanked Gibson and put up the receiver. On his way back to the inn from Uffington, he wondered at what point Willingham's death would bring attention round to Parkinson's empty cottage. Until it did, he would leave Hill to it.

He stayed away from the cottages, but by nightfall he was restless. He could feel the tension building, and Hamish, in his mind, was a bleak shadow that threatened to break through his guard.

He walked to Wayland's Smithy, back again to the inn, and from the road watched the moon rise. After a time he strolled on toward the White Horse, revealing itself as he neared it, and felt the tug of its spell. The graceful gallop was marvelous, and he thought about the hand that had created it, guiding the men who dug the sod from the chalk with antler spades until its dimensions were revealed. What must it have felt like to see it complete for the first time, shimmering in the moonlight, magic in its own way?

He was suddenly distracted by something he could sense but not clearly see. Surely there was someone at the foot of the horse? And instead of looking up, whoever it was had his back to the horse.

Rutledge stood very still, letting all his faculties tell him what was there.

Hamish said, his voice soft in Rutledge's ear, "Whoever it is, it isna' stirring. Else I'd hear it."

Rutledge was thrown back to the trenches, and scanning No Man's Land in the dark for any activity. Scanning until his eyes ached, and he had to rub them with his fingers before opening them again. His men's lives had depended on his alertness, his ability to see a sniper crawling to a vantage point, or men changing the watch along the line of trenches opposite, sometimes even parties going out to look for their wounded. Once or twice he'd caught the faint sounds of fresh men settling at the machine gun far across the pitted landscape. Hamish had been better than any of them at the game, his ears attuned to sounds most couldn't hear.

The slightest movement caught Rutledge's attention, dragging him back to the figure. No sound, just a minute change in position as if someone had been standing there too long and was beginning to feel stiff or chilled in the night air.

He waited, slowly dropping until he was squatting and no longer a silhouette against the sky.

There it was again. A figure in black. He couldn't tell if it was male or female. Only that it was as quiet as a carving, its shape altered by arms wrapped around its body, giving it a bulkier outline.

In the day of the White Horse, he'd have believed in ghosts or totems of a clan, he told himself. But this was human, this figure, and tiring.

After a bit, it seemed to lengthen, as if it too had been squatting or bent over, peering toward the cottages.

And then it began to move, away from Rutledge, back to the far side of the horse, and toward a clump of trees that grew across the road. He rose slowly to his feet, and followed in its wake.

He was closer now, and he'd been right. The figure was bent over, as if in pain, and its arms were wrapped tightly around its body.

Hamish said, "Yon motorcar."

Indeed there was one, left in the dark shadows cast by the trees.

A sound drifted back to him, human and grieving. A sob, he thought, that rose in spite of intense self-control and for an instant broke free before being smothered again.

He was closer still, the figure never turning to look back, never dreaming that someone followed it.

It reached the motorcar and leaned against a wing, as if struggling with some emotion, then it went forward to the grill and reached for the crank.

As the engine fired, Rutledge broke from the side of the hill and raced forward, catching the figure just as it turned toward the driver's door.

It fought, with tooth and nail and shoe, but he was stronger, saying over the sound of the engine, "I'm not going to harm you. I'll let you go, if you don't cry out. Neither one of us wants to be heard over there at the cottages."

There was a stillness, and then a nod. He stepped back, ready to move again if it was a trick.

He knew who his prisoner was. A woman. Rebecca Parkinson. And yet what he found almost incomprehensible was the pain he'd sensed in someone who had clearly hated her father and reveled in his death.

"What do you want?" The voice was husky in the darkness. "Who are you?" And there was fear in that question as well.

"My name is Rutledge, Miss Parkinson. You know me. We talked at your home."

"You're lying."

"No, truly, I was at Pockets—"

She threw her head back, and said, "I don't live at Pockets."

So the housekeeper was right about children. Here was the sister to Rebecca.

"I'm sorry. If you aren't Rebecca, what's your given name, Miss Parkinson."

"It's Sarah." Grudgingly spoken, he noted.

"Where do you live?"

"Near Porton Down. In one of the old cottages. What possessed you to attack me in that outrageous way?"

"I'm from Scotland Yard. I've been trying to speak to your sister, and she's done her best to avoid me. It's about your father."

She was still for an instant, and then she said, "My father's dead. At least to me he is, as he has been for the past two years."

"Yet you come here, to where he lived." He hazarded a guess. "And someone saw you here once before, knocking at his door. Then sometime later, sitting in what must have been this motorcar, alone and crying."

She appeared to be shaken by his knowledge of her movements. "Have you been watching me?" she demanded. "What is this? I don't understand why the Yard would take any interest in my father."

"He hasn't been seen for some time. We think he's dead, and that he may have been murdered."

He could hear the quick drawn breath, as the shock of his words hit her.

"I don't believe you."

"Nevertheless. His body has been found in Yorkshire."

She broke down then, turning away from him and burying her face

in her hands. He let her cry, standing patiently behind her until she
was calmer.

"I hated him," she said after a time.

"I think you must have loved him as well."

"How could I, after what he'd done to my mother? She killed herself, no matter how hard they tried to put a better face on it. *She killed
herself!* Do you know what it is to come home from a party and find
the police in your house, and everything at sixes and sevens, and then
you're asked to look at your mother's dead face and tell the police that
you recognize her? Rebecca and I said good-bye to her, and she was
smiling, she was *smiling,* and she insisted on kissing us, for luck she
said. And we went blithely away, waving to her, looking forward to the
party, and it never struck us, either of us, that she was different somehow. That perhaps she was saying good-bye in a very different way."

He said, "Where was your father when she died? At the house?"

"No, no, he was at the laboratory. He was always in the laboratory,
looking for a way to stabilize a gas so that it could be used in a shell
or trying to make it more potent, longer lasting, more dependable in
delivery. Everyone thought he was the cleverest man, a practical scientist. He not only could devise gases, he could take them to the battlefield. I heard them say so once, when they didn't know I was there
in the cottage he sometimes used, and they were waiting for him to
arrive. *Practical,* as if this horrid way of maiming and killing soldiers
was something to be studied for the most economical or useful way of
doing murder."

"The Germans used it first."

"What does it matter? It was inhumane. Oh, I'm *sick* of this business. If you have nothing more to say to me, I'm going home."

"You haven't told me why you came here to see your father. Why
you were standing there on the hill tonight. If you hate him so much,
why do you torment yourself like this?"

"I don't know," she said wearily. "I remember sometimes the man
who set me on his shoulders to see the Queen's carriage pass during

Victoria's Jubilee. Or held me on my first pony, until I stopped being afraid of falling off and could take the reins myself. Or bringing me chocolates on my birthday when I was twelve, and telling me they had come all the way from Belgium. Little things that had nothing to do with gassing soldiers or killing the cows by accident, or spending more and more time in his laboratory, lost in the things he could create there."

She caught her breath on a sob, then cleared her throat.

"There was something new he was working on, some terrible new possibility, that's why he wasn't there with us that night. Mother died, and he walked away from us and came to live here. Alone. I told myself it was recognizing what he'd done to her and to us. But later, I thought perhaps he was afraid to go back because in her will she'd asked that her ashes be scattered in the gardens under their bedroom windows."

18

If she had intended to shock him, Sarah Parkinson succeeded.

Rutledge had walked in those gardens, admiring them. He had seen how carefully they were maintained, and never guessed that they were, in effect, Mrs. Parkinson's memorial.

He said, "Is that why neither you nor your sister live at Partridge Fields?"

"Would you?" she demanded. "If every time you looked out at the gardens, you felt her presence? I thought it might be comforting, somehow, but it isn't. She's a restless, unhappy ghost, and we're afraid of her."

"Yet you or your sister—or both of you—keep the gardens the way they must have been when she was alive."

He could see her bite her lip. "I hate it. She's there, scattered about the beds, and we're caught up in her revenge. If we let the gardens go to seed, if they're overgrown and ugly, we're desecrating her grave. If we dig and plant and weed, we're touching her ashes. It's as if the flowers draw their strength from her bones and morbidly flourish. My father left it to us to decide what to do about the grounds. And it was the cruelest thing he did."

She walked to the door of the motorcar. "I'm tired, I want to go home. I've talked too much as it is."

"You must decide, between you, who will come to Yorkshire with me and bring your father's body back to Wiltshire."

"No. I'll have no part in any such thing. Let him stay where he is, unloved and unwanted."

She hadn't asked why her father had gone to Yorkshire, or had died there.

Hamish said, "It would ha' been easy for them to kill him. If he was lured to the house."

Were either of the women capable of murder? He rather thought that Rebecca Parkinson was. Her hatred was still white-hot and ran deep. There was grief mixed into Sarah's emotions. But she would surely have supported her sister after Parkinson had been killed. The only other choice would have been to refuse, then see Rebecca caught, convicted, and hanged.

But if the sisters had killed their father, why do it in Yorkshire?

Or had he got away the first time they'd tried, and they had gone after him?

A chilling thought.

The question was, how was he going to go about proving it?

"Did your father have enemies, anyone who would have liked to see him dead?" It was the standard question to put to survivors.

"Not that I know of. Although there was one man in London whom my father didn't trust. He told my mother once that he'd been invited to bring us up to London to dine with this man, and my father didn't want us to go. I only remember because Becky and I were so disappointed. But my father said that London was quite dull because of the war, and it wouldn't have been as exciting as we'd thought."

"What was this man's name?" Rutledge asked, although he had a very good idea.

"I don't think I ever heard it. My father referred to him as the Dreadnought. But that was the name of a ship, wasn't it?"

Deloran?

In the end he let Sarah Parkinson go, after asking how to find her if he needed her to answer more questions. He had no grounds on which to keep her.

But then as she put the motorcar in gear, Rutledge put a hand on her door. "There's been a murder in the cottages. A man called Willingham. Did he know your father, by any chance?"

"A murder? How dreadful." She shook her head. "I don't think my father would have come here to live if he had known any of his neighbors. He was running away. From the house, from Mother's ghost, from us—from the army. Possibly even from himself. Who knows? For that matter, who cares? It was selfish, whatever his excuse was."

Watching her motorcar out of sight, Rutledge found himself pitying the unwanted, still nameless body in Yorkshire.

Hamish said, "He made his own grave whilst he was still living."

And it was true, in many ways. But in the end, Rebecca and Sarah Parkinson would have no choice but to bring their father home.

If Mrs. Parkinson still haunted the house where she'd died, Parkinson would be satisfied to lie in the churchyard, far from the flower beds at Partridge Fields. But which name would be engraved on the stone over him?

If Rebecca and Sarah Parkinson denied that he was their father, Deloran would be only too pleased to add his own statement that the murder victim was an unknown unhappy man named Partridge, dead at the hands of person or persons unknown. And in a year or two all of this would be forgotten.

Brady might be brought in to testify, and disclaim any knowledge of an assignment to watch a scientist who had resigned prematurely from Porton Down. He was merely an ex-soldier, down on his luck and trying to sober up.

And Rutledge would be left looking a fool.

He walked back to the inn and retrieved his motorcar. It was late to be driving to Partridge Fields, but the roads were fairly empty and he made good time, keeping awake through sheer physical effort by the time he was twenty miles away.

He opened the gates and drove through them, leaving the car near the shed.

The house was dark, the gardens black in the moonlight, the brash colors of spring disguised as varying shades of gray.

The kitchen door, as he'd thought, was unlocked.

This was the country. No one came to rob the house, there was no need to lock doors.

Carrying his torch, he walked through the kitchen quarters and then through the formal rooms of the house.

The glancing beam of his torch illumined the brilliant colors of draperies and carpets and upholstery, the gold filigree around a mirror, the rich tones of polished walnut and mahogany, the shimmer of silk wallpaper and cut glass in the chandeliers.

Someone had had money. Mrs. Parkinson's dowry? Parkinson's wages from the government? A family inheritance? Enough at least for a comfortable life and a well-appointed home.

He moved quietly in the silent house, and avoided windows. Portraits watched him as he passed, and once a mouse scurried out of the wainscoting and across the floor, squeaking as it dived into the cold hearth.

Like the gardens, the house was meticulously maintained.

Even without Hamish's harsh reminder, Rutledge was well aware that he had no authority to open doors, look in drawers, and investigate the contents of desks, but he rather thought he would find nothing, even if he did.

Even so, he saw no trace of Parkinson here, although there were several photographs of a fair woman with two fair and pretty daughters set in silver frames. Looking at them, he could almost see the girls grow from room to room as the array of photographs marked the changes of years.

He studied Mrs. Parkinson's likeness. She was slim, very pretty, and her eyes reminded him of a doe, sensitive and vulnerable. She should have married a country squire, he thought, not a man whose training in chemistry had taken a far different turn from anything either of them could foresee.

Rutledge broke his own rule only once, looking in the wardrobe in what appeared to be the master bedroom. As he'd expected, it held only a woman's clothing, as if Parkinson had taken everything of his with him, leaving nothing behind because he never intended to come home again.

And reciprocally, his daughters had banned him from the house by carrying out their mother's wishes. He was shut out, lock, stock, and photographs. There were none that included him. Was that why the one on his desk was so precious to him?

"Taken the day we climbed the white horse . . ."

Rutledge inspected the lamps in the master bedroom, and turned the key gently, listening to the soft hiss of gas wafting into the room before shutting it off again. It would be a simple matter to close the doors and windows and lie there in bed, waiting to fall asleep and die. But then Mrs. Parkinson had been ready to die.

Had Parkinson been asked to come here for a reconciliation, and then drugged enough to keep him from waking up when someone slipped in, turned on the gas, and laid towels outside the doors? Retribution without pity, but without having to watch a father die.

Hamish said, "Aye, but no' in this room, and no' in this house. He wouldna' sleep here."

Which might explain why the body had been discovered in Yorkshire; but even if Parkinson had somehow been lured there, where was the gas jet that killed him? Even two young women would have a problem dragging a dead man out of a hotel without being noticed.

Hamish said, "Ye ken, it may ha' been one of Deloran's men who lured him to where he was killed."

Counting on the fact that the newspapers wouldn't concern themselves with a nobody's unfortunate death? Then why dress the body in mask and cloak, attracting attention to it?

Hard to believe that Deloran would stoop to murder, but then Rutledge was still in the dark about why precisely the man cared what happened to either Gaylord Partridge or Gerald Parkinson. It would be easier, surely, to discredit him than to murder him.

Aloud Rutledge said, "Then why send the Yard here, when Parkinson went missing? Drawing attention to him. Why not leave well enough alone?"

"To wash his hands. There's the watcher. He could ha' sworn that nobody knew where Partridge had gone, just as nobody kenned where he'd vanished before."

"Yes, well, I think tomorrow it's time to speak to Mr. Brady. Drunk or sober."

Keeping his torch from striking the glass, he went to the window and looked down on the dark gardens. Clouds were moving across the face of the moon as it set, and he could almost imagine something out there as the shadows shifted. Very likely the horse fountain, showing itself in ghostly white fragments as the shrubs moved in the wind. But add a little guilt to that, and he could understand how the family must have felt about this room and the gardens.

In the passage leading to the stairs, Rutledge paused to consider the nature of the silence around him. The ashes in the garden must have been the last straw, not the first. He had a strong feeling that this family had broken apart long before Mrs. Parkinson's suicide. What had really brought her to the brink of despair? It must have gone far beyond her belief that her husband was squandering his gifts and talents on work that he loved and she hated.

He reached the kitchen, made certain that he'd not tracked mud from the yard onto the stone flags by the door, and left the house exactly as he'd found it. Standing for a moment in the night's darkness until his eyes adjusted, he thought he heard an owl call from the trees beyond. Then he walked to the motorcar without looking back.

Hamish remarked, "It wasna' wise to come here."

"It could do no harm," Rutledge answered, going down the drive without his headlamps, and turning the bonnet toward Berkshire.

"Aye, so ye may think now. And later live to regret it."

I n fact, Hamish was right. Rutledge was eating a late breakfast at The Smith's Arms when the door opened and Rebecca Parkinson strode in.

"What the devil did you think you were doing," she asked harshly, "when you went to my mother's house in the night?"

Rutledge, caught off guard, said, "If there are no servants in the house to protect it, if doors are left unlocked, anyone can walk in. How many times did your father go back to that house without your knowledge? Or for that matter, the man he called Dreadnought?"

She opened her mouth to say something, and then shut it smartly. After a moment she asked, "What could you possibly know about Dreadnought?"

"His real name."

That took her aback. In the silence that followed, she tried to absorb the implications of what he'd said.

"My father disliked him intensely. It was personal and professional. He told me once that the name suited the man—he feared nothing and he used people for his own ends. If you've been sent here by Dreadnought, I'm not surprised that you would stoop to anything."

"I told you, I'm from Scotland Yard. But I have met the man. Now, why should you think that someone had been in the house at Partridge Fields?"

Returning to the grievance that had brought her here, she said, "The gardener at one of the houses down the road was coming home late last night from a wedding, and he saw lights moving from room to room. He's known my family for ages, my mother and he often exchanged plants. He came to find me this morning, to tell me that something was wrong. Something about the lights troubled him, and he was afraid to investigate. He's an old man and he may have thought it was my mother's spirit. But I knew better. It wasn't my mother's poor ghost, it was you. When you couldn't badger me, you went to the house on your own, thinking no one would learn of it."

He had been careful not to show a light. And he remembered the flicker of movement he imagined he'd seen in the shadows near the horse fountain. Had someone else been there after he left? Deloran might have had reasons of his own for taking the risk of searching the empty house. If so, what was he looking for?

"He wouldna' go himself, ye ken," Hamish remarked. "His hands are clean."

Rutledge said to Miss Parkinson, "But you yourself couldn't see evidence of someone there?"

"Of course not. You're a London policeman, you aren't going to leave muddy footprints in the passages. What I want to know is what you took away?"

"If I was there, it was without any legal right to take anything from the house."

"I should have known you wouldn't have the decency to tell me the truth."

Rutledge smiled faintly. "Yes, all right, I was there. But I touched nothing. I wanted to see what drove your father away from his home—why he chose to live where he did. I was hoping that if I could understand that, I could explain some of the other things I don't understand. Please, sit down, and let Mrs. Smith bring you a cup of tea. I have a few questions to ask you and we might as well get them over with."

She was still angry. "You went into my mother's *room*. Where she died. Why should I want to talk to you? I wouldn't give you that satisfaction."

When she had first confronted him, he'd noted how much like her mother she looked, but in the course of their conversation Rutledge could see how much stronger she was than her mother must have been. Her spirit, he thought, must have come from her father. However much she would fiercely deny it.

Before she could turn and stalk out of the inn, he said, "I can arrange to have you taken into custody to help us with our inquiries if you prefer that."

"On what charges?" she demanded. "I've done nothing except refuse to speak to you. And I can't be forced to speak, as you well know."

"On the charge that you murdered your father."

Rebecca Parkinson sat down. "That's utter rubbish."

"Yes, but I rather think I could prove it. It might be worth a cup of tea to find out what I know."

"I don't want tea. Whatever you have to say, it had better be said quickly, or I'm leaving."

"I told you the first time we met. We've found your father's body." It was blunt and intended to be.

Her angry flush faded. "He's alive and well, and living in those wretched cottages under the White Horse." Her denial wasn't completely convincing. As if she knew her father was dead but must keep up the pretense that it was a lie. Her vehemence on their first meeting had been stronger.

"But he went missing, you see. And now his body is lying unclaimed in a Yorkshire village. Doesn't that mean anything to you? Or the fact that he might have been murdered?"

"It has nothing to do with me." The line of her jaw was defiant.

"He didn't die where we found him. That's why we have to suspect murder. I'm here to make sense of what little we do know, and that means I have to follow him if I can every step of the way from those cottages to Yorkshire. To do that, I need information about his life, his family, his friends, his enemies. Whether you like it or not."

She said, "Make sense of whatever you like. Just leave me out of it."

"Do you hate your father so much that you'd prefer to see his killer go free?"

She glanced down, so that he couldn't see her eyes. "I've told you, I don't really care."

"Did you know that one of the other people in those cottages was murdered last night? A Mr. Willingham. I need to know what connection he might have had with your father."

She looked up then, startled. "I don't believe you."

"Ask Inspector Hill, in Uffington. He's handling that case."

Leaning back in her chair, she considered him, her mind working. "I don't know anyone named Willingham. A coincidence. It must be."

"That's possible, of course. But in such a small community two murders in a few weeks has to be regarded with suspicion. I'm forced to wonder what Mr. Willingham might have known about your father's disappearance. If he saw someone come for your father and take him away. The bicycle your father sometimes rode and his motorcar were both where he kept them. Surely your father didn't walk all the way to Yorkshire."

He thought her mouth was dry. She ran her tongue over her lips and said, "If you'll summon Mrs. Smith, I believe I'll have that tea now."

It was a surprising change of heart. Rutledge was wary.

He went to find Mrs. Smith, though Hamish warned him that Rebecca Parkinson would be gone when he returned. It was a risk he had to take.

He was relieved when he came back, tray in hand, to find she was still at his table.

Rutledge passed her the fresh cup, waited until she had added milk and sugar, then taken the first sip.

"I spoke to your sister last night."

She nearly choked. "I don't believe you. You don't even know where to find her."

"She'd come to stand on the hill by the White Horse. I don't know what it was she was thinking. But I distinctly heard her crying."

"Sarah has always had a soft heart. She's like my mother, taking in lost kittens and stray dogs, worrying about young men we knew who went to France and stayed there in unmarked graves."

"Still, I had the strongest feeling that she must know more about your father's death than she's comfortable with, and her conscience is tormenting her. It's rather too much of a coincidence, isn't it, that she came to grieve the night after Willingham died."

Rebecca Parkinson stood up so quickly she knocked over her cup and tea splashed onto the skirt of her dress.

"You leave my sister alone, do you hear me? Don't go near her again. Or I shall have you up for harassment. Do you understand me?"

"What are you afraid of, Miss Parkinson? That she'll break before you do? Murder doesn't always sit easily on one's conscience. But sometimes a second killing is necessary to protect the secrets of the first. The police may consider that possibility, you see, in investigating Willingham's. Whatever part she played in your father's death will eventually drive her to confess. What will you do to stop her?"

Rebecca Parkinson leaned forward, and with all the strength of her shoulder behind the blow, slapped Rutledge as hard as she could across the face. *"Leave my sister alone!"*

And then she was gone, slamming the door hard behind her.

Mrs. Smith came hurrying from the kitchen. "I heard such a noise—and look at the tea, spilled all over my clean floor! What happened?"

"I'm afraid the young woman who was here has a chink in her armor," he said. "And I've just found it."

R utledge walked down to the cottages and tapped lightly on the smith's door.

Slater, looking as if he hadn't slept, opened it and said, "I don't think Inspector Hill wants you to talk to me."

"Not about Willingham, no," Rutledge said, stepping inside before Slater could shut his door. "I'm here to talk about Mr. Partridge. Did you know that he had two daughters?"

"No, of course I didn't. He never talked about his family. I thought he must not have any. No one came to spend a Sunday afternoon with him, that sort of thing. It was just a guess that the girl who knocked at his door was his daughter. Mrs. Cathcart likes happy endings. For all we know, she might well have been the daughter of a friend. You would think, wouldn't you, that being alone would make the cottages a friendlier place, but it doesn't work that way."

"Is Hill still giving you trouble over Willingham's death?"

"He's told me I'll be taken in to sign my statement. I don't know when that will be. Or if he'll keep me once he has me there." He was morose. "I've not done anything wrong. But the sexton has said I'm a liar and a cheat. I don't see that that leads a man to murder, but Inspector Hill seems to believe it does."

"For what it's worth, I don't think he actually believes that you did this. But he has to look at all the possibilities. Did you know Willingham before he moved here?"

"I didn't know any of these people. Including Mr. Partridge."

"And what do the other inhabitants of the Tomlin Cottages have to say about the murder?"

"They aren't saying anything. No one works in their garden, even as warm as it is this morning. No one answers the door. You'd think we collaborated on the murder, drawing straws to see who did the actual stabbing. Like Julius Caesar, in Shakespeare's play, when everyone turns against him. I remember reading that, and thinking he should have known the Ides of March meant trouble. But I suppose there wouldn't have been a play at all, if he'd listened to his wife in the first place."

Rutledge smiled. "You cut through the chaff to the kernel." The smile faded. "Are you all right, Slater?"

"As best as I can be. But I'm too anxious to work. And if I can't work, in the end I won't eat either. No one will bring business to me if I'm under a cloud of suspicion."

"I must go to Brady's cottage," he said, "but if there's anything you need, let me know."

"How? If they take me away, there's nothing you can do."

"I can try," Rutledge replied simply.

He left the smith's cottage and walked on down the lane to Brady's. There was no answer to his knock, and he'd expected none. A stranger arriving here would have sworn that all the cottages were empty, their inhabitants fled. But behind the shut doors and the drawn shades of the windows, there were people who had nowhere else to turn.

Dublin came to greet him as he returned to his motorcar, rubbing herself against his ankles, and he bent down to pet her just as a sparrow flitted by and she turned to give chase.

What did Dublin know about the murder of Willingham? She prowled the cottages, looking for mice. Had she been outside Willingham's two nights ago when a murderer came to call?

Hamish said irritably, "It wouldna' matter if she did. She's no' able to tell ye what she saw."

He climbed to the muzzle of the horse and sat there, watching scudding clouds cross the sky. It would rain before long, and he'd be wet if he didn't leave while he could. But still he sat there, waiting for someone to stir. He could feel the eyes watching for him, wondering where he might turn up next, and whether or not he was doing his own work or Hill's.

And then Mr. Allen stepped out of his door. Rutledge could hear him coughing, the sound captured and bounced up the hill to where he sat. Allen puttered a little in his front garden, casting wary eyes toward his neighbors.

Cabin fever, Rutledge thought, watching him. And a small defiance in the face of death. *I'm alive, you haven't gathered me in yet . . .*

Or was it because they all knew that Rutledge was sitting here, watching, that they felt free to move about.

Quincy opened his door and set a bowl of water down for Dublin, and looked up at the building clouds.

Mrs. Cathcart timidly crept out, and moved a flower pot to where it better caught the waning sun.

Miller was next, putting something in the dust bin by the corner of his house, and then looking fixedly at Rutledge. As if to ask why he was still here, when it was clear that Partridge wasn't coming back.

Rutledge hadn't met the man, but it wouldn't do any good to hurry down to the lane. Miller would be inside long before that.

They were all accounted for, except for Brady. But he was the watcher, accustomed to peering between his curtains and not showing his face. Rutledge found it interesting that Brady was still here, when Deloran knew perfectly well that Partridge was never coming back. Just as Gerald Parkinson would never return.

It was, Rutledge thought, a fanciful public façade, Deloran keeping his watcher there to report to him and to make it appear that he himself believed Partridge was coming back. Or perhaps Brady had already been put out to pasture, and lived on here because it was his home. Rutledge expected the man would claim that, if he were questioned.

Rutledge sat there, listening to Hamish in his head, for another quarter of an hour. He hadn't seen so much as the corner of a curtain twitch in Brady's cottage. No sign of life that would attract Rutledge's attention and bring him down the hill to knock again.

A crow came to perch on Brady's chimneytop, scolding Dublin as she made her rounds. Mrs. Cathcart, seeing it, went quickly back inside. Quincy called to the cat, then shut his own door. Allen, still in the garden in front of his house, looked up at the sound of Quincy's door closing. And after a few minutes, his defiance turning practical as the first drops of rain danced on the flagstones that made up his garden path, he disappeared as well.

Rutledge came down the hill, feeling the heavy drops strike his shoulders with some force. They were only the forerunners of the storm, but the clouds had thickened to the west and rain would come in earnest in the next ten minutes or so.

Rutledge went up the lane between the cottages and knocked again on Brady's door, calling to him when it remained shut.

There was no answer.

Feeling a stirring of his intuition, Rutledge put his hand on the latch and lifted it.

The door wasn't locked.

He pushed it open, calling, "Brady, I know you're in there. I want to talk to you."

The crow flew away, cawing as he went, shattering the silence that sometimes foretells a storm.

Rutledge stood there, waiting. But there was no response from Brady.

He stepped inside, Hamish loud in his ears, and looked at the untidy room, dishes left on a table, books and papers scattered about, a pair of field glasses standing on the shelf under the window. From his vantage point Brady had a sweeping view toward the hill of the White Horse, and also of Partridge's cottage.

For an instant Rutledge wondered if Deloran was mad enough to send Brady to do his dirty work for him at Partridge Fields, then laughed at the thought. A man who drank as Brady was said to do couldn't be trusted with murder . . .

And then as his eyes adjusted to the storm-induced gloom of the sitting room, he saw Brady staring back at him, as if accusing him of trespassing.

But Brady was not accusing anyone of anything.

A knife protruded from his chest, and both his hands were wrapped around the hilt, frozen there by death.

19

It appeared to Rutledge, looking down at the body, as if Brady had stabbed himself, his grip on the blade almost like iron. Sitting in his chair, forcing the blade into the soft flesh under his rib cage, he appeared to have sliced through an artery.

And on the table beside him there was a sheet of paper. Rutledge could see the writing on it from where he stood, but couldn't manage to read the words.

His guess was that Brady had died sometime in the night, and the letter would express his fear of hanging, or a full confession.

Rutledge looked at the man's narrow face, unshaven chin, thin graying hair. There was depression in the circles under his eyes, indicating sleepless nights and watchful days, and nothing to show for it but a shabby cottage and a reputation for the bottle.

At his back, the rain had begun in earnest, and Rutledge turned to look at the ground behind him. Whatever tracks were there, the rain would quickly obliterate. Yet all he could see from where he stood were his own, and the mixed prints of Hill's men, trampling about as they came to interview Brady.

If the murderer had come up the garden path, he knew he would be safe.

If, that is, murder had been done . . .

He looked about the room, staying where he was in the open door. A gust of wind came up and whisked the sheet of paper from the table, sending it into the ash-strewn hearth behind it.

What would Hill make of this death? An easy solution to Willingham's murder? Whatever path the inspector took, it would give Rutledge insight into the man.

He closed the door against the rising wind and walked away. He would have to send the smith again to summon the police.

Slater was reluctant to go.

"Why me? He'll think I've had something to do with it, as sure as the dawn follows the dark."

"Because I must stay here to keep an eye on the cottage—"

"But no one would go in there. And I could as easily keep watch."

"Slater. Go on. I don't have my motorcar here, it's at The Smith's Arms. You'll find it there. And hurry."

"There's no need to hurry. Brady will still be there when Inspector Hill comes." Slater collected rain gear from the cupboard where he kept his clothes and then paused at the door. "You're safe enough, getting yourself involved in this. You're a policeman. Who is willing to believe me?"

And he was gone, out into the storm.

Rutledge turned so that he could watch the Brady cottage. The smith's house reeked of wood smoke. He'd never noticed it before, but the dampness outside somehow brought it to the fore.

Slater used fire and hammer for his work. It was evident everywhere Rutledge looked. The hinges of doors and cabinets, the bolts that held them closed, the tongs on the hearth, the scoop of the shovel used to take out the ashes. So many details he'd never had time to notice.

Even the latches of the windows had been replaced by wrought iron, and the candlestick holders on the windowsill were attractively turned. There was a boot scraper by the door, made in the shape of a hedgehog, the bristles of broom on his back looking like the bristles on the hedgehog's back.

Overhead a wrought-iron lamp dropped down out of the ceiling on a finely made chain, the sconces shaped like tulips, the candle in the fold of the petals.

Alone here, he realized how the smith's presence, tall and vibrant, filled the room. Now it seemed larger, outsized, because he wasn't there.

Rutledge kept his eye on the Brady cottage, saw the rain running hard off the roof and cascading onto the path and spreading out into the garden, only trickles at first, and then tiny lakes that came together and separated as the wind pushed them back.

By the time Inspector Hill came dashing in from the motorcar, his hair shining with rain, the shoulders of his coat dark with it, the clouds were thinning, the worst of the cloudburst passed.

He shook himself like a dog as he crossed the threshold, and said, "All right, I'm here. I'll deal with Brady. The rest of my men are following." He looked up into Rutledge's face and said, "You seem to bring death in your wake."

"You have it the wrong way round," Rutledge answered mildly.

"Too bad the rain has washed away any sign of footprints along the walk. But there may not have been any if we've got a suicide. Still, better safe than sorry, keep an open mind and all that."

"I looked, before I left the cottage. It was hard to pick out any print in particular. Too much traffic."

Hill grunted. "I hope the rain is finished before we go inside there. As it is, we'll be tracking in half the garden."

"Where's Slater?"

"He's still in your motorcar. I think he's half afraid I'm about to arrest him on the spot. Early days yet. I don't know whether to take it as a sign of guilt or just his way of looking at things." Suddenly he could hear himself speak. The rain had stopped. "All right, I'm off. You'll stay here?"

It was more a statement than a question.

He went out and splashed quickly up the lane to Brady's cottage, stopping on the threshold for a time and then disappearing inside, shutting the door behind him. He was in the cottage for several minutes, his men collecting at the bottom of the lane, awaiting instructions. Then he hurried back to Slater's cottage just as the sun broke hazily through the thinning clouds.

In his hand, protected by his coat, Hill held what appeared to be the sheet of paper that had fallen from Brady's table.

He came inside and offered it to Rutledge.

Rutledge scanned the words written there.

Willingham called me worthless and a disgrace. I don't stand for that from any man. I killed Partridge as well, patronizing sod that he was. I don't regret either of them. Find Partridge if you can. If you can't, you'll find me in hell. I won't hang, I've no taste for it. A knife is faster and cleaner. Bury me where you will. I don't care. It's over, and I'm just as glad.

There was no signature.

Rutledge looked up. "Can you be sure this is Brady's handwriting?"

"There are papers and notes all over the floor, but whether they can tell us conclusively or not that this is his, I don't know." He took the letter back. "Looks as if Brady were keeping a diary. Dates and times scribbled down."

Would Deloran wash his hands of Brady as easily as he had of Partridge?

Hamish replied, "He willna' care to have it known that this was his man."

Hill might believe what was in the note, but Rutledge did not.

What struck him was the reference to Partridge, but no admission that the body had been left in Yorkshire.

Half a confession . . .

Hamish said, "If Partridge's murder and Willingham's are solved sae easily, who will be best pleased wi' that?"

A very good question. Deloran for one.

And what about the two sisters?

Rutledge said aloud to Hill, "Do you think Brady killed Willingham? I'm not sure I can accept the admission that he killed Partridge." For one thing, Parkinson hadn't been killed with a knife.

Hill frowned. "That's the problem. Where's Partridge's body? Brady must have taken it away."

"Have you searched Partridge's cottage?"

"Not yet, but I'll see that it's done."

"I'd like to be there when you go in."

"I'm not certain—"

"It will be easy enough for me to obtain the necessary permission."

Hill grudgingly agreed, then asked, "What's this man Partridge to you? Did you have a suspicion that he's been murdered? Is that what brought you here in the first place?"

Rutledge chose his words carefully. "My instructions were to discover where he could be found, if he didn't return in a reasonable period of time."

"And he hasn't. Which may mean that what's on this sheet is the solution to your problems as well." He was probing.

"If I'm lucky," Rutledge agreed.

In the background, Hamish was reminding him that once more someone was using Partridge's disappearance for his own ends.

"I'll see to searching the Partridge cottage later in the day," Hill went on. "I'll set my men to asking the other cottagers when they last saw Brady. I doubt it'll be much use to me, but there you are. Has to be done." He rubbed his chin, as if something were on his mind, then thought better of speaking of whatever it was. "All right then. The doctor is on his way. The question will be whether or not Brady could have used that knife on himself. And after that I must ask myself why, if we had no inkling that he was involved with Willingham's murder, he felt compelled to confess."

Rutledge answered neutrally, "A very good question. Especially since you showed considerable interest in Slater, rather than the other residents. Brady was in the clear, still. But I'm told he was often drunk and not always thinking very clearly."

"True enough." Hill turned as a constable tapped lightly on Slater's door.

He nodded to the silent Rutledge. "The doctor is here," he informed Hill.

Slater finally brought himself to get out of the motorcar. He crossed to where the men were standing in his doorway and said, "Where will it end?"

"I'm not sure." Rutledge turned back to the room as Hill walked away. "I think we could use a cup of tea."

Slater came inside and began to prepare it. Rutledge quietly asked him, "Who lived in Brady's cottage before he moved here?"

"It was an elderly woman. Miss Chandler. A lawyer came to tell her a cousin had died and left her a goodly sum in his will. She didn't remember this cousin, but it wasn't surprising. She was a little daft, her mind going. Still, she thought she could recall her father telling her that someone in the family had gone to Australia to seek his fortune. I expect that was who died."

Quite a convenient windfall . . .

"Where did she go from here?"

"There's a nice home run by a Mrs. Deacon in the Cotswolds. She's well known for taking in elderly ladies without families. A bit pricey, but Miss Chandler could afford it now, couldn't she? She was very pleased. And she'd hardly got the good news when Mr. Brady came round asking about a cottage. They must have come to an agreement, because she left him most of her furniture."

"What did he offer as a reason for coming here to live?"

Slater brought in the tea tray. "How should I know? But she told me he was looking for a quiet life."

Deloran had been very clever. First the sizable bequest, and then someone there to take the cottage off Miss Chandler's hands at the right moment.

Rutledge took his cup from Slater, and said, "Did Partridge have any contact with Miss Chandler?"

"Fancy your asking that. I'd quite forgot. She was a typist, and the week before she left, he took her a handful of papers to type up for him. He had a machine and she told him she knew how to use it."

"Do you know the direction for Mrs. Deacon's house?"

"It's in the Cotswolds, a small manor house just outside Fairford. It's called Thornton Hall. I took Mrs. Chandler there in my cart, with her boxes and trunks. Why are you interested in what she typed for Mr. Partridge? Why is it important?"

Rutledge finished his tea. "There's no way of telling what's important and what isn't. Until all the information is in hand."

But Slater wasn't to be put off. "Why is it that people think I can't understand what's happening? Why do they think I'm easily distracted, like a child?"

Rutledge set his cup on the tray. "Mr. Partridge had another life before he came here."

"They all had other lives. Except for me." He shook his head. "No, that's not right. I'd lived in Uffington, hadn't I? I don't like remembering my life there. Still, I depended on the smithy for my livelihood, and I couldn't go very far."

Hamish was saying, the soft Scots voice just behind Rutledge's shoulder, "He's puzzled, and no one has the time to set him straight."

"Sometimes it isn't distance that matters. For Partridge I have a feeling it was the White Horse that brought him here, not the miles from where he'd lived before this."

"You don't believe that Brady killed Mr. Partridge, do you?"

"Let's say I'm keeping an open mind until all the facts have been collected."

"It's a waste of time going to Miss Chandler."

"Possibly. But I won't know until I speak to her."

He left, dashed through the puddles to where Slater had left his motorcar, and drove to the nearest road that would carry him up to Fairford.

Hamish kept him company along the way.

As it happened, the house he was looking for was three miles outside of the pretty little town, set just beyond a small grove of beech that had been planted sometime in the eighteen hundreds, judging from their size. Age had begun to take a toll, and three closest to the road looked to be near collapse.

Thornton Hall was a handsome stone house built in classical style, with a portico and dormers on the slate roof. A porch to one side had been closed in with long windows looking out over a large garden, and beyond that, fallow land rolled into the distance.

Mrs. Deacon wasn't what he'd expected.

A maid in crisply starched black that rustled as she walked led him through the hall to a small sitting room at the back of the house. A tall, spare woman with auburn hair rose to greet him and offer him a chair by the cold hearth. She took the other and nodded to the maid.

When they were alone, she asked Rutledge what his business was with Miss Chandler.

"I'm afraid it's private," he told her with a smile.

"Miss Chandler is a woman of means, but she's lonely and easily taken advantage of. I'd like to know that you won't upset her." Her gaze was sharp, her eyes detached.

"I have no designs on her wealth," he said. "The question might be, do you?"

A red flush flared across her cheeks. "I'm not in the habit of taking advantage of my guests, Mr. Rutledge. They are here because they have nowhere else to go. And I am here because this is my home, and the only way I can afford to keep it is to take in such guests. The property isn't productive now, and I have no other means of seeing that the roof's repaired, much less the plumbing functioning. Now I think you'd better leave."

"I'm sorry," he apologized, and meant it. "The business I have with Miss Chandler has to do with some typing she did for a man in the cottages where she used to live."

Her eyes didn't waver. "Then you'll have no objection if I stay while you speak to her."

"None at all."

Hamish said, his voice soft, "The dragon at the gate."

She rose again and led him down the passage to the enclosed porch where several women, most of them between their early sixties and late seventies, sat dozing or gossiping. They looked up with interest as Mrs. Deacon came into the room, smiling up at her as if pleased to see her. Then their eyes went directly to Rutledge, curiosity rampant.

"Is this the new doctor, then?" one asked.

"I'm sorry, no. A guest. Miss Chandler?" She spoke to a small woman swathed in shawls and seated in a large winged chair near the French doors. Needlepoint pillows at her back and on either side made it more comfortable for her, and Rutledge could see that she was well dressed, her clothes and hair and skin well cared for. Her eyes were a bright blue and still very clear. He hoped that her memory was as well.

She leaned forward a little, as if hard of hearing, and Mrs. Deacon said, "This young man is here to see you, Miss Chandler. Would you like to speak to him?"

"Is it my cousin from Australia?"

"No, this is Mr. Rutledge, Miss Chandler. He's here to ask you about a little typing you did for someone he knows."

She was crestfallen to discover it wasn't her cousin, and Rutledge spared a moment to think of Deloran's deception. But she brightened again as she said, "My fingers are getting a little stiff for the typing, young man. What is it you need?"

He took the chair across from hers so that she wouldn't have to look up at him. Mrs. Deacon remained standing. "I wonder if you recall Mr. Partridge? He lived in the Tomlin Cottages near the White Horse for a few weeks before you moved here."

She searched through the cobwebs of her mind and finally nodded. "Mr. Partridge. Polite, as I recall, and very pleased to learn I could type. Yes, I do remember him, now that you speak of him."

"Do you perhaps recall what it was you were asked to type for him? It appears to have been lost."

"Oh, that's a shame, truly. But I'm afraid my brain is a little addled these days. I'm sure I couldn't remember what I did well enough to type it again from memory. That must have been all of two years ago."

Hamish was saying, "It wilna' help." But Rutledge persevered.

"Was it a letter? Memoirs?" He tried to think of anything else that Partridge might have worked on. "Reports? Papers for a professional society?"

"Oh, yes, that's precisely what it was! How clever of you, Mr. Rutledge. Yes, indeed, it was a paper for a professional journal, I recall it now. He promised to send me a copy of the journal, when the paper appeared. I suppose he forgot. I never received it." There was disappointment in her face as she considered the matter. "I daresay it wouldn't have mentioned my name, I only typed it, but still . . ."

"Was the paper difficult to work on?"

"Quite so. A good many symbols had to be carefully inserted by hand. I didn't know what all of them represented, but I do remember how he insisted that they must be absolutely precise. He told me that others duplicating his work must know exactly what he knew, or it would be useless to try. It appears he'd made an interesting discovery in his laboratory just before he left his firm, and he wanted to report it to some society or other. As a last claim to fame and glory." She frowned. "Although truly, I thought he might be joking about that. He said it in such a wry way."

"Was he a man given to joking?"

"Far from it. He seemed withdrawn, as if he had a habit of living alone and had to remind himself sometimes to be jolly in company. Don't misunderstand me. He was quite professional, very clear in his instructions, and he went through the typed pages with great care to be sure everything was exactly as he'd set it out. I asked him if this discovery of his, however small, might be something mankind would be grateful to know about. 'In some quarters, perhaps,' he replied, 'it will be highly regarded.' I thought perhaps he meant in the medical field. He'd mentioned once working in a laboratory, you see. I was a great admirer of Madame Curie, and told him so. He answered that he could never aspire to her greatness, and I found I believed him."

Mrs. Deacon, standing to one side of the chair, put in, "Did you make a carbon copy for Mr. Partridge, my dear? If the original went to the society."

"No, he told me that wasn't necessary. There was only the original."

"And he paid you for this work?" Rutledge went on.

"Of course, with a nice little bit extra for finishing it quickly as well as accurately. I was planning to leave the cottage, you see. And he didn't want me to take the information with me. I suspect he felt someone else might see it and steal his idea. I told him it was safe with me. I knew nothing about science, and it was difficult enough, making certain I was exact, word for word."

Hamish noted that as she traveled back into the past, the strength of her memory grew. But could it be totally trusted? Rutledge ignored him.

Miss Chandler leaned back in her chair. "I thought he might find me and ask me to do other typing for him. I've missed it, and it kept my fingers nimble. He had a very nice machine, but it was borrowed, he said, and must be returned on time."

From the laboratory, very likely. But what had become of the paper? Knowing that Brady was watching him—and might even from time to time search the cottage—it would have been foolish for Parkinson to keep anything valuable there. And not at the house, where his daughters came and went. What would have felt like a safe place to him, where his work wouldn't be found?

It was possible that he'd long since taken the paper with him on one of his forays and put it in a bank vault or left it with someone he'd trusted. He hadn't had it with him in Yorkshire. And Rutledge hadn't found it in the cottage.

Hamish said, "Why did he write whatever it is doon? Much less gie it to someone to type."

A good question. A red herring? Or something Parkinson had been working on and hadn't quite finished, but knew that in time his earlier research might hold the key? A better way of killing armies was always a marketable commodity.

Miss Chandler was tiring. She made a little gesture with her hand, as if to apologize for failing him. "That's all, really. I wish I could do something to help. Mr. Partridge must be beside himself."

"It has been worrisome," Rutledge answered, sidestepping the issue of Partridge. "Thank you for seeing me, Miss Chandler. I wish you a pleasant evening."

"You won't stay and have tea with us?" She looked around the sun-room at the other women seated there, avidly listening. "We seldom have the pleasure of a young man's company."

"I'm afraid I've a long drive ahead of me."

"I have hoped against hope that someone from my cousin's family might come to England so that I can tell them how grateful I am to their father. But they haven't. I expect it's a long journey to make, just for an hour or so with an old woman."

He damned Deloran in his mind, yet could see that this woman was pleased with her good fortune and would be bereft if told the truth, that it was the need for her cottage and not an interest in her well-being that lay behind the sums she'd been given. He wouldn't put it past her to refuse the money.

"I'm sure they wish you well, even if they can't visit."

"How are my former neighbors?" she asked him then, searching for a reason to hold him there a little longer. "Will you give my regards to Mr. Allen and Mrs. Cathcart in particular? I've missed them, please tell them that. Mr. Miller was always kind to me as well."

"Yes, most certainly." He had reached the door when he turned and asked a last question. "Has anyone else come to ask you about the work you did for Mr. Partridge?"

"No one," she answered him, "knew about it. I've told you, he feared someone might steal his discovery."

He thanked her again, and Mrs. Deacon followed him to the foyer. "You can see that my guests haven't been cheated. Nor have I. I have my house still. And I would do it again, if I had to." She looked around her at the high coffered ceiling of the foyer, the pineapples in each square flecked with gold, at the paneling on the walls and the parquet flooring. "This is where I lived as a child. My brother inherited the house, you know. But he's dead, in the first fighting at Mons. I've been a widow for many years, and I longed to come back here. But his wife and I didn't see eye to eye." A brief triumphant smile touched her face. "It took every penny I possessed to buy her out. But I managed it. I don't know why I should feel required to defend myself to you. I expect it's because you doubted my motives. That was unkind of you."

He was reminded of the sunroom, a comfortable place for old bones on an April day when the rain had brought damp with it.

He smiled in return. "I misjudged the circumstances. I had reason to believe that perhaps Miss Chandler's good fortune was suspect. But I see it isn't. Do you remember the name of the solicitor who handled the inheritance for her? I should have asked."

"There was no solicitor. I was told she received the money directly from the solicitors in Australia and put it in her account in the bank." She held out her hand. "Good day, Mr. Rutledge. You would have made a good policeman. If you aren't one already."

He went through the door and she shut it behind him with a firm click.

Rutledge stood there for a moment. His work at the Yard, he

thought, had made him overly suspicious of goodness. He had seen so much that was evil.

Hamish said as he walked back to the motorcar, "Yon Mrs. Deacon is no' afraid of anyone. It's her strength."

Rutledge was late arriving at The Smith's Arms. Mrs. Smith had set his dinner on the back of the stove to keep warm. He hung his wet coat over the other chair to dry and sat by the fire in the bar, only half listening to the gossip of the lorry drivers and the locals who came regularly to sit and drink.

Most of it was of no importance.

Then Hamish said, "Hark!"

And Rutledge brought his attention back to the room in time to hear a farmer comment, "They took the smith to the police station today. I always said he was a danger. I wouldn't let him play with my son, would I, when they were in school together. Too big by half, and didn't know his own strength."

"It was a knife he used, not his hands," his companion reminded him.

"Yes, well, he killed them, didn't he?"

What had happened to Brady's confession? Had Hill already discounted it? Rutledge finished his meal and went out into the night, directly back to the cottages.

There was still a light in Quincy's cottage, and Rutledge knocked at the door.

"Who's there?" There was an undercurrent of alarm in the query.

"Rutledge. I need to talk to you."

"It's late." But there was the sound of the latch being lifted, and Quincy stood in the opening. The light behind him struck him from the left, throwing that side of his face in stark relief while the other half was deeply shadowed. It gave him an oddly malevolent look. "What's brought you here? Not another killing?"

"It's Slater. I heard at the inn that he'd been taken into Uffington by Inspector Hill."

"Shows how wrong gossip can be. No, Hill took him there to the doctor. He was using a hammer while they talked, working on one of those kettles he makes sometimes. They sell well at the summer fair. And he smashed his knuckles. Slater nearly passed out from the pain, and Hill called one of his men to get Slater into a car."

"Then all's well."

"Why do you think he's not guilty?" Quincy asked with some curiosity. "People like that often have a bad temper." He turned his head to look at the cat asleep on her favorite chair. "She's mine now, I expect. She didn't mourn long for Partridge. If I thought it would work, I'd make a gift of her to Mrs. Cathcart. God knows she needs something to calm her nerves."

"She's afraid."

"Aren't we all? But you're right, Mrs. Cathcart's fear is exacerbated by what happened in her life before she came here. She peers out the window at every newcomer. I've seen the curtains twitch. A pity, really. She'll die a tormented soul."

Which is probably what her husband had in mind, Rutledge thought.

"Did you ever see Brady go in or come out of Partridge's cottage?"

"No. He stayed away from Partridge as far as possible, considering he lived here as well. Look, do you want some coffee? I developed a taste for it in Guatemala. If you aren't going away, then you might as well come in."

"I'll take you up on the offer."

Rutledge stepped inside and shut the door behind him. The room where the birds were kept was in darkness, but the flickering light of the fire on the hearth glanced off iridescent feathers and glass eyes. He took the chair next to Dublin's and sat down. The night was just chilly enough to make the fire comforting, and he felt a drowsiness steal over him. Quincy was busy in the kitchen, and the cat had begun to purr.

Hamish urged him to keep awake, prodding at him with words.

Reminding him that the night watches in the trenches had meant life or death.

Rutledge asked him silently if he thought Quincy would poison the coffee, and Hamish gave him no answer.

"I'd give much to know what's going on here," Quincy was saying as he worked.

The rich scent of coffee beans in a grinder filled the room.

"So would Inspector Hill. Brady wrote a note before he died. At least it would appear he had. In it he claimed he'd killed both Willingham and Partridge."

"Willingham I can understand. There was no loss of love there. But Partridge was, if you forgive me, the goose with the golden egg. Brady was out of a job if he harmed the man."

"Quite." Rutledge reached out a hand to smooth the head of the cat as she stretched, her purr loud in the room. "You'll have to give Hill your full name on any statement, you know. It's a matter of form."

"I'm damned if I will. As long as I'm not a suspect, I'm giving him nothing."

"After so many years, do you really think your family cares where you're living? It's more to the point that you stay away from them."

"I signed an agreement, in front of witnesses. My brother might take it into his head to see that the letter and not the spirit of the law is carried out."

"And your parents?"

"Dead for all I know. It hasn't seemed worth my while to find out."

The coffeepot was on the stove, and the aroma was building.

"What did you do that was so unforgivable?"

"I was born. Do you have any sisters or brothers, Rutledge?"

"A sister."

"Close, are you?"

"Very."

"Well, it wasn't that way in my family. My brother hated me from the start. No, I swear it. He was a nasty piece of work in my eyes as well. We never got along, and just when he was rising in his firm, I was being sent down from Cambridge in disgrace. Too much drinking, too many women, my schoolwork suffering into the bargain. There was talk that I was the black sheep of a fine old name, and I wouldn't amount to much. And then I did the unspeakable—I met the woman my brother was planning to marry, and she liked me well enough. Perhaps a little too well, for she broke off their engagement. I like to think the contrast with him pointed up just how great a bastard he was. My father offered me a sizable sum paid to my account anywhere in the world except England, and I was young enough not to fancy taking a position in my father's firm. Going off to build the Panama Canal for the French seemed to be a fitting revenge, and off I went. Only the French died like flies, and the engineers died with them. So much for that."

He went for the coffee and brought a cup of it back with him, handing it to Rutledge. "I take mine black. There's not much choice, actually. I don't have sugar or milk." He fetched his own cup and sat down. "I don't know why I talk to you. I don't care for people as a rule. But before I know it, I'm telling my life story and thinking nothing of it. You're a bad influence."

Rutledge laughed. "So I've been told."

"*Did* Brady kill Willingham, do you think?" Quincy asked abruptly, changing the subject.

"He confessed to it."

"All right, for the sake of argument, what about Partridge?"

"I'm not as sure of that."

"Nor am I. Which makes me wonder if Brady isn't a scapegoat. And accordingly, I keep my door bolted at night now. I can protect myself. What's loose amongst us here?"

It was an echo of the question Slater had asked.

"There's no way of knowing."

"Well, if it's Slater, he won't be using that hand to kill anybody for a while. Then we have Allen, who doesn't have the strength left to overpower anyone, and Mrs. Cathcart, who is afraid of her own shadow. Which leaves in the suspect category Miller, Singleton, and me. Unless it's Partridge coming back from the grave. We haven't been shown his body, and that's something to be taken into account."

Rutledge couldn't tell if this was a fishing expedition or not. But Hamish was warning him to take care.

"I think Hill is planning to dig up the floor of Partridge's cottage tomorrow. To be certain he's not under it." It was a light answer, to avoid the truth.

It was Quincy's turn to laugh, but it rang hollowly. "Yes, well, I wish him luck." He drained his cup and held out his hand for Rutledge's. "I'll say good night. Thanks for coming by. I was in the mood for company."

It was said with an edge to it, as if he weren't particularly pleased to have been disturbed.

He let Rutledge out the door and bolted it behind him.

Rutledge went back to the inn and to bed. It was too late to see what Inspector Hill had to say about the murders.

In the night someone tried to burn Quincy alive in his cottage.

But he'd been telling the truth when he said he was armed. The shotgun blasted a hole through the door and peppered the front garden. Then he was outside, taking a broom to the rags someone had jammed under his door, pulling them apart in smoky masses. Those shoved through the broken windowpane in the bird room took longer to extinguish.

Damage was not as extensive as it might have been. Someone had counted on the door being unlocked, to make fire-starting easier. And when he found it wasn't, he had tried to improvise, determined to set the house ablaze.

For the rest of the night Quincy sat in his dark sitting room, the shotgun across his knees and the coffeepot at his elbow.

When Rutledge came back the next morning, Quincy said with an edge to his voice, "I want to make a statement."

20

As soon as it was first light, Quincy had been busy, as he told Rutledge with grim satisfaction. He had gone to Mrs. Cathcart's cottage and called through the door, "There's no harm done, no one killed. You're safe for what's left of the night."

Inside he had heard her crying, but he said bracingly, "You'll make yourself ill in there. Go to bed, sleep while you can. There's nothing to worry about in the light of day."

It was two hours later that he'd sent Slater for Hill and Rutledge.

"I'd be dead if it weren't for the cat. She smelled the smoke and was howling frantically to get out. And when I came down, I could hear whoever it was trying to stuff more rags against the door."

"Do you think you hit him?"

"I don't know, and could care even less. But I want to go on record that out the back window I saw a shape running toward the shadows of Singleton's cottage. He may be dead as well. Or he may have tried to kill me. And I'll swear to that in any fashion you like. I had a good look, it wasn't my eyes playing tricks."

"No feeling for size, shape?"

"None. But if Brady killed Willingham and then himself, who tried to burn me out, I ask you."

He was incensed about his door, and demanded that a constable take him directly into Uffington to find lumber that would cover the damage.

"That door is going to be bolted again by nightfall, or you'll be assigning a constable to sit on my threshold all night."

Hill said to Rutledge as Quincy and the constable left, "What do you think?"

"It could well be true." But then Quincy could have set the fire himself and then fired his shotgun through the panels of the door. And both policemen knew it.

Another constable came to report that Singleton was in his cottage and safe. "I had to knock three or four times," he added. "He was asleep."

"We'll attend to him later. See if he heard anything. But for now, Rutledge, I've cleared paperwork for the search of Partridge's cottage. If you're ready? We might as well get on with it."

They crossed the lane to the cottage and went in.

Nothing had changed since Rutledge had been there alone. But this time he kept an eye open for the papers that Miss Chandler had typed, while Hill was poking about looking for a body.

Neither of them had any success.

"Ye've been here before," Hamish reminded Rutledge. "And you found nothing then."

"I didn't know about the papers."

"Aye, that's true. But if ye'd seen them, ye'd ha' taken note. They werena' here."

Hill sat down by the desk and said with some heat, "I'd have felt better if he'd been here, dead. Nothing against Mr. Partridge, but it would have solved my problem for me. Now that note of Brady's looks damned suspicious."

Rutledge debated telling him about the body in Yorkshire, but held off. Hamish, looking ahead, told him in no uncertain terms that it was unwise.

All the same, he decided to wait until he was sure how the crimes were related.

"I don't know that Partridge is connected to this business. On the other hand, my presence here might have set off something we haven't got to the bottom of yet. The killings began after I identified myself as a policeman. Not before."

"Nonsense. A Scotland Yard inspector doesn't go about triggering murders. I haven't time for foolishness." He paused. "The doctor tells me that Brady could have killed himself, right enough. The way the old Romans used to fall on their swords. The chair was directly behind him, and the force of the blow drove him into it. Why would Quincy want to put that in doubt?"

Hill got up from the desk and moved restlessly about the sitting room. Rutledge remembered the crumpled beginning of a letter in the basket by the desk and went to look at it again.

But it wasn't there now. Of small importance—yet it told him that someone else had been through the house since he had been here.

Rutledge said, "I spoke to Quincy for an hour, more or less, last night. Coincidence? Or fear?"

They moved on to the shed where the motorcar was kept and Hill did a cursory search of the vehicle. But Rutledge, with a little better light now, looked at the tires and the boot, then thoroughly inspected the interior.

It gave up no more secrets to him than it had to Inspector Hill, but as he ran his hand over the rear seat, something was brushed to the floor of the motorcar. It was so small he had trouble finding where it had got to, but after a moment, his fingers finally retrieved it.

The tab from a 1917 small box respirator.

He could see, vividly, the slit in the mask that Parkinson had been wearing when he was found in the cloisters of Fountains Abbey. Just where this tab should have been.

It had caught on something and torn off.

Rutledge straightened up. Parkinson had been in this motorcar, along with the mask. And no one noticed the tab was missing as it was slipped over a dead man's face.

He would have given any odds that Parkinson had traveled to his death in this motorcar, and someone had seen to it that it was quietly returned to the shed where it belonged, when the journey was finished. In some ways, a motorcar was harder to hide than a body. It could be traced. Better to leave the impression that Parkinson had set out without it.

And that confirmed that Parkinson's death was deliberate, carefully planned and executed.

L eaving Hill to cope with his own case, Rutledge drove to Wiltshire, to the house called Pockets where Rebecca Parkinson lived.

She was there, and he had to bang on the door for nearly ten minutes before she finally opened it to him.

Something in his face must have alerted her, for the first words out of her mouth were, "I've told you. I've had nothing to do with my father for the past two years or more. It's useless, coming here. He put his work before his family, and now his family no longer cares. His sacrifice was in vain. The army didn't want him either."

"How do you know that?"

"For weeks before my mother died, he was obsessed, secretive, doing much of his work at night, making endless calculations. He hardly ate or slept. It was as if he were trying to convince himself of something—as if he'd lost his way but couldn't bring himself to admit it. In any other man I'd have said he was on the verge of a breakdown.

In his case, I think it was pride crashing. He wasn't as clever as he thought he was, and he was about to be found out."

"That's a rather harsh judgment."

"Is it? He resigned, didn't he? If he'd made a brilliant success of his work, do you think he'd have done that? Even in contrition over my mother's death? And the man in charge of the laboratory let him go. They'd have offered him a leave of absence, if he was so indispensable to them. The war wasn't over in the spring of 1918, and we weren't certain of winning."

"You don't know what it was he was working on?"

"I wasn't interested in his work. It had brought nothing but grief to us, and I hated it as much as I came to hate him. It took me a long time to reach indifference. But I have now."

He thought she hadn't. She was still passionate about her father and anything to do with him. The hate showed in her anger at the man.

Rutledge stood there, letting her feel the silence, willing her to betray herself.

As if to fill it before she couldn't stand it any longer, she said, "When my mother died, I hated him so much all I could think of was making him feel pain in a way he couldn't ignore. If he'd still been using his laboratory, I'd have burned it to the ground, and wouldn't have cared if he was there inside. When she asked that her ashes be scattered in the gardens she loved so much, I strewed them myself. I was half mad too, I think. I wanted to hurt him and I wound up hurting myself. Do you know what someone's ashes feel like? Do you know how they blow on the wind, and sometimes into your face or cling to your fingers in spite of everything? A gray powder, that was all that was left of my mother. And I diminished it by letting it soak into the damp ground, so that the house was uninhabitable. And now I'm afraid to go there because I'm afraid I'll see her ghost. I think, at the end, he did see her. That's why he couldn't stay there."

"What will happen to the house?"

"I don't know. I can't sell it—not after what I did. I can't live there. I can't let it go to wrack and ruin. I can't have brambles and weeds on my mother's grave. He ruined all our lives, and I don't really care what's become of him."

She turned her back to him, and he heard the catch in her voice when she added, "There's nothing I want in that wretched cottage where he went to live. As far as I'm concerned, you can burn it to the ground."

And then she was inside, on the point of shutting her door.

He said, "The motorcar as well?"

Her voice was weary when she finally answered. "Let them sell it. I have no need for it."

"Miss Parkinson. I shall have to speak to your sister. There's no way around it."

"Did she tell you where she lived? At Road's End, a house not very different from mine. It's not far from Porton Down. Ironic, isn't it? A friend offered it to her for a small rent, and she was upset with me, about the ashes. I can't blame her for not wanting to live with me." Rebecca Parkinson laughed harshly. "That house at Partridge Fields is worth a great deal of money. But the two of us have almost nothing to our names. A small inheritance from Mother, that's it. And I wouldn't touch my father's money if he offered it. If I thought it would solve anything I'd shoot myself. But it won't. Don't come back here again."

And she was gone.

He stood there for a moment longer, staring at the closed door. If one of the sisters killed Gerald Parkinson, which was it?

He thought that Rebecca had the stronger sense of abandonment and might in a fit of anger try to assuage it by killing her father. But surely in the heat of the moment, not two years later. Unless there was something he didn't know, some factor in their relationship that went so deep it had taken time to face. When she had, the only solution might have been murder.

And yet, Sarah, the weaker of the two, might have found she couldn't

live with her own pain and grief any longer and made the choice between killing herself, as her mother had done, or killing her father.

Rutledge turned and went back to the motorcar, driving on to the
house at Partridge Fields.

He walked through the grounds to the small garden with the horse
fountain. It was dappled in shade, this early, a mysterious and inviting
place to sit.

But he'd come not to sit but to look at the grass that surrounded the
fountain, squatting to see if there was any sign that someone had stood
here two nights ago. The grass was still dew-wet, and it was difficult
to judge. No one had trampled the green blades, no one had left a tidy
footprint in the moist soil of the shrubbery beds. Still, he'd have given
odds that walking here in the dark would lead to a misstep at some
point.

It took patience and careful, almost inch-by-inch inspection, but
he found something that might have been the half print of a heel just
where an edge of the grass walk met the soil.

Hamish said disparagingly, "A bird scratching. A beetle trying to
right itself. An owl after a mouse."

Rutledge got to his feet. "Possibly. But why haven't they scratched
over here—or there?"

"It's no' solid proof."

"No."

He left the shrubbery and stood where he could see the windows of
the master bedroom above the garden.

Here, at this house—in that room, for all he knew—lay the heart of
a family's collapse.

It was as if each of the Parkinsons gave more energy to hurting than
to healing.

For one thing, why had Mrs. Parkinson wanted her ashes buried
here, if she'd been wretched at Partridge Fields? The answer to that
was, she intended them to be a constant reminder to her husband of
everything she'd suffered.

He had no idea what she'd had in mind—an urn set on a marble square by the horse fountain, or ashes scattered in the central circle of the French-style beds where the roses grew. It had been Rebecca's decision in the first anguished days after finding her mother dead to spread them throughout the gardens.

Neither mother nor daughter, set on their acts of revenge, had considered how difficult it might ultimately be for Sarah or Rebecca to live here. Punishing Gerald Parkinson was paramount, shutting out every other consideration, and Rebecca was left to reap the whirlwind she had sown.

Where had all this passionate need to hurt started?

There was Parkinson's obsession with his work, putting it before his family. And his wife's morbid fascination with the destructive nature of what he did. These must have led to violent arguments, to turn her thoughts to suicide. Or had she been unstable most of her married life?

In that case, why hadn't her daughters spared a moment's sympathy for what their father must have had to endure?

There must have been something else, to send a sensitive mind into a downward spiral of depression and finally despair.

Had Parkinson lashed out physically, when he'd felt his back was to the wall? Striking his wife would have erased any sympathy Rebecca and her sister might have felt.

Then why hadn't Rebecca mentioned it in defense of her anger? Or Sarah dwell on that as she remembered a kinder father?

Rutledge thought, *It's time to ask Sarah what she remembers about her parents' relationship, not just her own with her father.*

But he spared five minutes to walk to the kitchen garden and knock at the door. No one came to open it, and he finally gave it up and went back to his motorcar.

He had some difficulty finding the small house where Sarah Parkinson lived. It stood at the end of a country lane and was no larger than Pockets and far more isolated.

Over a slight rise, he could just see the roof of a barn and tall chimneys.

Why couldn't the sisters live together? It would have made sense. Especially if money was a problem. Rebecca was protective of Sarah, but there wasn't the closeness one might expect under the circumstances of their mother's death and their father's desertion. Had the ashes been the only problem?

Sarah Parkinson was surprised to see him. She had come to the door at the sound of the motorcar and now stood on the threshold trying to decide whether to tell him to go away or invite him in.

"Good morning," Rutledge began. "I've come to see if you're all right."

"Don't worry, crying over the past won't lead me to do anything rash."

"I expect not. Still. May I come in? I'd like to talk to you."

He could watch the internal debate as she frowned, then said, "I don't expect I have much choice about it."

"We can stand here, if you'd rather."

"No. Come in. But I won't take your hat. You won't be staying long."

Rutledge smiled. "I want to ask you about your parents. If I come in, are you prepared to answer my questions? Otherwise this will be a waste of time for both of us."

She was disconcerted by his bluntness. "If I don't like the questions, I'll tell you."

"Fair enough."

The house was old and had seen hard use. But Sarah Parkinson had tried to make it comfortable and pretty, adding paint to the walls and curtains to the bare windows. A fine French carpet lay on the floor, and some furnishings were a little out of date, as if she'd scavenged them from her parents' attics. They were far better quality than the walls that enclosed them.

"Yes, I've come down in the world," she said, following his gaze. "I only have this house through the courtesy of a friend. It was the best she or I could do."

"I can understand that you don't want to live at Partridge Fields again. But what will you do with it?"

"It's the tomb of my mother. When Becky and I are gone, it can be torn down by people who don't know why we deserted it. Better that way."

"The housekeeper still comes to see to it. Who pays her to clean and sweep?"

"My father, I expect. I can't afford to keep her there."

"May I ask why you and your sister don't choose to live together? It would make sense."

"I think we both prefer the silence. If we were together, we'd talk too much about the past. We wouldn't be able to help it."

"Whose motorcar do you drive? Your own? Or Rebecca's?"

"It belongs to a friend of hers who went to France and came back without his legs. He didn't want to look at it any more, and told her she could drive it."

"But you borrow it from time to time?"

"When I can." She looked away from him, her gaze following a bee at the window. "It's a long walk for both of us to go anywhere. We trade days. It's not the life I'd have chosen."

"You're young. You'll marry in time and the past will seem less vivid."

"After what I've seen of marriage," she retorted, "I want no part of it. It leaves you terribly vulnerable. And in the end you hate each other. My father killed my mother as surely as if he'd held her head under the gas and made her breathe it in. I've never understood why he couldn't love her enough to stop what he was doing. She was so softhearted she couldn't bear to see a bird suffer. He knew that, but it didn't matter. He turned his back on her feelings and did what he wanted to do anyway, and in the end she died. When he saw what he had done, it was too *late*."

"Was it always that way? You remember your father being kind to you, but was he kind to your mother as well? When you were five, for instance, did you think they were happy?"

"I thought they were. More fool I. It must have been a pretense, for our sakes. I realize that now."

"They couldn't have pretended so perfectly that you didn't see the strain of their trying. Children are very perceptive. Think about when you were six—twelve. Think about birthday parties and holidays and long winter evenings together." He tried to suggest images that she could explore, and watched her face closely as she frowned, sorting through her memories.

"When I was four, we went to Cornwall for our holiday. I remember it well, it was the first time I'd seen the sea. And we watched moor ponies one afternoon, and in one of the harbors, there was a fishmonger with a tray of fish, silvery in the sun. We took our breakfast out to the rocks and watched the fishing boats coming in."

"Did your parents laugh? Hold hands with each other? Seem comfortable with each other? Or was there tension, sometimes raised voices?"

"I—yes, I think everything was all right. I rode on my father's shoulders when my legs were tired, and Becky held on to his coattails. Mama laughed, calling us a dragon, three heads, six arms, six legs. And we made up stories about the dragon, how he could run faster than anyone else, and lift twice as much and see before him and behind him at the same time, and my father made silly noises, while Becky laughed so hard she fell down and the dragon came apart."

She looked away, seeing a day she had buried in the past. "I loved my father more than anything, then. I had forgotten."

"And later?"

"We went to Kent when I was six, to visit an aunt. She told us there was a ghost in her house, but it was only mice behind the walls. The next summer, Mama was very ill and kept to her bed. I remember we had to be quiet, and there were nurses coming in to look after her. My father was worried, he sat in his study and I think he cried. His face was wet when I came in to kiss him good night."

Her gaze came back to Rutledge, startled and confused. "I had forgotten. It frightened me to see Mama like that, pale and helpless, and I didn't want to think about it. I don't remember her laughing for a long time even after the nurses had left and she was well again. That was after my father had begun to use the laboratory in the garden. He said he had more freedom there than at Cambridge. She railed at him once, calling him a murderer. She was so distressed, and she threatened to burn down the laboratory. And he told her that if she did, he would leave her."

Sarah Parkinson put her hands to her face, reliving that scene. "It was never the same after that. Never. There were no more holidays. Mama told me that it was because my father refused to leave his precious laboratory long enough to take us anywhere. That it meant more to him than we did, and because he spent so much of his time there, I knew it to be true. Sometimes he had his meals brought to him there. And I'd hear him come up the stairs at night long after we were in bed. I always waited for him to come in and say good night, but he didn't. I thought perhaps he'd stopped loving Becky and me."

"Why was your mother ill? Do you know?"

"I was never told. I have no idea."

"But it changed her—and her feelings toward your father."

Sarah Parkinson bit her lip. "I can't answer that. Although she must have been happy when we were in Kent. She and my father took long walks together, and I watched them from the windows. I was a little jealous, I expect. I know I felt left out. Why are you asking me these things? I've worked hard to forget most of it."

Rutledge didn't want to tell her that he'd come to find out if her father had struck her mother in arguments over the laboratory. Sarah at least had no memory of that. Or had suppressed any she did have. "I never had the opportunity to meet your father. The man who died in Yorkshire is a mystery to all of us."

"Why do you keep telling me that my father died in Yorkshire?" There was an element of defensiveness in her question. "How do you know where he died?"

"All right. The man who was found dead in Yorkshire. He's your father, whether you wish to acknowledge him or not." He rose to leave. "No one wants to claim his body. He'll be buried in a pauper's grave, without a marker."

"You can put the name he used in those cottages on his stone. It was the one he chose, and it shut us out completely. Why should I care about him now?"

"You came back to the cottages," Rutledge said as he walked to the door. "Why?"

Her eyes were bright with tears. "I'm looking for something I lost. But I can live without it. I learned the hard way to do that."

She didn't see him out. He closed the door as he went.

Hamish said, as the motorcar turned toward the cottages at Uffington, "She willna' change her mind. But when she's old, she'll have regrets to overcome."

"Unlike her sister."

"Aye, the elder. She learned to hate at her mother's knee."

"Her mother's child. As Sarah might well have been her father's favorite."

"Looking into the past hasna' given you a solution."

"Not yet."

Rutledge arrived at the cottages and walked down the lane separating them, turning in at Mrs. Cathcart's door.

She was reluctant to open to him, but in the end, her innate politeness won. She said, "That other policeman has been here, asking me what I've seen, what I know, how Mr. Brady struck me. I don't spy on my neighbors and I didn't know Mr. Brady well enough to answer him."

"Do you think Mr. Brady spied on his neighbors? I'm told he spent most of his time sitting at his windows, looking out."

"I expect he was lonely. Most of us are, you know. He did seem more interested in Mr. Partridge than he was in the rest of us, but then it was Mr. Partridge's cottage he could see best. Of course Mr. Willingham was always accusing Mr. Brady of staring at him. I can't believe either of them is dead. Do you think Mr. Partridge is as well? If I had anywhere else to go, I'd leave this place. I don't feel safe here, I'm terrified of being murdered in *my* bed."

He wished he could tell her that she had little chance of that. "Keep your door locked. Don't open it at night to anyone, no matter what he may say to you."

"I'd ask Mr. Slater to be sure my locks couldn't be tampered with. But he's hurt his hand, and it must be very painful. Will you look at my door and windows?"

He agreed and followed her through the rooms of her cottage testing the latches on windows and the main door. "If you're afraid, keep a light on. It will be a comfort."

"Do you think Inspector Hill is capable of doing anything about these frightening events? I've not been impressed by him. He's a local man, after all. And he doesn't know anything about us."

"He's making every effort."

"I'm not sure that's good enough." She tugged at her earlobe, clearly upset. "For a very long time, now, I've been afraid of dying," she confessed. "I always believed my husband would see to it that I was quietly disposed of. Now it may be a complete stranger who makes him the happiest man in England."

Rutledge said, "Would you prefer to stay at The Smith's Arms for several nights, until this business is finished? You're the only woman here. You might be more comfortable."

She said, the strain apparent in her voice, "I've considered that. I'd do it, if I could afford it."

"Let me have a word with Mrs. Smith. I think it might be possible to arrange."

Mrs. Cathcart said, "Please? Let me go with you? I've only to put a few things into my overnight case. When the sun begins to set, I can hardly breathe for fear."

Rutledge took pity on her and said, "Yes, of course. I'll wait."

It took her less time than he'd expected. She came out of her bedroom with a worn leather valise and handed it to him. "I'm so grateful. You can't imagine. There's no one I can turn to. I could smell the smoke at Mr. Quincy's cottage in the night, and at first I thought it was mine. Even so, I sat here, wondering what would be worse, burning to death or walking outside into the arms of someone with a knife. They say he prefers a knife. I thought Mr. Brady confessed."

She paused on the threshold, stricken by a thought. "It isn't Mr. Partridge, is it? Coming back here and attacking us? I've heard people can be struck down by a brainstorm, and not know what they're doing."

"You don't have to fear Mr. Partridge. I don't think he'll be coming back to the cottages."

She locked her door behind her but didn't look back as he helped her into the motorcar. He could feel her worry drain away until she was light-headed from relief.

It took him five minutes to convince Mrs. Smith that he had no ulterior motive in paying for Mrs. Cathcart's room. He also made her promise to say nothing about who was taking care of the account.

Then, as Mrs. Cathcart stepped into the inn, Mrs. Smith smiled at her and welcomed her, saying, "I'll bring up a cup of tea after I've shown you your room."

Mrs. Cathcart cast a grateful glance at Rutledge and followed Mrs. Smith up the stairs, answering questions about the two deaths as they climbed.

He went into the pub, sat down in the window seat, and tried to shut out Hamish's voice. The large room was empty of custom, and in the quietness Rutledge considered a possibility that had nagged at the edges of his consciousness for several hours.

Which of his daughters had Parkinson started a letter to, only to crumple it up and toss it aside as if the words he wanted wouldn't come?

My dear . . .

If it was Sarah, then he must have held out hope of some sort of reconciliation.

If it was Rebecca, he might well be trying to make amends for what she felt he'd done to her mother.

Hamish said, "But he didna' send it. Which brings up the question of whether he'd ha' gone with ither one o' them, if they'd come to his door late at night. And it must ha' been late—no one saw what happened."

"Interesting about the cars," Rutledge said. "The body was transported in Partridge's. Which suggests that the daughter without the car that night was the one who killed him."

"It's a long way on foot for ither o' them."

"A friend could have driven them to Uffington. It's an easy walk from there."

But what if the unfinished letter was simply a first draft, and Parkinson had after all sent what he'd written?

What if he had intended to sell Partridge Fields? Would that threat be the last straw for Rebecca?

My dear Rebecca, I am writing to tell you that I've decided that the time has come to sell the house and grounds. If there's anything in the house that you wish to have, please make arrangements to remove the item before I put the property on the market. . . .

And that would have brought Rebecca storming to his door in the middle of the night after struggling for hours to find a way to stop him.

Or look at it another way round.

The letter might have been very different.

My dear Rebecca, I'm writing to tell you that I've decided to move back to Partridge Fields now. I've made arrangements for the house to be refurbished and the gardens cleared and replanted. . . .

All that was necessary was to persuade their father to spend one night in the house while they argued over his plan. The rest would have been simple. Drug him, turn on the gas, and let him die while he slept.

But why then remove Parkinson from the house and carry his body to Yorkshire? Why not leave him there for the housekeeper to find, and let him be buried in the churchyard with his ancestors?

Perhaps they had left Parkinson where he died—and it was Deloran who had ordered the body moved, so that both Parkinson and Partridge were disposed of in one neat solution.

21

It was late, but Rutledge went back to Rebecca Parkinson's house. And even though she refused to answer the door, he stood outside and called her name.

"Miss Parkinson, I know you can hear me. If you won't come out, then we can conduct our business this way. I want you to give some thought to what is happening in Uffington. Inspector Hill has a confession that was found next to the body of a man Dreadnought set to watch your father for two years. In that confession, there's an admission by the dead man that he killed your father and then murdered another resident who might have seen this man going into your father's cottage the night he disappeared."

He waited, but Rebecca Parkinson neither came to the door nor answered him from inside.

Hamish said, "Ye're wasting your breath. If she didna' kill her father, she's verra' glad someone did."

Rutledge answered him in the silence of his mind. "We must have a family member make a positive identification of that body, even if we must exhume it. It's the only way I can think of to persuade either sister to take that step. We'll worry about murder after that. It's what every case is built on, the identity of a body."

Aloud, he said, "I'm bound to tell you, Miss Parkinson, that Inspector Hill isn't completely satisfied that the confession is in the dead man's handwriting. That must be verified. But if it is, and the confession is allowed to stand, there will be matters you and your sister must deal with. We've already found evidence that your father's motorcar was used to transport his body north, before being returned to the cottage. We'll need to prove once and for all that the man in Yorkshire is one Gerald Parkinson, not Gaylord Partridge."

Still there was no answer.

Rutledge began to doubt that Rebecca Parkinson was in the house after all. She could easily have gone out through the kitchen yard and walked away.

"Whether you like it or not, you will be faced with other issues. Who will pay the housekeeper's wages if your father is dead and his estate is left unsettled? Who will pay for repairing the drains and rooting out worm in the wood, and seeing to the roof? Are you prepared to stand and watch the house fall down for lack of money? Whether you want to touch your inheritance or not, you will find it will make a difference in what becomes of you and your sister, and the house at Partridge Fields."

He had hoped that that would be a telling argument in persuading her to identify the body. But the silence lengthened.

"At least give me the name of your father's solicitor, Miss Parkinson. I shall have to contact him. Meanwhile, you're letting your anger blind you. I think your mother would want to know that you and your sister were provided for."

But the bait was ignored.

No response, no angry outburst, no confrontation in the failing light, where he could try to read Rebecca Parkinson's face and define her reactions.

He'd learned long ago that when people could be persuaded to talk, even about something as simple as the weather, he had a better chance of building a bridge to the truth. Silence worked in favor of the suspect—if there was no conversation, there would be nothing to stumble over later.

Hamish said, "Ye ken, ye said fra' the start, this sister couldna be persuaded to work wi' the police."

Please God, Sarah would be a different sort. Certainly she was the more emotional of the two women. And probably the less stubborn.

In the end he left, driving back to Berkshire in the waning light of a spring evening.

It was just dark when he reached The Smith's Arms. Tired and dispirited, he had listened to Hamish for miles, and he wished only for peace.

As he walked into the inn, he stopped short.

Sitting quietly in the chair by the window, where sometimes he had eaten his breakfast, was Meredith Channing.

The surprise was so complete that he simply stood there, unable to imagine what had brought her here, how she had found him. Even Hamish hadn't warned him. And then he remembered that she was a friend of Frances's, and he asked quickly, "Is anything wrong?"

She rose to greet him, something in her face that frightened him. But then she said, "I thought it best to come and tell you about Simon Barrington. For your sister's sake."

"How did you find me?"

"I asked a friend to call the Yard. Sergeant Gibson was kind enough to give me your direction." She looked around, listening to the sounds of laughter and someone's harmonica making rowdy music in the bar. "Is there anywhere that we can be private?"

"The night is mild enough. We can walk, if you'd like."

She preceded him through the doorway, and said, "I passed

the White Horse as I was coming in. It's amazing. One of the most beautiful things I've ever seen. There's something about it that is—I don't know—rather fearsome. And yet not at all frightening."

"I've always admired it."

They turned in the direction of Wayland's Smithy. He said, "I saw Simon when I was in Lincoln. With another woman. I didn't know who she was."

"Yes, well, she's his sister, and she's been having an appalling time. He goes north every weekend, even midweek if it's necessary. He hasn't told anyone but his closest friends, people who know her too. Her husband's dead, you see, and she's ill, rather a dreadful illness I'm afraid, and he takes her to the doctor in Lincoln for treatments. I expect he doesn't know how long she may have to live, and if she does, how long she will need to convalesce."

"Why tell me this? Why not speak to Frances directly?"

"If I tell her, I'm betraying a confidence from a friend. But Frances came to me for answers, and I know how wretched she is. I'm hoping you'll find a way to assure her that it isn't personal."

"I'll do my best." He hesitated. "Is she in love with Simon, do you think? Or is this a passing fancy? I've been busy, and there hasn't been time to find out."

"I think she's lonely, and sometimes that palls. Simon is single, attractive, and of her own social set. If she isn't in love with him, she may believe she ought to be. And that could go a long way toward explaining her unhappiness."

He hadn't considered that possibility. It put matters in a different light.

They had reached the Smithy and stood beside it, gazing at it but not really seeing it. He thought that Frances was not the only problem that Mrs. Channing had brought with her.

After a moment she said, "I shouldn't have come. This could have waited."

"I'm glad you did."

In the darkness her face was a pale blur framed by her hair. "Ian. I only just heard about Jean Montroy's death."

He took a deep breath. "It was a surprise." Inadequate, but that was all he could manage.

"Yes, it must have been. I'm sorry."

Rutledge turned away, listening to the roar of Hamish's voice in his ears, and not understanding any of what he was saying.

"What did the poet say? That the saddest words of tongue or pen were what might have been? It's true. If we'd been married in the summer of last year, the child might have been mine. But it wasn't, and if she was happy, I'm glad. Her happiness was brief enough." He walked a short distance, then came back. "Who told you?"

"It was in the Canadian newspapers, of course, and a friend sent me the cutting. I wondered if you would like to have it."

He considered that, and in the end, said, "Thank you. No. At least not at present."

"Of course." She put her hand on one of the stones that formed the Smithy and said, apropos of nothing, "Whoever was buried here must have been famous in his day. I wonder what his life was like, and his death."

"I don't suppose there's any way to know. Although the local smith will tell you that there's still treasure to be found inside."

"Perhaps he's right. Well, it's late, and I must be on my way. I'm staying with friends a few miles from here, and they'll be wondering what's become of me."

They walked back to the inn in a comfortable silence, and he found it soothing. "Where is your motorcar? I didn't see it when I came in."

"I left it in the kitchen yard. Mrs. Smith thought it best." He could hear the amusement in her voice. "I don't think she quite agrees with women driving."

He turned the crank for her and said, as she pulled on her driving gloves, "Thank you for coming."

"I wasn't sure it was the right thing to do. Good night, Ian." And with that she drove out of the inn yard and went on her way.

He watched the rear light disappearing down the road before turning back to the main door and going inside.

Rutledge didn't sleep well. He was awakened by the sound of guns firing in the distance—artillery, German, he could tell—and realized after the first startled instant that they were in his head. He'd been dreaming about the Front, and it had stayed with him even though he had awakened from it. The inn was quiet around him, and he lay there listening to the night.

In the darkness he heard Hamish saying, "Why did a friend send yon widow a cutting aboot your Jean?"

It hadn't occurred to him to question that at the time, but it struck him as odd now. Why had she really come? To see how he was mourning Jean? Or to be certain that the news hadn't eroded his narrow margin of safety, his tenuous grip on sanity? He wasn't sure how much Meredith Channing knew about his war. Sometimes it seemed that she guessed more than he was prepared for anyone to know. But then she'd been at the Front, a nurse in the forward aid station closest to his section. She had seen men in every state between living and dying and somehow managed to keep her own sanity intact. There was a well of something there, understanding perhaps or sympathy, even knowledge. But no pity. He couldn't have borne that from anyone.

A rooster crowed in the distance, and Rutledge reached for his watch, lighting his lamp long enough to glance at it. Dawn would be breaking soon.

And with it, what? Another murder? Another day of chasing a truth that didn't want to be discovered?

Sometimes he thought that Gerald Parkinson would be happier in an anonymous grave rather than one where he wasn't wanted.

After a time he drifted again into sleep, his last thought one that had grown out of his conversation with Meredith Channing.

A murderer would have put Parkinson's body in Wayland's Smithy and called his death a suicide.

When he came down the next morning, Mrs. Cathcart was eating her breakfast at the table that was usually his, but he made no move to join her. She seemed to be in better spirits, and Mrs. Smith had been carrying on a running conversation with her as each dish was brought in. The subject under discussion was affairs at the cottages, and they had reached the point of debating whether Partridge was one of the victims or not.

"He's not been seen for some time. But the police were there, in his cottage, and nothing was said about finding him," Mrs. Cathcart was saying.

"He would come here sometimes to talk with the lorry drivers. The distance to this place or that, what accommodations might be had, what kind of weather he might expect. I didn't know for the longest time that he was from the cottages—I thought he'd come in from Uffington. Horrible to imagine him murdered. Are they quite sure of that?" Mrs. Smith asked over a rack of toast.

Rutledge asked, "Did he ever talk about his visit to Liverpool?"

It was Deloran and his men who had tracked Parkinson there. And Rutledge had never been satisfied that Parkinson hadn't lured them there, to keep his watchers from guessing what he'd really done during his brief absences.

But neither Mrs. Cathcart nor Mrs. Smith could answer that question.

Mrs. Smith was called away by two drivers just in, and Mrs. Cathcart was still sitting over the last of her tea when he left the inn.

Hamish said, "She believes her husband willna' think to look for her here."

It was true—The Smith's Arms was hardly a place where the Mrs.

Cathcarts of this world spent their days. But she seemed less anxious this morning, as if she had slept well enough.

Rutledge drove as far as the foot of the lane and pulled the motorcar to the verge. The sun was watery as he walked up to the cottage occupied by Mr. Allen. The smith had fashioned a wrought-iron *SIX* in a Gothic script for Allen's door, giving it a distinction the other cottages lacked.

The curtains twitched in the front window before the door was opened to Rutledge's knock.

"Taking precautions," Allen said in explanation as he moved aside to let Rutledge inside the small entry. "I'm dying but have no interest in hurrying the process."

"Miss Chandler, who once lived in Brady's cottage, sends you her regards. She was pleased to hear that you're still alive."

He smiled. "She didn't belong here. But beggars can't be choosers. I'd wondered if her good fortune was truly that."

"It appears to have been."

"I wish I were well out of here myself. This business of murder practically on one's doorstep is not good for any of us, I expect. I've found it hard to sleep. I spoke to Miller this morning, and he agrees, if we had anywhere else to go, we'd be off. I'm not up to travel, sadly. I'll have to take my chances."

"What does Miller think about events?"

"He's a rather timid man, and he overcomes it with bluster. Once you get past that, he's all right. Though I don't count him a friend, you understand. He's not convinced that Brady is our man. He favors poor Slater, telling me that he'd not be predictable in taxing situations. Miller says he grew up with one such and there was murder done because of a misunderstanding that got out of hand. I can't say that I agree. I've never seen Slater violent."

"That leaves you, Singleton, and Quincy to be cast as murderers."

Allen smiled. "I daresay I'm not in Inspector Hill's sights, given my health." The smile faded. "What's become of Mrs. Cathcart? I haven't seen her today. Has someone looked in on her?"

"Yes, she's fine. She was enjoying breakfast earlier."

"Is Partridge dead, as Brady claimed?"

"Yes, I'm afraid he is. But under rather different circumstances than Willingham's murder. It will take some time to learn what Brady's role was in his death. If any."

"I must say, I'd have not thought it of Brady. He was a weak man, in my view, troubled by his drinking and whatever it was that brought him here to live."

Rutledge prepared to take his leave, watching Allen's face sag with fatigue, one hand clutching the arm of a chair with white-knuckled fingers.

Allen was saying, "I'll tell you something about Partridge. For what it's worth. I wouldn't have, if there was a chance he was still alive."

Rutledge waited.

"I don't think that was his real name. I'd seen him at a party in Winchester several years ago, and although we weren't introduced, he was pointed out to me as one of the people doing some sort of hush-hush work for the government. There were a number of important guests at the dinner, and he seemed to know most of them. I never asked him about this, partly respecting his privacy and partly because I heard later that he'd fallen from grace and was in bad odor with the government. You can imagine my surprise when I looked out my door one morning and saw him walking down the lane. He was calling himself Partridge then, but for the life of me I can't remember how he was called at the party. Something similar, but I'd have remembered Partridge if it had been that. It's not a common name."

"And you said nothing about this to anyone else?"

Allen responded with irritation. "I told you. I respected his privacy."

"Later on, did you tell the friend who'd first pointed this man out to you that you'd seen him here in Berkshire?"

Allen's face flushed. "Only because I thought it might reassure him that all was well. I was in Winchester to see my doctor when I ran into him."

"How long after that did Mr. Brady come here to live?"

"A month, possibly less. There can't be a connection. I'd have sworn they didn't know each other." But Allen was no fool. "You aren't trying to say there's a connection, are you? That word spread, and that's why Brady came here? I refuse to believe it." But the dawning realization was shattering. "If your charge is true, why did the man wait so long to kill Partridge? Answer me that?"

"Brady's dead, and there's no way we can ask him."

Allen said again, "I refuse to believe my casual comments had anything to do with Brady or the murder of Partridge." He stepped forward, forcing Rutledge to move back outside the door, and shut it with firmness.

"That was how Martin Deloran found his missing scientist," he said to Hamish as he walked back the way he'd come.

A chance encounter, a remembered name and face, a chatty reference in a conversation, and somehow the news had reached Deloran's ears.

Hamish said, "Ye ken, Parkinson knew as soon as the watcher came, but didna' understand how it was that he'd been found."

"I'm sure of it."

He stopped to tap at Miller's door in Number 7.

This time to his surprise it opened. "The police have been and gone. I've nothing to say to you."

Rutledge said, "I happened to call on Miss Chandler, and she asked to be remembered to you and to Mr. Allen."

"Kind of you. Good day."

But Rutledge had his hand on the door to prevent it from closing. "I've also come to ask if you knew Mr. Partridge well."

"No one here knows anyone well. I thought you'd have learned that by now."

Rutledge studied the man. A thin face, hair graying early, a sturdy build. He could have been the conductor on a streetcar or a clerk in a shop. Middle-class with an accent that didn't betray his roots, one cultivated to win him a better position in the marketplace, but not completely natural to him. It was his eyes that were interesting. They were what many would call hazel, but the dominant color was a golden green and oddly feral. And they were guarded, as if someone else stood behind them, a very different man from the one the world saw at first glance.

Inmates of prisons sometimes had that shuttered look, surviving as best they could in a place where they were afraid.

Rutledge said, "Every cottage has windows. And there's nothing to see except the horse on the hill and the comings and goings of your neighbors."

"I don't watch from my windows."

But he had, like the others, and now he denied it, as the others had done. What was *his* secret?

Had he embezzled funds at his place of business? Or been passed over for promotion and lost his temper? Allen had called him a timid man, and Slater had said he was evil.

There was something here, something that Rutledge, an experienced police officer, could feel in the air.

"You saw nothing the night that Willingham was killed? Or on the night when Brady must have disposed of Partridge's body?"

"I didn't see anything when Willingham was killed. Thank God I was asleep. As for Partridge, I don't even know what night that was. But I can tell you that it was about three days since I'd seen him—he used to walk over to where the trees start and stand there looking up at the horse—when I heard the motorcar come back. It was close on three in the morning, and I was having trouble sleeping. I got up, thinking I might have a cigarette, and I stood there at the window watching someone open the shed door and then drive the motorcar inside. As a rule, Partridge shuts it straightaway, but this time I didn't see him walk around to the door as he usually did. The shed door stayed open."

"And in the morning?"

"The shed door was shut and all was quiet. I thought perhaps he'd slept in, after a long drive. I never saw him again."

When Rutledge didn't comment, Miller hesitated and then added, "The next night Brady went there to Partridge's door, knocked, and went inside. He stayed nearly an hour, and then hurried back to his own cottage. My guess at the time was that Partridge had been taken ill, but nothing came of Brady's visit."

Rutledge said, "No one else has given me this information."

Miller laughed harshly. "Even Quincy must sleep sometimes. I seldom sleep the night through. It's become a habit with me now."

Hamish said, "The truth? Or what ye want to hear?"

Rutledge considered his answer, both to Hamish and to Miller.

Miller added to the silence, hurrying to fill it again, "As far as I know, Mr. Brady didn't have anything with him when he left the cottage."

"And you'd be willing to swear to this under oath at the inquest, Mr. Miller? I wish I'd been told earlier, while Brady was alive."

A flicker of emotion passed across Miller's face. "You never came to ask."

"I was here several times. You failed to answer your door."

"Yes, well, these things happen." He waited with expectancy, as if he thought this time the man from London might leave.

Rutledge thanked him and went back to his motorcar.

To Hamish he said, "It's hard to say what Mr. Miller's motive was in telling me what he just did. Unless it was to speed the police in finishing their business here sooner than later. Offering us lies we want to hear."

He had caught that slight movement when he'd asked Miller about appearing at the inquest for Brady's death.

Miller hadn't expected his admission to be taken any further than a statement. Certainly not to be sworn to under oath and in public. And that rather reinforced the possibility that he hadn't told the truth.

Rutledge thought he understood now why Slater had called Miller an evil man. Those arresting eyes, coupled with an unfriendly nature and impatience or outright antagonism toward a man with a simple view of the world, must make the smith very uncomfortable in Miller's presence.

Hamish said, "It's no' likely that he showed you the same face he showed the ithers."

Rutledge had just reached his motorcar when Hill came down the road toward him and waved him to wait.

He got out of his motorcar and came across to Rutledge, his face sober. He said without preamble, "We managed to get our hands on something Brady wrote before he moved to the cottage. It was a list of what he wanted to bring with him. Somehow it had fallen behind the desk and out of sight. But it was enough for us to compare handwriting. If Brady wrote that list—and there's every reason to believe he did—then he didn't write the suicide note we found, confessing to the murder of Willingham and Partridge."

He held out a sheet of paper, and Rutledge took it.

The list wasn't long. But there were references to "my green folder," and later "my black coat" as well as clothing, books, and personal items. It ended with "the file MD gave me."

Martin Deloran . . .

"I wasn't completely convinced—" Rutledge began, but Hill interrupted him.

"That's as may be. The question is, what are we going to do about this? And I've brought two constables with me. They'll take turn about, watching the cottages day and night. Until we get to the bottom of it."

Two middle-aged men in uniform had stepped out of the motorcar behind him and were walking up the lane. They went into Brady's cottage and shut the door behind them.

"The list of suspects isn't long," Rutledge said, thinking about what Allen had said to him. "Quincy. Allen. Slater. Miller. Singleton."

"You've left out the woman."

"Do you really believe she could have wielded that knife?"

"I doubt it very much. But I'm not taking any chances." He marched off after his men, head down and mouth a tight line.

Rutledge turned the motorcar in the middle of the road and drove back to Partridge Fields.

It had represented many things in Gerald Parkinson's life.

A happy childhood for two young girls. A mother's illness. A father's obsession with his work. A death by suicide, and then a house left to stand empty.

But not abandoned. Rebecca Parkinson may have seen to the flower beds, but it was her father who made certain that the lawns were well kept, and someone was paid to clean and polish and see that the rooms stayed fresh.

Parkinson had even used the name Partridge, after the name of his house. Gaylord Partridge.

The gate was always closed and today was no exception. But he let himself in and walked around to the kitchen. He was in luck. The housekeeper was there—a dust pan and brush stood beside a mop and a pail of old cloths just outside the door. And from the kitchen he could hear a woman humming to herself as she worked.

He called to her, but she didn't immediately answer. He stood there, his back to the house, looking past the kitchen garden to the small orchard on the left and the outbuildings just beyond. Shrubbery, tall with age, partly blocked his view, but there appeared to be a small stable for horses, a coop for chickens, and a longer building where everything from carriages to scythes, barrows, and other tools could be stored. Leading to the buildings was a cobbled walk, to keep boots out of the mud when it rained, and someone had put a tub of flowers to either side.

He walked to the orchard, where plum and apple and pear grew cheek by jowl, and beyond there was another outbuilding, this one low, foursquare, and without grace. Apparently built for utility not beauty, it was one story so as not to be visible at the house over the tops of the orchard trees. A pair of windows was set either side of the door.

Someone had tried to make it prettier, for it had been painted green and there was a lilac avenue leading up the walk to it, three to either side. A silk purse and a sow's ear, Rutledge thought.

Hamish, regarding it with dislike, said, "The laboratory."

Rutledge went up to the windows and looked inside.

The workbenches in the center of the floor were too heavy to be overturned, but someone had taken an axe to them, and the rest of the room was littered with glass and twisted metal, broken chairs, and a scattering of tools and equipment. Someone had come in here and destroyed everything that could be destroyed, with a wild anger that hadn't been satisfied by mere destruction. It had wanted to smash and hurt and torment.

Who had done this?

Gerald Parkinson's late wife?

Or his daughters, hungry for a revenge they couldn't exact on their father?

Hamish said, "The elder one."

It was true. Rebecca Parkinson was riven by an anger that went bone deep, unsatisfied and uncontrolled.

But Sarah might have been jealous enough of her father's passion to hate the laboratory just as much.

He heard someone calling from the direction of the house and retraced his steps, coming out of the orchard to see the housekeeper standing in the doorway, a hand shading her eyes as she called.

"I saw your motorcar from the windows. Where have you got to? There's nobody here but me—" She broke off as she heard him approaching and turned his way.

"You mustn't wander about like this, it isn't right," she scolded him. "Policeman or no."

"I called to you. I could hear you humming in the kitchen," he said lightly, shifting the blame for his walk squarely onto her for not answering him.

"I was arranging fresh flowers for Mrs. Parkinson's bedroom and taking them up. I do sometimes. It cheers me."

"A nice touch," he said. "You must have been very fond of her."

"I was that, a lovely lady with gentle manners." She sighed. "It seems to me sometimes that I can still hear her voice calling to me." At his look of surprise she smiled wryly. "No, not her ghost, of course not. But her voice all the same, in my head, just as it used to be. 'Martha, do come and see what I've done with the flowers.' Or 'Martha, I think I'll take my luncheon in the gardens, if you don't mind making up a tray.' Little things I'd do for her and knew she'd appreciate. But that time's long gone, and I don't have anyone to spoil, not even Miss Rebecca or Miss Sarah."

"Do you recall when Mrs. Parkinson was ill—some years ago when her daughters were young?"

"I've told you, it isn't my place to gossip about the family."

"It isn't gossip I'm looking for," he said, "but something to explain what makes Gerald Parkinson's daughters hate their father. It might be traced back to her illness, for all I know."

"I don't think they hate him, exactly—"

"What else would you call it? I've spoken to both of them, and I'd be deaf not to hear the way they felt about him."

"Yes, well, I expect there's some hard feeling over poor Mrs. Parkinson's sudden death."

"On the contrary, I think it went back longer than that. Sarah Parkinson remembers how happy she was before that illness. But she was too young to understand what the illness was. Or why it changed her parents."

"Come in, then, I was just about to put the kettle on. You might as well have a cup with me."

She led the way into the kitchen and set the kettle on the stove. He could see that it was already hot, and she said, "I like to cook some-times when I'm working. Nothing but a bit of warmed-over soup and some tea, once in a while my bread baking for the week. This is a bet-ter oven than the one I have in my little house."

"No one objects, surely?"

"No. At least they've never said anything. Once when I'd done some baking I came back and found half my lemon cake gone. It wasn't all that long ago either. I expect Miss Rebecca was sharpish after working in the gardens."

"Mrs. Parkinson's illness?" he reminded her.

"I wasn't here then, as it happened. I left service to go and marry a scoundrel, and when I came back, looking for work, she took me on again. The interim housekeeper had just left without giving notice."

"Do you know why?"

"I was told she hadn't counted on being a nursemaid, but it was more than that, I think. Mr. and Mrs. Parkinson weren't getting on. He was spending more and more time in that laboratory of his, and she didn't leave her bed for a good two months after I came back. She'd lost her will to live, I thought, and I tried everything I could think of to bring her back to her old self. It wasn't until Miss Sarah caught the scarlet fever that Mrs. Parkinson got herself up and dressed and stayed up night and day with the child. I think that was the saving of her, but Mr. Parkinson, when I mentioned it to him, said that even great sorrows don't last forever. I took that to mean that Mrs. Parkin-son had lost a child she was carrying. I don't know why I thought that, except it was just the sort of thing that would break a woman's heart. No one ever *said*, in so many words. But they'd have liked a son, I'm sure, to carry on the name."

Hamish said, "Truth or only wishful thinking?"

It was something neither parent would discuss with a young girl, but a loss that would send the father to bury himself in his work and leave the mother to mourn for what might have been.

"Do you know if the doctor who cared for Mrs. Parkinson is still in practice?"

"My goodness, no, Dr. Butler died six years ago of a heart condition. His son was going to take over the practice, but then the war came along."

So much for verifying her supposition.

He drank his tea as the housekeeper rattled on about her work and the family she had served, small anecdotes that she had taken pleasure in remembering through the years.

"I don't expect you've ever seen a photograph of her. When they was first married, Mr. Parkinson said he'd like to have her painted. She was such a pretty thing, Mrs. Parkinson. Fair hair and blue eyes, a real English rose, you might say. It was a pleasure to look at her when she was all dressed up for a party or to travel up to London. Blue was her color, it brought out the softness of her skin, but she could wear most anything. They made a handsome pair, I can tell you. Him dark, her fair . . ."

When he'd finished his tea, he thanked her and rose to leave.

"I shall have to mention to Miss Rebecca and Miss Sarah that you were here," she told him as she saw him to the door. "If they ask. And if you could see fit to forget anything I may'uv said out of turn, it would be a kindness. But you being a policeman and all, it's not like gossiping with the greengrocer's wife, is it?"

He promised to respect her confidences, and walked back to his motorcar, thinking about what she'd told him.

A miscarriage could change the relationship of husband and wife. Most certainly if the doctors had told her she mustn't have another child. The emotional impact of loss and grief could have frightened children who didn't understand what had happened. They would certainly have felt the great distress wrapping their parents in shared sorrow, and they might have felt left out of it. Something like that could shake the safe world a child was accustomed to living in.

It went a long way toward understanding the sisters' anger and even explained to some extent why Mrs. Parkinson had finally killed herself, if she had never quite come to terms with her grief. But it didn't explain patricide.

Hamish said, "She died many years later."

"I don't know that time has anything to do with grief, but yes, it must have added to her burden."

He'd spoken aloud from habit, and caught himself up.

Hamish said, "Aye, ye can pretend I'm no' here, but you canna' turn around to see for yoursel'."

It was true, the one thing Rutledge dreaded was seeing the face of a dead man. However real Hamish was, he was lying in his grave in France. And if he was not . . . it didn't bear thinking of.

The housekeeper, Martha, might not have believed in ghosts, and for that matter, neither did Rutledge. The voice in his head had nothing to do with dead men walking. It was there because Hamish *had* died, and there was nothing he could do to change that. It was his punishment for killing so many of his own men, for leading them over the top and across No Man's Land and coming back without a scratch on him, while they fell and cried out and died. He'd had the courage to die with them, but Fate had decided to spare him, and scar him with the knowledge that his very survival mocked him.

22

When he got back to The Smith's Arms, Rutledge was surprised to find that the ex-soldier, Singleton, had come to the bar and was there drinking heavily.

It was Mrs. Smith who told him, her voice pitched not to carry but her concern very real.

"I don't want Smith to throw him out, it isn't good for business, and besides, he's likely drunk enough to take exception to it, and then where will we be? And for that matter, poor Mrs. Cathcart is in her room frightened of her own shadow, with him shouting down here."

As Hamish warned him to stay out of it, Rutledge pushed through the door and found Smith behind the bar, standing there grimly watching Singleton. He was talking with a lorry driver, and the man had pushed back from the table to escape the intensity of Singleton's vehement certainty that the world was going to the dogs, and before long they'd all be murdered in their beds.

Walking over to the pair, Rutledge greeted them with a nod and then said, "Singleton. I'd like to have a word, if you don't mind."

The ex-soldier looked up at him. "If it's about the murders, I have nothing to say. It's not a military matter, is it?"

"You're right. Still, you've more experience than most of the residents there at the cottages." He sat down, moving his chair slightly so that he could watch Singleton and his irate companion at the same time.

"Experience in what?" It was a low growl, as if Rutledge had accused him of the killings.

"Dealing with men. What if Hill is wrong, and Brady couldn't have killed himself or Willingham? Who do you think might be capable of it?"

Singleton shook his head as if to clear it. "Blame it on Partridge, if you like. It's as good a guess as any. Why else did he run off, and bring the police prowling about like ants?"

"Hardly like ants. Hill and his men have tried to be discreet."

"Yes, well, I'd had enough. I came here for a little peace. If Mrs. Cathcart can flee the scene, so can I."

"She's a woman, and nervous."

"I intend to stay the night."

"Mrs. Smith doesn't have a free room."

"Then I'll sleep here. All I need is a pillow and a blanket."

"I'm afraid that's not possible. Let me drive you home. You'll be safer in your own bed."

"Safe has nothing to do with it. There's no peace there any more. I wish Willingham had never died, or Brady for that matter, though I didn't like *him* at all. Smelled of trouble, the moment I saw him."

"He never disturbed you, to my knowledge," Rutledge pointed out.

"I'd have dealt with him if he had."

The lorry driver cleared his throat and started to get up. Singleton told him shortly to sit down and mind where he was. "You're drinking my round, and you'll finish it out of courtesy."

But the lorry driver said, "I've had all I can drink and still drive. You don't have another fifty miles to travel before you're done."

"I want company," Singleton retorted. "I've never liked to drink alone."

"You've got company," the driver pointed out but subsided in his chair, casting a pleading glance at Rutledge.

"Singleton. I'll ask Smith to give us a bottle and we'll finish it at the cottage."

Singleton considered him. "I told you, I wanted to get away from there."

"This is hardly the place to drown your sorrows."

"But it's where I am."

"Partridge is dead. His body was found some distance from here. It's likely he was murdered as well. But not necessarily by the same hand as Brady and Willingham."

Singleton's eyes sharpened. "You're lying. You can't have two murderers prowling the same patch."

"Why not? Murder is as individual as the man or woman who resorts to it. You've killed, you know that's true."

"What do you mean, I've killed?"

Rutledge thought, *He's beyond reasoning with.*

And Hamish said once more, "'Ware!"

"All right, Singleton, we're leaving." Rutledge got to his feet and pushed his chair back to the table. "Are you ready to come with me?"

It was not the conversational voice he'd been using, but the tone of an officer expecting his men to obey on the spot.

Surprisingly Singleton responded, standing and then gripping the edge of the table to steady himself.

"Give me a shoulder, man!" he appealed to Rutledge, and together they walked out of the bar. Mrs. Smith, standing in the shadows by the stairs, watched, and up on the landing, Mrs. Cathcart had wrapped her arms about her body as if to stop shaking. Rutledge got Singleton outside and into the motorcar.

They drove back toward the cottages, and Singleton was silent, brooding.

As Rutledge turned up the lane toward his cottage, the ex-soldier said, "It's Quincy, if you're looking for one of us to be the murderer. He's half mad anyway, with all those damned birds. Someone should fire the cottage with him in it."

"Someone did try. He got a shotgun barrel in his face."

"Then you've only to look at any one of us to see who it was."

"Quincy fired through the door. Apparently scaring the hell out of someone but not hitting him."

"I told you he was mad."

"Yes, probably you're right. Do you want me to come in with you?"

"No. You're not drinking my whisky and telling me lies."

"Suit yourself. Good day, Singleton."

He waited while Singleton made up his mind. After a moment, the man clambered down, threw a mockery of a salute in Rutledge's direction, and said, "It's the pain that gets to you after a while. It drives you mad."

"Were you wounded?" Rutledge knew Singleton had served in India.

"The disgrace, damn you. It turned my father against me, I'll tell you that. He never spoke to me again. His only son, disgraced before his regiment. And mine. But I didn't care any more. And he did."

He walked with surprising steadiness to his door and went inside. As Rutledge turned the motorcar, he was close enough to Number 7 to see Miller standing at his window.

What if Miller had been telling the truth, or part of it, that someone had brought Partridge's motorcar back to the cottage to make it appear that Partridge hadn't used it?

With the tab of the respirator found in the vehicle and Miller's story—if true—to show that the motorcar had been returned late at night by an unknown driver, the pieces of the puzzle were falling together. But Rutledge still hadn't determined where Parkinson had died. If it was in his own house, then the sisters were involved. If not, then it could have been Brady, or if Deloran didn't trust him, another of his minions. He hadn't died in the cottage. Had someone overpowered him while he stood in the trees looking up at the White Horse? It would have been easy, quiet.

Rutledge had come to know Rebecca and Sarah Parkinson. Letting their father die the same way their mother had killed herself smacked of a certain justice. If he took them into custody, and a jury found them guilty, he'd have to be present when they went to the gallows. And he was fairly certain that Rebecca would protect her sister to the end, claiming that she alone had carried out the murder, even if it had taken two of them to drag their father's body to the motorcar and drive it to Yorkshire.

The newspapers would make a sensation out of the trial. Parkinson's daughters would be vilified in print, their family's secrets dragged out into the open and dissected over tea and the butcher's counter and in the pubs.

He had better be damned certain that his facts were irrefutable before he tossed two young women to the wolves.

But for Parkinson's sake, his murderer or murderers had to be brought to justice. Even if he would have railed at the police for doing it.

Rutledge thought, *I've always spoken for the victim. This time the victim might well prefer to see me fail.*

Rutledge drove to Sarah Parkinson's house, waited at the door while she decided whether or not to answer his knock, and when she came at last, he went straight to the point.

"You have a choice, Miss Parkinson. Come with me to Yorkshire and identify your father's body, then help us solve the mystery of where and how he died. There have been two other deaths among the residents of the Tomlin Cottages, and so far we've managed to keep the two inquiries separate. But the fact remains that both of the dead men,

Mr. Willingham and Mr. Brady, had a very good view of your father's cottage. We've been told by another witness that your father's motorcar was returned after he went missing. This witness saw one person driving it, and since your father wasn't there the next morning, we have to believe that it was his killer who brought the motorcar back. Both Mr. Willingham and Mr. Brady were closer to the shed than our third witness. They could very well have seen the driver more clearly. If the police can't prove otherwise, then a connection will be made between your father's death and the other murders." He could see the color draining from her face. "It's been my experience, Miss Parkinson, that murdering another human being is easier after the first time. If you didn't kill those men, then we must assume it was Rebecca, trying to protect you."

"My sister did nothing of the sort! You're trying to frighten me. Go away."

"You can shut the door, if you like, and I'll leave. But what I've told you won't leave with me. It will echo in your head until you come to your senses and act to protect yourself. She's your sister, Miss Parkinson, but she's placed your own life at risk. Can't you see that?"

"You're wrong," she told him resolutely. "You are *wrong*—"

"Then tell me what the truth is and let me deal with it."

"There's nothing to tell." Her voice held a world of sorrow. "This business at the cottages has nothing to do with us. And you said yourself that my father's body—if it is his—was found a long way from here."

"Miss Parkinson, listen to me. Whatever happened, you must find the courage to speak out. If you're afraid of your sister, we'll protect you—"

"Why should I be afraid of her? She's done nothing. Nothing at all. And this talk about murders to cover up what witnesses saw is wild guessing, nothing else. Let this witness meet me face-to-face and tell me I was there. *I was not.*"

"But you can't speak for Rebecca, can you? If you weren't there, you can't prove or disprove that she might have been. Come in and give us a statement, tell us what you know. Let us set the record straight."

"If I sign a statement, you'll use it against Becky. She's the only family I have left. Do you think my mother would ever forgive me if I did something that would hurt Becky? Do you think I could forgive myself? My father is dead. There's nothing more I can do to hurt him, and nothing more he can do to hurt me. Let it go."

"Murder isn't something I can walk away from. When I leave here, I'm going to take a statement from the witness who saw your father's motorcar return three nights after your father left. The motorcar is there still. But in the rear seat I found something that you or your sister overlooked. It's a tab from the respirator he was—"

She moved so quickly he couldn't have forestalled her. The door was slammed, and he could hear on the other side the rasp of the bolt as it was shoved into place.

He had planted the seeds of doubt about her sister in Sarah Parkinson's mind. It was what he had come to do. But he felt unclean now.

"It was a cruel thing ye did."

"What would you have me do? Tell me," Rutledge demanded impatiently as he cranked the motorcar's engine. "Tell me how else I could show her the danger ahead, if she remains loyal to her sister. Hill will come round to thinking this same way. He's no fool."

"Would you betray your sister?"

"The circumstances here are different." But even as he denied it, he knew how much he loved Frances and would protect her.

"No' sae different in my view," Hamish said dryly, as if he'd read Rutledge's mind.

"You had no sisters or brothers. How can you be so sure what you'd have done in my shoes?"

"Aye, it's true. All the same, you'll no' get anywhere with this lass."

He had a strong feeling Hamish might be right. In the end, they could very well get away with murder if they could prove they hadn't touched Willingham or Brady.

And while it was essential to his evidence that they go to Yorkshire and positively identify Inspector Madsen's nameless body, they might decide to accommodate him, let him take them there, and in front of witnesses deny that it was Gerald Parkinson.

He was surprised that Rebecca at least hadn't considered doing just that. If she ever separated her anger from her best interests, it might still happen that way and her father would be buried as Gaylord Partridge. And as surely as the sun rose every morning, Martin Deloran would be delighted to support her testimony.

I t was time to put his case in writing. Rutledge drove back to the cottages to ask Allen to make a statement identifying Parkinson as the neighbor he'd known as Partridge.

It wasn't strong enough to overturn what Parkinson's own daughters told the court, but it might serve to cast doubt on their motives.

But when Rutledge arrived on Allen's doorstep, the man shook his head. He seemed to have aged in a matter of hours, the color of his skin mottled and his hands trembling. "I must rest. Come back this afternoon, if you please."

When Rutledge expressed concern, Allen reminded him, "There are good days and bad. And this hadn't been one of my better ones. They're farther and farther apart now. My doctor warned me, but of course one always supposes he'll be wrong. He wasn't."

He closed his door and Rutledge heard the click of the bolt as he locked it.

Rutledge walked away, thinking that Allen would have a difficult time when it came to giving evidence at a trial. But he would be believed, he was that sort of man. And the view of the jury might well be that a dying man had nothing to gain by lying.

The next statement he wanted was Miller's. Rutledge was surprised when the man answered the door. He explained what he needed.

Miller said, "I told you what I saw. I don't see any point in writing it out."

"What you told me is evidence in a murder inquiry. I can corroborate what you've said, but I can't speak for you. It was you who saw the motorcar come back. It was you who saw Brady go into the Partridge cottage. If both events happened the way you described them to me, you have nothing to fear."

"I'm not much for what follows, appearing in court."

"You'll be summoned to give evidence, whether you wish to or not. It's out of my hands."

"Oh, very well," Miller replied grudgingly. "Come again in half an hour, and I'll give it to you." He said, almost as an afterthought, "What was it you were badgering Allen about? Did he see something as well? Let him give you a statement in my place."

"It doesn't work that way, Miller."

Rutledge went to Quincy's cottage and at first thought that Quincy might not open his door. But he did, saying, "The minders, those two constables in what was Brady's cottage. What are they supposed to do? Arrest our killer as soon as he strikes again? They're not fit enough to run a man down."

A hot, spicy aroma filled the air behind him, distinctly un-English.

"They're Hill's men, here to keep the peace."

Quincy snorted. "Well, they're a damned sight too late for Willingham and Brady. And if Brady did the killing, what are we in need of minders for, tell me that? It's the fire setter who worries me."

"Early days yet, to be certain it was Brady." His curiosity got the better of him. "What are you making?"

"It's something I learned to cook in Mexico. Chili with chocolate cooked in it. Not bad. I admit to homesickness now and again. At least for the food. I've grown fond of a bit more flavor than boiled cabbage and boiled potatoes and boiled beef. I gather you're looking for something other than culinary lessons. And if it's character references you want, Dublin will do."

"Have you told me everything you could? Or is your fear of your brother finding out you're back in England locking up your tongue?"

"I don't know anything more than I've told you. I kept the cat when he wasn't here. We spoke from time to time and that was it."

"He never gave you anything to keep for him, while he was away?"

"Like state secrets, do you mean?" He grinned. "Hardly. He knew he couldn't trust me for the simple reason that I put myself above all else. I've a comfortable life here, and I'm not interested in setting it at risk. The kettle's on, if you want a cup of tea."

Rutledge followed him inside, and as Quincy worked, went into the room with the birds.

"You were lucky the cottage didn't burn down with you in it," he told his host. "It was a near thing."

"And I haven't got rid of the smell yet. Did you notice it? I expect that's why I decided to make chili. I brought spices back with me when I came to England, and they're running out. I need to find a way to stock them in again."

"Surely you left behind friends who could oblige you."

Quincy came back with the tea. "No, I didn't. I burnt those bridges. I didn't want someone showing up in England to surprise me. Here you are. What fascinates you about my birds?"

"How you killed them, before you mounted them."

"That's what Partridge asked me as well. Sorry to disappoint you, but I had others do it for me. I didn't like that part of it. But birds live and die, either by the hand of a small boy with a slingshot or in the jaws of a predator stalking them on the jungle floor. I knew what birds I wanted, and I paid to have them brought to me. I've told you."

So he had. But Rutledge still had his doubts.

Quincy said as he passed Rutledge sugar for his tea, "I borrowed the sugar from Allen, by the way. I knew you'd come calling again. All right, let's look at the broader picture. If I'd killed Willingham and

Brady, I'd have done it more efficiently. Taken my shotgun and seen them off quickly and with a minimum of fuss."

"And a maximum of noise."

"There's that," Quincy acknowledged. "But I'm not one for carving up my enemies with a knife. It's a favorite weapon in Central America, but I never took to it. The same holds for why I didn't kill these birds myself. I don't have to feel guilty every time I look at them for how they may have died."

"Everyone here has secrets. You said as much yourself. I know most of them now, and none of them appears to be worth a murder. Much less two."

"Yes, well, there are secrets and secrets."

"And yours might be that if your brother demands that you leave England again, you don't dare show your face in Central America."

Something flickered in his eyes, but Quincy said, "The world is wide, and there are other places to hide."

Hamish said, "He canna' return. Or he wouldna' ha' risked coming home."

Rutledge smiled. "There are ways to find out if there are warrants out for your arrest."

"I'm not so worried about the police, damn it. There's a family out for my blood and likely to have it if I'm not careful. It's easy to hire an assassin where people are poor and desperate. I'd never know the face of my murderer until he was on me. And so I paid a few bribes of my own and got out."

It had the ring of truth.

But that left Allen and Miller and Singleton. As well as Rebecca Parkinson.

"Ye forgot the smith," Hamish warned Rutledge.

He had. Finishing his tea, he asked, "What secrets did Willingham have?"

"That made him a victim? Who knows? If you caught the rough edge of his tongue, you might want to kill him on general principles."

Rutledge rose to leave. "But you were nearly a victim as well. After Brady died."

"Yes. We might need to ask ourselves, what set something in motion that can't be stopped? And that's why I sleep with the shotgun to hand. If he comes in here, I'll be ready for him."

It was an interesting remark, and it stayed with Rutledge after he left Quincy's cottage.

We might need to ask ourselves, what set something in motion that can't be stopped?

He climbed the hill and sat down on the chalk edge of the great horse's foreleg.

Secrets within secrets . . . Something set in motion that can't be stopped.

What had changed in this tiny hamlet of nine cottages over the past two years?

Partridge had come to live here, and then Allen had unwittingly given him away to someone who passed the news of Parkinson's whereabouts to Deloran. Brady had then taken over the cottage vacated by Miss Chandler, after her fortuitous "inheritance" from a cousin had allowed her to move elsewhere.

That had covered what, the space of a few weeks or months?

And after that, nine people had lived together in peace if not in harmony until Partridge went away and failed to come back.

He'd have thought, Rutledge mused silently, that the first death ought to have been Brady's. But Partridge had accepted his watcher and very likely proceeded to play with him by disappearing at intervals. *Better the devil you know . . .*

Partridge's death had stirred up something here.

Or was it Rutledge's appearance on the scene to find out where he'd gone and why?

That was more to the point. Whatever Inspector Hill wanted to believe.

Hamish said, "Else, someone came looking for what yon old lady had typed. When you didn't find it."

But Rutledge couldn't believe that Parkinson would have trusted anything of value to a curmudgeon like Willingham. Then again, why not? The least likely place might have been the most secure.

That still wouldn't explain Brady's death, even if Brady had gone to search Number 3 while he thought Willingham was asleep.

It all came round to what they'd seen the night Partridge vanished.

And—both deaths occurred after Rutledge had made himself known to Parkinson's daughters. That ought to have been included in his time line.

"Speak of the devil—" Hamish began.

Below Rutledge a motorcar went speeding by, and he recognized it—it was one that Sarah Parkinson borrowed from her sister.

It looked as if the things he'd said to her only this morning had sent her headlong to confer with Rebecca.

Rutledge went down the hill fast, reached his own motorcar, and set out in pursuit.

He wanted to be there when the sisters met.

Halfway down the hill he stopped. The door to Allen's cottage had swung open, and Allen himself stood there for an instant and then went sprawling head first into the front garden.

Rutledge changed course, and shouting for Slater or Quincy, raced to Allen's aid. No one came to help him. Not even the constables Hill had left on watch.

When he reached Allen, he could see that there was no need for help. The man was dying. Rutledge turned him over and lifted the thin shoulders into his arms, holding him.

Allen looked up, squinted at the sky, then slowly brought Rutledge's face into focus. "It's you," he said. "You won't get your statement after all. Sorry."

He lay back, trying to breathe. After a moment he said, "I don't regret going this way. I'm just grateful that I'm not alone. I always worried about that, you know. Silly, when I chose to live here by myself."

Rutledge said, "Is there anything I can do? Anyone you want me to contact?"

"It's all there, in my desk. You're a good man, Rutledge. Thank you for coming."

Allen began to recite the Twenty-third Psalm, breathless and yet not hurrying, as if he knew he had time. When he'd finished he said, "I didn't live a blameless life. But I never did anyone any harm. I expect God will take that into account."

Rutledge had seen men die, most of them young, and had held more than one frightened boy until it was over. Allen, worn and frail, had reached the end of a normal life span, but it made no difference. Watching was difficult. But he spoke quietly, steadily, to the dying man, and Allen answered as long as he was able. And then he was quiet, but still breathing. After an interval he said, quoting King Charles II, "I seem to be an unconscionable time a-dying." His chuckle caught on a small cough, and then he was gone, the light fading from his eyes.

Rutledge said, "Rest in peace. I hope you have found it wherever you are."

He could feel his leg cramping but went on holding Allen for some time, until Slater, returning from the direction of Uffington, saw them there and came on the run.

"What's happened?" he called as he reached them.

"Allen is dead. Time caught up with him, I think."

"Yes, he told me once that the doctor had given him six to eight months, but he was determined to live longer. And so he did."

He reached down and gathered the man's body in his arms, lifting him gently and carrying him into the cottage where he laid Allen on his bed.

Rutledge, working out the cramp in his leg, followed them.

"I'll go for Inspector Hill. Will you stay here?" Slater asked.

Rutledge thought of the sisters meeting, the danger that Sarah might stand in. It was already too late to get there in time.

He answered, "Go on. I'll wait."

23

For a time Rutledge stood by the hearth in Allen's cottage, listening to the ticking of the carriage clock on the mantelpiece.

The old man had been sitting in his chair when he realized that the end was near. A handful of papers had scattered across the floor as he struggled to his feet and dragged himself to the door to call for help. It must have taken enormous will to travel even that short distance. But he hadn't died alone in an empty house. It was even possible that from his windows he'd seen Rutledge sitting by the horse, and held on until the man from London got to him.

Rutledge gathered up the papers to set them neatly on the table beside the chair.

They were mostly letters from Allen's family, and he put them down without reading them. But among them he saw that Allen had begun his statement, writing out the first sentence in a trembling hand before realizing that his malaise that morning was the precursor to death.

The sheet below that one caught Rutledge's eye, for it was a list of the occupants of the Tomlin Cottages. Partridge's name had been struck off, and then Willingham's and Brady's. There was a question mark by Miller's, and the notation "The likeliest choice, I think. Mostly because he doesn't belong here."

Allen had been playing at amateur detective.

Beside Quincy's name was another notation. "Armstrong? Or perhaps Remington? Can't be sure, must write to Halloran and see . . ."

Next to Slater's name was an X as if Allen had crossed him off as a suspect. The notation beside it read, "He might manage one killing, but not a second. Not in his nature . . ."

And after Singleton's, he'd written, "Soldier, trained to kill. Still—"

It appeared that he'd come to no particular conclusion.

The door opened and Inspector Hill walked in. "You're sure Allen died of natural causes?"

Rutledge said, "Very likely. See for yourself." And Hill went into the bedroom. Rutledge pocketed the list Allen had made, then looked in the desk. As Allen had told him, there was an envelope with the words "To be opened after my death" written in the same hand as the list. Rutledge took it out and set it against a lamp, where Hill would notice it.

Slater was still outside, his face pale. Rutledge went out to him. "I know. It was what he wanted, all the same."

"What are we to do? I think these cottages are accursed. They shouldn't have been put here in the first place. It was a desecration."

"Slater. If I were you, I'd sleep at your smithy tonight, not in your cottage."

"I'm not afraid, if that's what you think."

"If you aren't here, you can't be accused."

The man's eyes widened. "But what about Mr. Quincy, and Miller? And Singleton. You can't leave them."

Inspector Hill came out of the cottage and cast a glance in the direction of Brady's where his men had been stationed. "Why the hell didn't they come? Slater said you were here alone."

"You'd better have a look."

Hill gave him an odd glance, then set out for Brady's cottage at a trot. He went through the door without knocking, and even from this distance, Rutledge could hear him shouting angrily at his men.

He came back, still furious, and said, "They thought it might be a trick. They were told to watch, and damn it, they *watched,* their eyes glued to the other cottages for any sign of trouble."

"There wasn't anything they could do."

"No. All right then, I'll take over here. Thanks." And he turned to go back into the cottage.

Rutledge walked down the lane with Slater. "Will you leave?"

"I'll think about it."

"Good man."

Quincy was standing in his doorway. "Allen, was it?"

"Yes," Rutledge answered shortly. He was still angry with Quincy for not coming to the man's aid.

"I'm glad you were there," Quincy said, and went back inside.

Rutledge left then, knowing it was too late but driving anyway as fast as he dared toward Pockets, the house where Rebecca Parkinson lived.

When he got there, Sarah's motorcar was gone. He wasn't surprised, but she hadn't passed him on the road, and he thought he knew where else she might have gone.

And he'd guessed right. She was at Partridge Fields, sitting in the motorcar just outside the gates, crying.

He pulled up behind her and got out. She looked up, and said, "You've done enough damage. Go away."

"I'm sorry."

"No, you're not. I went to Rebecca to ask what we were to do, she and I. And she said there was nothing we could do. If you arrested us, so be it."

"A charge of murder is a very serious matter."

He looked up. Rebecca Parkinson was peddling toward them on her bicycle. She hesitated when she saw Rutledge's car pulled in behind her sister's. And then she came on, resolute.

"Sarah? Are you all right? I was worried," she said, ignoring Rutledge.

"Yes, I'm fine."

"Come inside. It's one of Martha's days. She may still be here. She can make us some tea."

"I'm not sure I want to go in."

"Then why did you come?"

"There was nowhere else to go." It was said with great sadness.

"I know. Come along in, and it will be all right, I promise you."

Sarah cast a glance in Rutledge's direction. "What about him?" she asked her sister. "I don't think I can bear any more."

"If he comes after us, I'll have him up on charges of trespassing." Rebecca turned to Rutledge, challenging him to argue with her.

Leaving the motorcar where it stood in the middle of the road, Sarah opened her door and crossed to where her sister was still astride the bicycle.

Rutledge waited.

Sarah said, her back to him, "There's something you've forgotten, Mr. Rutledge. In your concern for my father, and whatever justice it is you seem to want for him, you didn't have to live in this house all your life. We did. Push too hard, and we could choose the way out that our mother chose, because right now there isn't much left of our future. If you really want justice, what about a little for us? As for those men in the cottages, I'm sorry about them, but I didn't know them, and neither did Rebecca. I won't take their deaths on my soul."

Rutledge said, "Your father is dead. He doesn't care now what you think of him, what you owe him, or what he made you suffer. For all you know, his own life was as wretched as yours."

Sarah started through the gate, still not looking at him. "Then we're even, aren't we, he and the two of us."

Rebecca followed her, propping her bicycle just inside.

There was triumph now in the glance she cast over her shoulder toward Rutledge.

Hamish said, "She's got her sister under her spell."

And they were gone up the path, walking side by side in silence.

Rutledge swore. It was as if they drew their strength from each other, secure in the knowledge that if neither of them confessed what they knew, there was nothing the law could do to them.

Hamish reminded him that one of the lorry drivers had seen a woman alone and crying in a motorcar drawn to the side of the road, near Wayland's Smith.

"I'll give you odds," he answered aloud, "that it was Sarah, while her sister returned their father's motorcar to the shed. Waiting to take her back to Pockets when it was finished."

The timing would be about right, although it would be hard to prove exactly which night that was. Or find the lorry driver who had seen her.

It was late, but there was still one thing he could do. He drove back to the crossroads and began searching for a doctor's surgery. If Butler had been called to attend Mrs. Parkinson during her pregnancy, he must be near enough to summon at need. And whoever took over his practice might still have Butler's records.

In a village not two miles distant to the west, he found the first of them, and then another just a little farther to the east. A third was due north. But none of them had treated the Parkinson family, or knew what had become of Dr. Butler's records.

He kept moving, first down this road and then that, and as the sun began to set, he turned on his headlamps, determined to find what he was after.

Hamish said, "They had money, the Parkinsons. They would ha' seen a London doctor."

"Not for measles or a fall or a sore tooth. There would have been someone closer who could be called."

"No' for the lost child. For the despair that followed."

Rutledge considered that possibility. But he'd got the impression that for many years Mrs. Parkinson had withdrawn into herself, shutting out her husband, and would never have been persuaded to see a London doctor of his choosing. It would have been an admission that they shared a grief. Mrs. Parkinson had hugged it to herself instead, and in the end, used her death as the ultimate punishment.

He gave up after another two hours. He was too far afield.

He was halfway back to Partridge Fields when he saw a house well off the road, sheltered by a small copse. Its lights were burning in the dark and a drive wandered in their direction. It was just outside the first village he'd tried.

What had caught his eye, in a flash of his headlamps, was not a doctor's board but a small, elegant stone pillar at the end of the drive. He'd almost passed by it a second time when he realized that the scrolled name inset into the pillar was THE BUTLERS. He backed up and turned into the drive, pulling up by the door.

The knocker was a worn brass caduceus, and he felt his hopes soar.

A woman answered, her face framed in soft waves of reddish-brown hair, and behind her, peering around an inner door, was a girl of about twelve.

"Betsy, dear—"

She stopped when she saw a stranger standing on her threshold.

"Oh, I do beg your pardon. I was expecting a friend, and she's late. Are you lost?"

"My name is Rutledge," he said, offering her his identification. She peered shortsightedly at it.

"Scotland Yard? Oh, dear. Perhaps I ought to call my husband." She turned to the girl. "Will you fetch Papa, darling? There's someone here to see him." She sounded uncertain.

The girl disappeared, and in a moment or two a man came to the entry. He was dressed in rough work clothes and there was paint on his hands and across his face.

"Sorry, we're doing up my mother's room. How can I help you, Mr.—er—Rutledge, is it?"

"Yes, from London. I'm looking for a Dr. Butler, who once practiced in these parts. Are you by chance related to him?"

"Good God, how did you ever find us? Yes, he was my father. Dead now, I'm afraid. I don't think he practiced after 1910."

"One of his patients was a woman named Parkinson. I'm trying to learn more about her, and the illness he treated. You don't, by any chance, have his records?"

Butler brushed a hand across his forehead, pushing his light brown hair out of his eyes and leaving another streak of paint there. "I doubt they'd do you much good. But yes, we do. Somewhere. In the attic, at a guess. Well, not his records, actually, those went to the man who took over his practice. And he's dead, as well, killed in the war, worst luck. I don't know who might have taken over from *him*. But my father kept a series of diaries, and they're boxed up just as he left them. Would that be of help?"

"If I'm lucky," Rutledge said.

"Do you need them now?" It was clear Mr. Butler would have preferred another time. "We'll be up all night with our painting. My mother arrives in the morning. This morning."

"It would be best."

"Let me clean up a bit first, then. Come in, man!"

Rutledge followed Butler into a sitting room and waited there for nearly three-quarters of an hour before Butler came back with a wooden box in his hand. Inside were rows of small leather-bound diaries, each with a year printed in gold on its spine.

Rutledge had been trying to calculate which year he was after, based on what Sarah Parkinson had told him about her holidays as a child. He pulled out a likely diary, but there was no mention of the Parkinsons at all save for a reference to a cough that had kept Sarah in bed for three weeks and a burn that the housekeeper, Martha Ingram, had sustained while cooking a Christmas goose.

Butler was sitting across from him, clearly anxious to get back to his painting, and Mrs. Butler, held by curiosity, sat quietly knitting and watching from across the room. The girl was nowhere in sight.

Rutledge had to go back two years before he found the diary entry he was after. There was a date, April 27, and then the notation "Mrs. Parkinson went into labor at two o'clock in the afternoon. All proceeding normally. Three weeks short of full term."

Was that the reference he'd been after? The housekeeper had distinctly told him there was a miscarriage. This child was nearly full term.

"Yon housekeeper wasna' there. She left to wed a scoundrel."

On the twenty-eighth there was a second entry. "Eleven in the morning. Boy survived only an hour. Gave Mrs. Parkinson a strong sedative and told the housekeeper, Mrs. Fortner, to sit by her through the night, until I can arrange for a nurse. Four o'clock same day, set Robert Dunning's leg after he was kicked by a horse. Five o'clock, Peggy Henderson brought in with a splinter in hand. Six-thirty, looked in on Mrs. Parkinson again. Sleeping. Nurse Meadows with her now, replacing Mrs. Fortner. Just as well, not impressed with housekeeper's skills. Had long talk with Parkinson, explaining situation. Question about who should see to burial. He left arrangements with me. I did what I could. Sad day for that family."

There was nothing else about treating Mrs. Parkinson, except for the daily visit to be sure she was recovering from the birth.

Rutledge scanned ahead.

Two months later there was a final entry. "Mrs. Parkinson refuses to leave her room. Have advised husband to let her mourn in her own fashion. Would have been easier if she hadn't heard the child cry and knew it lived. Better to have told her it was stillborn. But it was out of my hands."

The only other mention of the Parkinsons that year was a notation that Parkinson had come to Dr. Butler in July with cuts on his hands after an accident in his laboratory. "Self-inflicted" had been added to the terse notation. But Dr. Butler hadn't seen fit to elaborate.

The heartbreaking loss of a son recorded in a few dozen words written in a cramped but clear hand.

Rutledge went through the next year to be sure, but there was no other mention of the child or how the family had learned to cope. Whatever role Dr. Butler had played in Mrs. Parkinson's recovery was not given. These were reminders to himself, not a medical record.

He jotted down the dates and events, then closed the diary and thanked the Butlers. They were glad to see the back of him, he thought. Another woman had arrived with an armload of freshly ironed bed hangings, and Mrs. Butler had taken her directly upstairs.

He could hear her voice drifting down after her. "Betsy, you're a good friend to pitch in like this. I'd never have got them ready in time. There's just one wall left to paint—"

Butler followed Rutledge to the door, as politeness dictated, saying, "I don't suppose you found what you were looking for. Sorry."

"It was worth my time to read what was there." Rutledge thanked him and went out to his motorcar.

It was after midnight, in fact closer to two o'clock. He could feel the long day in his shoulders, and in the tension in Hamish's voice as they drove back to Berkshire.

There had been a living child. So much harder to forget, so much more of a tie for the grieving mother who had heard him cry.

It had been a wild-goose chase, as Hamish was pointing out, but Martha Ingram had been right in her supposition that while she was occupied with her short-lived marriage, there had been another child, a boy after two daughters. And when she returned to serve the family, Mrs. Parkinson had never told her the whole story.

He recalled the comment, "Had long talk with Parkinson, explaining situation."

And later, Gerald Parkinson had smashed something in his laboratory, cutting himself badly.

Things had gone wrong for him as well.

When he reached the inn, Rutledge went up to his bed and fell asleep almost at once. Hamish, silent at last, waited as he always did for the dawn.

There were no alarms in the night, and Mrs. Cathcart announced over breakfast that she was ready to return to her cottage.

Rutledge took her back, and on the way told her that Allen had died. She cried for him.

"Poor man. But he knew it was coming. If I had anywhere else to go, I'd leave here. But there's no hope of that and I mustn't even dwell on it."

He saw her safely inside, then stood there in the soft end of April morning light, looking up at the White Horse. There were workmen repairing the damage to Quincy's door, the blows of their hammers echoing against the hill and rebounding.

Legend had it that if someone knew the secret, he could stand on the ground below the hill and make his voice appear to come from the horse. Rutledge's father had told him that, but try as they would, they never found the spot. A priest or chieftain would have known where to look for it, and like the Delphic oracle, could have given his pronouncements the power of a god.

It was time to go back to London and report. But he was reluctant to leave until Inspector Hill had caught his murderer. What he would do about his own was another matter altogether. It hadn't worked to turn one sister against the other.

Slater called to him as he was walking home from the village, and Rutledge went to meet him.

"You were wrong. Nothing happened last night."

But Hill had left a message earlier at the inn for Rutledge, saying that he'd collected a sample of handwriting from each of the surviving inhabitants, and the results were unclear. The message ended with "Whoever wrote this confession must have tried to emulate Brady's hand or, at the very least, tried to disguise his own. Hard to say which."

"Nothing happened," Rutledge agreed. "But why take the risk? I'm not convinced Brady killed anyone."

Slater looked up at the horse. "I spent much of the night thinking about Mr. Brady. If he'd killed Mr. Willingham, he'd have tried to bluff his way out. He was that sort. Good at making excuses."

"Perhaps the point was to kill Willingham, and see that Brady took the blame."

"Willingham was free with his tongue, I grant you. And he never cared who he hurt," Slater agreed. "And if that's what's behind this business, he invited his own death. He's called me a simpleton and witless often enough. But I'm used to it. I've been called names all my life. I can't kill every man or woman who hurts my feelings."

"The attempt to burn down Quincy's cottage was probably a sham, to throw us off the scent. The question is, did Quincy set that fire himself?"

Slater said, "They should all be burned down. They were never meant for us. But then I'd have nowhere to go."

He went inside and shut his door, a lost and lonely man who would always draw spite because he was different.

Hill arrived just then, and said, "There's been a development."

"I got your message."

"Yes, well, the doctor says now that Brady couldn't have killed himself, no matter how it was made to look. The angle of the thrust is wrong. He conferred with a colleague."

"So two murders, and an attempted one, if you count the fire at Quincy's. I was just going up to speak to Miller. Would you like to join me?"

Hill shook his head. "It's Slater I'm interested in. That man's got the arm to wield a knife like that, and whatever he says, I think he was pushed over the edge."

"I'd like to look through Willingham's cottage."

"My men have been thorough."

"I'm sure they have. It won't do any harm to add another pair of eyes."

"Go ahead. All you'll find will be the sketches. Constable Smith saw them before I did. Nasty piece of work, but it explains, doesn't it, why we were so ready to believe that Brady had killed the man."

"What sketches?"

Hill said with a grin, "Didn't you know? He took aim at all his neighbors. Quite Hogarthian, really. Still, he knew his way around pen and paper—"

But Rutledge was already on his way, swearing under his breath.

Hamish was pointing out that it wasn't his case.

Rutledge ignored him.

There had been a constable on duty the first day, but he was gone now. Rutledge let himself in, shutting the door behind him.

It wasn't hard to locate the sketches. They were in the desk drawer in a folder tied by string.

He unwound the string and brought out a dozen or more pen-and-ink drawings that were as vicious as any he'd ever seen. Each one showed one of the residents involved in a scene that was often crude and at the same time close to the mark. Singleton as a soldier, Miller in the dock and later standing by the hangman, Mrs. Cathcart drunk in public, Allen craftily using his illness for pity, Quincy paying ragged children to bring him his birds, Slater creating teapots without handles, offering them for sale at a market fair, the sign below them reading STOLEN FROM CHURCHES.

Partridge was there, wearing a mask that was what the artist must have seen as his true self. It was goatlike, the real man cringing behind it. Scapegoat? Only Brady was missing from the collection, presumably because he would have taken his sketch when he killed Willingham. Only he hadn't killed anyone.

Rutledge stood there studying them. Hill was right, the draftsmanship was excellent, the content exceedingly vicious, and most certainly the work of a man who cared nothing for the feelings of others.

He was a recluse by habit and inclination. Charles Dickens might have used him for the model of half a dozen unsavory characters. Whatever had embittered him in his youth, he had slowly become a man to avoid. A nasty piece of work, indeed.

But had he created these sketches?

There was an imagination at work here that didn't fit Willingham as Rutledge had seen him. These had taken time to draw in such detail, and from Willingham Rutledge would have expected more dash and less drama. His temper flared too easily. These were secretive, closet vengeance, a pleasure taken in private, so that no one knew he'd been savaged on paper.

"A coward's work," Hamish said.

Quincy, for instance, could have taken pleasure in skewering himself and his neighbors. But there would have been more dark humor, Rutledge thought, not such earthy attacks, if it had been his hand holding the pen. There was no whimsy here.

Rutledge went on searching the desk, but couldn't find more of the paper that the artist had used nor the nibs that were necessary to carry out the design.

He went back through the drawings, remembering how Mark Benson had worked on the face of a dead man, the strokes, the intensity of concentration. Mrs. Cathcart was too emotional. Allen couldn't have killed either Willingham or Brady, no match for them physically. Slater worked with his hands, but not with ink or charcoal. It was a very different skill, a very different brain.

That left Singleton or Miller.

He considered the two men, then went back to the portrayal on paper. Miller in the dock. Yes, that went along with what Rutledge himself had suspected. It could be proved. The portrayal of Singleton was more like the recruiting posters Rutledge had seen at the start of the war—the Hun bayoneting innocent Belgian women and children and committing other atrocities. It had made excellent propaganda, men had volunteered in droves. And like most propaganda, there was not much basis in fact to support it. The emotional impact was all.

Hamish said, "He was trained to kill."

"So he was. But why should he attack Willingham or Brady, suddenly and without apparent warning?"

Rutledge put the drawings back in their folder and shoved them out of sight in the desk.

"We'll start with Mrs. Cathcart. Her cottage is near enough to have heard any exchanges."

She was reluctant to talk to him about Willingham. "He's dead, we should respect the dead."

"He was murdered, Mrs. Cathcart. There's a difference."

"There's that." She took a deep breath, then answered with a self-deprecating gesture. "He would say the cruelest things. I tried not to listen. He told me once that I was a self-centered woman with nothing to offer any man. That was when he was very angry because I'd had someone come and repair my roof. It was a noisy business, and he shouted at them to stop."

"And Quincy?"

"They got into a shouting match once, because Willingham called him a ne'er-do-well who had never worked a day in his life."

"Who else took the brunt of his tongue?"

"Mr. Miller, of course. Willingham called him a liar and a scoundrel, and said he should be locked up."

"What was that about?"

"I'm not really sure. Mr. Miller told Quincy it was because Willingham thought he'd seen Mr. Miller's photograph in a London newspaper. Some scheme to defraud. It was Mr. Singleton he annoyed the most, called him a toy soldier, a disgrace to the uniform. Mr. Singleton ignored him, but I saw his face, sometimes, and it would be twisted with his fury."

"Any truth to the charges?"

"I don't know. It hurts most when they're true, doesn't it? Hearing them shouted about like the town crier. I don't think anyone would have blamed Singleton if he'd taken on Willingham and beaten him until he took back every word." She flushed at her own vehemence. "I'm sorry, I could never like the man, though I wouldn't have wanted him killed."

"It might have been the only way to stop him."

"Yes, there's that. A pity, wouldn't you say? But I thought it was Mr. Brady who'd killed Willingham. Why are you interested in the rest of us?"

"Making sure we've got the right man," he said, and thanked her.

Hill was waiting. "What was that all about?"

"Mrs. Cathcart had heard some of Willingham's shouting matches. Did you find the Brady sketch in his cottage?"

"No, but then he'd have burned it, wouldn't he? If he'd been guilty."

"I don't think Willingham drew any of them. There was no paper, no special ink, no pens in his desk. How had he done them without the proper tools?"

"Look, Rutledge, we're doing our best. If you want to point a finger, then get on with it. If not, leave us to our work."

"Start with Singleton. He and Brady were both in the army. There might have been something there. Singleton might not have known that in the beginning. Brady kept his past to himself, I should think. When the truth came out, Singleton might have thought that Brady knew more than he should."

"Singleton makes no secret about being cashiered."

"He didn't, did he? Perhaps it was too late when he realized he'd been better off keeping his mouth shut."

"Then why kill Willingham first?"

"Willingham irritated everybody. Kill two birds with one stone, and put the blame on Brady before setting up his death."

Hill glared at him. "You're not serious."

"Do you have any better suggestion? Go talk to him, but watch your back if you're going to make accusations."

Hill looked at the cottages, the way they were set out, to give each one maximum privacy. "Willingham could have seen anyone going into Brady's cottage, couldn't he? A good soldier would have taken him out, then launched his main attack."

Rutledge walked back to his motorcar and said as he took up the crank, "Good luck."

Hill was dragging his feet. "I'll ask the army for information," he said. "I've been wrong once already. I don't relish a second time."

"Your decision," Rutledge agreed, and drove off.

Hamish said, "He doesna' believe you."

Rutledge answered, "I think he does. He's just covering his back."

He turned the car and went to call on Sarah Parkinson, on his way back to London.

24

Sarah Parkinson was just leaving her house when Rutledge drove up. She was riding the bicycle today.

"Miss Parkinson—"

"No. Go away." She mounted the bicycle and pushed off, leaving him there.

Rutledge turned the motorcar and caught up with her, slowing his speed to a crawl to match hers.

"I haven't come to talk about your father."

"I'm uncomfortable being hunted this way. Is this what the police do, drive you to distraction until you can't sleep or eat or think?"

"Put your bicycle into my motorcar and I'll take you to your sister, or to Partridge Fields. Wherever you're setting out to go."

He could see her hesitate. She wasn't as skilled with the bicycle as her sister, and she had wobbled once or twice.

"I can manage very well, thank you."

"You can't. Get down before you're hurt. I swear, I won't ask you any questions on the way."

The front wheel jerked and almost threw her into a bank of late thrift, where the road narrowed a little.

Rutledge sped up and cut her off.

Getting out, he said, "You shouldn't be riding this in your state of mind. Go on, let me put the bicycle into the back. I've given you my word."

She stopped just inches from where he stood.

"I may be your enemy," he said gently, "but accepting a lift from me doesn't convict you of anything but good sense."

"I hate you, did you know that?" she said with some force, but when he reached for the handlebars she dismounted and let him have the bicycle. He set it in the back, more concerned about invading Hamish's space than anything else, his hands shaking as he maneuvered it to fit.

Hamish chuckled derisively, saying only, "When I'm ready to be seen, ye canna' hide."

Rutledge got back behind the wheel, his mind on Hamish, and nearly choked the motor.

Sarah Parkinson said tartly, "You're no better driver than I am."

She was goading him, and she'd succeeded, but Rutledge kept his promise, only asking where she wanted to go.

"To Pockets, my sister's house."

He took off the brake and set out. As they passed the cottages, she shivered, as if her father's death were still too raw a reminder.

He said nothing, letting the silence grow heavy between them. Finally Sarah Parkinson said, "If you will let me out a mile before her house, I'll pedal the rest of the way."

"As you like."

It was almost as if the silence accused her. Again she broke it first. "You weren't there when my mother died. You can't even imagine how we felt. And my father standing over her, after we'd summoned him, and saying that it had been a long time coming. Then why hadn't he tried to prevent it? Why hadn't he made her happier when it *mattered*?"

He didn't answer her.

"Sometimes in the dark while I'm trying to fall asleep I can see all of it again. People talk about nightmares, but this was real, and it happens over and over again until I'm half sick, my head aching, my mind struggling to forget. You have no idea what that's like. You must sleep well at night, duty done, and you have no idea what it's *like*."

But he did. He wanted to tell her that she was wrong, others suffered as she did, and that his hovering spirits were as fearsome as hers.

She must have read something of it in his face, for she snapped, "Oh, don't sit there, pretending you can't hear me."

"Then I'd have to ask you if you killed your father to stop your nightmares. If it helped at all, to punish him for what he'd done to your mother and to you. I'd like to know. I can't kill my ghosts, you see. I left them all on the battlefield in France."

She stared at him. "You were in the war?"

"I was in France, yes." He fought to get himself under control. "It was worse than anything you can imagine. Worse, even, than finding your mother dead. And it went on for four years, relentless, without respite. And there was no one to kill except the Germans, and even that wasn't as easy as we'd thought. In the night sometimes you could hear them singing. Men's voices, homesick and as frightened as we were. And the next day you were firing at them, trying to make every shot count, and using your bayonet when you had to, and trying to stay alive one more minute, one more hour, and after a while, you didn't even care about that, only about not letting your men down, shaming them in the face of the enemy, trying to set a good example that they could follow. And the worst of it was, they trusted me, and I led them to slaughter as surely as if I'd been the judas goat at an abattoir. If you want to compare nightmares, Miss Parkinson, you've chosen the wrong man."

She sat there stunned, her face pale, and her hands shaking in her lap, the gloves she wore bicycling clenched into fists to stop it.

"You see, your righteous defense of your mother is all very well. But if you killed your father, you are a murderer as surely as any other murderer in the dock. Your excuse may seem important to you, but it never is enough. Death is a very final solution, Miss Parkinson, and no matter how you try to excuse it, if you took a life without provocation, you will hang as surely as the man who killed two people back at the cottages. No better, no worse. The same."

He suddenly realized that he'd lost track of where he was, where the motorcar was heading. The darkness through which he'd spoken began to recede and nothing was familiar, nothing as it should be. But then he recognized the tower of a distant church and knew he was on the right road.

Miss Parkinson was opening her door. He braked quickly to keep her from falling out into the road.

"I'll take my chances with the bicycle," she said, tears on her face. "I should never have trusted you to keep your promise."

Rutledge said, "You were the first to speak, if you remember. You were the one who said I didn't understand."

"It doesn't matter. I've had enough," she said, getting out as the motorcar came to a stop.

"Go look at yourself in your mirror, Miss Parkinson. And ask yourself if your mother will be avenged by letting your father be buried in a pauper's grave. It will be on your soul and not hers, if that's what you do."

He brought out her bicycle for her and set it on the road.

She took it, mounted, and pedaled off, her shoulders hunched, her head down.

This time he watched her go, not making any effort to stop her again.

Hamish said, "It wasna' well done."

"I think I'll stay here a while, and see who comes back. Sarah Parkinson or her sister."

He pulled the motorcar to the verge, staring across the fields at the rooftops of the next village, trying to interest himself in the people there. But all he could think of was what he'd said to the young woman disappearing in the distance.

It was all true. But who was he to judge her? Who was he to set his torment against someone else's and make comparisons? He'd known Sarah Parkinson for a matter of days. It wasn't his place. It wasn't his duty.

He waited some time, thinking she might come back this way. It was useless trying to talk to Sarah when her sister was present and he could see no point in continuing on to Pockets to confront the two together.

Rutledge drove back to the inn, abandoning his decision to drive to London. He couldn't remember the last meal he'd eaten, but he wasn't hungry.

Upstairs in his room he stood by his window, looking out at nothing that was visible.

Hamish said, "What if you're wrong about Singleton?"

"Then I'm wrong. The drawings were not Willingham's style. I'll stand by that."

"Aye. But of the lot, there's the man with the birds."

"There is. If I'm wrong about Singleton, then I shall have to look at Quincy more closely. It isn't his style either."

"Ye're no authority on drawing. There's a darkness in him."

It was true. He'd grasped his jeweled treasures in desperation, and he kept them with him because they were a talisman, in his eyes. Without hope, men go mad . . .

Small feathered defenses against the family that didn't want him and enemies that wanted to see him dead.

Which brought Rutledge back to Parkinson. Two men, Madsen

and Deloran, had tried to use his body for their own ends. Parkinson's two daughters refused to claim it. And until they did, the case couldn't be closed.

There were heavy clouds in the sky, shortening the day, and as the light faded, Rutledge considered turning on his lamp. And then decided against it.

Three lorry drivers were pulling in as another edged his vehicle back on the road. The men called to their departing colleague and then walked toward the inn, looking for food and something to drink. One of them was the man Rutledge had defeated at darts. Laughing, they made their way through to the bar.

In the distance he thought he saw a flash of lightning, but he could hear no thunder afterward. If there was a storm, it was far to the west still.

Hamish said, "Ye canna' sit here in the dark and pity yoursel'."

It wasn't pity but a need for peace, he thought. In a little while, he would have to decide what to do next.

He hadn't seen Sarah Parkinson pass along the road again on her way to her house. He thought it odd, by this time, unless she had decided to wait out the storm with her sister.

Rising, he went down the stairs and started through the door. One of the drivers was leaving, his lorry backing out of the yard and moving off down the road. Rutledge watched him go, then set out on foot for the White Horse. All was well there, lamps lit in the cottages belonging to Miller, Quincy, and Mrs. Cathcart, and a thin trail of wood smoke rose from her chimney. Singleton's cottage was dark. Then Slater came up from the village and went in his door.

The White Horse offered ambient light, and Rutledge walked its lines, as he had done with his father. Then he turned and went back to the muzzle, standing there watching the sky.

He thought it was nearly simultaneous, the flickering of fire he could see in Willingham's windows and Brady's. Then Partridge's were suddenly bright, with Singleton's not far behind. They were burning—

Rutledge raced down the hill, shouting for Slater and Quincy, but he knew it was useless. The five of them could do nothing to stop the cottages from burning.

He cursed himself for not bringing his motorcar, then remembered that Partridge's was in the shed next to the house.

Slater finally came to his door to see what the commotion was about, and Rutledge pointed. The smith turned to stare, then wheeled back to Rutledge.

Rutledge shouted, "Partridge's motorcar. Go for help, fast as you can."

Quincy had heard the shouting and came out to look. Then he was back inside, his door shut.

Hamish said, "He'll protect the birds."

Mrs. Cathcart answered his knock and was frightened when she saw the smoke and flames. Miller came out just then and swore as he realized that his house was in danger.

Rutledge knocked on Singleton's door, and waited, then opened it and went inside.

It was burning as well, but there was no sign of the ex-soldier.

Where had he gone?

Partridge's motorcar kicked over on the third try, and Slater was backing out, on his way to Uffington. Rutledge took Mrs. Cathcart with him, and called to Miller to come down as well, but he stubbornly stayed where he was. Quincy was occupied in the room where he kept his collection, and Rutledge pushed Mrs. Cathcart through the door, saying, "Help him."

It would keep her busy.

That done, he began to run toward the inn, thinking about his own motorcar standing there in the yard. Singleton was no fool. Under the cover of the fire he must have slipped away, and his best chance of putting some distance between himself and any pursuit was to go fast and far.

The motorcar was still in the yard when Rutledge, his heart hammering and his lungs burning, reached the inn. He wouldn't have put it past Singleton to take it. Another of the lorries was pulling out, and he shouted to the driver to wait. He was ignored. There was still one of the lorries left and he dashed inside, calling to Smith. But he stopped short in the bar.

Two lorry drivers were still there—and only one vehicle remained in the yard.

He said, forcing the words out, harsh and curt, "There's a fire at the cottages. Take your lorry to Uffington, pick as many men as you can and bring them back to help."

The drivers were on their feet, heading for the door, and then he heard shouting.

Rutledge said to Smith, "Have you seen Singleton?"

Smith shook his head. "I'll fetch something to drink. They'll be needing it. Is it bad, over there?"

"The fire may spread to the occupied cottages. Tell Mrs. Smith that she may need to make up beds for tonight."

And then he was gone, cranking his motorcar with such energy that the motor almost missed fire, then caught. His headlamps found the road as the lorry drivers demanded to know what had happened to the other vehicle. He didn't have time to tell them.

The lorry had headed west, away from the cottages, and he followed. Singleton was having trouble keeping it on the road at speed. By the time Rutledge caught him up, he could see the rear wheels swaying as Singleton took the curves.

Rutledge swore. To stop him meant finding a stretch where he could get ahead and block the road. He ran through the map in his mind, seeing where the bends would slow Singleton down, where he could gain time on the straightaway.

Singleton went through the next village far too fast, scattering people and brushing past a cart stopped at an angle in the road. The cart went winding, and someone cried out in pain.

Rutledge slowed, keeping Singleton in sight but trying not to hit anyone in his path. And they were out into the open again, moving far too fast for safety in the stormy light. Rutledge thought Singleton had a very good idea who was behind him, even if he couldn't see the motorcar for its bright headlamps.

There was a long straight stretch, enough for Rutledge to gun the motor and make an attempt to pass, but Singleton swung the lorry into his path, and it was all Rutledge could do to keep from plowing head-long into a stone wall where the road angled to the right.

Hamish was shouting now, telling him to watch what he was doing.

"Kill us both, and he'll go free," Hamish reminded him.

Rutledge fell back. For the next mile or two there was a double bend, first one way, then a short interval, then the other way.

He wasn't sure the lorry could make that at speed, but Singleton had got the hang of driving it now and in the dark made the adjust-ments necessary to keep his lumbering vehicle on the road, though it swayed dangerously, the load it was carrying sometimes shifting with the curves.

The road was straight again, houses and a barn flashing past, a roadside pub and then a long looping bend.

Singleton wasn't prepared for it. He swung the lorry too hard around the first part of the bend, then overcompensated as he began to slip sideways on the rough surface. Dust flew up from his wheels and he lost speed as he struggled to keep himself upright.

The bend ended in another short, straight stretch, and then a copse of trees loomed ahead at the next bend. And then in the lorry headlamps a single bicyclist stood out with shocking clarity.

He had been lucky this far, Singleton had. The road had been empty and he had had the time and the strength to keep the wheel under control. But his first reaction as he saw the bicycle was to swerve, his tires failed to grip, and the side and rear of the lorry began to slide inexorably toward the oncoming bicycle.

It was like slow motion. Rutledge could see the bicycle, and then as the lorry slowly lost traction, it blotted the rider from view. The scream of the brakes was almost human, and like a juggernaut the lorry moved on, across the road now, blocking it from verge to verge. In the glow of the headlamps the bicycle rose in a gleaming silver arc, rising above the truck like a winged thing, and then the silver faded and it was lost to view.

Rutledge was braking with all the power of his arm, knowing it wasn't going to be in time, that either the bicycle could catch him or he would slam at speed into the side of the lorry.

He fought the wheel, heard the bicycle crash into something just to the left of him, and saw himself sliding too, this time sideways, and his brakes could do him no good.

Somehow Rutledge managed to gun the motor at the last, forward momentum clashing with his sideways slide.

He wound up in a field by the road, came to a jarring stop, and was out of the motorcar while it was still rocking heavily.

The lorry was crashing into the wood, trees snapping as the weight of the vehicle mowed into them, metal rending with a high-pitched whine that was earsplitting.

He couldn't see what had become of the rider, and his greatest fear was that whoever it was had been caught beneath the lorry wheels and dragged.

Suddenly everything was quiet.

From the verge of the road he heard a whimper, and went quickly toward it, cursing himself for not bringing his torch. There wasn't a light for miles, it seemed, except for the lorry's headlamps and his own.

She was lying in stubble and high grass, and he stumbled over a stone and nearly went headfirst into her.

He and Hamish saw her at the same time.

It was Sarah Parkinson, and she was badly injured. He thanked the gods wherever they were that she was still alive, and knelt beside her. He didn't know what had happened to Singleton and he didn't care.

His hand touched blood, wet and warm at the side of her head, and then as he ran his hands down her body, he could feel the odd angle of one arm. Broken, he thought, but the head wound was more serious.

She moaned as he touched her, and he was afraid to move her until he knew the extent of her injuries.

Another motorcar was coming from the east, and Rutledge stood up, not sure that the driver could see the lorry and his motorcar in time to realize what had happened. He moved to Sarah Parkinson's feet, prepared to wave off the other driver, but the motorcar slowed, then stopped.

"Is anyone hurt?" It was a woman's voice, frightened but steady. "Hello?"

"Over here," Rutledge called. "Bring a torch, or fetch mine from my motorcar."

The driver got out and ran toward Rutledge's motor, rummaging for the torch. Rutledge had a fleeting thought about Hamish, from long habit.

She came racing back, nearly tripping on the rough ground, torch in hand, flicking it on and shining it inadvertently into his face.

She stopped. "Rutledge? What's going on?" she demanded, as if he had staged the accident to throw her off stride.

He said, "It's your sister. I don't think the lorry struck her, but she's here on the side of the road, one arm broken and a cut on her head. If there are internal injuries—"

Rebecca was beside him, pushing him away, shining the light on her sister's face.

"Sarah? For God's sake—*Sarah.*"

She began to work quickly, but there were tears spilling down her cheeks now and her voice began to quiver as she talked to her sister.

There was no response.

"I've killed her!" Rebecca Parkinson cried. "We had a quarrel, it was my fault—I shouldn't have let her go alone in the dark—I tried to find her again—"

Her sister moaned, and Rebecca bent over her trying to cradle her head.

"Don't move her," Rutledge cautioned. "We don't know the extent—you must go and find help at once. There's a village back the way I came, no more than three miles? Four? Go there and ask if there's a doctor."

"I won't leave her. It's my fault, I tell you."

He grasped her by the shoulders and shook her. "Hysteria wastes any time she has left. Get in the motorcar and go. There's a murderer loose here, he was driving that lorry, and you can't stay here alone. *Go.*"

She stumbled back to her motorcar and got in, pushing her foot down on the gas pedal with such force that the car leapt ahead as she turned it and he heard a wheel of the bicycle crunch under the tires. But she bumped over it and kept going, disappearing into the darkness with such abandon he wondered if she would make it herself.

He used the light to look for more injuries, and then bound Sarah's head with his handkerchief to control the bleeding. As he moved her slightly, she cried out. Her arm or her back? He had no way of knowing.

Speaking to her quietly, he tried to reassure her, but she seemed not to know where she was or what was happening.

"A blessing," Hamish said, at his shoulder.

Taking off his coat he rolled it and set it under the broken arm, then ran his hands down her legs. He could feel bloody bunches of stocking, blood soaking through her skirts, but there was no indication of a break on either.

She came to for a moment, and he said, "Rebecca is here. She's gone for help. Hold on. It won't be long."

"I hurt. All over."

He tried to smile. "That's good. It means you can feel. Stay quiet, I'll be here."

From the lorry he could hear the sound of a door creaking open.

Singleton was still alive.

He did nothing. Said nothing. And listened.

After a time a voice from the darkness called, "I can see you, even if you can't see me. I'll kill both of you if you try to stop me."

"You aren't my case. You're Hill's. Go on." He snapped off his torch.

"You aren't armed. I am."

"I said, go on."

He could hear footsteps crunching in the dirt of the road and then fading as Singleton reached the grass verge.

Hamish said, "He'll no' leave witnesses."

But Rutledge remained silent, listening from where he knelt at Sarah Parkinson's side.

To Hamish he said, "I'd swear he wasn't armed."

"You canna' chance it. He's Hill's case. You said so yourself."

"Yes."

He could hear the crank turning, and then the motor came to life. The driver's door shut. Singleton was backing Rutledge's car into the road. He could see the sweep of headlamps across the sky.

For an instant Rutledge thought Singleton might try to run them down, but the ground was too rough just where he was kneeling by Sarah, and the risk of doing serious damage to the motorcar was obvious.

And then the moment came where if Singleton was armed, he would fire.

Does he have a service revolver?

Many of the enlisted men had brought them home as souvenirs . . .

The motorcar idled in the road. Rutledge held his breath, keeping his back to Singleton, making sure that he was between the killer and the girl on the ground at his feet.

She said, "What's wrong? I heard a motorcar. Is it Rebecca?"

Rutledge didn't answer, counting the seconds as he waited.

And then Singleton was driving away, leaving them there in the night.

He could feel the tension in his back. To Sarah he said, "She'll be here soon."

It couldn't have been more than ten minutes later that Rebecca was back, braking hard, calling to her sister. A door opened. A man carrying his medical bag hurried toward them. Rebecca was maneuvering the motorcar until the headlamps shone directly on her sister, giving them light to work.

The doctor was there beside Rutledge. "What's most urgently needed?"

"The head wound. It's bleeding heavily."

Rebecca hadn't emerged from the car. Rutledge thought he could hear her teeth chattering over the sound of the engine.

"Head wounds generally do. Next?"

"Right arm. Broken, I think. Cuts and bruises. I don't know about her back. But she can feel pain. All over, she says."

"A good thing." He began to work, slowly at first and then with greater assurance as he learned the extent of Sarah Parkinson's injuries. He did what he could to brace the broken arm, put bandaging over the head wound, and then turned to Rutledge.

"She'll be all right, but I daresay there's concussion, and shock is setting in. We need to get her to hospital."

Rutledge said, "There's a rug—" But his motorcar was gone. He called to Rebecca Parkinson. "Do you have a rug, there?"

"Yes, I think—"

He could hear her getting out now, coming toward them. "Is she alive?" Her voice was under control, but tense with stress.

"She's all right," he told Rebecca and took the rug from her, helping the doctor wrap Sarah in it. Between them the two men carried her to the motorcar and lifted her into the rear seat. It must have hurt like the very devil.

The doctor got in after her and made certain she was comfortable. Then he turned to Rutledge. "Anderson's the name."

"Rutledge." He nodded to Rebecca. "I'll drive."

"All right, I'll direct you. Can we get around that lorry?"

"I think so."

"That's the fastest way. What's become of the driver? Is he dead?"

"He went for help."

Anderson nodded. "Then we needn't concern ourselves with him."

Sarah regained consciousness several times, complaining of feeling cold and hurting. Anderson reassured her, but Rebecca, next to Rutledge, didn't look back or answer her sister.

They drove into a medium-size town where there was a hospital of sorts near the church. It had, Anderson was telling him, been a lying-in hospital before the war and after that had been turned into a burn treatment center. "But most of the patients have been sent elsewhere now, and the town has taken it over."

"Where are we?"

"Salverton."

"I need to find a telephone as soon as possible. The lorry is still blocking the road."

"Yes, of course. The hotel just down that street should have one. Give me a moment to find someone with a stretcher. Then you can go."

Rutledge stayed until Sarah Parkinson was in a room on the first floor, nurses working over her with quiet efficiency. Rebecca, still silent, was with her. No one noticed as he slipped quietly out and went to the stairs.

The clinic had been a bank in an earlier life, Rutledge thought, noting the marble pillars in Reception and the ornate staircase sweeping up to the first floor. His footsteps echoed as he crossed to the door. A nursing sister passing through nodded to him.

He found the hotel, The White Hart, without any difficulty, put in a call to Uffington, and after a time heard Hill's voice on the other end of the line.

Rutledge gave the inspector a brief report, and asked about the cottages.

"We couldn't save the empty ones where the fire had been set inside. We couldn't get enough water to them. The rest, the ones still occupied, will be habitable. Where's Singleton?"

"I wish I knew. I told you, he left in my motorcar."

"He wasn't injured in the crash?"

"Not as far as I could tell."

"Surely you could have stopped him." Hill's frustration came to the fore, backed by anger.

"I couldn't leave the woman he ran down."

"But she'll live, you say?"

"It appears that way. Early days." He saw again the doctor's grave face as he examined the head wound and tested Sarah Parkinson's reflexes. "The next twenty-four hours will tell us."

"Where do you think Singleton went?"

"Where does he feel safe? I don't know. I expect he'll abandon my motorcar as soon as possible and find other means of transport. It could be a country bus or a train. One that isn't crowded, I should think."

"We haven't got enough men to watch train stations."

"No."

Hill said, "I delayed, waiting to hear from London. Singleton wasn't cashiered from an Indian regiment. That was all a lie. He'd been in the regular army, and was called up again in 1915. Seems he killed another soldier on the transport ship to France. Used a knife then, as well. He was put in irons, but somehow in the confusion when they docked, he got away. London thought he was still in France, hiding in the south, but he probably came home with the wounded, and just walked off. He must have thought Brady recognized him, and when you came nosing about, he was sure you were searching for him. We'll find your motorcar for you. Pray God we find Singleton too."

Rutledge walked back to the hospital. He found Rebecca sitting in the small waiting area down the passage from her sister's room. Someone had kindly brought her a cup of tea, but she was holding it between her hands as if she didn't know what to do with it.

He sat down across from her, waiting until she broke the silence.

"I told you, we quarreled. I should have never let her go back on that bicycle, but I was angry, I thought she deserved to suffer too. But not this, I never imagined *this*."

"There was no way you could."

"It's partly your fault. You upset her, more than you know. She didn't kill our father. Leave her alone."

"I'd come to the conclusion she hadn't. I don't think it's in her nature to kill."

"Are you saying it's in mine?" She looked up at him, holding his gaze, challenging him.

"I don't know. You must tell me."

"I haven't killed anyone," she said wearily. "At least not until tonight. She wouldn't have been on that road if I'd kept her at Pockets or even driven her home."

"What did you quarrel about?"

"She wanted to go to Yorkshire and bring home Father's body. I was just as happy to leave him there to rot."

"Why did he die?" He waited, and when she didn't answer, he said, "Look, you might as well tell me what happened. I know most of the story, and can guess the rest of it."

She gave him a withering glance. "Oh no. You couldn't in your wildest dreams guess what happened to Gerald Parkinson. I don't think any of us know."

A young nursing sister stuck her head round the door. "Your sister is awake, Miss Parkinson, and asking for you."

Rebecca got up and followed her. Rutledge, after a moment, went as well.

Sarah's head was bandaged, her face pale, and by morning she'd have a very black eye. Her arm was in a cast, and she lay there trying to stand the pain.

"They can't give me anything," she said as her sister came into the room. "Not until they're sure about the concussion. I can't tell you how much it hurts. I feel sick with it."

"I'm sorry, Sarah, truly—I had no way of knowing this would happen. I never meant for you to be hurt."

"I thought I was going to die. It was terrifying. When the lorry struck the bicycle, I was thrown through the air. Can you imagine watching yourself die? And when I landed, there was such pain. I didn't expect to live. But I did. For a reason. We might as well tell him, Becky. I want to get it off *my* conscience at least, but I can't say anything without your consent. Please, will you let me tell him?" Her eyes were pleading, but dry. As if she'd already cried as much as she could.

Rebecca answered her with a coldness that startled her sister. "I thought we swore. On Mama's memory. I thought it was agreed, Sarah."

"You sound like Father, you're as hard as he was."

Rutledge stepped forward before Rebecca could vehemently deny the charge.

"There's a solution here. I can take Rebecca into custody, and let the courts sort it out. The publicity will be painful, but that was your choice when you started all this."

"Go ahead," Rebecca told him defiantly.

Sarah said, "We neither of us killed him, you know. He was dead when we found him."

Rebecca opened her mouth to deny it, but Sarah went on relentlessly. "He'd come to the house sometime in the night. We found his motorcar there the next morning. He hadn't been there in two years, and we were horrified. When we went through the house looking for him, he was in Mama's room, lying on her bed, and the room was filled with gas. We shut it off, opened windows—but it was too late. He was already dead, and had been for several hours."

Her sister turned on her heel and went out the door.

Sarah watched her go, and then said, "It's all true. I'll swear to it under oath. What happened next was awful. We didn't want him to be found there. Not in Mama's bed. So between us we dragged him out of there and down the stairs." She began to cry. "Do you know what it's like to move a dead man? It was awful, but we were angry with him, and all we could think about was being rid of him. It was Rebecca's idea to drive him away from the house. We got him into his motorcar, found the opera cloak in the attic and wrapped him in it, pulled his hat down over his face, and set out. I think we drove all day and part of the night. By that time we were beginning to come to our senses, but Rebecca wouldn't take him back. I couldn't bear to dump him at the side of the road. I wouldn't have done that to a dog. And then we saw the wood. It seemed like a good idea, and we managed to get him that far. That's when I glimpsed the abbey just beyond the trees, and I made her help me carry him there. Heavy as he was. She wouldn't leave him in the nave. It was holy ground, and he didn't deserve it. So we took him into the cloister and left him there, and she put the gas mask on his face, because she said it was his epitaph."

He could picture them, the anger feeding on itself until they found the strength to do what had to be done. As the anger faded, a cold reality had set in, but Rebecca was still adamant. He had to be punished . . .

Sarah was saying, "When we got back to Berkshire, I waited by the side of the road in our motorcar, while Rebecca took his to the shed and left it, as if he hadn't gone far and would be back soon. I was so exhausted, so anxious, I began to cry, and she told me I was not very brave. But then I saw she'd been crying as well, and she swore it was because she hadn't killed him herself."

"Did you believe her?"

"Of course I did—I was there with her when we found him. She couldn't have been so shocked, if she'd already known. I saw her face. It wasn't a lie."

For the first time there was a ring of truth behind her words.

"Why does Rebecca hate your father so much?"

"She was older. She saw more. I don't know. You must ask her."

Sarah lay back against her pillows, exhausted. "Now it's done. Over with. I can sleep at night." She closed her eyes for a time, then said, "Are you still there, Mr. Rutledge?"

"I'm here."

"When I was hurtling through the air, all I could think of was, God, let me live, and I'll make amends, I swear I will."

"It wasn't a bad bargain."

He stayed with her for some time, asking that a few more details be cleared up, but he couldn't catch her in a lie or a mistake.

Afterward he found Rebecca in the waiting room, sitting there, he thought, like a martyr waiting to be led to the flames.

"I have no regrets." It was all she said.

"No, I expect not. What had he done to you, Rebecca, that you could hate so well? I'd like to understand why a daughter could be— as your sister just said—so cold."

She turned on him. "My mother lost a child when we were small. I didn't know why she was ill, only that she stayed in her room with the curtains drawn for week after week. But then one day when I'd been a nuisance, the housekeeper we had then, Mrs. Fortner, told me what no one wanted us to know. The child was born alive, a boy. And so badly deformed that no one could bear to look at him. He died almost at once, and it was a blessing. My mother told my father it was because of all the things he did in the laboratory—that he'd brought something home that maimed and killed their son. And nothing was ever the same again."

She broke down, alone and wretched and confused. "My mother was never the same either. And when she killed herself, she was holding the christening gown that was meant for my brother. Don't tell me it was long ago in the past! *She grieved for him until the day she died.*"

Rutledge said, "He was born full term and died from natural causes. There was nothing in the doctor's report to say he was deformed. I've read it."

"But he was. The housekeeper was there."

He remembered the words in the late Dr. Butler's diary. "Had long talk with Parkinson, explaining situation. Question about who should see to burial. He left arrangements with me."

What had that long talk been about?

And why had Parkinson slashed his hand in an angry moment in his lab?

Hamish said, "It isna' wise to tell the lass aboot that."

"I think your mother grieved for her son, and possibly even blamed your father for the child's death. That much must be true. But the housekeeper created a monster for reasons of her own. She left shortly afterward, with no notice given. It's likely your father discovered what she'd told you."

Rebecca said, "I never told Sarah. I never wanted her to know. But I can remember the day, and the words spilling out of the housekeeper's mouth, and her face leaning down to mine. I remember feeling sick, and not being able to eat my dinner. There must have been some truth to the story. Or my father would have come to me and tried to explain that Mrs. Fortner was lying."

"He may not have known how to explain such cruelty. He could have told himself you'd forget in time. Remember, your father had suffered a great loss too. He couldn't have been himself."

After a moment, she got slowly to her feet. "I must talk to Sarah—"

Rutledge caught her arm to stop her. "You don't intend to tell her this, do you? It would serve no purpose now."

"No. Never. I couldn't bear her to know." She left the room.

Rutledge went to find transportation back to Uffington. That done, he put in a call to the Yard.

Hamish said, "How can ye be sure it was suicide and not murder?"

"Because," Rutledge said, "it explains Rebecca's behavior. That's why she was ready to humiliate a dead man, because he wasn't there to hate any more. If he came back to Partridge Fields to be buried in a churchyard, like a decent man, then it was over, he'd won. To be abandoned in Yorkshire was to leave him outside God's grace, so to speak."

He said good-bye to Rebecca. Sarah was resting and didn't answer as he stepped briefly into the room. But Rebecca raised haunted eyes to his.

Then his driver was at the door and Rutledge left.

By the time he reached the inn, it was early morning, and Hill had left a message for him.

"Your motorcar is in Oxford. My sergeant will drive you there. As for Singleton, he was caught in the train station, as you'd expected. It's finished."

25

Rutledge arrived in London and went to his flat to change his clothes.

His first duty, he knew, was to go to the Yard and report.

After that he would find Frances and talk to her about Simon Barrington. He knew his sister. All she needed was to be told Simon hadn't deserted her. She'd be able to cope after that.

The Yard was bustling, the passages crowded. He asked Inspector Peterson as they met turning a corner what was happening and Peterson said, "There's been a murder in Kensington. It's taken most of our manpower to cover the ground. On top of everything else on our plate. Old Bowles is in a foul mood. Walk clear of him if you can."

Rutledge took the warning to heart. But there was no avoiding the upcoming meeting.

Chief Superintendent Bowles lived by the philosophy, rock everyone's boat but mine. Only it wasn't working today. He'd been called on the carpet for lack of progress.

Still, he sat there and listened to what Rutledge had to say about Berkshire, then nodded. "It's been a bugger here, everything at sixes and sevens. I want you ready to help Chief Inspector Johns with Kensington."

There was to be no respite, then. Rutledge said, "I'll do my best."

"See that you do." Bowles went back to the letter he'd been reading when Rutledge had knocked. Rutledge took that as his dismissal.

But Bowles stopped him at the door as he was about to open it.

"I explained matters to Martin Deloran after your preliminary report from Salverton. Whoever he may be when he's at home, Deloran's a nasty piece of work. This letter came an hour ago. Here, read it."

Rutledge took the letter from Bowles and scanned it quickly, then read it more slowly.

Martin Deloran was a bad enemy.

The letter said,

It has come to my attention that Inspector Rutledge is being considered for advancement to Chief Inspector.

My recommendation is that he is not ready for greater responsibility. His handling of the recent affair in Berkshire showed a lack of understanding of the facts and a grievous failure to follow instructions. The feeling in certain quarters is that Inspector Rutledge has not earned promotion at this time.

Rutledge looked at Bowles. "You know none of this is true."

"I don't care if it's true or not. I'm not going to fight him or I'll be brought down with you. I've told him that you went to Berkshire against my advice and I wash my hands of you."

"You told me that the Yard doesn't take orders. That murder was murder, wherever it occurs."

"So I did. It was a mistaken belief. You'll take your medicine like a man and not cause more trouble. That's an order."

Rutledge stood there, hearing what Bowles was saying. *If you think*

Deloran is a bad enemy, drag me into this and you'll discover what kind of enemy I can be.

Rutledge took his time replying. "I understand," he said, and left the room.

This time Bowles didn't stop him from going.

He walked out of the Yard and debated bearding Deloran in his den. But it was no use.

He went back to his flat. The mail had arrived in his absence, and he looked through it quickly before dropping it on the table by the door. And then he went back again to the large manila envelope that he'd glanced at and passed over. The return address was Slater, Andrew, Tomlin Cottages, Uffington, Berkshire.

He turned it over in his hands several times before opening it.

Hamish said, "Ye ken, he tried to tell you."

And I ignored him, Rutledge answered.

He set the packet on his desk and went into the kitchen to make himself a cup of tea, then changed his mind and came back to take it up again.

Inside there was no letter of explanation. Only a sheaf of paper that Miss Chandler had taken such pride in typing.

Rutledge read through it, following the chemistry as best he could.

Here was Parkinson's new discovery, with the admission that he hadn't completely worked out the formula to his satisfaction.

Another gas, this one deadlier than anything used in the war.

Rutledge saw Rebecca Parkinson's face, and then thought about Deloran's retribution for defiance.

By rights these pages should go to Deloran. For some reason Parkinson hadn't delivered them himself. Because of his wife's suicide, two years ago? Instead he'd had them typed, then had deliberately given them to Slater to keep for him, where Brady couldn't find them. And Slater had kept them faithfully until he knew for certain that Partridge was dead. Then he had passed them on to the only person he trusted.

Hamish said, "He'll be pleased, will Deloran. Ye'll be given your promotion after all."

Rutledge considered that.

Still holding the pages, he went into the kitchen, struck a match, and over the sink burned them to ash.

Parkinson knew what was in these sheets, and still he'd withheld them. It was enough for Rutledge.

Hamish said, "That was no' wise."

"It isn't a matter of wisdom." He watched the ash cool and turn gray-white. "Or spite. I've killed enough men to last me a lifetime."

It is a fact that most of the gas stockpiled until the 1950s was based on the World War I models. But in World War II the Germans were on the brink of new types of poison gas that were far more lethal than anything used in the trenches. And the Allies were quick to scoop them up and see where they led. We've been cursed with variations of them ever since.

Was it possible, scientifically, to be close to the same formulas as early as 1917? The answer is yes, that a clever mind accustomed to playing with poisons from around the world could have stumbled over something that didn't disable armies, it killed them fast and in great numbers. The amazing thing is not that it was possible then but that it took thirty years, once the can of worms was opened at Ypres.

Of course, early attempts might also have led to another dead end. Who can say?

The what-ifs of history can be fascinating.